Modern Critical Views

Modern Critical Views

Modern Critical Views

URSULA K. LE GUIN

Modern Critical Views

URSULA K. LE GUIN

Edited with an introduction by

Harold Bloom

Sterling Professor of the Humanities
Yale University

CHELSEA HOUSE PUBLISHERS
New York
Philadelphia

THE COVER:

Illustrating the great ordeal-sequence of *The Left Hand of Darkness*, the cover represents the two protagonists, Genly Ai and Estraven, making their way by sledge across the harsh terrain of the planet called Winter.—H.B.

PROJECT EDITORS: Emily Bestler, James Uebbing
ASSOCIATE EDITOR: Maria Behan
EDITORIAL COORDINATOR: Karyn Gullen Browne
EDITORIAL STAFF: Laura Ludwig, Linda Grossman, Peter Childers
DESIGN: Susan Lusk

Cover illustration by Liane Fried

Library of Congress Cataloging in Publication Data

Ursula K. Le Guin.
    (Modern critical views)
    Bibliography: p.
    Includes index.
    1. Le Guin, Ursula K., 1929–   —Criticism and
interpretation—Addresses, essays, lectures.
2. Science fiction, American—History and criticism—
Addresses, essays, lectures.   3. Fantastic fiction,
American—History and criticism—Addresses, essays,
lectures. I. Bloom, Harold.   II. Series.
PS3562.E42Z952   1986   813'.54   85-17510
ISBN 0-87754-659-2

Contents

Editor's Note

This volume gathers together what its editor considers to be the most illuminating criticism so far devoted to the fiction of Ursula K. Le Guin, arranged in the chronological order of publication. The editor's "Introduction" centers upon both *The Left Hand of Darkness*, her most widely esteemed novel, and upon her poetry, still too little known and appreciated.

The chronological sequence begins with David Ketterer's analysis of *The Left Hand of Darkness*, which expresses some reservations that later critics of the book address themselves to answering. Douglas Barbour's reading of the early Hainish novels also serves as a thematic introduction to some of Le Guin's later works. This opening phase of Le Guin criticism is rounded off by the general estimate of Robert Scholes, which sets her in the larger contexts of fantasy and of science fiction.

More detailed studies begin with Ian Watson's investigation of a characteristic Le Guin cognitive metaphor, the forest, in two of her best-known shorter pieces. Fredric Jameson's analysis of utopian narrative is deeply informed by his extensive knowledge of revolutionary literature. George E. Slusser's high estimate of the *Earthsea Trilogy* is given authority by his enormous erudition in the entire range of literary fantasy. With Gérard Klein's inquiry into the ethnology of Le Guin's work, another strand is uncovered in her complex pattern of intellectual sources.

T. A. Shippey returns us to the *Earthsea Trilogy*, with an expert essay upon magic and language. Le Guin's more conventional stories, *The Orsinian Tales*, are studied by James W. Bittner in an adroit reading which demonstrates that they are not anomalies in her work.

The remaining essays in this volume focus in depth upon what would appear to be Le Guin's principal achievements to date: *The Left Hand of Darkness*, *The Dispossessed* and *The Beginning Place*. Victor Urbanowicz explores the anarchist dialectics of *The Dispossessed*, while Eric S. Rabkin provides an acute analysis of the relation between perspectivism and free will in *The Left Hand of Darkness*, an analysis neatly complemented by Jeanne Murray Walker's consideration of myth and history in that novel. Susan Wood, Dena C. Bain and Barbara Brown all investigate, in different but supplementary ways, the closely entwined perspectives of feminism, utopianism, Taoism and androgyny in this most colorful and vital of Le Guin's works. *The Beginning Place*, Le Guin's most experimental and most recent novel, is examined by Brian Attebery in the context that he calls "Metafantasy." Finally, Carol McGuirk, in an essay written to conclude this volume, masterfully portrays Le Guin's optimism and humanism as elements that mark "the limits of subversion" both in *The Dispossessed* and in *The Left Hand of Darkness*. With McGuirk's eloquent demonstration of Le Guin's place in humanistic tradition, still wider perspectives are opened for the future of Le Guin criticism.

Introduction

I

In a recent parable, "She Unnames Them" (*The New Yorker*, January 21, 1985), the best contemporary author of literary fantasy sums up the consequences of Eve's unnaming of the animals that Adam had named:

> None were left now to unname, and yet how close I felt to them when I saw one of them swim or fly or trot or crawl across my way or over my skin, or stalk me in the night, or go along beside me for a while in the day. They seemed far closer than when their names had stood between myself and them like a clear barrier: so close that my fear of them and their fear of me became one same fear. And the attraction that many of us felt, the desire to smell one another's scales or skin or feathers or fur, taste one another's blood or flesh, keep one another warm—that attraction was now all one with the fear, and the hunter could not be told from the hunted, nor the eater from the food.

This might serve as a coda for all Ursula Kroeber Le Guin's varied works to date. She is essentially a mythological fantasist; the true genre for her characteristic tale is *romance*, and she has a high place in the long American tradition of the romance, a dominant mode among us from Hawthorne down to Pynchon's *The Crying of Lot Forty–Nine*. Because science fiction is a popular mode, she is named as a science-fiction writer, and a certain defiance in her proudly asserts that the naming is accurate. But no one reading, say Philip K. Dick, as I have been doing after reading Le Guin's discussion of his work in *The Language of the Night*, is likely to associate the prose achievement of Le Guin with that of her acknowledged precursor. She is a fierce defender of the possibilities for science fiction, to the extent of calling Philip K. Dick "our own homegrown Borges" and even of implying that Dick ought not to be compared to Kafka only because Dick is "not an absurdist" and his work "is not (as Kafka's was) autistic."

After reading Dick, one can only murmur that a literary critic is in slight danger of judging Dick to be "our Borges" or of finding Dick in the cosmos of Kafka, the Dante of our century. But Le Guin as critic, loyal to her colleagues who publish in such periodicals as *Fantastic, Galaxy, Amazing, Orbit* and the rest, seems to me not the same writer as the visionary of *The Earthsea Trilogy, The Left Hand of Darkness, The Dispossessed* and *The Beginning Place*. Better than Tolkien, far better than Doris Lessing, Le Guin is the overwhelming contemporary instance of a superbly imaginative creator and major stylist who chose (or was chosen by) "fantasy and science fiction." At her most remarkable, as in what still seems to me her masterpiece, *The Left Hand of Darkness*, she offers a sexual vision that strangely complements Pynchon's *Gravity's Rainbow* and James Merrill's *Changing Light at Sandover*. I can think of only one modern fantasy I prefer to *The Left Hand of Darkness*, and that is David Lindsay's *Voyage to Arcturus* (1920), but Lindsay's uncanny nightmare of a book survives its dreadful writing, while Le Guin seems never to have written a wrong or bad sentence. One has only to quote some of her final sentences to know again her absolute rhetorical authority:

> But he had not brought anything. His hands were empty, as they had always been.
>
> (*The Dispossessed*)

> Gravely she walked beside him up the white streets of Havnor, holding his hand, like a child coming home.
>
> (*The Tombs of Atuan*)

> There is more than one road to the city.
>
> (*The Beginning Place*)

> But the boy, Therem's son, said stammering, "Will you tell us how he died?—Will you tell us about the other worlds out among the stars—the other kinds of men, the other lives?"
>
> (*The Left Hand of Darkness*)

When her precise, dialectical style—always evocative, sometimes sublime in its restrained pathos—is exquisitely fitted to her powers of invention, as in *The Left Hand of Darkness*, Le Guin achieves a kind of sensibility very nearly unique in contemporary fiction. It is the pure storyteller's sensibility that induces in the reader a state of uncertainty, of *not knowing what comes next*. What Walter Benjamin praised in Leskov is exactly relevant to Le Guin:

> Death is the sanction of everything that the storyteller can tell. He has borrowed his authority from death. . . .
>
> The first true storyteller is, and will continue to be, the teller of fairy tales. Whenever good counsel was at a premium, the fairy tale had it, and where the need was greatest, its aid was nearest. This need was

the need created by the myth. The fairy tale tells us of the earliest arrangements that mankind made to shake off the nightmare which the myth had placed upon its chest. . . .

Elsewhere in his essay on Leskov, Benjamin asserts that: "The art of storytelling is reaching its end because the epic side of truth, wisdom, is dying out." One can be skeptical of Benjamin's Marxist judgment that such a waning, if waning it be, is "only a concomitant symptom of the secular productive forces of history." Far more impressively, Benjamin once remarked of Kafka's stories that in them, "narrative art regains the significance it had in the mouth of Scheherazade: to postpone the future." Le Guin's narrative art, though so frequently set in the future, not only borrows its authority from death but also works to postpone the future, works to protect us against myth and its nightmares.

I am aware that this is hardly consonant with the accounts of her narrative purposes that Le Guin gives in the essays of *The Language of the Night*. But Lawrence's adage is perfectly applicable to Le Guin: trust the tale, not the teller, and there is no purer storyteller writing now in English than Le Guin. Her true credo is spoken by one of her uncanniest creations, Faxe the Weaver, master of the Foretelling, to conclude the beautiful chapter, "The Domestication of Hunch," in *The Left Hand of Darkness*:

> "The unknown," said Faxe's soft voice in the forest, "the unforetold, the unproven, that is what life is based on. Ignorance is the ground of thought. Unproof is the ground of action. If it were proven that there is no God there would be no religion. No Handdara, no Yomesh, no hearth gods, nothing. But also if it were proven that there is a God, there would be no religion. . . . Tell me, Genry, what is known? What is sure, predictable, inevitable—the one certain thing you know concerning your future, and mine?"
>
> "That we shall die."
>
> "Yes. There's really only one question that can be answered, Genry, and we already know the answer . . . the only thing that makes life possible is permanent, intolerable uncertainty: not knowing what comes next."

The fine irony, that this is the master Foreteller speaking, is almost irrelevant to Le Guin's profound narrative purpose. She herself is the master of a dialectical narrative mode in which nothing happens without involving its opposite. The shrewdly elliptical title, *The Left Hand of Darkness*, leaves out the crucial substantive in Le Guin's Taoist verse:

> Light is the left hand of darkness
> and darkness the right hand of light.
> Two are one, life and death, lying

> together like lovers in kemmer,
> like hands joined together,
> like the end and the way.

The way is the Tao, exquisitely fused by Le Guin into her essentially Northern mythology. "Kemmer" is the active phase of the cycle of human sexuality on the planet Gether or Winter, the site of *The Left Hand of Darkness*. Winter vision, even in the books widely separated in substance and tone from her masterpiece, best suits Le Guin's kind of storytelling. Mythology, from her childhood on, seems to have meant Norse rather than Classical stories. Like Blake's and Emily Brontë's, her imagination is at home with Odin and Yggdrasil. Yet she alters the cosmos of the Eddas so that it loses some, not all, of its masculine aggressiveness and stoic harshness. Her Taoism, rather than her equivocal Jungianism, has the quiet force that tempers the ferocity of the Northern vision.

II

"Visibility without discrimination, solitude without privacy," is Le Guin's judgment upon the capital of the Shing, who in 4370 A.D. rule what had been the United States, in her novel, *City of Illusions*. In an introduction to *The Left Hand of Darkness*, belatedly added to the book seven years after its publication, Le Guin sharply reminds us that: "I write science fiction, and science fiction isn't about the future. I don't know any more about the future than you do, and very likely less." Like Faxe the Weaver, she prefers ignorance of the future, and yet, again like Faxe, she is a master of Foretelling, which both is and is not a mode of moral prophecy. It is, in that it offers a moral vision of the present; it is not, precisely because it refuses to say that "If you go on so, the result is so." The United States in 1985 still offers "visibility without discrimination, solitude without privacy." As for the United States in 4370, one can quote "Self," a lyric meditation from Le Guin's rather neglected *Hard Words and Other Poems* (1981):

> You cannot measure the circumference
> but there are centerpoints:
> stones, and a woman washing at a ford,
> the water runs red-brown from what she washes.
> The mouths of caves. The mouths of bells.
> The sky in winter under snowclouds
> to northward, green of jade.
> No star is farther from it than the glint
> of mica in a pebble in the hand,
> or nearer. Distance is my god.

Distance, circumference, the unmeasurable, god, the actual future which can only be our dying; Le Guin evades these, and her narratives instead measure wisdom or the centerpoints. Yet the poem just before "Self" in *Hard Words*, cunningly titled "Amazed," tells us where wisdom is to be found, in the disavowal of "I" by "eye," a not un-Emersonian epiphany:

> The center is not where the center is
> but where I will be when I follow
> the lines of stones that wind about a center
> that is not there
> > but there.
> The lines of stones lead inward, bringing
> the follower to the beginning
> where all I knew
> > is new.
> Stone is stone and more than stone;
> the center opens like an eyelid opening.
> Each rose a maze: the hollow hills:
> I am not I
> > but eye.

One thinks of the shifting centers in every Le Guin narrative, and of her naming the mole as her totem in another poem. She is a maze maker or "shaper of darkness/into ways and hollows," who always likes the country on the other side. Or she is "beginning's daughter" who "sings to stones." Her Taoism celebrates the strength of water over stone, and yet stone is her characteristic trope. As her words are hard, so are most of her women and men, fit after all for Northern or winter myth. One can say of her that she writes a hard-edged phantasmagoria, or that it is the Promethean rather than the Narcissistic element in her literary fantasy that provides her with her motive for metaphor.

In some sense, all of her writings call us forth to quest into stony places, where the object of the quest can never quite be located. Her most mature quester, the scientist Shevek in *The Dispossessed*, comes to apprehend that truly he is both subject and object in the quest, always already gone on, always already there. A Promethean anarchist, Shevek has surmounted self-consciousness and self-defense, but at the cost of a considerable loss in significance. He represents Le Guin's ideal Odonian society, where the isolated idealist like Shelley or Kropotkin has become the norm, yet normative anarchism cannot be represented except as permanent revolution, and permanent revolution defies aesthetic as well as political representation. Shevek is beyond these limits of representation and more than that, "his hands were empty, as they had always been." Deprived of the wounded self-regard that our primary narcissism converts into aggression, Shevek becomes nearly as colorless as the actual personality upon whom he is based, the physicist Robert Oppenheimer. Even Le Guin cannot have it both ways; the ideological anarchism of *The Dispossessed* divests her hero of his narcissistic ego, and so of much of his fictive interest. Jung is a better psychological guide in purely mythic realms, like Le Guin's Earthsea, then he is in psychic realms closer to our own, as in *The Dispossessed.*

III

Le Guin's greatest accomplishment, certainly reflecting the finest balance of her powers, is *The Left Hand of Darkness*, though I hasten to name this her finest work *to date.* At fifty-five, she remains beginning's daughter, and there are imaginative felicities in *The Beginning Place* (1980) that are subtler and bolder than anything in *The Left Hand of Darkness* (1969). But conceptually and stylistically, *Left Hand* is the strongest of her dozen or so major narratives. It is a book that sustains many rereadings, partly because its enigmas are unresolvable, and partly because it has the crucial quality of a great representation, which is that it yields up new perspectives upon what we call reality. Though immensely popular (some thirty paperback printings), it seems to me critically undervalued, with rather too much emphasis upon its supposed flaws. The best known negative critique is by Stanislaw Lem, who judged the sexual element in the book irrelevant to its story, and improbably treated in any case. This is clearly a weak misreading on Lem's part. What the protagonist, Genly Ai, continuously fails to understand about the inhabitants of the planet Winter is precisely that their sexuality gives them a mode of consciousness profoundly alien to his (and ours). Le Guin, with admirable irony, replied to feminist and other critics that indeed she had "left out too much" and could "only be very grateful to those readers, men and women, whose willingness to participate in the experiment led them to fill in that omission with the work of their own imagination." Too courteous to say, with Blake, that her care was not to make matters explicit to the idiot, Le Guin wisely has relied upon her extraordinary book to do its work of self-clarification across the fifteen years of its reception.

The book's principal aesthetic strength is its representation of the character and personality of Estraven, the Prime Minister who sacrifices position, honor, freedom and finally his life in order to hasten the future, by aiding Genly Ai's difficult mission. As the ambassador of the Ekumen, a benign federation of planets, Ai needs to surmount his own perspective as a disinterested cultural anthropologist if he is to understand the androgynes who make up the entire population of the isolated planet alternatively called Gethen or Winter. Without understanding, there is no hope of persuading them, even for their own obvious good, to join with the rest of the cosmos. What is most interesting about Ai (the name suggesting at once the ego, the eye, and an outcry of pain) is his reluctance to go beyond the limits of his own rationality, which would require seeing the causal link between his sexuality and mode of consciousness.

The sexuality of the dwellers upon the planet Winter remains Le Guin's subtlest and most surprising invention:

> A Gethenian in first-phase kemmer, if kept alone or with others not in kemmer, remains incapable of coitus. Yet the sexual impulse is tremendously strong in this phase, controlling the entire personality, subjecting all other drives to its imperative. When the individual finds a partner in kemmer, hormonal secretion is further stimulated (most importantly by touch—secretion? scent?) until in one partner either a male or female hormonal dominance is established. The genitals engorge or shrink accordingly, foreplay intensifies, and the partner, triggered by the change, takes on the other sexual role (? without exception? If there are exceptions, resulting in kemmer—partners of the same sex, they are so rare as to be ignored).

The narrator here is neither Ai nor Le Guin but a field investigator of the Ekumen, wryly cataloging a weird matter. Her field notes add a number of sharper observations: these androgynes have no sexual drive at all for about 21 or 22 out of every 26 days. Anyone can and usually does bear children, "and the mother of several children may be the father of several more," descent being reckoned from the mother, known as "the parent in the flesh." There is no Oedipal ambivalence of children toward parents, no rape or unwilling sex, no dualistic division of humankind into active and passive. All Gethenians are natural monists, with no need to sublimate anything, and little inclination towards warfare.

Neither Le Guin nor any of her narrators give us a clear sense of any casual relation between a world of nearly perpetual winter and the ambisexual nature of its inhabitants, yet an uncanny association between the context of coldness and the unforseeable sexuality of each individual persists throughout. Though Lem insisted anxiety must attend the unpredictability of one's gender, Le Guin's book persuasively refuses any such anxiety. There is an imaginative intimation that entering upon *any* sexual identity for about one-fifth of the time is more than welcome to anyone

who must battle perpetually just to stay warm! Le Guin's humor, here as
elsewhere, filters in slyly, surprising us in a writer who is essentially both
somber and serene.

The one Gethenian we get to know well is Estraven, certainly a
more sympathetic figure than the slow-to-learn Ai. Estraven is Le Guin's
greatest triumph in characterization, and yet remains enigmatic, as he
must. How are we to understand the psychology of a manwoman, utterly
free of emotional ambivalence, of which the masterpiece after all is the
Oedipal conflict? And how are we to understand a fiercely competitive
person, since the Gethenians are superbly agonistic, who yet lacks any
component of sexual aggressiveness, let alone its cause in a sexually
wounded narcissism? Most fundamentally we are dualists, and perhaps our
involuntary and Universal Freudianism (present even in a professed Jungian, like Le Guin) is the result of that being the conceptualized dualism
most easily available to us. But the people of Winter are Le Guin's shrewd
way of showing us that all our dualisms—Platonic, Pauline, Cartesian,
Freudian—not only have a sexual root but are permanent because we are
bisexual rather than ambisexual beings. Freud obviously would not have
disagreed, and evidently Le Guin is more Freudian than she acknowledges
herself to be.

Winter, aside from its properly ghastly weather, is no Utopia.
Karhide, Estraven's country, is ruled by a clinically mad king, and the
rival power, Orgoreyn, is founded upon a barely hidden system of concentration camps. Androgyny is clearly neither a political nor a sexual ideal
in *The Left Hand of Darkness.* And yet, mysteriously and beautifully, the
book suggests that Winter's ambisexuality is a more imaginative condition
than our bisexuality. Like the unfallen Miltonic angels, the Gethenians
know more than either men or women can know. As with the angels, this
does not make them better or wiser, but evidently they *see* more than we
do, since each one of them is Tiresias, as it were. This, at last, is the
difference between Estraven and Genly Ai. Knowing and seeing more,
Estraven is better able to love, and freer therefore to sacrifice than his
friend can be.

Yet that, though imaginative, is merely a generic difference. Le Guin's
art is to give us also a more individual difference between Ai and Estraven.
Ai is a kind of skeptical Horatio who arrives almost too late at a love for
Estraven as a kind of ambisexual Hamlet, but who survives, like Horatio,
to tell his friend's story:

> For it seemed to me, and I think to him, that it was from that sexual
> tension between us, admitted now and understood, but not assuaged,
> that the great and sudden assurance of friendship between us rose: a

friendship so much needed by us both in our exile, and already so well proved in the days and nights of our bitter journey, that it might as well be called, now as later, love. But it was from the difference between us, not from the affinities and likenesses, but from the difference, that that love came. . . .

The difference is more than sexual, and so cannot be bridged by sexual love, which Ai and Estraven avoid. It is the difference between Horatio and Hamlet, between the audience's surrogate and the tragic hero, who is beyond both surrogate and audience. Estraven dies in Ai's arms, but uttering his own dead brother's name, that brother having been his incestuous lover, and father of Estraven's son. In a transference both curious and moving, Estraven has associated Ai with his lost brother-lover, to whom he had vowed faithfulness. It is another of Le Guin's strengths that, in context, this has intense pathos and nothing of the grotesque whatsoever. More than disbelief becomes suspended by the narrative art of *The Left Hand of Darkness*.

IV

That Le Guin, more than Tolkien, has raised fantasy into high literature, for our time, seems evident to me because her questers never abandon the world where we have to live, the world of Freud's reality principle. Her praise of Tolkien does not convince me that *The Lord of the Rings* is not tendentious and moralizing, but her generosity does provide an authentic self-description:

> For like all great artists he escapes ideology by being too quick for its nets, too complex for its grand simplicities, too fantastic for its rationality, too real for its generalizations.

This introduction could end there, but I would rather allow Le Guin to speak of herself directly:

> Words are my matter. I have chipped one stone
> for thirty years and still it is not done,
> that image of the thing I cannot see.
> I cannot finish it and set it free,
>   transformed to energy.

There is a touch of Yeats here, Le Guin's voice being most her own in narrative prose, but the burden is authentic Le Guin: the sense of limit, the limits of the senses, the granite labor at hard words, and the ongoing image that is her characteristic trope, an unfinished stone. Like her Genly Ai, she is a far-fetcher, to use her own term for visionary metaphor. It was also the Elizabethan rhetorician Puttenham's term for transumption or metalepsis, the trope that reverses time, and makes lateness into an earliness. Le Guin is a grand far-fetcher or transumer of the true tradition of romance we call literary fantasy. No one else now among us matches her at rendering freely "that image of the thing I cannot see."

DAVID KETTERER

Ursula K. Le Guin's Archetypal "Winter-Journey"

As distinct from the general recognition that a relationship exists between mythology and any form of literature, science-fiction criticism has recently made much of science fiction as a peculiarly significant vehicle for myth. Unfortunately this idea is being taken rather too literally by a growing number of science-fiction writers, with the result that their work, far from being the articulation of a "new mythology," to use a current critical cliché, consists essentially of the sterile revamping of the old. It is not of course totally erroneous to speak of science fiction as a "new mythology," but what I wish to deplore is the lack of particularity that generally accompanies such assertions. New-mythology critics are curiously loath to offer specific examples, although possible exhibits are certainly at hand. There is for instance what might be called the "terminal beach" myth, to appropriate Ballard's title, the notion being that, just as, in Darwin's view, the transposition of life from the sea to the land allowed for the genesis of humanity, so the end of man might appropriately be envisaged as taking place "on the beach," to utilize Nevil Shute's title. H. G. Wells is perhaps the originator of this "myth." His time traveler's glimpses of Earth's end are from "a sloping beach," while, in a short story entitled "The Star" (1897), the destruction that follows in the wake of that errant body is depicted as follows: "Everywhere the waters were pouring off the land, leaving mud-silted ruins, and the earth littered like a storm-worn beach with all that had floated, and the dead bodies of the men and brutes, its children."

In Northrop Frye's formulation, the mythic basis of any fiction, aside from the occasional reworkings of an O'Neill or a Sartre, should exist irrespective of an author's intentions and in a severely displaced relationship to the story line. In science-fiction novels such as *The Einstein Intersection* (1967) and *Nova* (1968), by Samuel R. Delany, and some of Roger Zelazny's work, there is no doubt as to the author's conscious awareness of his mythic source material and very little attempt at displacement aside from matters of environment. Inevitably in such fictions the logic of plot development is at the service of a mythic structure, and suffers accordingly. *The Left Hand of Darkness*, by Ursula K. Le Guin, the 1969 Hugo *and* Nebula Award winner, is a further case in point. But something is gained here, because, to a degree, this work functions as a science-fiction novel about the writing of a science-fiction novel and is particularly informative for that reason. Since the various fictional genres can be meaningfully defined in relation to basic myths or to segments of myth, the mythic concern of Le Guin's novel, in spite of its attendant deleterious effects on the narrative, does have its point.

As I have argued [elsewhere], science fiction is concerned with effecting what might be termed an epistemological or philosphical apocalypse. A new world destroys an old world. Given that this apocalyptic transformation involves the mythic structure of death and rebirth, for which the cycle of the seasons is the model, we can speculate as to why Gethen, the new world in *The Left Hand of Darkness*, enjoys such an inhospitable climate that the place is known, in English, as Winter. At the same time perhaps we can hypothesize some connection with Frye's "mythos of winter," by which he distinguishes the duplicitous modes of irony and satire, as opposed to the unitary, "apocalyptic" mode of romance. Science fiction draws very much on the combination of satire and romance, and the concepts of unity and duality are, as I shall indicate, central to the theme of Le Guin's book.

II

The Left Hand of Darkness tells a story set in the distant future. Genly Ai has spent two unprofitable years in the nation of Karhide, on the planet Gethen, his mission being to persuade Gethen to join the Ekumen, a loose confederation of eighty or so worlds. Because of a political dispute over the desirability of joining the Ekumen and doubt as to its very existence, Ai's Gethenian friend, Estraven, one time senior councilor to Argaven XV, the mad king of Karhide, is exiled and replaced in office by his opponent, Tibe. The king gives Ai the impression that Estraven has been exiled not for promoting the Ekumen's cause, as officially stated, but for working against it.

His faith in Estraven undermined and otherwise generally frustrated, Ai tries his cause elsewhere within the Great Continent, which is divided between Karhide and the rival nation of Orgoreyn, to the northwest. At this point Estraven has already begun his exile, in Orgoreyn. The central portion of the narrative chronicles, in more or less alternating chapters, the respective yet linked careers of Ai and Estraven in Orgoreyn. Ai has the more eventful time. He crosses over at a disputed border area known as the Sinoth Valley, and his first night's sleep in Orgoreyn is interrupted by a raid from Karhide that leaves Ai without his passport (an inspector having kept it for the night) to join a group of refugees from the raid, who, also lacking identification papers, are incarcerated in a windowless cellar. The machinations of Shusgis, First Commensal District Commissioner of Entry-Roads and Ports, extricate Genly from this predicament and bring him to the Commissioner's home in Mishnory, the largest city on Gethen. In Mishnory, Genly runs into Estraven, from whom he learns something of the danger of his situation. Apparently Shusgis is a representative of the Domination faction, which is opposed to the Free Trade faction. In short, Shusgis is opposed to the Envoy's mission, and is actually an agent of the Sarf, a police organization that controls the Free Trade faction. Consequently Genly is imprisoned again, this time at the Pulefen Farm and Resettlement Agency, in the frigid northwest of Orgoreyn.

With the help of Estraven, who has, to a degree, controlled Genly's progress (he plays a part in arranging that Genly feel disposed to leave Karhide when the king begins to favor an unfriendly faction), the Envoy escapes. The concluding third of the book traces their tortuous journey "north through the mountains, east across the Gobrin, and down to the border at Guthen Bay"—the Gobrin being the notorious ice sheet and the border being that fronting on Karhide. Estraven had sent word to King Argaven of the Envoy's arrest on the assumption that Argaven, ignoring Tibe's advice, would inquire and would be falsely informed by Mishnory of Genly's unfortunate death. Estraven later believes that, on discovering Genly's presence in North Karhide, Argaven, now aware of Orgoreyn's duplicitous treatment of the Envoy, would be sympathetic to Genly's mission and enable him to safely call down his star ship, which has all the time been circling Gethen. Except that Estraven, a traitor in his own country, is shot attempting to cross the border back into Orgoreyn, everything, however unlikely, happens as planned: Gethen joins the Ekumen.

III

That an "intelligible" summary of the often arbitrary action of Le Guin's novel is possible without any mention of what it is that makes the Gethenians especially distinctive, especially alien—namely their unique form of bisexuality—argues against the book's structural integrity. The truth of the situation appears to be that Gethenian sexuality, like Gethen's climate, has less to do with the surface plot than with the underlying mythic pattern of destruction or division and creation or unity. Making sense of the novel, and this is its essential weakness, depends upon an act of dislocation on the part of the reader and seeing what should be implicit as explicit, seeing the way in which the mythic structure rigorously, almost mechanically, determines the various turns of the plot. The Gethenians alternate between periods of twenty-one or twenty-two days when they are sexually neuter, neither male nor female, and six-day periods of *kemmer*, when they become sexually active and take on sexual identity. When a Gethenian in kemmer has located a partner in a similar condition, intercourse is possible. During the successive phases of kemmer, one of the parties will develop male sexual organs and the other, female, depending upon how they react to one another. It is therefore possible for any Gethenian to become pregnant. Incest, except between generations, is allowed, with minor restrictions.

It is proposed that, as a result of their ambisexuality, Gethenians are much less prone to the dualistic perception that conceivably is related to the permanent male/female split that characterizes most other forms of humanity: "There is no division of humanity into strong and weak halves, protective/protected, dominant/submissive, owner/chattel, active/passive." Commenting on the Orgota (i.e., of Orgoreyn) word translated as "commensal," "commensality," for almost any form of group organization, Genly remarks on "this curious lack of distinction between the general and specific applications of the word, in the use of it for both the whole and the part, the state and the individual, in this imprecision is its precisest meaning." As one of the Handdarata Foretellers (whom Genly consults at one point), Estraven is "less aware of the gap between men and beasts, being more occupied with the likenesses, the links, the whole of which living things are a part." Genly concludes, "You're isolated, and undivided. Perhaps you are as obsessed with wholeness as we are with dualism."

This Gethenian peculiarity is epitomized by the book's title, which is extracted from "Tormer's Lay":

Light is the left hand of darkness
and darkness the right hand of light.

Here is capsulized the destruction of unity and the reemergence of unity out of a disparate duality, a movement implicit in the thesis-antithesis-synthesis structural arrangement of the book and a movement basic to my theoretical definition of science fiction. From the Gethenian point of view, a unified Gethenian reality is destroyed by the knowledge of the much larger reality of the Ekumen confederation prior to being incorporated in that larger unity. Likewise, the reader's terrestrial vision is destroyed and then reintegrated to the extent that, during the reading process, he accepts the world of Gethen with its aberrant sexuality and the apocalyptic suggestion that both Gethen and Terran civilization were experiments by superior beings on the planet Hain. Le Guin's book effects a philosophical apocalypse in the three ways that science fiction can: by presenting a radically different image of man, by pointing to the existence of a previously unsuspected outside manipulator, and thirdly, as a consequence, by radically altering man's vision of human reality. The sense of mystical unity that "Tormer's Lay" initially suggests suffers an interim disorientation because of the paradoxical equation of the concrete with the abstract and the reversed correlation of light with the left hand, given the sinister associations of left, and of darkness with the right hand. But, almost immediately, the traditional association between the female and the left and between the female and primal darkness helps reintegrate the breach.

IV

The state of division that Genly brings to Gethen is dramatized by means of a series of widening objective correlatives. Estraven, the first alien to whom we are introduced, is presented twice by Genly as "the person on my left," hence somewhat apart and unfamiliar. The king of Karhide, being mad, is presumably divorced from his true self and thus a symbol of disorder and chaos. Hence the efficacy of deception and the rise of Tibe to power, Tibe who is spoken of as possessing the non-Gethenian trick of hate. Of course the major analogy for the state of duality, division, and destruction resides in this piece of information from Estraven: "You know that Karhide and Orgoreyn have a dispute concerning a stretch of our border in the high North Fall near Sassinoth." We are told, "If civilization has an opposite, it is war," with the implication that we infer the opposition between order and chaos. In normal times war is unknown in

Gethen, perhaps because of the lack of continuous sexual differentiation. It is hypothesized that war may "be a purely masculine displacement-activity, a vast Rape."

In Orgoreyn both Genly and Estraven are in exile, a condition of separation, Genly from his kind and Estraven from his homeland, although, in some ways, faction-ridden Orgoreyn is a mirror image of Karhide just as Gethen is an inverted image of Earth. As Estraven is approaching the shore of Orgoreyn, he observes, "Darkness lay behind my back, before the boat, and into darkness I must row." For Genly the experience in Orgoreyn is also that of darkness, darkness betokening the destruction of reality, death and chaos. The raid that issues from an unspecified border town of Karhide appears to be a dream. After supper in Siuwensin, Genly "fell asleep in that utter country silence that makes your ears ring. I slept an hour and woke in the grip of a nightmare about explosions, invasions, murder, and conflagration." This is the moment of apocalypse. Although Genly has mentioned waking, he continues to speak of what is happening as a dream: "It was a particularly bad dream, the kind in which you run down a strange street in the dark with a lot of people who have no faces, while houses go up in flame behind you, and children scream." From this moment until Genly's revival or rebirth from his mock death (arranged by Estraven to aid the escape from Orgoreyn), unreal in a literal sense but real in a symbolic sense, the reader cannot be totally sure that everything is not a dream. But this intervening loss of a stable reality, one of the more subtle aspects of the book, is exactly appropriate as an analogy for the destructive effect the apocalyptic transformations of science fiction have on conventional reality. Thus it is that *The Left Hand of Darkness* may be viewed as a science-fiction novel about the theoretical definition of science fiction.

In his "dream," Genly is incarcerated with a group of refugees in a windowless "vast stone semi-cellar": "The door shut, it was perfectly dark: no light." Genly is metaphorically "in the dark" for most of the time in Orgoreyn, as witness his ambiguous description of Mishnory, the capital city: "It was not built for sunlight. It was built for winter." Yet, at the same time, Genly felt as if he had "come out of a dark age" in Karhide. This sense of unreality is subsequently confirmed by Genly's description of the buildings of central Mishnory: "Their corners were vague, their façades streaked, dewed, smeared. There was something fluid, insubstantial, in the very heaviness of this city built on monoliths, this monolithic state which called the part and the whole by the same name."

Later, confined in a windowless truck on his way to Pulefen Farm, Genly begins to understand the chaotic nature of Orgoreyn:

> It was the second time I had been locked in the dark with uncomplaining, unhopeful people of Orgoreyn. I knew now the sign I had been given my first night in this country. I had ignored that black cellar and gone looking for the substance of Orgoreyn above ground, in daylight. No wonder nothing had seemed real.

Genly is suffering the sense of dislocated confusion attendant upon his awareness of a new world—the lack of co-ordinate points: "One's magnetic and directional substances are all wrong on other planets; when the intellect won't or can't compensate for that wrongness, the result is a profound bewilderment, a feeling that everything, literally, has come loose." This is, of course, also a description of the apocalyptic sense of disorientation that the reader of science fiction experiences and that is perhaps the major reason why he reads the stuff. This experience is not unique to science fiction; it is just more purely expressed in the science-fiction form. Indeed the repeated references to the truck as a "steel box," "our box," and "existence in the steel box" are surely reminiscent of Private Henry Fleming's experiences, in a sense apocalyptic, in *The Red Badge of Courage*, as a member of an army that is referred to as a directionless "moving box." And it is surely not accidental that Estraven's first job on arrival in Orgoreyn involves running "a machine which fits together and heatbonds pieces of plastic to form little transparent boxes," symbols presumably of unconscious containment, isolation, alienation, separation, and hence destruction and chaos. As a final analogy to the import of dualism, the mock death of Genly and the deaths of Estraven and of King Argaven's son all betoken the destruction of an old world of mind in the face of a radically new vision.

V

The extent to which the mythic pattern of death and rebirth underlies the action of the novel is reinforced by the "myths" injected into the book in relation to various aspects of the plot. The myth of the "Place inside the Blizzard," in which two brothers, one then dead, who had vowed kemmering to one another, are momentarily reunited, bears on the later action. Hode, the dead brother, seized the other, Gethenen, "by the left hand," which as a consequence, was frozen and subsequently amputated. The Place inside the Blizzard is clearly a mystic point where life and death may be united. It subsequently transpires that Estraven had vowed kemmering to his now-dead brother although, as Estraven reflects, his "shadow followed me." Later, as anticipated, Estraven and Genly find themselves "inside the blizzard," a kind of still point. This mythic configuration culminates at the novel's conclusion, when Genly is introduced to Sorve Harth, the child of the two brothers, now both dead. Thus life and death are one, an intuition rather clumsily underscored by the book's final lines, Sorve's question to Genly regarding Estraven: "Will you tell us how he died?—Will you tell us about the other worlds out among the stars—the other kinds of men, the other lives?"

Estraven, in fact, has a family history of bringing unity out of discord through "treachery," as is indicated in the Romeo-and-Juliet-like mythic story of "Estraven the Traitor." The matching hands of two mortal enemies make for a reconciliation. This is the myth Estraven re-enacts with Genly. Although they are aliens to each other, they become as one, particularly when Estraven exhibits a capacity for telepathic communication or "bespeaking," as it is appropriately termed. In this way, the mind expansion attendant upon the awareness of a new reality is made both metaphoric and literal. Why speak of telepathic communication as the "Last Art" if not to insinuate the possibility of an apocalypse of mind? And although it is not possible to communicate telepathically anything other than the truth, Estraven believes at one point that it is his dead brother Arek bespeaking him rather than Genly.

Later, as a consequence of his telepathic awareness, Genly, hearing Estraven's words, believes that he himself spoke them. This is a confusion that the reader is made to share, since, although most of the story is told from Genly's point of view, several chapters, without warning, are narrated from Estraven's perspective. Genly explains: "The story is not all mine, nor told by me alone. Indeed I am not sure whose story it is; you can judge better. But it is all one, and if at moments the facts seem to alter with an altered voice, why then you can choose the fact you like best; yet none of them are false, and it is all one story." What confusion exists is designed to augment the impression of unity. There is a similar gain in Chapter 7, "The Question of Sex," where Le Guin plays on the reader's expectations by delaying, until the end of the chapter, the revelation that the anthropological notes by Ong Tot Oppong are the work of a woman.

Unity of awareness is also enjoyed by the Handdarata Foretellers, who are introduced in the chapter of injected myth called "The Nineteenth Day," which illustrates the rather vague nature of their prophecies, a vagueness Genly recognizes when he consults them. The Foretellers are controlled by Faxe the Weaver, who brings the various disparate and chaotic forces together like "the suspension-points of a spiderweb." Indeed the weaving imagery, which permeates the book and may be related to the triangular netlike structure created by the relationship of unity to duality, finds its nucleus here. Genly feels himself "hung in the center of a spiderweb woven of silence," "a point or figure in the pattern, in the web." The act of putting together a novel and creating an aesthetic unity can be imaged as a weaving process. Thus Genly speaks of forgetting "how I meant to weave the story." Estraven, making his way to rescue Genly from Pulefen Farm, travels by caravan "weaving from town to town." Traveling between two volcanoes, Drummer and Dremegole, the hissing sound of Drummer, which is an eruption, "fills all the interstices of one's being." These "interstices" may be seen as objectified by the "crevasses" or "crevassed area" to which repeated references are made during the journey across the ice; objectified also by the indirect, crisscross path that Genly and Estraven travel, invariably turning "east-northeast by compass" or "a little south of east" and almost never directly north, south, east, or west. On a larger scale, what is referred to as the "shifgrethor" relationship in Gethenian society appears to be a theoretical network or unformulated pattern of right behavior, rather similar in fact to that web of worlds known as the Ekumen, which is not so much a "body politic, but a body mystic" modeled on the process of evolution. In view of the importance of webbed relationships to the awareness of a new unity, it is in no way accidental that Faxe the Weaver, at the end of the book, is likely to take Tibe's place as the Prime Minister of Karhide.

VI

The *Left Hand of Darkness*, which begins with a chapter entitled "A Parade in Erhenrang" and ends with chapters entitled "Homecoming" and "A Fool's Errand," is primarily concerned with the journey from Karhide to Orgoreyn, "One Way" or "Another Way," and back to Karhide following "The Escape" from Pulefen Farm. Physically the journey describes a jagged clockwise circle. I mention its being clockwise because the book, beginning and ending in late spring, covers a temporal cycle. What is being dramatized is the ultimate unity of space and time. Since Gethen is known as the planet Winter, when Genly speaks of his and Estraven's "winter-journey" it is intended that the reader infer the identification of space and time—it is a journey across and through Winter with, as I have intimated, all the associations of Frye's mythos of winter. The period of death and destruction here symbolized by winter is occasioned by the conjunction of an old and a new world of mind, the basic concern of science fiction.

The journey to and across the ice is replete with imagery suggestive of the forces of creation. Two injections of Gethenian myth point the way. "On Time and Darkness" explains that "Meshe [note the net implications] is the Center of Time," Meshe being the founder of the Yomesh cult, which broke from the Handdarata. Genly experiences something of this insight traveling by truck with a group of prisoners to Pulefen Farm: "We drew together and merged into one entity occupying one space." One member of the group dies. It is significant that just before Estraven's death, Genly is "taken by fits of shuddering like those I had experienced in the prison-truck crossing Orgoreyn." Once again it should be apparent that all the narrative action illustrates the two basic structures of division/ duality and unity. The sense of temporal unity at Meshe is perhaps the inspiration for the Gethenian method of numbering the year backward and forward from the present year, which is consequently always at the center.

"An Orgota Creation Myth" provides a second pointer. We are told, "In the beginning there was nothing but ice and the sun," a notation that explains the landscape through which Genly and Estraven have just passed. The previous chapter ends with a reference to "the veiled sun, the ice." In the process of reaching the blindingly white Gobrin Glacier, white with all the implications of fusion and unity that the color holds for Poe at the polar conclusion of his *Narrative of A. Gordon Pym*, Genly and Estraven have made their way between the two volcanoes of Drummer and Dremegole, Drummer in eruption. The impression is of "the dirty chaos of a world in the process of making itself." The creation myth concludes with a reference to Meshe, "the middle of time," which explains the environment of the next chapter. On the Gobrin Glacier, Genly feels himself and Estraven to be "at the center of all things." It is "On the Ice" that Genly truly comes to recognize Estraven as both man and woman. "Until then I had rejected him, refused him his own reality." The telepathic experience and the experience "Inside the Blizzard" follows his understanding. This mutual understanding, which is equivalent to a re- birth, is symbolized by changes in the environment as "that bland blind nothingness about us began to flow and writhe" and the incident in which Genly "delivers" Estraven from a crevasse into which he falls to emerge with a vision of "Blue—all blue—Towers in the Depths." The crevasses become the cracks in an eggshell, with Genly and Estraven both inside and outside.

This unifying sense of a microcosm and macrocosm is dramatized by the arrival of the Ekumen star ship. It is as if the world view of the Ekumen and that of Gethen are collapsed together. Genly plans his call to the ship with a consciousness of setting "the keystone in the arch." One thinks perhaps of Hart Crane's bridge or the bridge on Jupiter in the first volume of Blish's *Cities in Flight* but more particularly of the keystone ceremony with which *The Left Hand of Darkness* opens, which is now seen for its symbolic significance. From among the stars, which have earlier been likened to "far cities," the approaching ship is quite literally "one star descending"; I say literally because it represents "the coming of a new world, a new mankind." For the reader, a metaphorical conflation of Earth and Gethen has already taken place encouraged by King Argaven's initially disconcerting reference to Gethenians as "human beings here on earth" and by Estraven's similar reference to Gethen as "this earth." In addition Genly points out, "Fundamentally Terra and Gethen are very much alike. All the inhabited worlds are."

My point has been that Le Guin's use of duality and unity as mythically connotative of destruction and creation is in fact a way of talking about the relationship between new and old worlds of mind and that this relationship is at the theoretical basis of science fiction. As such, *The Left Hand of Darkness* is a skillfully integrated, perhaps I should say woven, piece of work, although my criticism that the plot is unfortunately subordinate to the overly conscious use of mythic material remains. The world of the novel, like the snowbound ecology of Gethen and the snowy metaphors it gives rise to, is developed with a consistency that at least equals Frank Herbert's sandbound world of *Dune*. Mention of "a snow-worm" recalls the sand-worms of *Dune* (1965), which figure so prominently in the plot of that novel. But Le Guin's single and singular reference is perhaps indicative of that loss of dramatic surface incident compelled by her rigorous adherence to a mythic design insufficiently displaced. To use a repeated Gethenian image of unity, the wheel of Le Guin's plot turns rather too inexorably and predictably in its seasonal and mythic groove.

DOUGLAS BARBOUR

Wholeness and Balance in the Hainish Novels

The five stories by Ursula K. Le Guin
with which this essay is directly concerned—*Rocannon's World* (1966),
Planet of Exile (1966), *City of Illusions* (1967), *The Left Hand of Darkness*
(1969), and "The Word for World is Forest" (1972)—are all set in what
may be called the Hainish universe, for it was the people of the planet
Hain who originally "seeded" all the habitable worlds of this part of the
galaxy and thus produced a humanoid universe that is single, expanding,
and historically continuous, but at the same time marvelous in its variety,
for each planetary environment caused specific local mutations in its
humanoids as they adapted and developed. The result is a universe full of
"humans" who display enough variety to provide for any number of alien
encounters, and since any possible stage of civilization can be found on
some particular planet, new definitions of "civilization" can be made in a
narrative rather than a discursive mode.

In *Rocannon's World* and *Planet of Exile* Le Guin sketches in the
background of the League of All Worlds, which is preparing to fight an
Enemy from some distant part of the galaxy, and prepares the reader for
City of Illusions, which is the story of the man who will eventually
"rescue" humanity from the Shing, the mind-lying aliens. *The Left Hand
of Darkness* is set in an even further future when the Shing have been
defeated and most of humanity has once again united, this time in the
Ekumen of Known Worlds—a subtler and humbler title than the former

From *Science-Fiction Studies* 3, vol. 1 (Spring 1974). Copyright © 1974 by R. D.
Miller and Darko Suvin.

one. "The Word for World is Forest," being set in the first year of the League, brings the Hainish universe comparatively close to our own time.

Besides the continuous time-space history, these narratives are bound together by a consistent imagery that both extends and informs meaning. Although Le Guin has used particular images which emerge naturally from the cultural and ecological context of her imagined worlds as linking devices within each work, she has also consistently used light/dark imagery as a linking device for the whole series. Again and again, good emerges from ambiguous darkness, evil from blinding light. Thus there is a specific local imagery in each novel, and a pervasive light/dark imagery in all of them.

In *Rocannon's World* the local image is the "Eye of the Sea." This jewel, the efficient cause of Semley's actions in the "Prologue," appears throughout Rocannon's adventures until, when he has accomplished his task, he gives it, as a final sign that he has found his home, to the Lady Ganye, who, at the end of the story, appears as "his widow, tall and fair-haired, wearing a great blue jewel set in gold at her throat."

The light/dark imagery is more pervasive and more complex. From the very beginning the interdependence of light and darkness are made clear. Take Kyo's explanation of the difference between his people and the Gdmiar: the Fiia chose to live only in the light, the Clayfolk chose "night and caves and swords" (Chap. 7), and both lost something by their choice. The image of the Fiia dance, "a play of light and dark in the glow of the fire" (Chap. 7), reflects a pattern which Rocannon realizes had existed between Kyo and himself. This *dance* of shadows and light is the proper image for their interplay in all Le Guin's work: both the light and the dark are necessary if any pattern is to emerge from chaos (see *Left* Chap. 16). When Rocannon meets the Ancient One, he must enter the "dark place" to gain the gift of mind-hearing (Chap. 8). Later he enters the FTL ships on "a night when of all the four moons only the little captured asteroid . . . would be in the sky before midnight" (Chap. 9). The success of his mission, the explosion destroying the enemy base, is marked by "not the light but the darkness, the darkness that blinded his mind, the knowledge in his own flesh of the death of a thousand men all in one moment" (Chap. 9). Clearly and consistently light/dark images dance through the whole novel.

The title of the first chapter in *Planet of Exile*, "A Handful of Darkness," refers to Agat's dark hand against Rolery's white one. The alliance of farborns and hilfs, of black and white, is touched on through-out the novel: Agat's and Rolery's growing love is imaged in these terms. As Rolery "seemed to hold against her palm a handful of darkness, where his touch had been," so Agat "recalled briefly . . . the light, lithe, frightened figure of the girl Rolery, reaching up her hand to him from the dark sea-besieged stones" (Chap. 3). Rolery feels a "little rush of fear and darkness through her veins" (Chap. 5) because she is a natural telepath and has been "bespoken" by Agat; later, when Agat is attacked and wounded and sends out calls for help, "Rolery's mind went quite dark for a while" (Chap. 6) and she is the one to find him. Both are young and fear the Winter, for they have only "known the sunlight" (Chap. 5). That oncoming 5000-day cold spell provides some of the local image patterns of this novel, as do the customs of the Askatevar, but the light/dark imagery weaves its way from book to book.

"Imagine darkness. In the darkness that faces outward from the sun a mute spirit woke. Wholly involved in chaos, he knew no pattern." Thus begins *City of Illusion*, and thus begins Falk's book-long search for the correct pattern, one made up of light and darkness as all good patterns must be. Naturally enough, in a story of lie and paradox, light and dark seldom carry ordinary meanings. Falk begins and ends in darkness, yet the two darknesses are opposed: the first a mental chaos, the last an important part of the whole pattern he has sought. As the images gather, we begin to see the pattern, and the play of paradox and illusion within it. The old Listener's warning about "the awful darkness of the bright lights of Es Toch" (Chap. 3) presents one of the central paradoxes, one Falk must resolve if he is to survive. In Es Toch it is "the word spoken in darkness with none to hear at the beginning, the first page of time" to which Falk turns as he tries to outmaneuver the Shing (Chap. 8).

The two major local images are the "patterning frame" (Chaps. 1, 5) and the "Way" of the "Old Canon" (i.e., the *Tao-te ching*). References to Falk as a stone within the frame appear throughout the story, as do quotations from and allusions to the *Tao*. Falk-Ramarren's final recognition that "there's always more than one way towards the truth" (Chap. 10), which is his personal resolution of the dark/light pattern, is an "open" one. Yet it has been implicit in the imagery of the patterning frame and the *Tao*, which has been very carefully organized, and which leads directly to the novel's final paragraph:

> On the screen dawn coming over the Eastern Ocean shone in a golden crescent for a moment against the dust of the stars, like a jewel on a great patterning frame. Then frame and pattern shattered, the barrier was passed, and the little ship broke free of time and took them out across the darkness.

"Tormer's Lay," from which *The Left Hand of Darkness* takes its title (Chap. 16), suggests the importance of the light/dark image pattern in that novel. When Ai finally comes to accept and love Estraven as a whole person, he shows him the Yin-Yang symbol: "Light, dark. Fear, courage. Female, male. It is yourself, Therem. Both and one. A shadow on snow." (Chap. 19). This list of opposites yoked together expresses precisely the deep meaning that the image pattern points to; it clearly owes much to the Tao sensibility of Chuang Tzu who similarly yokes opposites together on the Way.

When Estraven says that the word *Shifgrethor*, which Ai has found impossible to understand, "comes from an old word for *shadow*" (Chap. 18), a clear light is cast back across the novel, illuminating passage after passage where shadows or the lack of them are mentioned with particular emphasis—even Ai himself had said of the Orgota that it was "as if they did not cast shadows" (Chap. 10). This sequence of images is solidly grounded in Gethenian psychology and philosophy, yet it simultaneously fits into the larger pattern that connects all the novels. In *Left Hand* shadow images concerned with personal integrity indicate what kind of person is being referred to; they are also deeply embedded in the ecology of the planet, the warm shadows of the hearths opposing the snow, the terrible cold, so bright with danger: no wonder the Handdara is a "fecund darkness" (Chap. 5).

The essential unity of light and darkness is always implicit in the imagery, as in the description of the Foretelling: "Hours and seconds passed, the moonlight shone on the wrong wall, there was no moonlight only darkness, and in the center of all darkness Faxe: the Weaver: a woman, a woman dressed in light" (Chap. 5). The Foretelling emerges from the Darkness, the very darkness the Handdara rely on, as is shown by their "short and charming grace of invocation, the only ritual words" Ai ever learns of them: "Praise then darkness and Creation unfinished" (Chap. 18). "Dothe," the special strength Handdarata can call up in their bodies, is the "strength out of the Dark," and "thangen," the sleep of recovery, is "the dark sleep" (Chap. 14). Yet Faxe the Weaver shines with his own light, even in noon sunlight (Chap. 5). As the Lay says, "Two are one . . . like the end and the way" (Chap. 16).

Having heard Estraven recite Tormer's Lay, Ai speaks of the difference between Gethenians and Terrans:

> "You're isolated, and undivided. Perhaps you are as obsessed with whole-ness as we are with dualisms."
> "We are dualists too. Duality is essential, isn't it? So long as there is *myself* and *the other*."
> "I and Thou," he said. "Yes, it does, after all, go even wider than sex. . . ."
>
> (Chap. 16)

As wide as the universe of meaning itself, the images say: wholeness and duality, together and separate at once, a pattern of life itself, woven through an artist's fictions, the matrix of her vision.

As the discussion of imagery has shown, Le Guin's artistic vision is multiplex, dualistic, and holistic. That she has never sought simplistic philosophical solutions for the human problems she explores in her narratives, could be demonstrated in her first three books, but I wish to concentrate here on her artistic handling of balance as a way of life in *The Left Hand of Darkness* and "The Word for World is Forest."

Very few science fiction books have succeeded as well as *The Left Hand of Darkness* in invoking a whole environment, a completely consistent alien world, and in making the proper extrapolations from it. Le Guin has chosen a form that allows for various kinds of "documentation": six of the twenty chapters (not to mention the Appendix) are documents separate from the actual narrative—three "Hearth tales" (Chaps. 2, 4, 9), a report on Gethenian sexuality (Chap. 7), excerpts from a sacred book (Chap. 12), and "An Orgota Creation Myth" (Chap. 17)—each placed so as to aid our understanding of the narrative at a particular point in its progression. And the narrative itself is a document, consisting partly of Ai's transcription of passages from Estraven's notebook and partly of Ai's direct report to his superiors in the officialdom of the Ekumen. The whole is a masterful example of form creating content.

Quite early in the story, immediately after a "hearth tale" concerned with their Foretellings, Ai spends considerable space reporting on his experiences at a Handdara Fastness, and it soon becomes obvious that he considers the Handdara a religion of considerable profundity. I think it is safe to assume that Le Guin means us to agree with this opinion, partly because of the way in which Handdara thought reflects the *Tao-te ching*, which is explicitly drawn upon in *City of Illusions*. In *Left Hand* the basic Handdara religious philosophy is influenced by the specific paraverbal talent the Gethenians have, yet there are many allusive connections between this invented religion and Taoism.

"The Handdara," says Ai, "is a religion without institution, without priests, without hierarchy, without vows, without creed; I am still unable to say whether it has a god or not. It is elusive. It is always somewhere else." Similarly, the *Tao-te ching*:

> The thing that is called Tao is eluding and vague.
> Vague and eluding, there is in it the form.
> Eluding and vague, in it are things.
> Deep and obscure, in it is the essence.
> (Chap. 21; translation by Wing-tsit Chan)

Although Taoist-influenced Zen Buddhism has many points in common with the Handdara, Le Guin has created in this "elusive" religion something that is still alien as well as very human. The Handdara's "only fixed manifestation is in the Fastnesses, retreats to which people may retire and spend the night or a lifetime" (Chap. 5). Ai visits the Otherhord Fastness to investigate the "foretellings" for the Ekumen; these predictions, which must be paid for, are apparently completely true. Ai arrives a skeptic and departs a believer, having participated unwillingly in the Foretelling by virtue of his own paraverbal talent. He remarks that although the humanoids of the Ekumen have certain paraverbal abilities, they have not yet "tamed hunch to run in harness; for that we must go to Gethen." But this chapter also reveals basic Handdara beliefs and attitudes which later clarify Estraven's behavior, for he has been Handdara-trained. The response of young Goss to what Ai intends as an apology for being "exceedingly ignorant"—"I'm honored! . . . I haven't yet acquired enough ignorance to be worth mentioning."—is important in that it introduces the central doctrine of Handdara life:

> It was an introverted life, self-sufficient, stagnant, steeped in that singular "ignorance" prized by the Handdarata and obedient to their rule of inactivity or non-interference. That rule (expressed in the word *nusuth*, which I have to translate as "no matter") is the heart of the cult, and I don't pretend to understand it.
>
> (Chap. 5)

Most readers will sympathize with Ai's last small complaint, but these ideas have much in common with the Tao of both Lao Tzu and Chuang Tzu. *Tao* (Chap. 37) says, "Tao invariably takes no action, and yet there is nothing left undone," and Chuang Tzu writes: "I take inaction to be true happiness, but ordinary people think it is a bitter thing. . . . the world can't decide what is right and what is wrong. And yet inaction can decide this. The highest happiness, keeping alive—only inaction gets you close to this." The time that Ai spends at the Otherhord Fastness is the happiest he has known.

The Handdarata, Estraven tells Ai, are perhaps, in comparison with the Yomeshta of Orgoreyn, who are somewhat further into the pattern of the ecology-breaking cultures of other worlds, "less aware of the gap between men and beast, being more occupied with likenesses, the links, the whole of which living things are a part" (Chap. 16). This preoccupation with wholeness and likenesses is found throughout the *Tao*, for the Way unites all things. Tormer's Lay, which Estraven recites for Ai in Chap. 16, brings to a focus the light and dark imagery which has operated with such poetic sublety throughout; it also expresses in highly charged and culturally consistent imagery the ideas of wholeness and balance which have been implicit in the language of the novel:

> Light is the left hand of darkness
> and darkness the right hand of light.
> Two are one, life and death, lying
> together like lovers in kemmer,
> like hands joined together,
> like the end and the way.

Light and darkness sharing the world and our apprehension of it: this is a deeply Taoist insight, but it is also a deeply holistic/artistic one. On Athshe, the world of "The Word for World is Forest," it is one of the bases of life for the natives, and a lost fragment of old knowledge for the Terran colonists. Here Le Guin departs from any obvious use of Taoism; instead, she approaches the theme of balance, of the light and darkness joined together, through a highly dense and specific creation of an ecology and culture inextricably entwined, and through the ideas of Dement and Hadfield on the nature of dreams. In creating a culture in which people balance their "sanity not on the razor's edge of reason but on the double support, the fine balance of reason and dream" (Chap. 5), she has also created a powerful image of holistic duality. The sanity and balance of Athshean society, the Athshean's awareness of "the whole of which living things are a part" (*Left Hand* Chap. 16), stands in stark contrast to the emotional and mental imbalance of the Earth-imperialist colonial culture which represents a logical extension of certain present-day technological and political trends. Despite the fact that the Earthmen come from all parts of the globe (ironically, their leader, Colonel Dongh, is from Viet Nam), they are all imbued with the attitudes of the "Judeo-Christian-Rationalist West," as Haber will so fondly call it in Chap. 6 of *The Lathe of Heaven* (1972).

The Terran colonists are xenophobic despite their knowledge of other star-traveling humanoid races (the story is set in the period in which the league of All Worlds is first founded): they still believe they are kings of the universe. They have no desire to understand, or, more important, learn from the hilfs. With the sole exception of Lyubov, the military men of the colony see the Athsheans as "creechies," animal-creatures; that is, as non-human and therefore to be treated as animals. Although the group is presented in general terms, the foci of interest are the individual psychologies of Davidson and Lyubov. These are extreme types, at opposite ends of the Earth-human spectrum, and in each we can see those attitudes and behavioral mannerisms which, in a mixed way, are the heritage of a civilization given over to the acquisiton of material goods and power, the attitudes of which are fixed in the Hobbesian vision of man. Davidson's nearly incoherent "reasoning" provides a spectacular instance of how a man's psychosis (in this case, paranoia) correlates to the excessive exploitation of a world's inhabitants and natural resources. Lyubov's tortured soul-searching, eager reaching out to others for knowledge, and final refusal of Selver's proffered gift of dreaming, reveal a mild, humane, liberal, and finally weak man. Selver, the Atheshean who becomes a "god" and acts with violence to protect his people when necessity so dictates, reveals by contrast the weakness of Lyubov's position.

These contrasts of character are partially exposed in light/dark imagery and partially translated into balance/imbalance imagery. The brightness of Don Davidson's mind, intense, paranoid, and in love with the fire that kills others, especially "creechies," is frighteningly unbalanced. Seeing "water and sunlight, or darkness and leaves" only as opposites, he chooses to "end the darkness, and turn the tree-jumble into clean sawn planks, more prized on Earth than gold" (Chap. 1). Earthmen, trying to balance their sanity "on the razor's edge of reason," fail to comprehend "the fine balance of reason and "dream" and thus live in fear of the dark forests of the Athsheans, where "into wind, water, sunlight, starlight, there always entered leaf and branch, bole and root, the shadowy, the complex" (Chap. 2). The complex is that fusion of light and darkness which represents wholeness. The concept of living in both dream-time and world-time reflects this wholeness. Lyubov's reflection on his original fear of the forest and his gradual acceptance of it reveals how much the Earthmen, from a technological, well-lit, treeless Earth, have lost in their relentless pursuit of power. They would clean out the forest, burn it off, to let the light shine on the barren ground that they mistakenly believe will bear growth again. Driven by the "yumens" to struggle for survival, the Athsheans have "taken up the fire they feared into their own hands: taken up the mastery over the evil dream: and loosed the death they feared upon their enemy" (Chap. 8). Truth is complex, dark and light at once, and the various images attached to the forest, that place of no revelation, "no certainty," all contribute to our understanding of this. The Athsheans are at home in the complex, and sit under a big tree to meet with the yumens: "The light beneath the great tree was soft, complex with shadows" (Chap. 8). This complexity is deeply embedded in their culture, in which everyone lives in both times, that of the dream and that of the world.

Although specific references to darkness and light are not as numerous as in some of the other stories, the pattern is definitely there, in the ambiguous forest, behind the words and images that do appear. In a very important sense, the disturbed balance of dream-time and world-time is the local image-system in this work.

Selver, recognizing the necessity of armed resistance (of fighting a war of liberation, that has obvious parallels with Third World struggles, especially that in Viet Nam), is the dreamer who becomes a god, translating to his people the terrible but necessary new dream of killing one's own kind (for the Athsheans, unlike the yumens, have recognized the essential oneness of the two races). Their survival depends upon it, but their innocence has been forever lost, and he recognizes what a terrible price that is to pay for freedom (Chap. 8). Le Guin's handling of this specific political problem is remarkable, at least in the world of popular science fiction, for its intellectual toughness: Lyubov's death results directly from his "liberal" inability to face the reality of the situation as the Athsheans have seen it. Selver survives, together with his people, because he rigorously follows the logic of the situation to its necessary conclusion: fight or be exterminated.

Le Guin's fictions are all imbued with great sympathy for the strange "human" cultures they present. Nevertheless, the Athshean culture of "Forest" is her clearest example yet of a culture presented as in basic and violent conflict with present-day "Earth-normal" standards but still as unequivocally the saner of the two. Thus the culture of the Athsheans, the ecology of Athshe, and the profound connections between them, are the focus of this novella. The ecological balance of Athshe, though not quite precarious, is delicate, as is revealed in Chapter 1 by the complete devastation of an entire island and indirectly by Davidson's thoughts on the exploitative value of this "New Tahiti." The Athshean vision emerges in a thick poetic prose at the beginning of the first Selver chapter (Chap. 2) in a description whose beauty and complexity stand in stark contrast to the prose associated with Davidson or even Lyubov. The forest is presented in a series of concrete images; then there is this:

> Nothing was dry, arid, plain. Revelation was lacking. There was no seeing everything at once: no certainty. The colors of rust and sunset kept changing in the hanging leaves of the copper willows, and you could not say even whether the leaves of the willows were brownish-red, or reddish-green, or green.
> Selver came up a path beside the water, going slowly and often stumbling on the willow roots. He saw an old man dreaming, and stopped. The old man looked at him through the long willow-leaves and saw him in his dream.

We have been introduced to the ecology from within, and to the major aspect of the culture: all that follows will merely fill out the sketch before us until it is a full portrait.

The clan system that is tied into tree names, the small village systems, the special male and female roles that have been devised to maintain the society, the major part that dreaming plays in the lives of the Athsheans, their use of "a kind of ritualized singing to replace physical combat" (Chap. 3), and many other aspects of their culture, are all brought out as the novella progresses. Lyubov explains the Athsheans in this way:

> "They're a static, stable, uniform society. They have no history. Perfectly integrated, and wholly unprogressive. You might say that like the forest they live in, they've attained a climax state. But I don't mean to imply that they're incapable of adaptation."
>
> (Chap. 3)

But even though he sees that the Athsheans might be able to adapt to meet the challenge of the Earthmen, he does not really know their culture.

The most important aspect of Athshean culture is the use of dreams. Selver says that Lyubov, despite his attempts to understand Athshean ways, "called the world-time 'real' and the dream-time 'unreal,' as if that were the difference between them" (Chap. 2). Le Guin's extrapolations from Hadfield's theories have resulted in a marvellously different culture in "Forest." If it lacks "progress," Athshean culture possesses in abundance the sanity Earth culture so obviously lacks. Lyubov's thoughts on this matter in Chapter 5 add some interesting scientific "facts" to the speculative enterprise, yet all he can see is that the Athsheans have learned to dream in a brilliant and complex fashion. The Athsheans, however, see the situation in different terms: they have learned to *live*, sanely, in both times.

The whole question of sanity, or balance, is argued in the concrete terms of fiction throughout the novel. There are two forms of art on Athshe, dreaming and singing, and both are specialized cultural activities which serve to nullify aggression against other humans. The Athsheans recognize necessity for controlling one's dreams, for dreaming properly, but the devastating impact of the Terrans has resulted in a deep cultural trauma:

> "And all men's dreams," said Cora Mena, cross-legged in shadow, "will be changed. They will never be the same again. I shall never walk again that path I came with you yesterday. . . . It is changed. You have walked

on it and it is utterly changed. . . . For you have done what you had to do, and it was not right. You have killed men.

(Chap. 2)

Having done what "was not right," Selver has become a god—"a god that knows death, a god that kills and is not himself reborn"—and for the Athsheans such a person is "a changer, a bridge between realities" (Chap. 2). The concept is clarified further by Lyubov's hesitant articulation of the implications of "sha'ab, translator" to the point where he sees that Selver is "A link: one who could speak aloud the perceptions of the subconscious. To 'speak' that tongue is to act. To do a new thing. To change or to be changed, radically, from the root. For the root is the dream." (Chap. 5). Although Selver's godhead enables him to lead the Athsheans to victory over the Terrans, it is a burden that brings him nothing but pain, loss, and insanity, and at the end he renounces it. That he should be allowed to do so is a significant example of the sanity of his culture.

His culture's sanity—the awareness that balance must be sought where dark and light meet and mix, in the ambiguous center where simple-minded "we-they" solutions fail—emerges organically from its total context in the fictional world of the novel. Yet that balance, though no longer clearly Taoist, is paralleled in the Taoist insights of *City of Illusions* and *The Left Hand of Darkness*, in the teachings of the Handdarata in the latter book, in the joining of the races in *Planet of Exile*, and in the lessons learned by Rocannon in *Rocannon's World*. For Le Guin's artistic vision, her deep understanding of the real meaning of culture, has always been ambiguous, multiplex, subtle, and dualistic/holistic in the sense that it has always recognized the cultural relativity of "truth." Always, in her work, the representatives of different cultures meet, interact, and, in the cases that count, learn of each other (often through love) that they are equally human, part of the great brotherhood of "man."

ROBERT SCHOLES

The Good Witch of the West

Though it is appropriate to recognize
that some writers work with minimal distortion of contemporary probabili-
ties and project carefully into the near future while others move into
much more distant territory, within each of these areas there are certain
writers who have succeeded in blending speculation and narration superbly. . . . If I were to choose one writer to illustrate the way in which
it is possible to unite speculation and fabulation in works of compelling
power and beauty, employing a language that is fully adequate to this
esthetic intention, that writer would be the Good Witch of the West.

In the Land of Oz, all the good witches come from the north and
south, the wicked witches from the east and west. But we do not live in
the Land of Oz and must take our witches as we find them. Ursula
Kroeber Le Guin, born in California and a resident of Oregon, is very
much of the west, and the literary magic she works is so dazzling as to
make the title of "good witch" almost literally appropriate. (And perhaps I
should add that the one photograph of her that I have seen pictures a
woman of an appropriate formidability.) Since 1966 she has published
nine novels, three of them designed especially for younger readers, and all
of them likely to appear in the section reserved for science fiction and
fantasy in your neighborhood bookstore. She has been compared to C. S.
Lewis, with some appropriateness, especially as concerns her juvenile trilogy, but that comparison fails ultimately because she is a better writer than
Lewis: her fictions, both juvenile and adult, are richer, deeper, and more
beautiful than his. She is probably the best writer of speculative fabulation

working in this country today, and she deserves a place among our major contemporary writers of fiction. For some writers, the SF ghetto serves a useful protective function, preserving them from comparison with their best contemporaries. For Ursula Le Guin, as for others, this protection, and the sense of a responsive, relatively uncritical audience that goes with it, may have been helpful during her early development as a writer. But with *The Left Hand of Darkness* (1969) she displayed powers so remarkable that only full and serious critical scrutiny can begin to reveal her value as a writer. It is my intention here to initiate such scrutiny, concentrating on that excellent novel but glancing also at her other fiction, especially at the first volume of her trilogy for young people.

The Earthsea trilogy consists of *A Wizard of Earthsea* (1968), *The Tombs of Atuan* (1971), and *The Farthest Shore* (1972). These books have been compared to C. S. Lewis's chronicles of Narnia, especially by English reviewers, for whom this constitutes considerable praise. But the comparison is misleading. Lewis's books are allegories in the narrow sense of that much abused word—his Lion *is* Christ, and the whole structure of the chronicles is a reenactment of Christian legend. The fundamental story is fixed, and the narrative surface becomes simply a new way of clothing that story and retelling it as a heroic adventure. The ultimate value of such allegorizing, then, must reside in the permanent value of the legendary pattern itself, raising the question of how the story of Christ functions cognitively to help us understand our world and live in it. My own feeling in this matter is that Lewis's narratives work on us because we are preconditioned to be moved by that particular material, with its legend of a redemptive sacrifice—preconditioned by our particular cultural heritage rather than by the shape of the world itself. In other words, this kind of allegory is leading its readers toward a stock response based on a preestablished and rigidly codified set of values. But there is another kind of allegory—allegory in a broader sense—which is more speculative and less dogmatic. Ursula Le Guin, in the Earthsea trilogy, relies on the mythic patterns of sin and redemption, quest and discovery, too, but she places them in the service of a metaphysic which is entirely responsible to modern conditions of being because its perspective is broader than the Chistian perspective—because finally it takes the world more seriously than the Judeo-Christian tradition has ever allowed it to be taken.

What Earthsea represents, through its world of islands and waterways, is the universe as a dynamic, balanced system, not subject to the capricious miracles of any deity, but only to the natural laws of its own working, which include a role for magic and for powers other than human, but only as aspects of the great Balance or Equilibrium, which is the order of this cosmos. Where C. S. Lewis worked out a specifically Christian set of values, Ursula Le Guin works not with a theology but with an ecology, a cosmology, a reverence for the universe as a self-regulating structure. This seems to me more relevant to our needs than Lewis, but not simply because it is a more modern view—rather because it is a deeper view, closer to the great pre-Christian mythologies of this world and also closer to what three centuries of science have been able to discover about the nature of the universe. No one, in fact, has ever made magic seem to function so much like science as Ursula Le Guin—which is perhaps why it is no gross error to call her work science fiction, and also why the term *science fiction* seems finally inadequate to much of the material it presently designates in our bookstores and other rough and ready categorizations.

A *Wizard of Earthsea* is the story of the making of a mage, the education and testing of a young man born with the power to work wonders but lacking the knowledge to bring this power to fruition and to control its destructive potential. Ged's education is begun by his first master, Ogion, on his home island of Gont. This education continues and becomes more formal when he studies at the School for Wizards on Roke. What he learns there is manifold, but much of it is contained in this one speech by the gentle instructor in illusion, the Master Hand:

> "This is a rock: *tolk* in the True Speech," he said, looking mildly up at Ged now. "A bit of the stone of which Roke Isle is made, a little bit of the dry land on which men live. It is itself. It is part of the world. By the Illusion-Change you can make it look like a diamond—or a flower or a fly or an eye or a flame—" The rock flickered from shape to shape as he named them and returned to rock. "But that is mere seeming. Illusion fools the beholder's senses; it makes him see and hear and feel that the thing is changed. But it does not change the thing. To change this rock into a jewel, you must change its true name. And to do that, my son, even to so small a scrap of the world, is to change the world. It can be done. Indeed it can be done. It is the art of the Master Changer, and you will learn it when you are ready to learn it. But you must not change one thing, one pebble, one grain of sand, until you know what good and evil will follow on that act. The world is in balance, in Equilibrium. A wizard's power of Changing and of Summoning can shake the balance of the world. It is dangerous, that power. It is most perilous. It must follow knowledge and serve need. To light a candle is to cast a shadow. . . ."

To be a wizard is to learn the "true names" of things. But the number of things in the world, the difficulty of discovering their names, set limits to magical power, even as the boundaries of scientific knowledge set limits to the power of science. As the Master Namer puts it,

Thus, that which gives us the power to work magic, sets the limits of that power. A mage can control only what is near him, what he can name exactly and wholly. And this is well. If it were not so, the wickedness of the powerful or the folly of the wise would long ago have sought to change what cannot be changed, and Equilibrium would fail. The unbalanced sea would overwhelm the islands where we perilously dwell, and in the old silence all voices and all names would be lost.

Finally, the greater knowledge, the greater the limitations—a view which is voiced by the Master Summoner after Ged has abused his youthful powers and unleashed a shadow of terror into the world:

You thought, as a boy, that a mage is one who can do anything. So I thought, once. So did we all. And the truth is that as a man's real power grows and his knowledge widens, ever the way he can follow grows narrower: until at last he chooses nothing, but does only and wholly what he *must do*. . . .

Ged's quest, after his recovery (for the shadow wounded him gravely), is to find the shadow and subdue it, to restore the Balance that he has upset by working his power in a way beyond his knowledge. His quest is both an adventure story and an allegory which clearly raises the parallel to Lewis's Narnian allegory. For Ged must try to redeem his world, too. He must struggle with an evil power and suffer in the process. The difference is that Ged himself is the sinner who has made this redemption necessary. In C. S. Lewis's universe, which is the traditional Christian universe, God functions like Maxwell's demon, to distort the natural balance of the universe. God accepts the blame for man's sin without accepting the responsibility, leaving the world forever unbalanced, with man forever burdened by a debt that cannot be repaid. In the case of God, however, the redemption of the individual will restore the Great Balance, making the world harmonious again. Ged's final sacrifice will save both himself and the world equally, and at once. There is no eternity, no heaven in this universe, though the spirits of the dead are not lost; there is only the balance, in which death defines life as the darkness defines the light.

Ged's magic is useless to him against the shadow, because he does not know its true name, while it knows his. Finally, it is through an exercise of intuitive logic that he determines the shadow's name. Knowing how it knows his name, he then knows its:

Aloud and clearly, breaking that old silence, Ged spoke the shadow's name, and in the same moment the shadow spoke without lips or tongue, saying the same word: "Ged." And the two voices were one voice.

The shadow was himself, his own capacity for evil, summoned up by his own power. To become whole, he had to face it, name it with his own name, and accept it as a part of himself. Thus by restoring the balance in himself, he helped to restore the balance of his world. The poetry of this balance shines through Ged's words, which are Ursula Le Guin's, as he explains the sources of power to a little girl.

> It is no secret. All power is one in source and end, I think. Years and distances, stars and candles, water and wind and wizardry, the craft in a man's hand and the wisdom in a tree's root: they all arise together. My name and yours, and the true name of the sun, or a spring of water, or an unborn child, all are syllables of the great word that is very slowly spoken by the shining of the stars. There is no other power. No other name.

Is this magic? Religion? Science? The great gift of Ursula Le Guin is to offer us a perspective in which these all merge, in which realism and fantasy are not opposed, because the supernatural is naturalized—not merely postulated but regulated, systematized, made part of the Great Equilibrium itself. And of course, this is also art, in which the sounds of individual sentences are so cunningly balanced as the whole design, in which a great allegory of the destructive power of science unleashed, and a little allegory of an individual seeking to conquer his own chaotic impulses, come together as neatly as the parts of a dove's tail. If Ursula Le Guin had written nothing but her three books for young people, her achievement would be secure, but she has done much more, capped, for the present, by her extraordinary accomplishment in *The Left Hand of Darkness*, which in its complexity and maturity shows what in the trilogy makes those books juvenile. It is not simply that their style is legendary, and it is certainly not that their world is falsified or prettified in any condescending way. It is simply that in such a world of substance and essence all cultural and social complications are stripped to the bone. In her most mature work, Ursula Le Guin shows us how speculative fabulation can deal with the social dimensions of existence as adequately as the most "realistic" of traditional models—or perhaps more adequately in some important respects. For she does not present us with the details of a social chronicle but raises questions about the nature of social organization itself. She is not so much a sociologist as a structural anthropologist, dealing with the principles rather than the data of social organization. Her method, of course, is distinctly fictional, fabulative, constructive. She offers us a model world deliberately altered from the world we know, so as to reveal to us aspects of the "known" that have escaped our notice.

The concepts that rule the construction of *The Left Hand of Darkness* are those of likeness and unlikeness, native and alien, male and female. The questions asked are about the ways that biology, geology, and social history control our perception of the world and our actions in it. The convention of representation adopted in this novel is one of the most fundamental—in some hands the most hackneyed—of the SF tradition: the alien encounter. The first stirrings of speculative fabulation were marked by stories of voyages to strange lands with different customs, and these were answered later by reciprocal tales of strangers from China or Mars or Wherehaveyou visiting our Western world. Such fictions have always offered opportunities for the distortion of habitual perspective that enables cognition—and not merely recognition—to take place. In some hands the merely monstrous aspects of the alien encounter have been emphasized. In others, the eyes of narrator and author have become so bemused by the new social spectacle that narrative development virtually disappears, yielding to description and meditation. In many the observer, who is usually the narrator, becomes a mere eye, losing all personality, even all fleshly attributes, in the process. One of the sources of Jonathan Swift's undying power is his refusal to allow Gulliver to become a bodiless eye. And the sources of Ursula Le Guin's achievement in *The Left Hand of Darkness* lie in her ability to maintain a powerful narrative interest in characters who grow richer and more interesting to the very last words of the book and who themselves embody the larger problems and ideas that are being investigated.

The events of the novel take place on a remote planet in a corner of the known universe, at a time in the distant future when our earth, Terra, is just one of many earths or inhabited planets, in many solar systems, organized by a quasi-governmental body called the Ekumen. This planet, Gethen, was first called Winter by observers from the Ekumen secretly landed upon it because it is experiencing an ice age similar to those Earth experienced in the remote past. As the novel begins, a single ambassador from the Ekumen has landed openly on the planet, seeking to encourage the various countries on Gethen to join one another in establishing a trade and cultural exchange with the rest of the known universe. All the action in the novel takes place in two countries: Karhide, which is essentially feudal in its social and political systems, and Orgoreyn, which has a bureaucratic government something like a modern totalitarian state. In both countries all forms of social and personal life are affected by the sub-arctic weather patterns and by the one physical feature which distinguishes Gethenians from all other known human beings: their peculiar sexuality.

The Gethenians are all bisexual or hermaphroditic, but their sexuality is periodic, like estrus in animals, rather than continual, as in human beings. In a periodic monthly cycle they come into a brief period of heat or "kemmer," in which they experience a sexual drive much stronger than the human and then return to asexuality for the bulk of the month. All Gethenians have both male and female sexual equipment, and it is a matter of chance which organs become activated during their kemmering, the activation resulting from a couple's touching so that each couple becomes a heterosexual pair, but not always in the same way. Thus every person may become a father or a mother, and between periods of kemmer will not be either one sex or the other but something neutrally located between the two. One of the first secret investigators of Gethen reported on this as follows:

> The fact that everyone between seventeen and thirty-five or so is liable to be . . . "tied down to childbearing," implies that no one is quite so thoroughly "tied down" here as women, elsewhere, are likely to be— psychologically or physically. Burden and privilege are shared out pretty equally; everybody has the same risk to run or choice to make. Therefore nobody here is quite so free as a free male anywhere else. . . . When you meet a Gethenian you cannot and must not do what a bisexual naturally does, which is to cast him in the role of Man or Woman, while adopting toward him a corresponding role dependent on your expectations of the patterned or possible interactions between persons of the same or the opposite sex. Our entire pattern of socio-sexual interaction is nonexistent here. They cannot play the game. They do not see one another as men or women. This is almost impossible for our imagination to accept. What is the first question we ask about a new-born baby?

I submit that such a deliberate variation on human sexuality can help us to see the realities of her own sexual situation more clearly, and to feel them more deeply, than any non-imaginative work of sociology or "realistic" fiction. But this is only a beginning. This passage is couched in the clear but impersonal language of a trained social observer. It *is* sociology, though fictional. But this voice is only heard once in the novel, and it is one among a half dozen distinct voices through which we apprehend the world of Winter. We hear the bardic voices of folk-tellers, the cryptic voices of religious mysticism, and above all we hear the voices of the two main characters, who draw our human concern more intensely as the story progresses. One is the voice of Genly Ai, the Mobile or ambassador of the Ekumen to Gethen. The other is that of Therem Harth rem ir Estraven, one of the few men on Gethen with the foresight and imagination to accept the ambassador for what he is and seek to aid him in his mission. On one level, the story is the story of Ai's mission, his attempt to bring Gethen into the Ekumen, with Estraven's assistance. On another, it is simply the story of two human beings, two aliens, seeking to communicate with one another through cultural and biological barriers. On the level of the mission this is an exciting story, but not more so than many other works of science fiction. On the personal level, this is a richer and more moving tale than most. But the great power of the book comes from the way it interweaves all its levels and combines all its voices and values into an ordered, balanced, whole. In the end, everything is summed up in the relationship between the two main characters, and the narrative is shaped to present this relationship with maximum intensity.

Estraven, wrongly declared a traitor in his native land of Karhide, rescues Genly Ai from an Orgota concentration camp, where he is on the point of death. Together they flee nearly a thousand miles across the glacerized cap of the planet, toward a problematic safety. Isolated in this way, they must learn to understand one another truly or die, the mission they have both sacrificed so much for dying with them. This situation in this setting would challenge any writer's ability to describe a natural scene so stark and so important, to narrate an adventure so simple and physical, and at the same time to deepen the characterization of the adventurers rather than allow their personalities to be overwhelmed by the awesome scenery and the power of the adventurous trek itself. For Ursula Le Guin this challenge becomes an opportunity to bring together the main concerns of the work. Against Winter's most wintry aspect a human and cultural drama is brought into high relief. The adventure is presented alternately through the final report of Genly Ai to the Ekumen and the journal kept by Estraven for his family. And each of them tells the story of their struggle with the elements and their coming to know and accept one another. As Estraven puts it, looking back at their past misunderstandings before they begin their trek: "Mr. Ai, we've seen the same events with different eyes." But where this earlier had led only to blurred focus and confusion, by the end of the novel it gives to both of them a depth of perception that neither could have attained alone.

Here is the way Estraven sees his companion:

> There is a frailty about him. He is all unprotected, exposed, vulnerable, even to his sexual organ which he must carry always outside himself; but he is strong, unbelievably strong. I am not sure he can keep hauling any longer than I can, but he can haul harder and faster than I—twice as hard. He can lift the sledge at front or rear to ease it over an obstacle. I could not lift and hold that weight. . . . To match his frailty and strength, he has a spirit easy to despair and quick to defiance: a fierce impatient courage.

This is, of course, simply the description of a manly man, who seems mercurial to one who maintains a placid, sexless perspective. On another occasion, the envoy is close to tears, and Estraven notices this:

> He looked ready to cry but did not. I believe he considers crying either evil or shameful. Even when he was very ill and weak, the first days of our escape, he hid his face from me when he wept. Reasons personal, racial, social, sexual—how can I guess why Ai must not weep? Yet his name is a cry of pain. For that I first sought him out in Erhenrang, a long time ago it seems now; hearing talk of "an Alien" I asked his name, and heard for answer a cry of pain from a human throat across the night.

And finally, coming into the period of kemmer, with its heightened sexuality, the Gethenian contemplates the other:

> The trouble is of course, that he is, in his curious fashion, also in kemmer: always in kemmer. A strange lowgrade sort of desire it must be, to be spread out over every day of the year and never to know the choice of sex but there it is; and here am I. . . . After all he is no more an oddity, a sexual freak, than I am: up here on the ice each of us is singular, isolate, I as cut off from those like me, from my society and its rules, as he is from his. There is no world full of other Gethenians here to explain and support my existence. We are equals at last, equal, alien, and alone.

And from his alien perspective Genly Ai comes finally to perceive Estraven in a new way, and to accept his difference:

> And I saw then again, and for good, what I had always been afraid to see, and had pretended not to see in him: that he was a woman as well as a man. Any need to explain the sources of that fear vanished with the fear; what I was left with was, at last, acceptance of him as he really was. Until then I had rejected him, refused him his own reality. He had been quite right to say that he, the only person on Gethen who trusted me, was the only Gethenian I distrusted. For he was the only one who had entirely accepted me as a human being: who had liked me personally and given me entire personal loyalty: and who therefore had demanded of me an equal degree of recognition, of acceptance. I had not been willing to give it. I had been afraid to give it. I had not wanted to give my trust, my friendship to a man who was a woman, a woman who was a man.

They come together then as friends, though not sexually, for, as Ai puts it, "for us to meet sexually would be for us to meet once more as aliens. We had touched, in the only way we could touch." And they remain friends until death parts them, Ai and Therem, I and Thou.

So truly does Genly Ai enter into the worldview of his friend, that when his mission finally succeeds, and members of his own species, friends whom he has known before, land on Gethen, he finds their alien presence overpowering:

> Out they came, and met the Karhiders with a beautiful courtesy. But they all looked strange to me, men and women, well as I knew them. Their voices sounded strange: too deep, too shrill. They were like a troupe of great, strange animals, of two different species: great apes with intelligent eyes, all of them in rut, in kemmer. . . . They took my hand, touched me, held me.

After this he retires to his room and is soothed by a Gethenian physician: "His quiet voice and his face, a young, serious face, not a man's face and not a woman's, a human face, these were a relief to me, familiar, right." We may remember Gulliver here, in the stable talking to his horses, and this may lead us to smile. But this scene is still a touching and a meaningful one. It leads us away from Swift's hatred of the bestial in man and toward a love of the world's possibilities for intelligent life. This meaning is reinforced in the last lines of the book. The envoy visits the parent and child of his dead friend on their ancestral estate, to bring them the story of the great adventure, and the book closes with the words of young Estraven, which are full of the same generosity of spirit and openness to life that had made Therem so remarkable:

> "I should like to hear that tale, my Lord Envoy," said old Esvans, very calm. But the boy, Therem's son, said stammering, "Will you tell us how he died?—Will you tell us about the other worlds out among the stars— the other kinds of men, the other lives?"

This eagerness for the future, this willingness to embrace the Other, is surely a major force in all science fiction, though it has seldom been presented with such eloquence as in this book. And it is as surely something we need, to face the future ourselves. We need also the ultimate wisdom of *The Left Hand of Darkness* about the nature of opposition, which is the extreme form of otherness. An experience of Ai and Therem on the ice brings this wisdom home to them and to us. At one point a curious cloud cover arises, leaving them in a hazy light but taking away color and shadow. In this white world they cannot continue on their way, can barely maintain balance, and can scarcely perceive the crevasses that threaten them with death. When they stop and make camp, Ai complains of his own fear, and Therem replies, "Fear's very useful. Like darkness. Like shadows. . . . It's queer that daylight's not enough. We need the shadows, in order to walk." And Ai thinks of a Gethenian folk poem, the Lay of Tomer, which Estraven had recited for him, and of a symbol which has had a history on many worlds. He borrows Estraven's journal and draws the symbol on one of its pages, explaining,

It's found on Earth, and on Hain-Davenant, and on Chiffewar. It's yin and yang. *Light is the left hand of darkness* . . . how did it go? Light, dark. Fear, courage. Cold, warmth. Female, male. It is yourself, Therem. Both and one. A shadow on snow.

As in the Earthsea narratives, Ursula Le Guin remains the poet of the Great Balance, but here the balance as a tension, an opposition like the halves of an arch, is emphasized. "To oppose is to maintain," Estraven says, and so says the creator of Estraven. Thus male is defined by female and female by male, light by darkness and darkness by light. As the Master Hand said on Roke, "To light a candle is to make a shadow." And thus for us to see what it is to be human, as opposed to merely male or female, we need a non-human shadow, a world other than our own. And this is the value of the harmless illusion worked by this Mistress of Fiction in *The Left Hand of Darkness*. The book contains far more riches than I have been able to consider here—in fact I have left whole aspects of it unconsidered, but this discussion should serve to suggest what kind of book it is and what kind of writer its author has become. I have ignored also, her four previous adult novels, which, though no one has quite the completeness and complexity of this one, are able and interesting fictions, especially *Planet of Exile*, in which the encounter of alien races is particularly well managed, though now we may see this merely as preparaton for the bigger book which followed. Her most recent novel, *The Dispossessed*, is a rich and remarkable work of utopian speculation—one of the most satisfying fictions ever achieved in that ancient and difficult speculative genre. With each book she writes, Ursula K. Le Guin places us more deeply in her debt.

IAN WATSON

The Forest as Metaphor for Mind: "The Word for World is Forest" and "Vaster Than Empires and More Slow"

In the Afterword to "The Word for World is Forest" (WWF) Le Guin remarks that writing this story was "like taking dictation from a boss with ulcers. What I wanted to write about was the forest and the dream; that is, I wanted to describe a certain ecology from within, and to play with some of Hadfield's and Dement's ideas about the function of dreaming-sleep and the uses of dream. But the boss wanted to talk about the destruction of ecological balance and the rejection of emotional balance." The story accordingly describes the conflict between the forest-dwelling natives of the planet Athshe—who possess a sane and balanced, if (to a prejudiced eye) "primitive," social order—and the Terran colonists who exploit and brutalize them and their world.

The Terrans, having already reduced Earth to a poisoned wasteland, regard the forests of Athshe purely as a source of lumber, and the native Athsheans as a pool of slave labour. The Bureau of Colonial Administration on Earth may issue benevolent guidelines, and a hilfer (high intelligence life form specialist) such as Raj Lyubov be genuinely concerned with native welfare, woodlands and wildlife; but, till the coming of the ansible instantaneous transmitter, there is no means of

From *Science-Fiction Studies* 3, vol. 2 (November 1975). Copyright © 1975 by R. D. Miller and Darko Suvin.

investigating complaints or introducing reforms within less than half a century. Thus the tone is set by the Terran military on Athshe, represented at its most paranoid and oppressive by Colonel Davidson. "They bring defoliation and they call it peace," to amend Tacitus.

The analogy between Terran conduct on Athshe and the American intervention in Vietnam is explicit, ironically underlined by the provenance of Earth's Colonel Dongh—and a considerable relief from other reflections of America's war experiences in SF, which, albeit the moral is one of futility and savagery, nevertheless frequently intoxicate the reader with the gungho mood of combat and the lavishly presented technology *per se* (as in Joe Haldeman's widely admired set of stories, collected as *The Forever War*). At the same time, the obvious Vietnam analogy should not blind one to other relevant contemporary analogies— the genocide of the Guyaki Indians of Paraguay, or the genocide and deforestation along the Trans-Amazon Highway in Brazil, or even the general destruction of rain-forest habitats from Indonesia to Costa Rica. Le Guin's story is multi-applicable—and multi-faceted.

The political facet aside, WWF is a vivid presentation of the dynamics of a sane society which lives in harmony with its natural environment because its members are themselves in psychological equilibrium. The Athsheans practice conscious dream control, and having thereby free access to their own subconscious processes, do not suffer from the divorce that Terrans exemplify between subconscious urges and conscious rationalizations. To the Athsheans, the Terrans—deprived of this dream knowledge—seem to be an insane people, their closest approach to self-knowledge being the undisciplined confusion brought on by the hallucinogens they entertain themselves with obsessively (the "drug problem" faced by American forces in Vietnam is here savagely presented as the military norm).

The Athsheans' proficiency in the dream life is directly imaged by their physical residence in the dark tangled forests of the planet: these latter function metaphorically as a kind of external collective unconscious. The Terrans, whose unconscious is an impenetrable jungle in which they are far from being at home, react to the Athshean forest with confusion, fear and dislike. Deforestation is their technological response to the mysteries of the wood. Indeed, one might fairly argue that the metaphorical significance of the Terran deforestation is primary and the economic or factual significance quite secondary:

> men were here now to end the darkness, and turn the tree-jumble into
> clean sawn planks, more prized on Earth than gold. Literally, because

gold could be got from seawater and from under the Antarctic ice, but
wood could not; wood came only from trees. And it was a really
necessary luxury on Earth.

(Chap. 1)

The paradox of "necessary luxury" neatly capsulates the confused thinking
of the Terrans, and goes some way towards explaining the essential
implausibility of hauling loads of wood over a distance of 27 light years;
but on balance, just as the metaphorical sense precedes the economic in
this passage, so it does in the story as a whole, intensely verisimilar
though the story is in presentation.

The metaphorical structure operates on a primary opposition of
light and darkness: the arid light outside the forests, where the aggressive
and exploitative Terrans feel falsely safe, and the shiftingly many-coloured
darkness within, where the integral Athsheans wake and dream. The
forest paths are "devious as nerves" (Chap. 2)—a neural simile which
supports the impression that the forest itself is conscious; that it represents the subconscious mind, the dark side of awareness. Being tangled
and dark, no superficial reconnaissance of it is possible—no fast overflight
surveys beloved of Herman Kahn's "flying think tanks" (Kahn's thermonu-
clear catechism is rehearsed by the rabid Colonel Davidson, reflecting "by
God sometimes you have to be able to think about the unthinkable"
[Chap. 7]). "Nothing was pure, dry, arid, plain. Revelation was lacking.
There was no seeing everything at once, no certainty" (Chap. 2). Lyubov,
initially oppressed by the world-forest with its impenetrability and "total
vegetable indifference to the presence of mind" (Chap. 5), eventually
comes to terms with the forest (and its implications), and reflects that,
whereas the name "terra" designates the soil of his own world, "to the
Athsheans soil, ground, earth was not that to which the dead return and
by which the living live: the substance of their world was not earth, but
forest. Terran man was clay, red dust. Athshean man was branch and
root" (Chap. 5). The Athshean word for "dream," indeed, is the same as
the word for "root."

Out of the original impetus to write about forest and dream, then,
has come a world-forest that—while nonsentient itself—nevertheless functions metaphorically as mind: as the collective unconscious mind of the
Athsheans. However, the story (at "the boss's" behests) is oriented politically and ecologically; hence it must be primarily verisimilar rather than
metaphorical. Consequently there is a surplus of energy and idea, attached
to the central image of a forest consciousness, which cannot find a full
outlet here. At the same time, WWF is exploring an alternative state of
consciousness, in the conscious dream; yet this is not a paranormal state of

mind—something which Le Guin has treated extensively in her previous Hainish-cycle works. The "Forest mind" theme, controlled and tempered to politics and ecology in WWF, finds its independent outlet only within a *paranormal* context, in another long story of this period, "Vaster Than Empires and More Slow" (VTE). The two stories are closely linked thematically—the latter involving a general inversion of the situation of the former. If, as I suggest in SFS #5, Le Guin's 1971 novel *The Lathe of Heaven* represents a discharge of paranormal elements built into the framework of the Hainish cycle, then, outside of that cycle, VTE represents a parallel working-out of a conflict between verisimiltude and metaphor in WWF. VTE uses the paranormal element from the Hainish cycle as a way of validating a forest-mind which is a verisimilar actuality rather than a metaphor.

Whilst Earthmen in general are regarded as insane by the Athsheans, the Extreme Survey team of the second story are of unsound mind by the standards of Earth—and Hain, and any other world. Only people who are radically alienated from society would volunteer for a trip lasting five hundred years, objective time. The most alienated of them, Osden, is paradoxically an empath. He possesses the paranormal skill "to pick up emotion or sentience from anything that felt." Unfortunately, the feelings of his fellows only serve to disgust him. Le Guin adds that properly speaking this faculty could be categorised as a "wide-range bioempathic receptivity"—which seems to be a way of suggesting that this is not in fact a paranormal skill, comparable to telepathy, since all human beings possess a certain degree of what can only be termed, "bioempathic receptivity" in relation to kinesic body-signals and pheromone scent-signals (even though most of the time they are unaware of this consciously). However, the fact that a teachable technique for telepathy exists (on Rocannon's World, otherwise Fomalhaut II—locale of Le Guin's first Hainish novel) is deliberately introduced into the story at this point, to rout the skeptic voice that would separate empathy off from telepathy. As the events of the novel *Rocannon's World* are supposed to take place some 300 years after the events of this story, the paranormal comparison is conceivably more important than strict adherence to chronology. But in any case, sharing "lust with a white rat, pain with a squashed cockroach and phototropy with a moth" is hardly classifiable as a natural talent. Clearly this represents a qualitative leap into the beyond of the paranormal—a movement away from a mere extension of everyday (if rarely noted) experience, to a radically different level of perception.

The psychological disconnectedness of the VTE survey team contrasts sharply with the total connectedness of the vegetation on World

4470. There is nothing but vegetation on this world—tree, creeper, grass; but no bird or beast, nothing that moves. The interconnected roots amid creepers function as slow neural pathways binding the whole complex of forest and prairie into a slow vegetable consciousness, whose awareness is a function of this connectedness.

It is aware; yet not intelligent. Slowly realizing the presence of rootless, mobile intruders in its midst, the vegetable mind reacts with an anxiety that grows to terror in the minds of the survey team as they sense it, and which is only absorbed and transcended by the empath Osden. His only psychological defence against the flood of feelings from others, that threaten to swamp his own personality, is to reject these others, and then masochistically thrive on his own rejection by others which this provokes. Thus rejection becomes his salvation.

One might clearly relate Le Guin's use of the forest as metaphor for a mental state to Henry James' use of a similar image in his story "The Beast in the Jungle." Not only does a lurking "psychic beast" lie in wait for James' protagonist John Marcher, to be sensed also by Le Guin's Porlock as "something moving with purpose, trying to attack him from behind." Not only does John Marcher's response, of hurling himself violently facedown in his hallucination, as though he has been physically leapt upon, pre-echo what happens to Le Guin's Osden. But even the very nature of Marcher's beast—which represents a lifelong atrophy of affect, of emotional cathexis with other people and the outside world—parallels Osden's autism.

At the same time, one can find in previous SF several "forest-minds" and vegetable intelligences. Perhaps the most lucid and insightful are Olaf Stapledon's Plant Men in *Star Maker* (1937). Stapledon's "vegetable humanities" are specifically associated with the mystical, and even the redemptory. ("Till sunset he slept, not in a dreamless sleep, but in a sort of trance, the meditative and mystical quality of which was to prove in future ages a well of peace for many worlds.") Stapledon is here closest to Le Guin in mood of the various arboriculturists of SF—and it is Stapledon, that mystical atheist, who remains the writer best able to articulate the sense of cosmic mystery as well as to indicate the nature of possible higher-order intelligences, or superminds, without falling into either naive bravura, or will to power. Van Vogt, who, with his assorted slans, silkies, nexialists, etc. can be relied on for operatic, mystificatory demonstration of the will to power, has described in his short story "Process" a forest-mind that is slow-thinking, yet fast-growing, a ravening leviathan of hostility, yet slothful and stupid, a forest replete with contra-dictions which visiting spacemen (who remain invisible) insert their impervious ship into, from time immemorial, to steal some riches (in the form of uranium) and fly away. This story, by contrast with Le Guin, is *unconscious* metaphor. The tangled, fearsome, stupid forest "reads" quite blatantly as the hidden, unconscious area of the mind, into which the masterful creative consciousness plunges—well-armoured—to extract necessary wealth; and the story remains an absorbing one, for all its contradictions, precisely because it is about the process of creation, and at the same time about Van Vogt's own willful refusal to be analytically aware of this. The story is about the betrayal of full consciousness.

Van Vogt's short story "The Harmonizer" describes a supertree which angrily manufactures a stupefying perfume whenever its "sensitive colloids" catch "the blasts of palpable lust" radiated by any killer—whether carnivorous animal, or hate-drunk soldier. Such trees, deposited on Earth by a spacewreck, are responsible for the disappearance of the dinosaurs. Latterly, their one survivor, re-emerging after 80 million years, halts World War III, introducing a malign, brainwashing pseudo-pacificism. This time, the tree is overtly associated with the militant spread of a form of consciousness. A similar manipulatory—though paranormal—situation occurs in Kris Neville's short story "The Forest of Zil," where a world-forest responds to Terran intrusion by retrospectively cancelling the time-line of Homo Sapiens, sending a creeping ontological amnesia back along the time axis. Manipulatory, too, is the symbiotic diamond wood forest in James H. Schmitz's short story "Balanced Ecology." It too encapsulates both violence and somnolence—twin associations which link these four stories, suggesting that the subconscious, the time of sleep, is indeed underlying these various tree-minds in one form or another, and that the time of sleep, furthermore—when dreams take place—is feared as a time of ignorance and violence. This can certainly not be said of Stapledon's treatment of the theme—nor of Le Guin's.

Theme and image, event and illusion, bind Le Guin's two forest-mind stories together. The title of "Vaster Than Empires and More Slow" is but one of a series of references to the work of Andrew Marvell, especially his poem "To His Coy Mistress": "My vegetable love should grow/Vaster than empires, and more slow." Another allusion to this same poem occurs at the end of the story ("Had we but world enough and time . . .") while another familiar line from the poem presides over Lyubov's headache in WWF: ". . . ow, ow, ow, above the right ear I always hear Time's winged chariot hurrying near, for the Athsheans had burned Smith Camp . . ." (Chap. 3). Again, in VTE, Osden's reflecting that the vegetation of World 4470 is "one big green thought" echoes the famous "a green thought in a green shade" from Marvell's poem "The Garden."

The second story also picks up the military argot of WWF where Colonel Davidson is obsessed with the idea of people going "spla"—crazy. Osden uses the word more than once of the effect the forest is producing; while the comment that "the chitinous rigidity of military discipline was quite inapplicable to these teams of Mad Scientists" recalls the behaviour of the Terran military on Athshe, at the same time as it turns it upside-down.

The hallucinatory quality of Athshe—a world "that made you day-dream" (Chap. 1)—recurs in the "Hypnotic quality" of the woods of VTE World 4470, where imagery binding root and dream is reinforced. The woods are dark, connected; nightmare passes through the roots as the visitors are sensed; the visitors themselves relapse increasingly into sleep, to dream dreams that are "pathless" and "dark-branching." When awake, the visitors are still scared "blind." The path leading Osden to his self-sacrifice commences with a fall in the forest that injures his face, and lets his blood mingle with the root-nerves. Thereafter his countenance is "flayed" by scars that parallel the injured face of Selver the Athshean, beaten up by Colonel Davidson. But Selver, the flayed one, becomes thereby a "God" in Athshean terms—dreamer of a powerful new collective dream. Osden too, through psychic identification with the "immortal mindless" forest—an idiot God absorbed in its own Nirvana beyond Maya, the changes of the world—transcends the human level, and at the same time becomes a "colonist" of World 4470. This word, the very last of the story, would seem an odd choice indeed for Osden's fate as castaway did it not reflect back to the ambition to colonize Athshe—which the Terrans signally fail to achieve, precisely because of their disconnectedness. Osden succeeds where they failed; but only in a mystic apotheosis achieved by a paranormal "wild talent"—a fictive dimension ruled out of court by the politically conscious, this-worldly "boss" of WWF, and henceforth to be purged from the Hainish universe of Le Guin.

However, it is apparent from this story that there is an authentic "mystical" strain in Le Guin—an authentic strain, as opposed to the various gimmick-ridden mystifications that frequently pass for mysticism in our times, from the conjuring tricks of Uri Geller or the "grokking" of Charles Manson, via the musico-hagiology of the pop Orient, to the opening of the third eye of confused Western disciples by cult gurus. Whether this authentic mystical strain is necessarily radically at odds with the socio-political strain, as metaphor may be at odds with verisimilitude, is another matter. It might be truer to say that this mystic element has hitherto been falsely expressed through the traditional paranormal gimmickry of SF and that it is here in the process of breaking free (though it is not yet free). Just as *The Lathe of Heaven* is discharging the tension generated by use of the paranormal in the Hainish cycle, so VTE, structurally attached as it is to the politically "correct" partner story presided over by the "boss," may be seen now as an attempt to discover a permissible locale for the mystical—stripped, as it were, of a phoney mysticism of supermen and superminds. Hence the caginess as to whether Osden's empathy is paranormal or not; hence the need to remark on this and draw the problem to our attention.

The story opens (in the original version at least) with a meditation on the nature of eternity as experienced during NAFAL time-distortion starflight, which is directly compared to the time, outside time, of dreams: "The mystic is a rare bird, and the nearest most people get to God in paradoxical time is . . . prayer for release," comments Le Guin, coining a phrase clearly suggested by the "paradoxical sleep" of the dream researchers. The story ends with a return to this same keynote mood. Osden is absorbed into the eternity, the no-time sought by those rare birds, the mystics:

> He had taken the fear into himself, and accepting had transcended it. He had given up his self to the alien, an unreserved surrender, that left no place for evil. He had learned the love of the Other, and thereby had been given his whole self. But this is not the vocabulary of reason.

The final sentence is revealing. Le Guin has inverted the main values of WWF to give suppressed material a verisimilar outlet. She has swung as far away as possible from the military domain into the realm of the "speshes" (specialists). Dream has become nightmare, and sleep a form of catatonic withdrawal from reality. She has made her visitors to the stars overtly mad. She has created an alien life-form—as opposed to the various humanoids of Hainish descent, that have been her theme hitherto. She has pushed beyond the limits of Hainish expansion to describe a world that has nothing to do with Hain. Forest as metaphor of mind has here been translated into narrative reality. The grudging military surrender of the Terrans on Athshe has become the "unreserved" spiritual surrender of Osden, who thus becomes the only true colonist: not so much of World 4470—for how can one man colonise a world?—as of the Beyond, of the dream time (*pace* Raj Lyubov's shade stalking Selver's dreams). Yet, in the end, this transcendent territory is unchartable by rational discourse. Stripped to the bare minimum of the paranormal trappings that do duty for it elsewhere (however successfully—one thinks of Genly Ai's encounter with Foretelling in *The Left Hand of Darkness*, Chap. 5), it is inarticulable. Or rather, to draw a distinction that Wittgenstein draws, it may be shown forth, but not stated. The ending of VTE recalls the terminal aphorism of

the *Tractatus:* "What we cannot speak about we must pass over in silence."
The essentially silent world forest of VTE shows forth, yet cannot state,
the para-rational elements implied by WWF though sternly suppressed in
that story.

It might seem, then, that whilst the mystic area of experience may
be an authentic area, there is nothing profound one can say about it.
Least of all should one attempt to do so by invoking the paraphernalia of
the paranormal from the lumber-room of SF, for this only alienates one
from the physical—and the social—universe. Yet the sense of insight into
the infinite is not thereby necessarily lost. It returns, in *The Dispossessed,*
with Shevek's creation of a General Theory of Time—within a context of
positive social, political and emotional practice. It returns, having been
chastened by the "boss" of WWF, and then by contrast—in the partner
story VTE—allowed free rein to test out the mystic Pascalian silences
where the vocabulary of reason becomes void. To the world-forests of
these two stories, both metaphors for mind—one overt, one covert—
corresponds Shevek's Theory: which is, within the verisimilar setting of
the book, also *metaphorical* to a large extent. Yet, whereas the forest-mind
is presented as something concrete that lies in wait out there for us,
Shevek's Theory arises only out of the complex dialectic of his own life as
scientist and utopian. As he discoveres his own unity, so his theory
becomes possible; and only so. This is the vocabulary of reason—which
turns out to have far greater scope and depth than that other vocabulary,
of unreason, or parareason. But it is a vocabulary of a *subversive* reason,
which has therefore had first to pass through the false, non-reasonable and
by themselves noncognitive expressions of parareason. The two forest
minds of WWF and VTE are—beyond their instrinsic interest as bases for
two shrewd and powerful stories—necessary stages in a development from
ur-SF to the mystico-political theory of time and society in *The Dispossessed.*

FREDRIC JAMESON

World-Reduction in Le Guin: The Emergence of Utopian Narrative

Huddled forms wrapped in furs, packed snow and sweaty faces, torches by day, a ceremonial trowel and a corner stone swung into place. . . . Such is our entry into the other world of *The Left Hand of Darkness* (LHD), a world which, like all invented ones, awakens irresistible reminiscences of this the real one—here less Eisenstein's Muscovy, perhaps, than some Eskimo High Middle Ages. Yet this surface exoticism conceals a series of what may be called "generic discontinuities," and the novel can be shown to be constructed from a heterogeneous group of narrative modes artfully superposed and intertwined, thereby constituting a virtual anthology of narrative strands of different kinds. So we find here intermingled: the travel narrative (with anthropological data), the pastiche of myth, the political novel (in the restricted sense of the drama of court intrigue), straight SF (the Hainish colonization, the spaceship in orbit around Gethen's sun), Orwellian dystopia (the imprisonment on the Voluntary Farm and Resettlement Agency), adventure-story (the flight across the glacier), and finally even, perhaps, something like a multi-racial love-story (the drama of communication between the two cultures and species).

Such structural discontinuities, while accounting for the effective-ness of LHD by comparison with books that can do only one or two of

From *Science-Fiction Studies* 3, vol. 2 (November 1975). Copyright © 1975 by R. D. Miller and Darko Suvin.

these things, at once raise the basic question of the novel's ultimate unity. In what follows, I want to make a case for a thematic coherence which has little enough to do with plot as such, but which would seem to shed some light on the process of world-construction in fictional narratives in general. Thematically, we may distinguish four different types of material in the novel, the most striking and obvious being that of the hermaphroditic sexuality of the inhabitants of Gethen. The "official" message of the book, however, would seem to be rather different than this, involving a social and historical meditation on the institutions of Karhide and the capacity of that or any other society to mount full-scale organized warfare. After this, we would surely want to mention the peculiar ecology, which, along with the way of life it imposes, makes of LHD something like an anti-*Dune*; and, finally, the myths and religious practices of the planet, which give the book its title.

The question is now whether we can find something that all these themes have in common, or better still, whether we can isolate some essential structural *homology* between them. To begin with the climate of Gethen (known to the Ekumen as Winter), the first Investigator supplies an initial interpretation of it in terms of the resistance of this ice-age environment to human life:

> The weather of Winter is so relentless, so near the limit of tolerability even to them with all their cold-adaptations, that perhaps they use up their fighting spirit fighting the cold. The marginal peoples, the races that just get by, are rarely the warriors. And in the end, the dominant factor in Gethenian life is not sex or any other human being: it is their environment, their cold world. Here man has a crueler enemy even than himself.
>
> (Chap. 7)

However, this is not the only connotation that extreme cold may have; the *motif* may have some other, deeper, disguised symbolic meaning that can perhaps best be illustrated by the related symbolism of the tropics in recent SF, particularly in the novels of J. G. Ballard. Heat is here conveyed as a kind of dissolution of the body into the outside world, a loss of that clean separation from clothes and external objects that gives you your autonomy and allows you to move about freely, a sense of increasing contamination and stickiness in the contact between your physical organism and the surfaces around it, the wet air in which it bathes, the fronds that slap against it. So it is that the jungle itself, with its non—or anti-Wordsworthian nature, is felt to be some immense and alien organism into which our bodies run the risk of being absorbed, the most alarming expression of this anxiety in SF being perhaps that terrible scene in Silverberg's *Downward to Earth* (Chap. 8) in which the protagonist discovers a human couple who have become hosts to some unknown parasitic larvae that stir inside their still living torsos like monstrous foetuses.

This loss of physical autonomy—dramatized by the total environment of the jungle into which the European dissolves—is then understood as a figure for the loss of psychic autonomy, of which the utter demoralization, the colonial whisky-drinking and general dissolution of the tropical hero is the canonical symbol in literature. (Even more relevant to the present study is the relationship between extreme heat and sexual anxiety—a theme particularly visible in the non-SF treatments of similar material by Catholic novelists like Graham Greene and François Mauriac, for whom the identification of heat and adolescent sexual torment provides ample motivation for the subsequent desexualization experienced by the main characters.)

Ballard's work is suggestive in the way in which he translates both physical and moral dissolution into the great ideological myth of entropy, in which the historic collapse of the British Empire is projected outwards into some immense cosmic deceleration of the universe itself as well as of its molecular building blocks. This kind of ideological message makes it hard to escape the feeling that the heat symbolism in question here is a peculiarly Western and ethnocentric one. Witness, if proof be needed, Vonnegut's *Cat's Cradle*, where the systematic displacement of the action from Upstate New York to the Caribbean, from dehumanized American scientists to the joyous and skeptical religious practices of Bokononism, suggests a scarcely disguised meditation on the relationship between American power and the Third World, between repression and scientific knowledge in the capitalist world, and a nostalgic and primitivistic evocation of the more genuine human possibilities available in an older and simpler culture. The preoccupation with heat, the fear of sweating as of some dissolution of our very being, would then be tantamount to an unconscious anxiety about tropical field-labor (an analogous cultural symbolism can be found in the historical echo of Northern factory work in the blue jeans and work-shirts of our own affluent society). The nightmare of the tropics thus expresses a disguised terror at the inconceivable and unformulable threat posed by the masses of the Third World to our own prosperity and privilege, and suggests a new and unexpected framework in which to interpret the icy climate of Le Guin's Gethen.

In such a reading the cold weather of the planet Winter must be understood, first and foremost, not so much as a rude environment, inhospitable to human life, as rather a symbolic affirmation of the autonomy of the organism, and a fantasy realization of some virtually total disengagement of the body from its environment or eco-system. Cold *isolates*, and the cold of Gethen is what brings home to the characters (and the reader) their physical detachment, their free-standing isolation as separate individuals, goose-flesh transforming the skin itself into some outer envelope, the sub-zero temperatures of the planet forcing the organism back on its own inner resources and making of each a kind of self-sufficient blast-furnace. Gethen thus stands as an attempt to imagine an experimental landscape in which our being-in-the-world is simplified to the extreme, and in which our sensory links with the multiple and shifting perceptual fields around us are abstracted so radically as to vouchsafe, perhaps, some new glimpse as to the ultimate nature of human reality.

It seems to me important to insist on this cognitive and experimental function of the narrative in order to distinguish it from other, more nightmarish representations of the sealing off of consciousness from the external world (as e.g. in the "half-life" of the dead in Philip K. Dick's *Ubik*). One of the most significant potentialities of SF as a form is precisely this capacity to provide something like an experimental variation on our own empirical universe; and Le Guin has herself described her invention of Gethenian sexuality along the lines of just such a "thought experiment" in the tradition of the great physicists: "Einstein shoots a light-ray through a moving elevator; Schrödinger puts a cat in a box. There is no elevator, no cat, no box. The experiment is performed, the question is asked, in the mind." Only one would like to recall that "high literature" once also affirmed such aims. As antiquated as Zola's notions of heredity and as naive as his fascination with Claude Bernard's account of experimental research may have been, the naturalist concept of the *experimental novel* amounted on the eve of the emergence of modernism, to just such a reassertion of literature's cognitive function. That his assertion no longer seems believable merely suggests that our own particular environment—the total system of late monopoly capital and of the consumer society—feels so massively in place and its reification so overwhelming and impenetrable, that the serious artist is no longer free to tinker with it or to project experimental variations. The historical opportunities of SF as a literary form are intimately related to this paralysis of so-called high literature. The officially "non-serious" or pulp character of SF is an indispensable feature in its capacity to relax that tyrannical "reality principle" which functions as a crippling censorship over high art, and to allow the "paraliterary" form thereby to inherit the vocation of giving us alternate versions of a world that has elsewhere seemed to resist even *imagined* change. (This account of the transfer of one of the most vital traditional functions of literature to SF would seem to be confirmed by the increasing efforts of present-day "art literature"—e.g., Thomas Pynchon—to reincoprorate those formal capacities back into the literary novel.)

The principal techniques of such narrative experimentation—of the systematic variation, by SF, of the empirical and historical world around us—have been most conveniently codified under the twin headings of *analogy* and *extrapolation*. The reading we have proposed of Le Guin's experimental ecology suggests, however, the existence of yet a third and quite distinct technique of variation which it will be the task of the remainder of this analysis to desribe. It would certainly be possible to see the Gethenian environment as extrapolating one of our own Earth seasons, in an extrapolation developed according to its own inner logic and pushed to its ultimate conclusions—as, for example, when Pohl and Kornbluth project out onto a planetary scale, in *The Space Merchants*, huckstering trends already becoming visible in the nascent consumer society of 1952; or when Brunner, in *The Sheep Look Up*, catastrophically speeds up the environmental pollution already underway. Yet this strikes me as being the least interesting thing about Le Guin's experiment, which is based on a principle of systematic exclusion, a kind of surgical excision of empirical reality, something like a process of ontological attenuation in which the sheer teeming multiplicity of what exists, of what we call reality, is deliberately thinned and weeded out through an operation of radical abstraction and simplification which we will henceforth term *world-reduction*. And once we grasp the nature of this technique, its effects in the other thematic areas of the novel become inescapable, as for instance, in the conspicuous absence of other animal species of Gethen. The omission of a whole grid-work of evolutionary phyla can, of course, be accounted for by the hypothesis that the colonization of Gethen, and the anomalous sexuality of its inhabitants, were the result of some forgotten biological experiment by the original Hainish civilization, but it does not make that lack any less disquieting: "There are no communal insects on Winter. Gethenians do not share their earth as Terrans do with those older societies, those innumerable cities of little sexless workers possessing no instinct but that of obedience to the group, the whole" (Chap. 13).

But it is in Le Guin's later novel, *The Dispossessed* (TD) that this situation is pushed to its ultimate consequences, providing the spectacle of a planet (Anarres) in which human life is virtually without biological partners.

> It's a queer situation, biologically speaking. We Anarresti are unnaturally isolated. On the old World there are eighteen phyla of land animal; there

are classes, like the insects, that have so many species they've never been able to count them, and some of these species have populations of billions. Think of it: everywhere you looked animals, other creatures, sharing the earth and air with you. You'd feel so much more a *part*.

(Chap. 6)

Hence Shevek's astonishment, when, on his arrival in Urras, he is observed by a face "not like any human face . . . as long as his arm, and ghastly white. Breath jetted in vapor from what must be nostrils, and terrible, unmistakable, there was an eye." (Chap. 1). Yet the absence, from the Anarres of TD, of large animals such as the donkey which here startles Shevek, is the negative obverse of a far more positive omission, namely that of the Darwinian life-cycle itself, with its predators and victims alike: it is the sign that human beings have surmounted historical determinism, and have been left alone with themselves, to invent their own destinies. In TD, then, the principle of world-reduction has become an instrument in the conscious elaboration of a utopia. On Gethen, however, its effects remain more tragic, and the Hainish experiment has resulted in the unwitting evolution of test-tube subjects rather than in some great and self-conscious social laboratory of revolution and collective self-determination:

> Your race is appallingly alone in its world. No other mammalian species. No other ambisexual species. No animal intelligent enough even to domesticate as pets. It must *color* your thinking, this uniqueness . . . to be so solitary, in so hostile a world: it must affect your entire outlook.
>
> (Chap. 16)

Still, the deeper import of such details, and of the constructional principle at work in them, will become clear only after we observe similar patterns in other thematic areas of the novel, as, for instance, in Gethenian religion. In keeping with the book's antithetical composition, to the two principal national units, Karhide and Orgoreyn, correspond two appropriately antithetical religious cults: the Orgota one of Meshe being something like a heresy or offshoot of the original Karhidish Handdara in much the same way that Christianity was the issue of Judaism. Meshe's religion of total knowledge reflects the mystical experience from which it sprang and in which all of time and history became blindingly co-present: the emphasis on knowing, however, suggests a positivistic bias which is as appropriate to the commercial society of Orgoreyn, one would think, as was Protestantism to the nascent capitalism of western Europe. It is, however, the other religion, that of Karhide, which is most relevant to our present argument: the Handdara is, in antithesis to the later sect, precisely a mystique of darkness, a cult of non-knowledge parallel to the drastic reductionism of the Gethenian climate. The aim of its spiritual practice is to strip the mind of its non-essentials and to reduce it to some quintessentially simplified function:

> The Handdara discipline of Presence . . . is a kind of trance—the Handdarate, given to negatives, call it an untrance—involving self-loss (self-augmentation?) through extreme sensual receptiveness and awareness. Though the technique is the exact opposite of most techniques of mysticism it probably is a mystical discipline, tending towards the experience of Immanence.
>
> (Chap. 5)

Thus the fundamental purpose of the ritual practice of the foretelling—dramatized in one of the most remarkable chapters of the novel—is, by answering *answerable* questions about the future, "to exhibit the perfect uselessness of knowing the answer to the wrong question" (Chap. 5), and indeed, ultimately, of the activity of asking questions in general. What the real meaning of these wrong or unanswerable questions may be, we will try to say later on; but this mystical valorization of ignorance is certainly quite different from the brash commercial curiosity with which the Envoy is so pleasantly surprised on his arrival in Orgoreyn (Chap. 10).

Now we must test our hypothesis about the basic constructional principle of LHD against that picture of an ambisexual species—indeed, an ambisexual *society*—which is its most striking and original feature. The obvious defamiliarization with which such a picture confronts the *lecteur moyen sensuel* is not exactly that of the permissive and countercultural tradition of male SF writing, as in Farmer or Sturgeon. Rather than a stand in favor of a wider tolerance for all kinds of sexual behaviour, it seems more appropriate to insist (as does Le Guin herself in a forthcoming article) on the feminist dimension of her novel, and on its demystification of the sex roles themselves. The basic point about Gethenian sexuality is that the sex role does not color everything else in life, as is the case with us, but is rather contained and defused, reduced to that brief period of the monthly cycle when, as with our animal species, the Gethenians are in "heat" or "kemmer." So the first Investigator sent by the Ekumen underscores this basic "estrangement-effect" of Gethen on "normally" sexed beings:

> The First Mobile, if one is sent, must be warned that unless he is very self-assured, or senile, his pride will suffer. A man wants his virility regarded, a woman wants her femininity appreciated, however indirect

and subtle the indications of regard and appreciation. On Winter they will not exist. One is respected and judged only as a human being. It is an appalling experience.

(Chap. 7)

That there are difficulties in such a representation (e.g., the unavoidable designation of gender by English pronouns), the author is frank to admit in the article referred to. Still, the reader's failures are not all her own, and the inveterate tendency of students to describe the Gethenians as "sexless" says something about the limits imposed by stereotypes of gender on their own imaginations. Far from eliminating sex, indeed, Gethenian biology has the result of eliminating sexual *repression*:

Being so strictly defined and limited by nature, the sexual urge of Gethenians is really not much interfered with by society: there is less coding, channeling, and repressing of sex than in any bisexual society I know of. Abstinence is entirely voluntary; indulgence is entirely acceptable. Sexual fear and sexual frustration are both extremely rare.

(Chap. 13)

The author was in fact most careful not merely to *say* that these people are not eunuchs, but also—in a particularly terrifying episode, that of the penal farm with its anti-kemmer drugs—to *show* by contrast what eunuchs in this society would look like (Chap. 13).

Indeed, the vision of public kemmer-houses (along with the sexual license of utopia in TD) ought to earn the enthusiasm of the most hard-core Fourierist or sexual libertarian. If it does not quite do that, it is because there is another, rather different sense in which my students were not wrong to react as they did and in which we meet, once again, the phenomenon we have called world-reduction. For if Le Guin's Gethen does not do away with sex, it may be suggested that it does away with everything that is *problematical* about it. Essentially, Gethenian physiology *solves* the problem of sex, and that is surely something no human being of our type has ever been able to do (owing largely to the non-biological nature of human desire as opposed to "natural" or instinctual animal need). Desire is permanently scandalous precisely because it admits of no "solution"—promiscuity, repression, or the couple all being equally intolerable. Only a makeup of the Gethenian type, with its limitation of desire to a few days of the monthly cycle, could possibly curb the problem. Such a makeup suggests that sexual desire is something that can be completely removed from other human activities, allowing us to see them in some more fundamental, unmixed fashion. Here again, then, in the construction of this particular projection of desire which is Gethenian ambisexuality, we find a process at work which is structurally analogous to that operation of world-reduction of an imaginary situation by *excision* of the real, by a radical suppression of features of human sexuality which cannot but carry a powerful fantasy-investment in its own right. The dream of some scarcely imaginable freedom from sex, indeed, is a very ancient human fantasy, almost as powerful in its own way as the outright sexual wish-fulfillments themselves. What its more general symbolic meaning in LHD might be, we can only discover by grasping its relationship to that other major theme of the novel which is the nature of Gethenian social systems, and in particular, their respective capacities to wage war.

It would seem on first glance that the parallelism here is obvious and that, on this particular level, the object of what we have been calling world-reduction can only be institutional warfare itself, which has not yet developed in Karhide's feudal system. Certainly Le Guin's work as a whole is strongly pacifistic, and her novella "The Word for World is Forest" is (along with Aldiss' *Dark Light-Years*) one of the major SF denunciations of the American genocide in Vietnam. Yet it remains an ethical, rather than a socioeconomic, vision of imperialism, and its last line extends the guilt of violence to even that war of national liberation of which it has just shown the triumph: " 'Maybe after I die people will be as they were before I was born, and before you came. But I do not think so' " (Chap. 8). Yet if there is no righteous violence, then the long afternoon and twilight of Earth will turn out to be just that onerous dystopia SF writers have always expected it would.

This properly liberal, rather than radical, position in Le Guin seems to be underscored by her predilection for quietistic heroes and her valorization of an anti-political, anti-activist stance, whether it be in the religion of Karhide, the peaceable traditions of the "creechies," or in Shevek's own reflective temperament. What makes her position more ambiguous and more interesting, however, is that Le Guin's works reject the institutionalization of violence rather than violence itself: nothing is more shocking in TD than the scene in which Shevek is beaten into unconsciousness by a man who is irritated by the similarity between their names:

> "You're one of those little profiteers who goes to school to keep his hands clean," the man said. "I've always wanted to knock the shit out of one of you." "Don't call me profiteer!" Shevek said, but this wasn't a verbal battle. Shevek knocked him double. He got in several return blows, having long arms and more temper than his opponent expected: but he was outmatched. Several people paused to watch, saw that it was a fair fight but not an interesting one, and went on. They were neither

offended nor attracted by simple violence. Shevek did not call for help, so it was nobody's business but his own. When he came to he was lying on his back on the dark ground between two tents.

(Chap. 2)

Utopia is, in other words, not a place in which humanity is freed from violence, but rather one in which it is released from the multiple determinisms (economic, political, social) of history itself: in which it settles its accounts with its ancient collective fatalisms, precisely in order to be free to do whatever it wants with its interpersonal relationships—whether for violence, love, hate, sex or whatever. All of that is raw and strong, and goes farther towards authenticating Le Guin's vision—as a return to fundamentals rather than some beautification of existence—than any of the explanations of economic and social organiztion which TD provides.

What looks like conventional liberalism in Le Guin (and is of course still ideologically dubious to the very degree that it continues to "look like" liberalism) is in reality itself a use of the Jeffersonian and Thoreauvian tradition against important political features of that imperializing liberalism which is the dominant ideology of the United States today—as her one contemporary novel, *The Lathe of Heaven*, makes plain. This is surely the meaning of the temperamental opposition between the Tao-like passivity of Orr and the obsession of Haber with apparently reforming and ameliorative projects of all kinds:

The quality of the will to power is, precisely, growth. Achievement is its cancellation. To be, the will to power must increase with each fulfillment, making the fulfillment only a step to a further one. The vaster the power gained, the vaster the appetite for more. As there was no visible limit to the power Haber wielded through Orr's dreams, so there was no end to his determination to improve the world.

(Chap. 9)

The pacifist bias of LHD is thus part of a more general refusal of the growth-oriented power dynamics of present-day American liberalism, even where the correlations it suggests between institutionalized warfare, centralization, and psychic aggression may strike us as preoccupations of a characteristically liberal type.

I would suggest, however, that beneath this official theme of warfare, there are details scattered here and there throughout the novel which suggest the presence of some more fundamental attempt to reimagine history. What reader has not indeed been struck—without perhaps quite knowing why—by descriptions such as that of the opening cornerstone ceremony: "Masons below have set an electric winch going, and as the king mounts higher the keystone of the arch goes up past him in its sling, is raised, settled, and fitted almost soundlessly, great ton-weight block though it is, into the gap between the two piers, making them one, one thing, an arch" (Chap. 1); or of the departure of the first spring caravan towards the fastness of the North: "twenty bulky, quiet-running, barge-like trucks on caterpillar treads, going single file down the deep streets of Erhenrang through the shadows of morning" (Chap. 5)? Of course, the concept of *extrapolation* in SF means nothing if it does not designate just such details as these, in which heterogenous or contradictory elements of the empirical real world are juxtaposed and recombined into piquant montages. Here the premise is clearly that of a feudal, or medieval culture that knows electricity and machine technology. However, the machines do not have the same results as in our own world: "The mechanical-industrial Age of Invention in Karhide is at least three thousand years old, and during those thirty centuries they had developed excellent and economical central-heating devices using steam, electricity, and other principles; but they do not install them in their houses" (Chap. 3). What makes all this more complicated than the usual extrapolative projection is, it seems to me, the immense time span involved, and the great antiquity of Karhide's science and technology, which tends to emphasize not so much what happens when we thus combine or amalgamate different historical stages of our own empirical Earth history, but rather precisely *what does not happen.* That is, indeed, what is most significant about the example of Karhide, namely that *nothing* happens, an immemorial social order remains exactly as it was, and the introduction of electrical power fails—quite unaccountably and astonishingly to us—to make any impact whatsoever on the stability of a basically static, unhistorical society.

Now there is surely room for debate as to the role of science and technology in the evolution of the so-called West (i.e., the capitalist countries of western Europe and North America). For Marxists, science developed as a result both of technological needs and of the quantifying thought-modes inherent in the emergent market system; while an anti-Marxist historiography stresses the fundamental role played by technology and inventions in what now becomes strategically known as the Industrial Revolution (rather than capitalism). Such a dispute would in any case be inconceivable were not technology and capitalism so inextricably intertwined in our own history. What Le Guin has done in her projection of Karhide is to sunder the two in peremptory and dramatic fashion:

> Along in those four millennia the electric engine was developed, radios and power looms and power vehicles and farm machinery and all the rest

began to be used, and a Machine Age got going, gradually without any industrial revolution, without any revolution at all.

(Chap. 2)

What is this to say but that Karhide is an attempt to imagine something like a West which would never have known capitalism? The existence of modern technology in the midst of an essentially feudal order is the sign of this imaginative operation as well as the gauge by which its success can be measured: the miraculous presence, among all those furs and feudal *shiftgrethor*, of this emblematically quiet, peacefully humming technology is the proof that in Karhide we have to do not with one more specimen of feudal SF, but rather precisely with an alternate world to our own, one in which—by what strange quirk of fate?—capitalism never happened.

It becomes difficult to escape the conclusion that this attempt to rethink Western history without capitalism is of a piece, structurally and in its general spirit, with the attempt to imagine human biology without desire which we have described above; for it is essentially the inner dynamic of the market system which introduces into the chronicle-like and seasonal, cyclical, tempo of precapitalist societies the fever and ferment of what we used to call *progress*. The underlying identification between sex as an intolerable, wellnigh gratuitous complication of existence, and capitalism as a disease of change and meaningless evolutionary momentum, is thus powerfully underscored by the very technique—that of world-reduction—whose mission is the utopian exclusion of both phenomena.

Karhide is, of course, not a utopia, and LHD is not in that sense a genuinely utopian work. Indeed, it is now clear that the earlier novel served as something like a proving ground for techniques that are not consciously employed in the construction of a utopia until TD. It is in the latter novel that the device of world-reduction becomes transformed into a sociopolitical hypothesis about the inseparability of utopia and scarcity. The Odonian colonization of barren Anarres offers thus the most thoroughgoing literary application of the technique, at the same time that it constitutes a powerful and timely rebuke to present-day attempts to parlay American abundance and consumers' goods into some ultimate vision of the "great society."

I would not want to suggest that all of the great historical utopias have been constructed around the imaginative operation which we have called world-reduction. It seems possible, indeed, that it is the massive commodity environment of late capitalism that has called up this particular literary and imaginative strategy, which would then amount to a political stance as well. So in William Morris' *News from Nowhere*, the hero—a nineteenth-century visitor to the future—is astonished to watch the lineaments of nature reappear beneath the fading inscription of the grim industrial metropolis, the old names on the river themselves transfigured from dreary slang into the evocation of meadow landscapes, the slopes and streams, so long stifled beneath the pavements of tenement buildings and channeled into sewage gutters, now reemergent in the light of day:

> London, which—which I have read about as the modern Babylon of civilization, seems to have disappeared. . . . As to the big murky places which were once, as we know, the centres of manufacture, they have, like the brick and mortar desert of London, disappeared; only, since they were centres of nothing but "manufacture," and served no purpose but that of the gambling market, they have left less signs of their existence than London. . . . On the contrary, there has been but little clearance, though much rebuilding, in the smaller towns. Their suburbs, indeed, when they had any, have melted away into the general country, and space and elbow-room has been got in their centres; but there are the towns still with their streets and squares and market-places; so that it is by means of these smaller towns that we of today can get some kind of idea of what the towns of the older world were alike,—I mean to say, at their best.

Morris' utopia is, then, the very prototype of an aesthetically and libidinally oriented social vision, as opposed to the technological and engineering-oriented type of Bellamy's *Looking Backward*—a vision thus in the line of Fourier rather than Saint Simon, and more prophetic of the values of the New Left rather than those of Soviet centralism, a vision in which we find this same process of weeding out the immense waste-and-junk landscape of capitalism and an artisanal gratification in the systematic excision of masses of buildings from a clogged urban geography. Does such an imaginative projection imply and support a militant political stance? Certainly it did so in Morris's case; but the issue in our time is that of the militancy of ecological politics generally; I would be inclined to suggest that such "no-places" offer little more than a breathing space, a momentary relief from the overwhelming presence of late capitalism. Their idyllic, yet elegiac, sweetness, their pastel tones, the rather pathetic withdrawal they offer from grimier Victorian realities, seems most aptly characterized by Morris' subtitle to *News from Nowhere: "An Epoch of Rest."* It is as though—after the immense struggle to free yourself, even in imagination, from the infection of our very minds and values and habits by an omnipresent consumer capitalism—on emerging suddenly and against all expectation into a narrative space radically other, uncontaminated by all those properties of the old lives and the old preoccupations, the spirit could only lie there gasping in the fresh silence, too weak, too *new*, to do more than gaze wanly about it at a world remade.

Something of the fascination of LHD—as well as the ambiguity of its ultimate message—surely derives from the subterranean drive within it towards a utopian "rest" of this kind, towards some ultimate "no-place" of a collectivity untormented by sex or history, by cultural superfluities or an object-world irrelevant to human life. Yet we must not conclude without observing that in this respect the novel includes its own critique as well.

It is indeed a tribute to the rigor with which the framework has been imagined that history has no sooner, within it, been dispelled, than it sets fatally in again; that Karhide, projected as a social order without development, begins to develop with the onset of the narrative itself. This is, it seems to me, the ultimate meaning of that *motif* of right and wrong questions mentioned above and resumed as follows: "to learn which questions are unanswerable, and *not to answer them*: this skill is most needful in times of stress and darkness." It is no accident that this maxim follows hard upon another, far more practical discussion about politics and historical problems:

> To be sure, if you turn your back on Mishnory and walk away from it, you are still on the Mishnory road. . . . You must go somewhere else; you must have another goal; then you walk a different road. Yegey in the Hall of the Thirty-Three today: 'I unalterably oppose this blockade of grain-exports to Karhide, and the spirit of competition which motivates it.' Right enough, but he will not get off the Mishnory road going that way. He must offer an alternative. Orgoreyn and Karhide both must stop following the road they're on, in either direction; they must go somewhere else, and break the circle.
>
> (Chap. 11)

But, of course, the real alternative to this dilemma, the only conceivable way of breaking out of that vicious circle which is the option between feudalism and capitalism, is a quite different one from the liberal "solution" —the Ekumen as a kind of galactic United Nations—offered by the writer and her heroes. One is tempted to wonder whether the strategy of *not* asking questions ("Mankind," according to Marx, "always [taking] up only such problems as it can solve") is not the way in which the utopian imagination protects itself against a fatal return to just those historical contradictions from which it was supposed to provide relief. In that case, the deepest subject of Le Guin's LHD would not be utopia as such, but rather our own incapacity to conceive it in the first place. In this way too, it would be a proving ground for TD.

GEORGE E. SLUSSER

"The Earthsea Trilogy"

The *Earthsea Trilogy* has generally been ignored by commentators on Le Guin. Some may have been deterred by the silly publishing classification which designates the books as "children's literature." More likely, though, the trilogy has simply seemed a world apart, self-contained, obeying the laws of the high fantasy genre, and having little in common with the Hainish "mainstream." Such logic may apply to writers whose world view is incoherent or inconsistent, but not to Le Guin. *Earthsea* does stand apart to the extent that it forms a carefully balanced whole. But, more essentially, it creates a universe which is parallel to that of the Hainish novels, one in which major themes are not simply mirrored or reflected, but carried forward and developed in new ways. The problems of individual responsibility, of folly, evil and the search for self-hood, are examined throughout these books in all their purity.

The first novel in the series, *A Wizard of Earthsea*, was published in 1968, one year before *Left Hand of Darkness*. The second, *The Tombs of Atuan*, appeared in 1971, slightly before *The Lathe of Heaven*, a work in which Le Guin abandons the Hainish world for a contemporary one, Portland, Oregon of the not-too-distant future. It is hard to imagine two books more different. The last Earthsea novel, *The Farthest Shore* (1972), came out the same time as the long novella, *The Word for World is Forest*. Here again, in appearance at least, are two widely divergent books, one set in a beautifully realized world of purest epic fantasy, the other in a thinly disguised Vietnam of the future. The period between *Left Hand* and

From *The Farthest Shores of Ursula K. Le Guin*. Copyright © 1976 by George E. Slusser. The Borgo Press.

the publication of the next major Hainish novel, *The Dispossessed* (1974), seems one of experimentation and turmoil. Actually, it is one of bifurcation: on one hand, Le Guin pursues the intricacies of balance in a fantasy setting which bears no resemblance whatever to our contemporary world; on the other, she examines the need to come to grips with the problems of the day, to take the Hainish epic—whose cultural high point is reached in LHD—back beyond *Roconnon* to its barbaric, American past.

For Le Guin, *Left Hand* is a crossroads. In that novel, evil is less an individual will to power than a collective one. This vision apparently gives rise to a series of works in which social systems are the villains, the disrupters of balance. Captain Davidson in *Word* is not an individual but a type—the tool of the exploitative capitalist society he represents. Even the power-mad Dr. Haber in *Lathe* is only the incarnation of a sort of liberal reformism familiar to us all. There are, however, both individuals and societies in *Left Hand.* In Ai's youthful arrogance, in the pride that brings him to misunderstand Estraven and his world, we see the potential for a much different approach to the problem of evil. It is this emphasis on man's growing awareness of the capacity for evil within him, that is developed in *Earthsea.* Neither Ged the Hero, nor his adversary, Cob the Unmaker, represent anything but themselves; what they serve or disserve directly is the Equilibrium. And they are responsible, ultimately, to themselves alone.

The Dispossessed will mark a return to more subtle interplay between society and the individual. In redressing this balance, the role of *Earthsea* is not to be minimized. During these experimentive years, it provided a counterweight to what was otherwise an excess of pessimism. Le Guin appears to have been swept along by the results of the Vietnam War; her indictment of our own destructive evil, the technocratic state and the machine without individuals, is impassioned and yet too simplistic at the same time. Le Guin herself, in an afterword to *Word*, sees the danger of being driven by a "boss" dictating to her, of moral considerations usurping artistic ones: "But the boss wanted to talk about the destruction of ecological balance and the rejection of emotional balance. He didn't want to play. He wanted to moralize. I am not very fond of moralistic tales, for they often lack charity." And in actual fact, this tale sounds a new note of despair. The seed of evil has been sown in Edenic "New Tahiti"; its people now know how to kill one another. And this world is not claimed by the League, but abandoned to its own destiny. After ravaging it, man has but one alternative left—to leave it alone. In another story from this period, "Vaster than Empires and More Slow," the hero chooses mystical union with a sentient forest world over human society, the unity of this vegetable being is preferable to the mental chaos of his fellow men, to whom his empathic powers give him access. Here is a colonist of one, a man who goes over to the "enemy" and abandons mankind. During this period of Le Guin's career, only the Earthsea books prove the value of positive individual action. The three novels celebrate the ability of one man, Ged, to overcome his pride and fear, and defeat an adversary who has succumbed to both, and then, from the base of his heroic combat, to project a new society of peace and justice to replace the old world of disunity and violence.

The difference between the Earthsea novels and the others of the same period is, most fundamentally, one of style. In an essay written in 1973, "From Elfland to Poughkeepsie," Le Guin talks about writing fantasy stories: one's writing style, she says, should be neutral, with few modernisms or archaisms sprinkled in; it should attempt to create a world never before seen in the clearest, most direct langauge possible. "In fantasy there is nothing but the writer's vision of the world. There is no borrowed reality of history, or current events . . . There is no comfortable matrix of the commonplace to substitute for the imagination, to provide ready-made emotional response . . . To create what Tolkien calls 'a secondary universe' is to make a new world. A world where no voice has ever spoken before." Fortunately, voices have spoken before in the world of Earthsea. But the voices are those of myth, of the epic tradition itself. Through its language, the trilogy purifies and starts anew. But though they avoid the harsh "Poughkeepsie" speech of the Davidsons and Habers, the books do not avoid moral degradation, nor do they mitigate the power of evil. *Earthsea* is a work of high style and imagination. *The Farthest Shore* is a work of genuine epic vision.

Ged is a fully developed hero, and interestingly, one of a new sort. Le Guin's earlier heroes were scientists or statesmen. Ged is a "mage." In her essay, "Dreams Must Explain Themselves" (1973), Le Guin tells us her mage is an artist—the trilogy is an artist-novel. Traditionally, the artist is the most private of heroes; the struggle to create is primarily a struggle with self, with one's own powers and the need to control them and their consequences. The scientists and "observers" of earlier novels occupy an intermediate position between men of action and the artist. But in Le Guin the pull is always toward action. Both Rocannon and Genly Ai are drawn into an active role through contact with a man of action. Ged is a loner. *Wizard* tells the story of a private battle; the two books which follow show the hero moving toward companionship and collaboration. The quest in *Farthest Shore*, though undertaken in the same secretive, unassuming spirit as always, has profound public implications. The artist no longer travels alone; and the one he takes with him is not another mage, but a young prince, trained not in the arts, but with the sword. Le Guin's portrait of the artist looks forward, in a sense, to her new hero, Shevek, in *The Dispossessed.* Shevek is the scientist with an artist's temperament, the creative genius. Ged learns that, although the magician is safe on Roke, the wizard's school, real creation begins only when he has left the ivory tower and gone forth into life. Shevek also sees that he cannot simply formulate a revolutionary theory, and send out the book containing it. He must also go with it, and fight for his ideas, assuming public responsibility for his act of genius.

In "Dreams Must Explain Themselves," Le Guin describes the thematic progression of the three Earthsea novels. *Wizard* deals with the hero's "coming of age." It is a novel of initiation and apprenticeship. The subject of *Tombs* is "sex"; it relates a "feminine coming of age." In broader terms, its theme is love. The third novel, *Farthest,* is about death, "a coming of age again," says Le Guin, "but in a larger context." This is the hero's last and greatest adventure. First an apprentice, then a master, Ged-grown-old now takes a new apprentice with him, thus completing the epic chain. The adventure is also, in a way, a return. Young Ged became a man by accepting and absorbing the shadow of his own death. Now he goes to fight a man who has refused death, who has been possessed by his shadow.

The central theme of all these novels is the nature of human evil. The exploration takes place within the same limits as always: the universe is still a creative, dynamic balance, Yin and Yang, not a Manichean contention between light as good and darkness as evil. Evil is still explicable as a misunderstanding of the dynamics of life. What has become awesome, however, is the power one man, each man, wields, potentially and actually, to disrupt the balance. The setting in *Left Hand* is realistic; here it can only be called allegorical. Ged is both an ideal hero in an idealized world order, and an everyman. His powers seem exceptional, and yet he wins his greatest battles with means we all possess. *Earthsea,* in its sharp, limited vision, explores in depth the question of individual responsibility. To deny death is to turn from life. But worse still is to project an anti-shadow, abstracting personal fear into a general virtue, and making fear of death into a quest for eternal life.

The image of the shadow dominates *Wizard,* as it does *Left Hand.* Like all of Le Guin's heroes, Ged is an alien, an orphan in the spiritual sense, ignored by his insensitive parent. Like the odd ones of myth and fairy tale, this child of innate gifts is sired by ordinary people. The "mage born" is adopted by the wizard Ogion and made his apprentice. But in his god-given gift lie the dangers of pride and ambition, and to these Ged succumbs. His attempt to raise the dead, to prove his power through an unnatural act, looses the terrible shadow upon him. He had been warned by Ogion that danger surrounds power as shadow surrounds light. Like all men, Ged must learn his limitations the hard way, and bear the consequences of his act. These consequences, fortunately, also have their limits; if it were not so, the balance would have long since failed. Young Ged is foolish, not wicked; but he releases a force which nonetheless seeks to possess him, to turn him into an instrument of evil. The novel narrates his struggle with the shadow—first his attempts to flee, then his resolve to hunt it down, and finally his confrontation and victory.

But what is the nature of Ged's struggle? The enemy is a shadow, part of the hero himself, something from within. And, yet, Ged moves in a world where things seem to be working against him, leading him to ruin. He is pursued by a hostile destiny. It is the young witch girl on Gont who, daring Ged, first suggests raising the dead. This leads him to read the fatal runes in Ogion's book. Jasper again dares him—and this time he raises the dead, and releases the shadow with it. Then there is the mysterious messenger who directs him to Osskil, where the shadow nearly takes his life. These figures exist—we see and hear them. But as "antagonists," they too are shadows, of Ged's own mind. He comes close at one point to believing in fate. This is more than illusion; Ged is fooling himself. For in seeking "causes" outside of himself, he avoids the look within. His own pride and fear have invested neutral shapes with purpose and hostile will in an attempt to cast the weight of responsibility onto something beyond him. In the final episode on the open sea, the man is alone with his shadow. Before he finally absorbs it, it changes shape. What passes before him is his own life. One of the shapes is Jasper; but he also sees his father, and Pechvarry his friend. The shadow is formed of his own acts and choices, and in accepting it, he accepts responsibility for them. For he, not Jasper or any other man or force, must bear the blame for what he does.

At first reading, the mood cast by *Wizard* is strange and dream-like; we seem to fluctuate between objective reality and the hero's mind. The shadow is loosed into a very real world—an Archmage dies sealing the breach—but is gradually drawn back towards Ged. The hero's adversaries are sometimes phantoms of his own creation, and sometimes real powers, like the dragons and the Lord of Terrenon. Behind this fluctuation lies a carefully controlled pattern. The traditional novel of apprenticeship shows the hero first learning, then doing. But Ged is the sorcerer's apprentice—he does before he learns, and his first deed is misbegotten.

For this mistake he is not sequestered; instead he becomes a mage, and is sent forth, master of his craft, but still ignorant of its implications. Again and again. life forces him to act first and learn later. Confronting the problem of action, he comes to see a deeper truth: to do great deeds, one must be whole oneself. And one is whole only by knowing one's limits.

Ged learns that what is done counts less than the spirit in which it is done. Tired of waiting in fear on the archipelago where he has become mage, Ged goes recklessly forward to brave the dragon, hoping to force the shadow into the open. But along with these private motives goes a public duty—he goes to prevent the dragons from invading his islands. Though he defeats the worm, it comes close to defeating him in turn. He has won the right to one mastery, one only. The dragon tempts him by offering the name of the thing that pursues him. Ged does not fail the archipelago, but the choice is painful. Self has gotten in the way of the deed, and the gift cannot be given freely. The Stone of Terrenon tempts him too in the same way, with that illusive name. To know something's true name is to have power over it. Ged realizes that one can act freely, without reservations, only when such temptation is put aside. To do so, he must accept in himself the thing whose name he seeks—death. The hardest task for Ged is not the heroic deed; it is the act of mind which necessarily denies his exceptional nature, and places him on a level with all the rest—the acceptance of his common mortality. What he has begun, all men begin and finish—their lives.

But what is the nature of evil in *Wizard?* What does the symbolism of darkness signify? Earthsea contains many "dark powers"—the Stone of Terrenon, the dragons. But these are primeval, inhuman powers; beside them and over them man has built up civilization. The use of the Old Speech, for instance, binds a man to truth, but dragons can twist true words to false ends, because this language is theirs. These true-namers are fundamentally indifferent to man, they are un-man. In order to exist, man must strike a balance with them. They cannot be conquered, but they must be contained: Ged names and fixes the dragon, and the stone is sealed in the fortress. They must not be served, because, in seeking to rule these forces, man enslaves himself to them—he consents to darkness. In the same way, Ged, wishing to rule over death by his conjuring, consents to it, and so becomes its prey.

But just what is this "shadow" he releases? Does it represent Death, a figure that walks among us; or is it a figure of his mind, the "shadow of his own death"? Ged flees the shadow, and it nearly claims him. Is he the victim of his own fears? The Otak dies to remind us that the struggle is not entirely in the mind. Ged pursues the shadow, and runs aground, nearly perishing. Finally, he stops running or searching; he knows that neither can escape their fate. When they have finally come to the time and the place destined for their last meeting, then they will meet. This other is Death, but the hero does not meet it here. But what does he encounter on the sand inside the ocean? The place is nowhere if not in the mind. And the act is inconclusive in terms of conquest or defeat: Ged neither loses nor wins, but in naming the shadow of his death with his own name, he makes himself whole again as a man. The evil here is neither death nor the darkness; it is rather Ged's refusal to grant these things their rightful place in the balance of nature. Only the whole man, who has accepted death, is free to serve the powers of life. Yet for all of this, Le Guin does not intend death to lose its sting or its reality. The ambiguity of the shadow is purposeful, for it reminds us that the mind is not everything. Death is, as Ged affirms in a moment of gloom, more than fear or a misunderstanding of life. It is a power as well, perhaps the only one that has any real hold on man.

It is significant that the struggle with the shadow is not mentioned in the epic poem celebrating the mage's life, whereas the journey to the tombs is. The first merely lays the foundation for deeds, the second is the true public act. In *Tombs*, Ged goes to the Kargad lands, home of the savage blond barbarians who raid Gont in the earlier novel, to recover the lost half of the ring of Erreth-Akbe from the tombs. As long as the ring remains divided, Earthsea will know neither unity nor peace.

Ged goes seeking neither fame nor fortune. His goal is a quest for knowledge. The two halves of the ring joined together form the "lost rune." To know the "true name" of a thing in Earthsea is to know its essence; so it is here. The true nature of unity is no longer understood because its sign is lost. This loss occurred long ago, when the attempts of the mage Erreth-Akbe to unify the world were defeated, and Earthsea slipped back into faction and darkness. This is no Christian fall which will end in a redemption. Ged follows Erreth as another man of wisdom and moral courage who attempts to bring harmony to a world. The tension between making and unmaking is constant and ongoing; man's continuing responsibility is to oppose the forces of disorder. The task is neverending, and utterly necessary. Against the permanence of chaos, mankind forms chains: the task passes from Estraven to Ai, from Erreth to Ged. In *Left Hand*, these forces of unmaking were collective bodies; in *Tombs*, their locus is an opposite sort—the tomb, the void. Yet significantly, this heart of darkness supports temples erected to a "God-King," maintained by a new political tyranny of "divine rights," and an oppressive priesthood.

The ring has been broken in two; one half was scattered to the winds, the other buried in the tombs. The world seems permanently in the grip of fear and greed. A false unity has been imposed on men by laws and priests. True harmony, in Le Guin, comes only from the gift freely given. The half of the ring in the world was thought buried at the ends of the earth—on a nameless sandbar along with the pair of royal siblings—and yet it returns. Ged is accidentally shipwrecked on the island in *Wizard*. Though rendered a near-savage from isolation, the woman nonetheless reaches out to mankind, and gives Ged the fragment. A chain of gifts begins which leads the hero to Selidor in the extreme west, where the dragon reveals to him the meaning of the object, then back to Atuan in the farthest east where, in the bowels of the tombs, the priestess Tenar gives him with the other half of the ring his greatest gift—his life.

At the heart of the public deed, we find a very private experience. The real drama is not Ged's, but Tenar's. She is faced with the same ordeal that Ged faced in *Wizard*—the coming of age. But she has no Ogion to guide her, and no school of wizardry to teach her. Her world is one that has sunk into ignorance and perversion. The proper balance of light and darkness, death and life, has been upset. Tenar is a person of great natural strength and imagination, but the priestesses guide her to darkness and denial of life. All feelings are repressed; her mind has nothing open to it but the dark labyrinth beneath the tombs. Ged's initiation began with water to life and a name. Tenar's name is taken from her in a grotesque ceremony in which the proper relationship between life and death is willfully inverted. A figure in white wields the sword of sacrifice, while one in black stays the hand at the last minute, and claims Tenar for the darkness. Thus, ironically, she becomes "the reborn"—her name is replaced by that of the "immortal" priestess Ahra. But this is eternal death, not life; the living are entombed, "eaten," swallowed by darkness: the dead become their master. In the case of the young child Tenar, it is Blake's "marriage hearse," the corruption of life at its source.

Ged is taken prisoner in the tombs. Tenar, the master of prisoners, holds him, and yet is fascinated by the presence of life in her dark domain. She will not yield him up to the God-King's priestess and death. Through their mutual contacts she comes, gradually, to see she is the one imprisoned, and not Ged. This mage shows her the marvels of the wide world beyond, but she claims superiority over him in the knowledge of her domain: "You know everything, wizard. But I know one thing—the one true thing!" Tenar is an intrepid explorer. She has gone farther than anyone else in the labyrinth, and now she pursues Ged with the same intellectual passion—she would know. It is only because her mind is great that she can make the breakthrough. Suddenly, she realizes Ged has gone farther than she even in her own realm of darkness. Seeing the scars on his face, she sees that "he knew death better than she did, even death." Their relationship is not only inverted, it changes levels as well. What was prisoner and jailer now becomes pupil and teacher. Ged knows one more thing—her name—and he gives it back to her. Only now, in accepting this gift, is she truly reborn. It is fruit from the tree of knowledge, for with her name the undying one must accept her mortality. The burden of life, she will discover, is a heavy one.

Once more, freedom comes only through acceptance of limitation. This is symbolized by the ring itself. Unlike the chains of the tombs, this "ring" is an armband which, in being joined and bound together, will free mankind. Tenar calls Ged a thief when she first meets him. But, just as the first half of the ring was freely given, this one must be too. It is Tenar who ultimately gives Ged both the ring and his freedom. In the tombs, literally, there is freedom only in joining. Tenar is surprised that Ged's magic seems powerless there. He must use it to keep from succumbing to darkness. But fighting the inner battle, he has not the strength to take the ring and return. Neither person alone, in fact, has the power to return to the light. Their only hope lies in the bond of mutual trust. The Ged who had lost faith in himself in *Wizard* was saved by a friend's kindness. Now Ged gives Tenar her name and life; in return, she gives him back water and life: "It was not the water alone that saved me. It was the strength of the hands that gave it." The union of these two is that of minds reaching out across the void. The result is a flood of light: from Ged's staff and hands a "white radiance" shows the walls of the great vault to be diamonds. Their opposite (the image runs through this novel and the next) is the spider, self-sufficient, weaving his futile web out of himself in dry, dark places.

Once again, darkness is emptiness, a negative thing with the power neither to make nor unmake. The tomb merely contains Ged and Tenar; it collapses of its own accord when they leave. Evil occurs only when men serve this darkness, and there are many degrees of evil in *Tombs*. When Tenar escapes into the world she feels a need to entomb herself again for the evil she has done. Ged tells her she was but "the vessel of evil"—it is now poured out: "You were never made for cruelty and darkness; you were made to hold light, as a lamp burning holds and gives its light. I found the lamp unlit . . ." More evil is the force that misuses this gift for life. But perversion is no absolute either; the priestess Kossil has corrupted herself. Her evilness can no longer be poured out, for she has taken the vessel within, and made of her mind a labyrinth. Her fear causes her to deny even the darkness, negating the order of things she has served all these years. The other servants of darkness have only wasted their lives: Thar's dignity, Manan's love, could find nothing to fulfill them. Kossil serves the destructive God-Kings, who have replaced the natural order with expediency and venality. Light is forbidden in the tomb, yet Kossil brings her feeble candle. She is no spider. The tomb collapses on her, digging by candlelight at empty graves, "like a great fat rat."

In a sense the last Earthsea novel, *Farthest Shore*, again plays out the struggle of *Wizard*, but this time on a different level, and in what appears a much more perilous and imperilled universe. Through the earlier novel there runs a deeper faith in the balance of things—it will right itself eventually, no matter what. Even if Ged had succumbed, and become an instrument of darkness, Vetch was still there to sink the boat. Ged had no intention of going to Iffish, his friend's home; a fortunate "chance" simply took him there. In FS, however, such checks and balances seem to have failed. A great wizard has yielded to the darkness, and his actions menace the equilibrium in Earthsea. To some extent, this wizard is again Ged's shadow, since Ged is largely responsible for the man's actions. Out of anger and vanity, Ged had once challenged a renegade mage named Cob, who had debased the summoning of the dead to a carnival trick, and dragged him to the wall that separates the land of the living from that of the dead. "Oh, a lesson you taught me, indeed," Cob later tells Ged, "but not the one you meant to teach! There I said to myself: 'I have seen death now, and I will not accept it.' "

Cob begins turning people from the natural rhythm of things by offering them eternal life. Against this irrational lure, knowledge is impotent—there must be power as well. The rune of peace has been procured, but the world remains divided. Without a central authority, a king on the throne, men and islands fall easy prey to him who would be Anti-King. The new leader will be young prince Arren, who comes to Roke and agrees to go with Ged to seek out the source of this evil.

Their journey takes them south, then west to land's end. At first, the object of their search is vague: it is a "break," a "breech." They seek a place, then a person, and eventually realized that what they are looking for is ultimately in themselves. Evil, in *Farthest Shore*, is more than ever "a web we men weave." The Anti-King is present in each man's mind, and their journey is that of each man to his death. But at the same time, it is also a journey through a series of real lands, people, and things; ultimately, it is a journey to Cob—an evildoer is destroyed, the breach in the universe is healed. The devastation is not only in their minds; real people are ravaged, leaders turn aside from duty, their lands fall to waste. More purposefully than ever, allegory functions here on several levels; the result is almost Dantesque. Symbolic levels are not only beautifully woven together, but firmly rooted in a concrete world which at every moment claims a reality of its own.

Ged soon realizes that he is not leading but following. Young Arren, although he accompanies the mage, is going his own way—to kingship, to the center of things. The path is, as usual, a circuitous and unexpected one. It takes him less to heroic deeds (his sword remains sheathed until the final adventure) than to out-of-the-way places: it is a true odyssey. To achieve their goal, both must cross the dry land of death. But this is a crossing Ged is ill-prepared for; the old man is at the end of his possibilities, and has already accepted death in the sunlight. Arren, however, is young; gradually he discovers his fear of death, and his desire for life. "It is your fear, your pain I follow," Ged tells him. But Arren in turn needs Ged and his wisdom of life. The task accomplished only through a bond of trust and love: "I use your love as a man burns a candle."

The physical journey may be read as a projection of Arren's fears, doubts and hopes. The trip south ends in a deadpoint—a slack sail and a paralyzed will. All along there is, significantly, little wind from Ged's magic. Arren in fact begins to doubt his power: what use is it? What can an old man and a boy do alone? *Farthest Shore* reflects Le Guin's interest in dreams. Arren dreams again and again—always visions of promise which end in chaos and darkness. The silk fields of Lorbanery become entangling spider webs. He hears the call to "come" during the seance with the drugged wizard Hare, and plunges deep into darkness. Later Roke itself falls victim to the same blight: students and masters begin to doubt their magic, recourse to crystal balls yield visions of unmaking, the Master Summoner loses himself in darkness. Arren becomes totally twisted around: he believes Ged is seeking death, and allies himself with the madman Sopli in the boat, whose madness is fear of death, water, and life itself. After the attack by the savages which wounds Ged, he himself is caught in the web of inaction; reality becomes a dream: "I could think of nothing, except that there was a way of not dying for me, if I could find it." Yet he cannot move, and life flows from him as from a broken scab.

The turning point is their rescue by the raft people, who beyond all land have built life and community over the abyss of the sea. Arren first believes this world a dream; but it is real, and the Long Dance is danced here as in all other lands of Earthsea; its people know joy and death. Here the young man learns that to refuse death is to refuse life—their relation is easy to see on the rafts, but is the same everywhere.

More importantly, Ged shows him that no one is immune to this evil: "What is a good man . . . one who has no darkness in him? Look a little farther. Look into yourself! Did you not hear a voice say 'Come'? Did you not follow?" Arren is now freed to act; when the singers fail at the Long Dance, he can complete the song. But for him there is more to achieving self-hood than there was for young Ged. He is to be the king; the evil must be rooted out of the kingdom before he can rule. All nature comes to his aid, as helpful now as it was recalcitrant before. The dragon flies before them as their guide, and magewind fills the sails. The ancient powers join with men to combat the ultimate perversion. As with the tombs of Atuan, but on a vaster scale, the land of the dead is part of the balance. Cob has violated it.

The last pages of *Farthest Shore* are filled with a series of unforgetable images. Arren sees the dragons flying, and experiences a burst of joy in life, just as Estraven saw the fire mountains in the face of ruin, and thanked life for the gift. The "fierce willed concord" of the dragons' patterned flight, the beauty formed of a triad of "terrible strength, utter wildness and grace of reason," is the essence of life, to be gloried in. Orm Embar, the great dragon, dies impaled on the enemy's staff, like Mogien diving selflessly, and gives his life to save balance itself. Here, on the very spot where his ancestor Orm died fighting against man, he now dies fighting alongside him. More moving, however, is the confrontation with Cob at the heart of dryness. Under Ged's questions, his powers melt away, revealing the utter desolation of one who has traded the supreme gift, life, for nothing. He is withered, ugly, a spider of dust; he is blind when even the shades of the dead see, nameless when even they have names: when my body dies, Ged tells him, "I will be here, but only in name . . . in shadow . . . Do you not understand?" Death does not diminish life. It is *there.* "Here is nothing, dust and shadows." Cobb is between, in limbo. And when he finally cries out for life, he sees that he has already forfeited it. Cob's tragedy, as with the Shing, is one of profound error: his "eternal life" is a colossal lie, and he is the first to be duped by it. This lie comes close to destroying mankind. It is not, however, an alien lure; it is man's deepest temptation.

Wisdom can heal the breach, but physical strength alone can make the return journey—Ged must rely on Arren to help him cross the Mountains of Pain and return to life. The young man, who failed Ged once before, now sets his will, and they escape back to the ocean shore, to water and life. To refuse death was to refuse life; in *Wizard*, here, the acceptance of death becomes a thirst for life. In his final voyage to the underworld, Arren, like the young Ged before him, learns what it is to be a man: "Only to man is given the gift of knowing he will die . . . Would you have the sea grown still and the tides cease to save one wave, yourself?"

The thrust of this epic is not simply "pre-Christian"; it is quite un-Christian, un-Western, in its naturalism, its reverence for the balance of life, and its refusal of transcendental values. The story is Arren's—his deed, like Ged's, is the acceptance of his own limits, his achievement of selfhood. He meets victory for the first time standing "alone, unpraised, at the end of the world." His victory is the act of closing his hand over a piece of dark stone from the Mountains of Pain. He thus accepts pain, and yet encapsulates it, enclosing it in warm life. Neither Ged nor Arren retreat from life in order to find it. Ged's "making" is the control of natural powers. More significantly, his successor is not a mage, but a king; the sword he wields may only be in the service of life, but it is nontheless a sword. Power has become more and more necessary to the world of Earthsea. In this shift of focus from artist to ruler, Le Guin affirms the primacy of the social realm.

GÉRARD KLEIN

Le Guin's "Aberrant" Opus:
Escaping the Trap of Discontent

Ursula K. Le Guin's opus, in parti-
cular the novels of the Hainish cycle, does not seem to fit into the general
trend in American SF towards discontent and pessimism. Her two most
accomplished books, *The Left Hand of Darkness* and *The Dispossessed*, both
take place in a distant future whose concerns and conflicts do not appear,
at first sight, to coincide with those of the contemporary world. One
would be tempted to classify them, and the four other episodes of the
Hainish cycle, among works of pure imagination, of escapism, which it is
fashionable to disparage. But I would venture to suggest—without any
pretence of proposing a complete explanation of Le Guin's structure—
that, in spite of appearances, her work does refer to a constituted science,
and even further, to an ideology of this science, in the purest tradition of
SF. The latter assertion seems to me to be of importance since I believe
that the durable relationship which SF has, for better or worse, muddled
through to establish between science (or technology) and literature, between rational knowledge and art, is of real cultural validity. Therefore, a
break in this relation (which some would call the emancipation of speculative literature from science) is a real regression which has its counterpart, and even its origin in society.

Le Guin separates herself from most of her colleagues on the
question of the future unity of human civilization. For a long time,
certainly since the last century, the theme of progress has appeared

---

Translated by Richard Astle. From *Science-Fiction Studies* 3, vol. 4 (November 1977).
Copyright © 1977 by R. D. Miller and Darko Suvin.

indissolubly linked to a tendency towards the standardization of cultures, towards the constitution of a single and unique human civilization, of which the great—and terrible—dream of a World State is perhaps the most current but not the least naive manifestation. This is a utopia cultivated as much on the Right as on the Left. In the SF mode, an ideology of science and technology serves as the unifying principle. The received—and much too simplistic—idea that truth (scientific, but before that, religious) is *one*, that each problem has one and only one "best" solution, impregnates a whole naive way of looking at social development. We have seen in my previous article the meaning of this unity for the social group that is the bearer of SF, anxious to accede to power by the universalization of its values. Thus, plurality is in general posited in the SF future only as an irreducible opposition: the Alien, the Extra-Terrestrial, the other, remains most often an enemy—unless the reverse happens, and he becomes a model. When agreement is established, with or without conflict, it is at the price of reduction to identity. Most works of contemporary SF, when they contain a utopian element, are haunted by a specter, that of orthodoxy—be it benevolent or malevolent, be it sorrowfully submitted to—or charismatically advocated and enforced.

Le Guin, for her part, challenges all orthodoxy in advance, in the sense that in all her works she posits a diversity of solutions or rather of responses, a plurality of societies, and furthermore that history is made where cultures come into contact: in *Rocannon's World* as in *The Left Hand of Darkness*, and more clearly in the recent *The Dispossessed*. What pre-exists the universe of the Hainish cycle is the breaking up of the Hainish culture, just as what pre-exists human history is the differentiation of cultural experiences. The theme of the planet Hain which seeded all the habitable worlds in that part of the galaxy is a myth of foundation, prior to all narrative. In the logic of the opus, the history of Hain before its fragmentation cannot be described. In this sense, Hain is Eden, the place of an abolished unity, foreclosed, prior to all real life.

This is clearly not a simple convention intended to explain the presence of more or less modified humans on a large number of worlds, for such a "cosmic" diversity is reproduced on each of the worlds Le Guin describes. The particular result is that for humanity no crisis can be final. Not without irony, Le Guin emphasizes that he who mistakes his own crisis for that of the whole human civilization is singularly limited by ignorance. Thus, in *The Dispossessed*, Le Guin's intention is clearly not simply to contrast two societies, one much resembling America today and the other having several traits in common with present-day China or perhaps with the Israel of the great dream, that is to say, before independence. Much less is it her intention to take a side—although the sympathies of the author, as someone exercising her subjectivity within the limits of her creation, appear evident enough—but rather to show that the two societies equally belong to human possibility. Despite their apparent separation they maintain close historical ties, in particular in their reciprocal fantasy representations, if only because the anarcho-collectivist society of Anarres comes out of the liberal bourgeois society of Urras at the same time as it rejects the latter's ethical defects. For Le Guin, what matters in the last instance is their difference which introduces the possibility of a dialogue, of a commerce (in the largest not necessarily economic, sense of the term), of an exchange which will allow the invention of the *ansible*, instrument of communication *par excellence*.

This difference also introduces a possibility, essential for Le Guin, of ethical judgement issuing from a practical confrontation and not from a system of moral rules deduced from any metaphysics. Without the experience of Anarres, the planet where an anarcho-collectivist society has established itself, Shevek would not be able to produce an ethical judgement, would not be able , that is, to condemn the social inequalities of Urras from the point of view of his subjectivity, moulded by a particular society. It is this distance as well as the experience of Anarres that provides the Urras revolutionaries with something special, a point-of-view larger than the strict defence of their class interests would require: the hope, the idea that it is possible to conceive of and to construct another society.

Thus Le Guin's work presents, in my view, an important concept which speaks against the ideology of necessity so pervasive in SF—namely that, socially and sociologically speaking, the possibility of hope, the idea of change itself, resides in the experience, the subjectivity of the other. The point is not, of course, in copying the other's solution, but in reacting to it with one's own individual and social subjectivity. *History is neither a succession nor an accumulation of experiences, but a confrontation of experiences*; it cannot be linear, even though chronology appears to invite linearity. Further, it becomes absurd to condemn a society or to propose an eternal model, even one conceived as evolving.

We here touch on a partial meaning of the beautiful short story, "The Ones who Walk Away From Omelas": all societies, be they the most utopian, the most perfect ones you can dream of whatever your dreams, carry in their depths their own denial, a fundamental injustice. Not because humanity is bad (metaphysically) but because every society, like a language, functions on the basis of a system of oppositions, and tends within itself to recreate and to perpetuate difference, including the difference between that which is subjectively experienced as good and as bad. Le Guin gently and somewhat unexpectedly introduces into SF a social relativism—which is by no means an electicism nor a skeptical cycnicism after the manner of Vonnegut.

This social relativism suggests several reflections. A specter, I have said, haunts SF and, beyond it, our civilization itself, a specter which Le Guin helps to exorcise: that of the ideal society or rather of the ideal of society. This specter ridiculously clothes itself in scientific hand-me-downs or rather in pseudo-scientific metaphor appropriated from natural sciences. If we are to believe those zealots, from their various ideological perspectives, there exists a precise solution to all human problems, in particular social ones: the main question is to utilize the science which would supply these solutions. This is what is implied in the works of Van Vogt and Asimov; indeed, the latter does not seem to make clear distinctions among machines, robots and human beings. In less extreme and seemingly less naive forms, panaceas are proposed which tend to demonstrate, scientifically, that it would suffice to add to or to take away from human culture a given element in order for humanity to know peace, happiness, and prosperity, just as one can admittedly protect oneself from an illness with a vaccine. All these propositions, some of which can seem quite generous, are based on the hypothesis of the objectivity of the social realm (in the sense that one speaks of the objectivity of the physical world, which only non-physicists still assert), and exhibit thus a strong odor of metaphysics: the world is understood to have been made in a certain manner whose laws it would suffice to know and respect in order to gain mastery over it. Philip K. Dick did much to shake such a confidence in "reality," but it was Le Guin who introduced the consequences of its destruction into the practice of conjectural literature. In fact, the "objectivist" hypothesis implied that social mechanisms can be thought of in abstraction from those who make them up and from the evolving cognition they have of their environment. However, history is made not by mechanical interaction of social molecules, definable once and for all, however complicated that definition might be, but by dialectical interactions among subjects, bearers of cognitions which are certainly limited but which change in function of their experiences. Further, the absence of a "total social science" does not result from a lack of cognition that might be reduced by a specialized effort, but from the fact that, while the process of interactions of knowing subjects unfolds, such a science is not constitutable; and were the process to stop, there would be no one to constitute it.

A scientific attitude toward society and history implies a reconciliation between subjectivity and science, and also an acceptance of the fact that all science is, in the final instance, subjective, that is to say relative to an observer-operator who knows and acts within a particular situation, marked by his point-of-view. In this perspective, history can be best be defined as the space of interaction of these relative, operative cognitions. By "subjects" it must be clear that one does not necessarily mean individuals, as liberal theory would have us believe, but social groups as well, indeed entire societies. Furthermore, this subjectivity does not imply that all propositions—even the most absurd ones—are arbitrarily equivalent: such an equivalence could be posited only by reference to an unattainable absolute. Reality is. The subjectivity of which we speak concerns simply the limited cognition a subject can have of the environment within which it acts and evaluates. This cognition can of course be more or less wide and more or less adequate to reality; but it is subject to change above all because it bears on a reality which is largely a function of the no less evolving cognitions of other subjects. It is the condition of social science, as of all the other sciences, to be an infinite process. But contrary to the other sciences, there is no one who can boast of comprehending its whole extent at a given moment, since it is diffused among all the cognizing subjects.

What Le Guin proposes in place of an unobtainable "total social science," what marks her originality in contemporary SF—indeed in literature—is not the idea that humanity progresses, in the sense that it goes from savagery to civilization, but that it is involved in a process of learning by means of its own differences and contradictions. And the stages of the process are perhaps emphasized in the course of her opus, with a willful naiveté tinged with malice, by humanity's progressive acquisitions of psychic powers. In a certain sense, the telepathy which appears in *Rocannon's World*, followed by mind-lying and the mental control which annuls it in *City of Illusions*, and finally by precognition in *The Left Hand of Darkness*, metaphorically reproduce humanity's invention of language, father of the lie, then of logic, and finally of a comprehensive theory of history and therefore of the future. That these "powers" come from the unconscious should perhaps be understood (at least in part) as signifying that such inventions are not born solely of the exercise of reason, but of a process of which the terms, particularly but not exclusively the social ones, remain largely unknown by the subjectivities which make history.

Ethics, which occupies a central place in the universe of Le Guin, is in fact a taking account of the behaviors, points of view, and ethics of others. Without any reference to a transcendence, man is "naturally" for

Le Guin an ethical animal insofar as he can integrate into his own consciousness, through language, a part of the lived experience—in particular the social situations—of others. He is not a nomad. Contrary to other animals which entertain only ecological relations among themselves and with the world, he also develops social relations. It does not seem to me inexact to say that ethics represents from then on a sociological pre-knowledge or pre-cognition, that it introduces a theoretical and practical science in the course of constitution, by which man changes from a sociable to a sociological animal. It is then evident that where ethics is lacking, where this pre-knowledge is faulty, social problems, even a grave crisis, cannot but arise. Such a flaw can manifest itself in two ways: the return to a fixed conception—absolute, theological, or metaphysical—of morality which claims to coincide with human ethology; or the rejection of the points-of-view of other subjects and the obsessive pursuit of self-interest. In both cases a false and formalized knowledge of man denies and obliterates an authentic pre-knowledge. Both cases are represented, in antagonistic or allied pairs, in our world: the prophets of doom are not completely wrong when they announce a moral crisis, a weakening of human values; but what they call for with their pleas of law and order is just as surely at the opposite pole from a rebirth of an ethics as the disordered, blind, indeed frenzied demands of those they condemn. Indeed, humanity only solves its problems to the extent that each subject, each man, becomes to the extent of his experience, a "sociologist," and it cannot advance more quickly, on this terrain, than the slowest ship in its convoy.

All, or nearly all, of Le Guin's works describe such a crisis and the conditions for the appearance of an ethics in this precise sense. Further, for Le Guin, man is an ethical animal *also* in the sense that he has the collective possibility of inventing and experimenting with social behavior in the same way that he can invent and experiment in other scientific fields. History is not for her a series of more or less glorious events, but it has *this* direction. It produces ethics as it produces language, and—as in the linguistic domain—each subject acts in the ethical domain without needing to know all its elements and their interrelations but, at any given stage, *as though* he were aware of them. True history is in the unconscious. *The unrenounceable and inaccessible mastery of history lies in the elucidation of that unconscious.*

Thus, a very long history has aged the Hainish, has made them wise and loaded them with guilt: they had tried everything. But why does that guilt, heavy and sad, persist, even though they have collectively recognized their errors and attempted to correct them? Perhaps it is necessary to remember Freud's distinction between hate (*la Haine!*) and love: "Hate, as a relation to objects, is older than love. It derives from the narcissistic ego's primordial repudiation of the external world with its outpouring of stimuli." The guilt of the Hainish is a reminiscence of the hate which they originally unleashed. These Hainish, so precisely, so evocatively named, once caused the differentiation of the human race and, in a complex process only alluded to by Le Guin, conceived hate for the others, for those different ones whom they had themselves made, who were themselves. They committed, then, inexpiable crimes, which later, when they could bear the difference and found themselves again facing the same objects, changed into guilt. Yet by differentiating humanity they rendered possible, much later, knowledge or cognition, that is to say love, but at the price of an unremitting anguish which recapitulates simultaneously the initial withdrawal and the recognition. The Hainish destroyed by the force of hate the shell of a pre-ethical Eden, which cannot be re-entered, and they can only forever repent.

One can allow, along this line, that Hain could be the symbol, not only of our culture, split between permanent fragmentation and the destruction of the different, but also of the bourgeoisie in the act of breaking up, of differentiating itself into eventually antagonistic social groups, if not into castes, at the cost of its more or less explicit egalitarian utopia and of the illusion of its universal mediation of (or of its power over) social reality. If so, this class becomes, by its very disappearance, the bearer of history and of civilization. Thus Le Guin completely overturns the problematic of the social group. It must disappear so that there may be life, growth, trying out and enrichment. This experience of dissolution and social death is by her localized, reduced, contained in the Hainish sentiment of guilt, in their anguish, in their nostalgia, of which the original reasons have become unconscious. One is tempted to write that, through the Hainish, Le Guin—contrary to her colleagues—mourns for that threatened social class, which she even sees as the occasion for an extraordinary revitalization whose description and comprehension are her only interest. This crisis, our crisis, is at the beginning and not at the end, behind and not before, and it is pregnant with other crises which lead to the growth of ethics in the unconscious, to cognition, to tolerance and to the possibility of love. The unconscious is doubly figured here, in the author who as it were conceals her problem in it and extracts from it a novelistic solution, and in her opus.

Can we go one step further? The fecundity of Hain, which seeded all the human planets, conceals perhaps something like a shadow of the famous "original scene," that of the coitus of the parents from which a whole brotherhood arises. Whereas most other SF writers behave as though they do not really accept the "birth" (or rather the unmasking) of other social categories, whether dominant (the "Big Brother," the neo-feudals) or dominated (the "younger sons," the proletariat or sub-proletariat), Le Guin accepts all its consequences, beginning with the very apparition of the Other. She also sees the benefits of this ineluctable inequality: a rena-scence of values other than the market ones. This is doubtless why neo-medieval societies play such a role—but not an exclusive one—in her work, and why she attaches such importance to nobility, to honor, like the "shifgrethor" of the Karhideans in *The Left Hand of Darkness*. Inci-dentally, does she not write, "Karhide is not a nation but a family quarrel" (LHD, Chap. 1)? But conversely, does not the acceptance of the Other, then of the hate-filled brotherhood, finally of cooperative posterity, signify that Le Guin has incorporated the "original scene," has taken it up as a woman, has installed herself as mother? Perhaps it is out of this condition— and in particular out of her female condition—that she can say this thing earlier and better than her masculine colleagues. In this sense, Hain is also Le Guin herself. Thus we see the myth of Hain resonating on three different levels without any self-evident relation between them: a personal level, where the guilt and the hate sustained by the contemplation or the fantasy of the "original scene" and by its products, eventual brothers and sisters, finds itself re-elaborated in adulthood and in some way positively turned around into genitality, that is to say into love and parentage, in the typically feminine manner of creative fragmentation; a social level, that of the downfall and breakup of the social class to which Le Guin belongs, which can be understood, assumed, and admitted as positive precisely by reason of work performed on the personal level; and finally, of course, a novelistic level, where the two preceding ones intermingle and at the same time speak to each other and express themselves. Everything hap-pens as though the successful and fortunate solution of a personal conflict allowed envisaging, with a realistic optimism, the still unreachable solu-tion of a social problem, for which the work is precisely the substitute, in short, a metaphorical child. It is rare, in my experience, that one sees with such clarity these different pathways, inscribed on each of these levels, deployed and resonating among themselves (though we have here, I submit, a widely distributed, possibly general, artistic phenomenon). One catches a glimpse, without really being able to grasp it, of the particular conditions for the production of such a work: a happily resolved childhood, an active feminine genitality, a belonging to a precise moment of a social class in crisis, and of course the necessary talent, intelligence, and culture. Let one of at least the first three circumstances be different, and the result would be completely different. Of course, the constitution of Le Guin's opus is not simply a product of these circumstances, but itself plays a very dynamic role in the ordering of their relations.

One finds again the function of the unconscious as the place where history inscribes itself in *The Lathe of Heaven* (1971), which, however interesting, is doubtless not the best of Le Guin's works. Curiously, she herself seems to experience a particular difficulty in situating it. She sees little here, she says in an interview, but a fable on "normality." She reversed here the roles of a psychiatrist and his patient: the former moves towards madness through the fantasy of his patient, namely the omnipotence of his dreams, while the latter acquires mastery over his "power," the realization of his dream-desires through successive disastrous experiences provoked by the increasing megalomania of the doctor who wishes to take advantage of that power to remake the world. Within our argument, this work covers two gaps in Le Guin's work. The unlivable near future finds itself here described in terms very similar to those we have encountered in other writers, notably Dick and Brunner. But above all, this novel raises an ethical problem, here in the unconscious, closely related to what I indicated above: the problem of interference [in the pattern producing sense in which light waves interfere with each other—trans.] between centers of consciousness (*conscience*) and of actions (here between the doctor and his patient) conceived as being at the origin of experience, of growth, and of cognition. The doctor goes mad because he does not recognize in the other an autonomous center, he comes to consider him as a machine, a mediating thing by means of which he can exert pressure on the real. Inversely, the patient becomes sane to the extent that he recognizes others have the same creative power as his own, though most often they lack the awareness or the experience which comes from having too long served as mediating objects. Thus the real world is that where autonomous desires encounter, recognize, and interfere with one another. The alienated world is that where one's desire develops with neither restraint nor opposition and exhausts itself in solitude. One recognizes here the problematic of the early Dick, which finds privileged expression in *Eye in the Sky* (1957). The place given to the dream in *Lathe* sufficiently indicates that there is no immediate, intrinsic solution to the problem posed to the social group in the near future. Here psychic powers, the extraordinary, a miracle in short, that is to say the impossible, would be needed. But at the same time, if one agrees to pass from narrative-as-representation (here of a false reality) to narrative-as-metaphor, this call to the powers of dream asserts there is no solution but in something which goes beyond rationality and individual will: the constant remodeling of the world by the dreamers' desires, the permanent interference of the actor's desires, in the social world. And the role which falls to George Orr is in some way a metaphor of the artist in our world, who at the same time invokes a false solution (the work of art) and reveals, by means of the formulated dream, the true solution to come. As Ian Watson notes in a slightly different perspective, *Lathe* is really a transitional work in Le Guin's work. She has here clearly expressed something which only appears by its absence in her preceding works, namely, the unconscious, and as in doing this she doubtless felt some resistances she leaned on a great precedent, that of Philip K. Dick. But her discomfort is felt in the relatively stiff construction of her work.

If one allows Watson's astute thesis according to which *Lathe* was for Le Guin the means to resolve the "schismogenic" tension accumulated in the works of the Hainish cycle between the growing recourse to the paranormal and the concern with sounding psychological and moral depths, it is all the more interesting to see the paranormal—which I have designated above as a metaphor of humanity's successive acquisitions in the domain of its self-cognition—developing in autonomous fashion and being charged with effects without the author's knowledge. From a certain point of view, it is not a question of a metaphor, since the image possesses a reality and a force of its own in the psyche (*psychisme*) of its author, but in fact all truly poetic metaphors, which go beyond the level of a device of style, present this double efficacy. It is as though for a time the image in the author's preconscious and the "meaning" in her consciousness develop parallel to each other, so that an unconscious operation on the image can give birth to a conscious thought at the level of meaning. At the end of such a development, when the evolution proper to the preconscious image renders it unusable in the chain of thought and inadmissible by consciousness as lacking pertinence to reality, each follows its own destiny, the one of fantasy, the other of reasoning. But in this divorce the image loses its effectiveness in the real world and the thought its force in the affective domain and, no doubt, even the very possibility of its prolongation. I will go so far as to say that the artist makes use of one part of the unconscious as a kind of analogical calculator which he feeds with "facts" and which returns "results" after the intervention of a "model" partially analogous to reality but entirely unknown and inaccessible to the artist. Insofar as the analogy to reality is acknowledged by consciousness, there is thought. Otherwise, before and after this acknowledgement, there is fantasy. It is in this sense that dreams can have a certain heuristic value and that they even exercise, although much less directly than in *Lathe*, a certain influence on reality. I would even willingly believe that style, taken in the very large sense of all aesthetic organization, from the general structure of the narrative to the idiosyncracies of the writing, is as it were a residue of this unconscious work, the signature of this process. Abstract thought pretends no longer to need it and to allow a summary indifferent to the form, but that is only achieved by denying its own origins which it knows perhaps too well, for it comes from a place where it was nothing but "style," nothing but contour or container without distinguishable content. The "style" of *Lathe*, in this sense, is felt in the exaggeratedly fantasmatic content of the work, poorly tolerated by the author's rigorous consciousness which reduces or deforms it.

One must obviously also ask oneself whence comes this rigor, or rather from what exterior models it borrows its criteria. These criteria are very important, since they determine the limits of what consciousness (*conscience*) will admit, of the "pertinence to reality" and therefore of fantasy. In the case of Le Guin and many other SF writers, it seems to me that such *cultural notions are borrowed from a science*, or at the very least from a more or less ideological, more or less informed, notion of a science. And it is perhaps the source of these borrowings that best distinguishes SF writers from other writers who seem to borrow their models from the dominant ethics, from "popular" philosophy, or from earlier literary discourse on reality—if not from the form itself of that discourse.

For Le Guin, in any case, the source is clear and precise: it is ethnology, and furthermore such a conception of ethnology which tends on the one hand to relativise cultures with respect to each other and on the other hand, less fashionably, to place the emphasis on the relations cultures entertain among themselves. At least as much as on their respective particularities. This idea is clearly expressed in a booklet by Lévi-Strauss, *Race and History*, which appears to foreshadow quite precisely Le Guin's implicit theses in the Hainish cycle, without my suggesting for all that that it inspired her. In this essay Lévi-Strauss made an effort to generalize starting from his science, and he drew from it—surrounding it, certainly, with many precautions—a comprehensive ideology of human civilization (a pursuit which goes well beyond the requirements of science and already touches on those of a creative writer). This ideology, based on the attainment of an authentic science, struggles, let us recall, against a monstrous ideology, supported by an illusion of science, namely, racism.

From a great number of passages from *Race and History* which could easily be adduced in support of the parallel to Le Guin, one is of particular interest: "It would seem," Lévi-Strauss writes in his third chapter, consecrated to ethnocentrism, a chapter on which many SF writers might profitably meditate, "that the diversity of cultures has seldom been recognized by men for what it is—a natural phenomenon resulting from the direct or indirect relationships between societies." By this criterion one measures the difference which separates utopia from SF. *The former never acknowledges the natural phenomenon of cultural diversity. It proposes a unique model of social organization in space and in time.* SF is much more circum-spect and realistic: it easily acknowledges difference as a fact, but often, at least in its optimistic period, only to finally refuse it by making history the agent of conformity. It is nevertheless vital to emphasize that from Stanley Weinbaum to John Brunner by way of Hal Clement and many others, numerous authors have shown, in a more or less sketchy but often optimistic manner, a collaboration of different races and civilizations which preserves their specificity. This is an attempt to substitute for colonization a more acceptable model of relations among different peo-ples, and in doing so they proceed, as did Lévi-Strauss, from its intrinsic practical interest rather than on moral considerations.

This is also one reason for the frequency of anti-utopias in SF, anti-utopias which often admit of no little ambiguity when they protest against that reduction to identity which the homogeneity of science and technology would produce, and against that project of political standard-ization which in fact is brought about not only by totalitarianisms but by bourgeois society itself. Thus, these anti-utopias are proffered outside science and the middle-class and often directed against both of them as though they were, by themselves, responsible for that menace, which they are not. The "ecological" catastrophe establishes itself in this sense in the forefront of anti-utopian literature, since it claims to denounce the conse-quences of a paradoxical utopia of progress. But in reality (see my first article) it expresses the fear of a dispersal of the social group bearing SF, and of its reduction to an undifferentiated mass. An extreme point of view of the same nature is presented by Stanislaw Lem (*Solaris, The Invincible*) who makes this natural phenomenon of irreducible diversity a source of pessimism by stripping it of all inclination toward communication. In Lem's universe foreign races pass by without in any way being able to understand each other; it is difficult not to discover there at least a nostalgia for a lost unity, for a humanism and perhaps for socialism. Thus, from the classical utopia to Lem, by way of SF, one passes from *one* monadic system to a *plurality* of monadic systems, isolated and closed. *Utopia and SF are literatures which consider the problem of cultural diversity, whether in order to exclude it, or to reduce it, or again to deny its benefits,* as with Lem, or *finally to exalt it,* as does Le Guin. No other novelistic genre seems to have concerned itself with this subject to that extent.

However, the American SF that has more or less accepted social relativism has often been a fearful reaction to the bursting of the American Dream, to the loss of power of the social group bearing SF, to the dissolution of its element into a working class envisaged (wrongly) as undifferentiated—in a word, to a reduction to the inferior. Almost alone, Le Guin seems to see in this bursting of the bubble the precondition of a new differentiation, of a rebounding of history. It is in such an attitude that lies her major similarity to European (including British) SF, which has always been subtly different from the American SF precisely in its relationship to differentiation. European SF has been created in a social context clearly much more diverse, and conserving the mark of much more ancient and deep inequalities, than the U.S. one. The ancient pessimism of European SF can thus be explained by the fact that their social group has never been able to entertain the illusion of an accession to power. However, the political masking of power relationships and the theatrical importance allotted to the individual's word have led some of the European SF writers to prophesying. What the Americans are discovering today, Europeans such as Brunner, Ballard and Aldiss have long known. Yet today, this old experience of inequality perhaps hinders the Europeans more than the Americans to see what is hidden in the new constellation of social possibilities, and immures them in social pessimism.

As for Le Guin, when in *The Dispossessed* she gets beyond the problematic of the ecological or pseudo-ecological crisis of the end of human civilization, she can no longer elude the political formulation of the problem. So she finally reintroduces into SF the possibility of debate on the form of future society. In her "ambiguous utopia" she presents two solutions to the present equation: one "neo-feudal," resembling the most probable near-future of America and perhaps of the Soviet Union, and one anarcho-socialist. Without doubt one must read Anar-res as the thing (*res*) of the *anar*-chists, and urras = USSR (URSS in French) plus USA. She does not ask us to choose. She only asks us to reflect.

It remains to propose a conjecture. It is that beyond the grounding in a science facilitated by her family environment, by her development, and without doubt by the historical culture of her husband, Le Guin has known how to surpass the crisis of her environment by proposing a world without a central principle, without a unifying system, without domination, because she is a woman, and as such the obsessional affirmation of the power of the phallus little concerns her. Perhaps she has thus indirectly suggested what a female culture might be, a-centric, tolerant, released, at last, on the occasion of the present crisis, from the male cultural pattern of repetitive conquest.

T. A. SHIPPEY

The Magic Art and the Evolution of Words: "The Earthsea Trilogy"

In C. S. Lewis's *That Hideous Strength*, the changing relationships between magic, science, and religion are expressed in a conversation between Dr. Dimble (a teacher of English) and his wife. Dr. Dimble remarks:

> "if you dip into any college, or school, or parish—anything you like—at a given point in its history, you always find that there was a time before that point when there was more elbow-room and contrasts weren't so sharp; and that there's going to be a point after that time when there is even less room for indecision and choices are more momentous. . . . The whole thing is sorting itself out all the time, coming to a point, getting sharper and harder."

This process of increasing distinctiveness is partly moral, partly practical; the drive of Dr. Dimble's argument is towards justifying the use of magic (in the person of Merlin) against science (as represented by the diabolist National Institute of Co-Ordinated Experiments), and he maintains it by asserting first that magic was in Merlin's time not opposed to religion, though now unlawful for Christians, and second, that when it had real power it was less occult and more materialistic than it is now generally taken to be. "Merlin," he concludes, "is the last vestige of an old order in which matter and spirit were, from our point of view, confused." In Merlin's day, then, magic, science, and religion were not the separate things they have since become.

From *Mosaic* 2, vol. 10 (Winter 1977). Copyright © 1977 by University of Manitoba Press.

The conversation, as one would expect from Professor Lewis, contains a good deal of semantic truth. The word "science" itself is defined in the *Oxford English Dictionary* as "A branch of study which is concerned . . . with observed facts systematically classified and more or less colligated by being brought under general laws," and a definition of this kind is now what most people think of when they use the word. It is, however, only the fourth heading offered by the *O.E.D.*, and is recorded in that sense only from 1725. A man using the word in the fourteenth century, say, might mean no more than "mastery of any department of learning" (*O.E.D.*'s heading no. 2). If that were the case, the distinction between "art" and "science" (now so critical in universities) would be hard to perceive; and the area we now call "scientific" might be inextricably confused with the area governed by the *ars magica* or "magyke natureel." The modern distinction between "astrology" and "astronomy" is not recorded till around 1480, while "alchemy" is still jostling "chemistry" a century later. To give a literary example, Chaucer is his *Franklin's Tale* explains the story's central fantastic event by referring fairly impartially to "magyk natureel," to "sciences By whiche men make diverse apparences," to "illusioun," to "apparence or jogelrye," even to "supersticious cursednesse"; the man who works the miracle is indifferently a "clerk," a "philosophre," a "magicien." This Chaucerian lack of distinctiveness is no doubt part of what Lewis's Dr. Dimble had in mind.

The point, however, should be of interest to critics as well as to semanticists or historians, for the very sharpness and hardness of modern concepts raises inevitable problems for the writer of fantasy. "There is a desire in you to see dragons," remarks one character in Ursula Le Guin's *Earthsea* trilogy to another, and he seems to speak for and about many modern readers and writers. But however great their desire, all modern people, apart from very young children, have dragons classified irrevocably as fictional/fantastic, along with wizards, runes, spells, and much else. The writer of fantasy in the present day, then, does not have the Chaucerian freedom, and is always faced with the problem of hurdling conceptual barriers. He knows that magic, in particular, cannot be assumed, but will have to be *explained*, even defended from the scepticism now intrinsic in the word's Modern English meaning. Of course this restriction offers a corresponding opportunity, one which, like the problem, would be ungraspable by a medieval author: the modern fantasist, by his explanations and his theories, is enabled like Dr. Dimble to comment on the real world, to create novel relationships, to suggest that the semantic "grid" of Modern English is after all not universal. His art is rescued from the standard jibe of "escapism"—"It's only a story!"—by its covert comparisons between "fantastic" and "familiar": the story embodies argument as well.

Such creation of relevance from what appears to careless readers as unbridled fantasy is embodied as well as anywhere in modern literature by Ursula K. Le Guin's trilogy of books, A *Wizard of Earthsea, The Tombs of Atuan, The Farthest Shore*: and significantly enough it is based on a semantic point. The archipelago-world of the trilogy (we never find out where or when it is) is devoid of science, but based on magic. Mrs. Le Guin identifies the workers of magic reasonably indifferently as wizards or witches or sorcerers, but there is one term she does not use, and that the commonest of all in Modern English: a worker of magic is never described as a "magician." The reason, of course, is that this term has a familiar current sense, deprecatory if not pejorative, "a practitioner of legerdemain." The word has been much affected by the rise of "scientist"; it contains strong suggestions that magic is no more than a "pretended art," as the *O.E.D.* so firmly insists—an affair of rabbits up sleeves and deceptive mirrors. A "magician," then, is barely superior to a "conjurer" or a "juggler." Mrs. Le Guin, accordingly, makes consistent use of the base-form from which "magic" itself is derived, "mage," from Latin *magus*; and from it she creates a series of compounds not recorded in the *O.E.D.* at all, "Archmage," "magelight," "magewind," "magery" etc. The point may seem a trivial one, and yet is close to the trilogy's thematic centre. The continuous and consistent use of words *not* familiar to the modern reader reminds him to suspend his judgment: his ideas, like his vocabulary, may be inadequate, or wrong.

This, indeed, is the basic point repeated through the first half of the first book in the sequence, A *Wizard of Earthsea*. Definitions of magic are repeatedly implied, or stated, and then turned down or disproved: the definitions bear a close resemblance to those current in our world. "You thought," says one of the characters to the hero, Ged, "that a mage is one who can do anything. So I thought, once. So did we all." The idea is immediately reproved as boyish, dangerous, the opposite of the truth (which is that a mage does only what he must); nevertheless we recognise it immediately, familiar as we all are with such phrases as "it works like magic," which imply that magic is effortless, unlimited. The magic of Earthsea, though, is given moral boundaries; in an earlier scene it was given intellectual ones. There Ged, still a boy and only just exposed to magic, finds himself facing a piratic invasion with the men of his village. In this situation he naturally wishes for some blasting stroke of magic, and rummages in his spells for one that might give him some advantage. "But need alone is not enough to set power free," the author reminds us: "there must be knowledge." The maxim gains added point by being a total reversal of a standard and familiar modern theory of magic, the anthropological one, stated most clearly by B. Malinowski, that magic is in essence a cathartic activity, called forth by stress, and working in so far as it produces confidence. "Science is founded on the conviction that experience, effort, and reason are valid; magic on the belief that hope cannot fail nor desire deceive." But Ged understands perfectly well the difference between desire and fulfilment, hope and fact. He is, in short, not the self-deluding savage whom Malinowski regards as the appropriate and natural practitioner of magic.

Ged is in fact at all times rather precisely placed within a framework of anthropological theory. For Malinowski's "cathartic" notion is not the only influential modern explanation of magic. Even more widespread were the "intellectualist" theories of Herbert Spencer, E. B. Tylor, Sir James Frazer, and others, by which magic was, as it were, a crude and mistaken first step in the evolution of man towards science and the nineteenth century, a "monstrous farrago" indeed, but nevertheless one based on observation and classification, if not experiment: something closer to science than to religion (so Frazer argued) because based on the assumption that the universe ran on "immutable laws." It may seem that the magic of Earthsea can be reduced to a kind of unfamiliar technology in this way, since it depends on knowledge and has severe limits to its power, but that too would be wrong. For the very first thing that Mrs. Le Guin does in the trilogy is to show us one way in which magic differs profoundly from science: it all depends on who does it! Ged, as a boy, overhears his aunt saying a magic rhyme to call her goat. He repeats it, ignorantly and by rote—and calls *all* his goats, calls them so strongly that they crowd round him as if compressed. His aunt frees him, promises to teach him, but at the same time puts a spell of silence and secrecy on him. Ged cannot speak, indeed, when she tests him; but he laughs. And at this his aunt is afraid, to see the beginnings of strength in one so young. All this, evidently, is not like our experience of science. A light turns on, an engine starts, regardless of who is at the switch; but spells are not the same. A mage, then, is knowledgeable, like a scientist; but his knowledge needs to be combined with personal genius, a quality we tend to ascribe to artists. And unlike both, his skill (or art, or science) has some close relationship with an awareness of ethics—something we expect, not of a priest perhaps, but of a saint.

It is the oscillation between concepts of this kind (and they are all familiar ones, even if readers do not feel a need to voice them consciously) which draws one on into A *Wizard of Earthsea*, searching for conclusions; and the book is evidently a *Bildungsroman*, a story of a sorcerer's apprenticeship, where one's attention is simultaneously on the growth of personal maturity, as one would normally expect, but also on the acquisition of technique. Once again, the basic processes of magic in Earthsea depend on a concept brought to prominence by early modern anthropology: what one might call the "Rumpelstiltzkin" theory. This is, that every person, place, or thing possesses a true name distinct from its name in ordinary human language; and that knowing the true name, the *significant*, gives the mage power over the thing itself, the *signifié*. The theory behind this simple statement is expressed in many ways and at some length all the way through *A Wizard of Earthsea*. One of Ged's first lessons from the mage Ogion (a lesson whose inner meaning he fails to understand, equating it with mere rote-learning) is on the names of plants. Later, and better educated, he spends much time at the Wizards' School of Roke learning lists of names, and nothing more, from the Master Namer, Kurremkarmerruk. Even at the end of the book he is still explaining the ramifications of the theory to casual acquaintances (and more relevantly, of course, to us). A key point, for instance, is the distinction between magical illusion and magical reality; it is relatively easy for a mage to *appear* to take another shape, or to make people see stones as diamonds, chicken-bones as owls, and so on. But to make this appearance real is another matter. Magic food and water do not really solve problems of provisioning, for though they may satisfy eye and taste, they provide neither energy nor refreshment. That is because the thing transformed retains its real identity, which is its name. As the Master Hand (or instructor in illusion) observes at one point:

> To change this rock into a jewel, you must change its true name. And to do that, my son, even to so small a scrap of the world, is to change the world. It can be done. . . . But you must not change one thing . . . until you know what good and evil will follow on the act. The world is in balance, in Equilibrium. A wizard's power of Changing and of Summoning can shake the balance of the world. It is dangerous, that power. It is most perilous. It must follow knowledge, and serve need. To light a candle is to cast a shadow. . . .
>
> (WE, ch. 3)

As with the definitions of magic, what is said here is in the end strikingly dissimilar to early modern statements of the importance of names, above all in its concern for morality, and its sense of philosophical considerations outweighing mere technology. Sir James Frazer opened his chapter on "Tabooed Words" by saying firmly if carelessly that the reason why "the savage" thought there was a real bond between *signifant* and *signifié* was that he was "unable to discriminate clearly between words and things." The statement is an echo of Bacon's remark, so close to the development of self-consciously scientific attitudes, that the "first distemper of learning" comes when men "study words and not matter," a remark rapidly hardened into a simple opposition between words and things. Sir Francis probably believed in the truth of Genesis 2:19–20, which would give him pause; but Sir James had no real doubt but that things were always superior to words. What Mrs. Le Guin is clearly suggesting, though, is that this promotion of the thing above the word has philosophical links with materialism, industrialisation, the notion that, to modern men, "Nature is a machine to be worked, and taken to bits if it won't work as he pleases." In her imagined world, the devotion to the word rather than the thing is bound up with an attitude of respect for all parts of creation (even rocks), and a wary reluctance to operate on any of them without a total awareness of their distinct and individual nature. To the Master Namer even waves, even drops of water, are separate, and not to be lumped together as "sea"; for the mage's art depends on seeing things as they are, and not as they are wanted. It is not anthropocentric.

Mrs. Le Guin puts this over more fully and more attractively than analytic criticism can hope to, and, as has been said, it is for much of the time the explanations of technique, limitation, and underlying belief-structure which hold the attention of even young readers. The questions remain: "Where does the background stop and the story start? What is the story really *about*?" By asking these one sees that the semantics and the explanations and the detailed apprenticeship of Ged are all necessary preparations to allow the author to approach a theme which cannot be outranked in importance by those of the least "escapist" of "mainstream" fictions, and which can perhaps nowadays only be expressed in fantasy: matters, indeed, of life and death. This theme has been adumbrated by the Master Hand's statement quoted above, and by the mage Ogion's summary of the magical and anti-scientific viewpoint: "being . . . is more than use. . . . To speak, one must be silent."

For the temptation which runs as a thread through the account of Ged's apprenticeship is to act, to exploit his power, to reject the wise passivity of the true mage. He shows this from his first appearance, when he calls the goats, not because he wants them, but to *make them come*; his instinct is fostered by the witch-wife who is his first teacher; and it leads him to repeated acts of mastery when he attempts to summon the dead (to please a girl), and *does* do so (to outdo a rival). This instinct is not entirely selfish, for he acts several times for others' benefit, saving his village from the pirates, saving his later "parishioners" from the threat of a dragon. But it *is* always dangerous, exposing Ged three times to bouts of catalepsy, and furthermore inhibiting his development and causing him to be sent away twice (affectionately enough) from his mentors at Re Albi and at Roke. It is dangerous not just because it breaks the rules of magery, including the often-mentioned but dimly-defined concept of Equilibrium, but because light and speech draw their opposites, shadow and silence: which are, quite overtly, terms for death. In seeking to preserve and aggrandise himself (and others) Ged draws up his own extinction. The point is made clearly enough when Ged (like the Sorcerer's Apprentice) reads his master's book for a necromantic spell, discovers a shadow watching him, and is saved only by his master's return; and again when (like Marlowe's Dr. Faustus) he calls up the spirit of the most beautiful woman known to history, to show his power, and—unlike Dr. Faustus, though in line with the severer morality of Earthsea—calls with it a shadow-beast, which savages him and pursues him ever after. In a way, though, the most powerful scene of the book is a relatively incidental one when Ged, from pure disinterested affection, breaks the first rule of magic healing and tries to bring back the dying son of his friend from the land of the dead. This "undiscovered country" is visited spiritually, but conceived physically, and its almost casually undramatic nature makes a stronger impact than any charnel-scene:

> . . . he saw the little boy running fast and far ahead of him down a dark slope, the side of some vast hill. There was no sound. The stars above the hill were no stars his eyes had ever seen. Yet he knew the constellations by name: the Sheaf, the Door, the One Who Turns, the Tree. They were those stars that do not set, that are not paled by the coming of any day. He had followed the dying child too far.
>
> (WE, ch. 5)

Ged turns back up the dark hillside and climbs slowly to the top, where he finds the "low wall of stones" (why "low"? we wonder) which marks the boundary between life and death. And there he finds the shadow-beast waiting. Nevertheless, it is not that which is frightening, but the land of the dead itself, with the little boy running uncatchably downhill into it: a conception lonelier and less humanised than the Styx which Aeneas crosses with his golden bough, and yet closer to Classical images than to the familiar Christian ones of Heaven and Hell.

It may be said that the fear of this dim place underlies the whole of the *Earthsea* trilogy, to be faced directly in the last book. But the land of the dead also acts as an ultimate support for the structure of ideas already outlined. Ged's temptation is to use his power; it is a particularly great temptation to use it to summon the dead or bring back the dying; he rationalises it by wishing to "drive back darkness with his own light." And yet the respect for separate existences within the totality of existence, which is inherent in magic dependent on knowing the names of things, resists the diminution of others which comes from prolongation of the self, extension of life. One might say that the darkness has rights too. So the nature of his own art is against Ged, and his attempts to break Equilibrium with his own light only call forth a new shadow. The shadow, as has been said, appears in the "Sorcerer's Apprentice" scene, becomes tangible and ferocious in the "Dr. Faustus" scene. The questions that agitate Ged and the reader from then till the end of the book are: "What is it? Has it a name?"

On this last point opinions are divided. Archmage Gensher says it has no name. Ogion, the dragon of Pendor, and the sorceress of Osskil, all insist that it has. Their disagreement is one of philosophy, not of fact. For Mrs. Le Guin is evidently no Manichaean; her powers of darkness are essentially negative (shadow, silence, not-being) rather than having a real existence that is simply malign. It follows that the shadow-beast, being absence rather than presence, should be nameless. But Ogion says "*All things have a name.*" The puzzle is resolved in the only possible compromise when Ged, after being hunted by the beast and then turning to hunt it instead, catches up with it in the desolate waters beyond the easternmost island. As he catches up, the water turns to land; evidently, to the dry land, the "dark slopes beneath unmoving stars," which we have seen before as the land of the dead. Here man and shadow fight, *and fuse*; the land turns back to sea; for each has spoken the other's name simultaneously, and the names are the same, "Ged." The shadow, then, is equal and opposite to the man who casts it; it does have a name, but not one of its own. And the scene rounds off the definitions of magic, the debate over names, the running opposition of death and life. Mrs. Le Guin glosses it (via Vetch, Ged's companion) by saying:

> And he began to see the truth, that Ged had neither lost nor won but, naming the shadow of his death, had made himself whole. . . . In the *Creation of Éa* which is the oldest song, it is said, 'Only in silence the word, only in dark the light, only in dying life: bright the hawk's flight on the empty sky.'

The key words are perhaps *his* and *empty.* The first tells us that Ged's call to resist death would, in the end, not be selfless but self-preserving; the beast was born of fear. The second reminds us that—since the sky *is* empty, hiding no divinity—the fear is justified, but has to be accepted as Ged accepts and fuses with his shadow. Yet the emptiness that frames his mortality also enhances it. *He* is the bright hawk, of the last image, for his use-name is "Sparrowhawk." The story then makes a clear final point, needing almost no critical exegesis. What should be realised further and more consciously, however, is first that this point about the nature of existence is in harmony with the earlier discussion of the nature of magic, with its restrained if not submissive philosophy; and second that all the philosophical implications of *A Wizard of Earthsea* exist in defiance of twentieth-century orthodoxies, whether semantic, scientific, or religious. It is an achievement to have created such a radical critique and alternative, and one so unsentimentally attractive.

One final way in which the book may be considered is indeed *as* an alternative, one might say a parody or anti-myth if the words did not sound inappropriately aggressive. Ged's re-enactment of the scene of Helen and Dr. Faustus has already been noted, as has his return from the land of the dead, reminiscent of the *Aeneid* in its difficulty—*hoc opus, hic labor est*, as the Sybil says (VI, 129)—though different in being done without a golden bough. To these one might add the final scene. For one of Sir James Frazer's great achievements in *The Golden Bough* was to create a myth of wasteland and fertility rite and king who must die, a myth mighty yet, as one can see just from book-titles. The regenerative aspect of that myth, as Miss Jessie Weston restated it, was the "freeing of the waters," the clearing of the dry springs. In Ged's sudden return from the dry land of the dead to the open sea, we have a version of it; yet it is typical that with the "glory of daylight" that is restored to him comes "the bitter cold of winter and the bitter taste of salt." The weakness of Sir James's myth was that it asked us to accept a cyclic process as rebirth; and Mrs. Le Guin knows the limits of such consolation. More positively, there is another aspect in which *The Golden Bough* is rejected by *A Wizard of Earthsea*. Sir James entitled his third volume—which contains the discussion of names—"Taboo and the Perils of the Soul"; and his account of true- and use-names was accordingly entirely about psychic dangers and the universal mistrust of savages. But Ged and his companions, once again, are no savages, for all their habits of nomenclature. Repeatedly in the book we have moving scenes where characters, instead of concealing their names as is normal and advisable, *reveal* them to each other in gestures of trust and affection. Vetch saves Ged at a black moment by this gift; at Roke the Master Doorkeeper tells his name to all graduands, in a mildly comic *rite de passage*. And that is the final impression that Earthsea gives: a world surrounded by the ocean in space and by the dry land of the dead in time, but still bright, warm, and fearless, removed from both the insecure exploitativeness of modernity and the meaningless murderousness of Frazerian antiquity. It offers a goal rather than an escape.

In a story so concerned with the fear of death and the assertion of life, one must expect to find strong statements of pathos, as with the pointless and unstoppable death of Ioeth, the little son of Ged's fisherman-friend. Throughout *A Wizard of Earthsea*, however, pathos is very rarely caused by deliberate, human cruelty; and what cruelty there is comes not from the Inner Lands, but from the eastern empire of Karego-At. The pirates who raid Ged's village at the start are Kargs; and when Ged, pursuing his shadow, finds himself wrecked on a desert island, the two wretched creatures he finds living there are maroons, left by the Kargs as a move in some dynastic struggle. There is, again, a pathetic scene as the female member of the pair shows Ged her two treasures, a broken ring and the embroidered silk dress she was wearing when abandoned as a baby, and presses the former on him as a gift. But the sense of human cruelty is restated when Ged offers to take them away, and the man refuses: "All his memory of other lands and other men was a child's nightmare of blood and giants and screaming. Ged could see that in his face as he shook his head and shook his head" (*WE* ch. 8). It is an extreme move, then, to set the second book of the trilogy in Atuan, one of the four islands of the empire; and to use it as a setting for discussion of another element not represented in the first book, the nature of religion. The change may be felt the more sharply by a modern American or European if he sees it further as a move from strangeness towards familiarity: for the Kargs are more like us than are Ged's people from the Inner Lands. They are white, for one thing, while Ged is brown. They are fierce, hierarchic, imperialistic, slave-owning. They have an organised state religion, and indeed an organised state, both unfamiliar in the rest of Earthsea. And offically at least, they do not believe in magic. "What is this magic they work?" asks one character in *The Tombs of Atuan*, to be told firmly "Tricks, deceptions, jugglery." And again: "How do they get the power? . . . Where does it come from?" "Lies" is the orthodox answer; "Words," suggests another, more open-minded but not much better-informed (*TA* ch. 4). The Kargs, in fact, agree with the *O.E.D.* They are the first sceptics to appear in Earthsea.

This is perhaps not too apparent in the opening scenes, which once more oppose pathos to cruelty. The book begins with a mother watching the child who is soon to be taken from her; and goes on to describe the "installation" of the child as priestess of the cult of the Nameless Ones, a cult which depends on the theory that as each priestess dies she is reborn as a girl-baby, who has then to be identified and brought back. The ceremony of dedication is purposely a cruel one, in which the child is symbolically sacrificed, and progressively deprived of family, and name, and membership of humanity. Once Tenar is made priestess she has to be called Arha, "the Eaten One," because the Nameless Ones have eaten her name and soul; she cannot be touched, either in affection or (and this is cruel too) in punishment. Kargish religion appears horrific, then, both in our terms, which exalt family life and individual rights, and in the values we have learnt from A Wizard of Earthsea, values which depend so ultimately on the right to be called by one's proper name. But, as has been said already, Mrs. Le Guin thinks that even the darkness has rights, and as the book unfolds we are forced to consider what all this cruelty is *for*, what is its basis in reality. The option exercised by Frazer, of looking on at savage foibles with amused contempt, is not left open.

For there are depths even beneath the horror of Kargish religion. The cults of the Nameless Ones, and the Godking, and the God Brothers have, after all, some good points. They offer an escape, in particular, from the fear that haunts A Wizard of Earthsea and The Farthest Shore, the fear of exile to the dry lands of the dead. The Kargs do not believe that they will go there. Kossil, priestess of the Godking and in general representative of all that is worst in Atuan, regards the inhabitants of the magelands with a scorn which does not rise to pity, because they are subject to death as she is not: "They have no gods. They work magic, and think they are gods themselves. But they are not. And when they die, they are not re-born. . . . They do not have immortal souls" (TA ch. 4). Her last sentence is a terrible one, redefining humans as animals, but it shows the assurance her religion offers. The real fear beneath Kargish religion is to have that assurance taken away, to have the whole thing exposed as a tragic mistake, or swindle, and the threat which Arha, accordingly, fears most is that of atheism—even if this is a warm and affectionate atheism like that of Earthsea mages or many modern agnostics. To this threat she is exposed in the persons of three sceptics: her friend/subordinate Penthe, her teacher/rival Kossil, her liberator/seducer Ged.

The first of these is easily subdued. Penthe does not believe in religion, which she knows, on the sensible ground that the Godking is only human. On the other hand she believes in magic, of which she has no experience, in an entirely credulous way: "they can all cast a spell on you as easy as winking." The "solidity" of Penthe's unfaith frightens Arha for a moment, and shows that reason can still work even in the stronghold of superstition. But her opinions are evidently not generally reliable, and she is soon brought to heel by a touch of fear. Arha makes her point, that

"Penthe might disbelieve in the gods, but she feared the unnamable powers of the dark—as did every mortal soul" (*TA* ch. 4). Kossil provides tougher opposition. As the story proceeds, we realise that she too fears the dark, but has little belief in the religion she herself represents (the cult of the Godking), except as a focus of secular power. And she, unlike Penthe, is consistently sceptical even about her own fear, and is prepared to put matters to the test. It is almost the turning-point of *The Tombs of Atuan* when Arha discovers Kossil in the Undertomb—the place most sacred to the Nameless Ones, where light is totally prohibited—digging in the ground to discover whether Arha has really killed her prisoner, Ged, and doing it *with a lantern burning.* And the Gods do not react. Ahra is converted to atheism on the spot, and weeps because of it, because "the gods are dead." The true turning-point, however, is the reaction of Ged. He too has brought light into the holy place, searching for the lost half of the Ring of Erreth-Akbe—the ring the maroon gave him was the first half—and he has been trapped as a result, provoking a crisis of conscience for Arha, who ought to kill him but cannot. Nevertheless his attitude is very different from Kossil's or Penthe's. Neither superstitious like the latter nor incredulous like the former, he expresses firm belief in the Nameless Ones, and asserts that it is only his magic power that is keeping them from a violent reaction.

All this leaves a modern reader slightly baffled. The story drives him to identify with Arha, and to accept Ged's authority. The one tells him that the dark gods exist, the other's grief makes him want to believe it. But he is more likely, intellectually, to agree with Kossil and Penthe, and to be repelled in any case by the cruelties inflicted on Arha in the name of the religion she serves. So who is right, about the Nameless Ones, about reincarnation, about souls? As with the anonymity or otherwise of the shadow-beast earlier, there are questions with quite objective answers at the core of *The Tombs of Atuan.* Nor are the new answers very dissimilar. Ged's central statement is that the Nameless Ones are powers, but not gods, and that their strength has two sources. One is the innate cruelty of the universe—a concept familiar to us since the time of Darwin. The other is the human reaction to that fact, the impulse to propitiate and sacrifice and offer scapegoats. Just as the shadow-beast was born of Ged's fear of (his own) death, so the Nameless Ones feed on the institutionalised cruelty, itself born of fear, which took Tenar from her mother and made her Ahra, the Eaten One. They would exist without worship, but their worshippers make them stronger. Ged's essential point, and Mrs. Le Guin's, is that though the universe cannot be denied, and loss of one kind or another is therefore inevitable, what can be controlled is the placatory impulse which seeks to control death but in practice makes an institution of it. Pathos is always with us, in short, but cruelty can be stopped.

This is a satisfying conclusion for the reader of *The Tombs of Atuan*, because it suggests that all its main characters have seen some part of the truth, Penthe and Kossil in rejecting the value of organised religion, Arha in believing that it must nevertheless have some basis. It must be said, however, that in spite of the novel's overt theme of liberation, there are implications at the end at least as grim as those at the start. The hope of future life is gently taken away, for one thing, when Arha sees her mother (whom she does not recognise) in a dream. Her mother comes to her in the quasi-angelic form which she has decided is representative of the souls of the damned, those who are not reborn, even though (according to Kossil) Arha's mother, as a gods-fearing Karg, would naturally be reincarnated and not be among the damned at all. Still, Kossil is wrong. And it is a further ironic twist that the vision of this lost relation should signal precisely the abandonment of belief in metempsychosis, since it contradicts the old "intellectualist" theory of Herbert Spencer, that the concept of the soul and of religion itself took its rise from seeing dead people in dreams. But Ged has no consolation to offer here, any more than he has over the book's final tragedy, which is that in order to escape Ged has to kill the only person who ever loved Arha in her priestess-life, and whom she continually threatened and tormented in return. Losses are not recovered in Earthsea, and even as the book ends with its vision of flags and sunlight and towers, one may recall Arha's furious outburst earlier:

> It doesn't matter if there's oceans and dragons and towers and all that, because you'll never see them again, you'll never even see the light of the sun. All I know is the dark, the night underground. And that's all there really is. That's all there is to know, in the end. The silence, and the dark. You know everything, wizard. But I know one thing—the one true thing!
>
> (TA, ch. 7)

Maybe she spoke truer than she knew. Certainly the story's last act contains a kind of sacrifice, and Arha's wish (which is overruled) to be cast out of humanity like the wretched Kargish maroons.

There are, of course, some warmer elements in the story, clustering for the most part round what magic is allowed to appear. By his gift of insight Ged restores Arha's name, Tenar, to her; and one might think that by doing so he has made himself able to exploit her. But in a neat scene near the end, after they have escaped the earthquake which is "the anger of the dark," we see that Ged does not use magic just to preserve himself. He calls a rabbit to him by using its true name, to show Tenar. But when she suggests eating it—and they are both hungry—he rejects the idea as a breach of trust. Presumably he has felt the same scrupulosity about her. So there are intimations of courage and self-mastery in the book, indeed prominent ones. They cannot, however, conceal the conclusion that while Mrs. Le Guin felt that early modern anthropologists had not been able to provide satisfactory theories of magic, she could on the whole agree with their models of the genesis of religion. Like Ged, Sir James Frazer thought that "religion consists of two elements . . . namely, a belief in powers higher than man and an attempt to propitiate or please them." The latter without the former gives us ritualism (Kossil), the former without the latter approximates to Ged's standpoint, in Frazerian terms a "theology" without a "religion." Frazer found it difficult, in fact, to *find* real examples of belief coupled wtih indifference, but there is a further analogue of sorts to Ged in the person of Frazer's contemporary and fellow agnostic, T. H. Huxley. In a famous passage he insisted that social progress depended "not on imitating the cosmic process . . . but on combating it," a view harsher and more self-reliant than Ged's, but projecting a similarly moralistic humanism. In this respect at least scientist and magician agree (as Frazer insisted they should). But there is no room in the agreement for those who wish to intercede with the universe, or think there is anything to do with the Nameless Ones except ignore them, or else rob them and run.

The movement of the first two books of the trilogy is then on the whole downwards, into a deepening gloom, and towards us, towards familiarity. It is continued and even accelerated in the last book, *The Farthest Shore*, which describes what things are like when the magic starts to run out. Earthsea begins to resemble America in the aftermath of Vietnam: exhausted, distrustful, uncertain. This is conveyed in a series of interviews with wizards who have lost their power, and who try, not to seek help, but to justify themselves to Ged, now grown old, and his young companion Arren. The first one they meet is a woman, once an illusionist, who has turned instead to being a saleswoman and employing in that trade the more familiar arts of distraction and hyperbole. She has, in short, become a conjuror, and defends herself dourly: "You can puzzle a man's mind with the flashing of mirrors, and with words, and with other tricks I won't tell you. . . . But it was tricks, fooleries. . . . So I turned to this trade, and maybe all the silks aren't silks nor all the fleeces Gontish, but all the same they'll wear—they'll wear!' They're real, and not mere lies and air . . ." (*FS* ch. 3). She has a point, even a business-ethic; but her equation of magic with mumbo-jumbo has robbed the world of beauty. She distinguishes herself sharply, furthermore, from the drug-takers who now for the first time appear in Earthsea, but when Ged speaks to one of these he insists similarly that eating *hazia* helps you because "you forget the names, you let the forms of things go, you go straight to the reality" (*FS* ch. 3). There is something ominous about the "reality" both speakers oppose to "names" and "words"; one remembers the subjection of "words" to "matter" discussed earlier. The point is sharpened by a third experience on the silk isle of Lorbanery, where the inhabitants insist that magic has never existed, and that things are the same as ever, but where the workmanship has become notoriously "shoddy," economics is rearing its ugly head, and a "generation-gap" appears to have been invented. In the end even the innocent Raft-folk who never touch inhabited islands are affected, as their chanters fail to carry through the ritual dance of Sun return; their forgetting the old songs represents the breach of tradition, the failure of authority, which has been, in some sense, the inheritance of the Western world since the mid-nineteenth century. Earthsea, in a word, has grown secularised; and we recognise the condition.

The root of the process is told us many times, and is entirely predictable from the two preceding books. It is the fear of death, the voice that cries (so Ged puts it) "*let the world rot so long as I can live!*" But the fear of death has been on or near Ged since the first few pages of *A Wizard of Earthsea*. The new if related factor in *The Farthest Shore* is more precisely the hope of life. A wizard has arisen who is able, for the first time, to go through the land of the dead and out the other side, to return to the world after his own death. His example, and the promise it offers, give those who know of it a new hope; but their preoccupation with that hope makes them fear the future more and love the present less, while their wish to preserve themselves is inherently destructive of the Equilibrium through which name-magic works. Besides, the breach that the wizard has made is imagined as a hole through which the magic of the living world runs out, so that the change affects even the ignorant.

There is, to a modern reader, something almost blasphemous in these statements about the dangers of eternal life. In the final confrontation near the exit from the dead land, the reborn wizard boasts:

> I had the courage to die, to find what you cowards could never find—the way back from death. I opened the door that had been shut since the beginning of time. . . . Alone of all men in all time I am Lord of the Two Lands.
>
> (*FS* ch. 12)

Opener of gates, conqueror of death, promiser of life—one can hardly avoid thinking of Christ, the One who Harrowed Hell. Probably one has been thinking of Him since the dark lord first appeared, holding out "a tiny flame no larger than a pearl, held it out to Arren, offering life" (FS ch. 3). And yet in Earthsea the one who brings the promise is a destroyer; the Christian of *Pilgrim's Progress*, who flees from his family with this hands over his ears, shouting "Life, life, eternal life!," now reappears as the wizards who abandon their trade and turn the world to shoddiness and gloom. The gifts of magic and of religion could hardly be more fiercely opposed. Yet the weakening of magic in Earthsea resembles the weakening of religion here. For there is a consistent image which underlies *The Farthest Shore*, and which seems to be taken from another book about the failure (and reattainment) of belief, Dostoyevsky's *Crime and Punishment*. There the morbid, sensual, ghost-haunted *roué* Svidrigaylov propounds his personal theory of eternity. Raskolnikov has just said "I do not believe in a future life"—a statement that holds no terrors. But Svidrigaylov replies:

> And what if there are only spiders there, or something of the sort. . . .
> We're always thinking of eternity as an idea that cannot be understood,
> something immense. But why must it be? What if, instead of all this, you
> suddenly find just a little room there, something like a village bath-house,
> grimy and spiders in every corner, and that's all eternity is.

Raskolnikov rejects the idea as horrible and unjust. How can you tell, asks Svidrigaylov. "I, you know, would certainly have made it so deliberately!" Ged's enemy seems close to Svidrigaylov, especially in that both have an abnormal terror of death; and his promise of eternity is inextricably spidery. His use-name, to begin with (he has forgotten his true-name) is Cob, the old English word for spider. And when Arren dreams, he dreams of being in a dry, dusty, ruined house, full of *cob*-webs which fill his mouth and nose; the worst part of his dream is realising that the ruin is the Great House of the wizards of Roke. After Ged is wounded, Arren's paralysis of the will is like being wrapped in fine threads, and he thinks "veils of cobweb" are spun over the sky. When the witch of Lorbanery confesses her failure of power, she says that the words and names have run out of her and down the hole in the world, "by little strings like spider-webs out of my eyes and mouth." The action begins with the Master Patterner of Roke watching a lesser patterner, a spider. There are many other contributory references. All suggest the entrapment of life in something powerful yet tenuous: if Cob has his way, both the lands of the dead and of the living will become like Svidrigaylov's bath-house, dry, dusty, covered by his personal web.

In both works faith (whether in magic and Equilibrium or in Christianity and eternal life) is wrecked by doubt, a parallel which ought to clear Mrs. Le Guin of the charge of wilful blasphemy. She is implying, not that Christianity leads to morbidity, but rather that the present inability of many to believe in any supernatural power lays them open to fear and selfishness and a greedy clutching at hope which spoils even the present life that one can be sure of. Her striking presentation of the land of the dead, so alien to either Christian or Classical concepts, seems also to have a root in the great lapse of faith of the late nineteenth century. For in *The Farthest Shore* Ged and Arren have actually to pass through this country, and see it as a strange analogue of the land of the living: people, streets, houses, markets, movement—but no emotion. Arren saw "the mother and child who had died together, and they were in the dark land together; but the child did not run, nor did it cry, and the mother did not hold it, nor even look at it. And those who had died for love passed each other in the streets" (*FS* ch. 12). The last sentence offers no eternal cure for the pathos of parting we so often see in Earthsea. But it is also strongly reminiscent of the A. E. Housman poem so popular in the 1880s and 1890s:

> In the nation that is not
>   Nothing stands that stood before.
> There revenges are forgot,
>   And the hater hates no more;
> Lovers lying two and two
>   Ask not whom they sleep beside;
> And the bridegroom all night through
>   Never turns him to the bride.

To be dead = not to be: that is Housman's faith, and Earthsea's orthodoxy. Cob's blasphemy is to try to cure that stable situation, from the ignoble motive of fear and with the joyless and desiccated result already indicated. Yet one hardly likes to blame him, for the dead land is a dreadful image, and it seems only natural to shrink from it, as indeed many others have done in the trilogy beforehand—Ged trying to recall the dead, the Kargs inventing reincarnation as a protection. Mrs. Le Guin has no trouble in convincing us that loss of faith is unfortunate, nor that joy in life is a proper goal. What is difficult is persuading us that the latter can co-exist with the former, or (to put it in the symbols of her trilogy) that magic is worthwhile even when it promises no immortality. The solution, for the last time, turns on an objective realisation, about names.

It is significant that Cob (like Arha) has forgotten his true-name, but that Ged, who says he can remember it, never restores it to him. The failed wizards whom Ged interrogates insist steadily that to be reborn you have to give up your name, but that it does not matter because "A name isn't real." Blasphemy again, by Earthsea standards, but as always with Mrs. Le Guin, even the worst characters are not simply wrong. They are right to say that names and new life are mutually exclusive. For the simplest way to describe the shades in the land of the dead is to say that they are names, which go there and must stay there. Whether one should say they are *only* names is doubtful, and one has an almost insoluble problem in translating such statements into our own terms. Perhaps one should say that a man's name is his self, his sense that he is who he is; once the man is dead this never returns. This means that those who take Cob's promise are deceived. What they get is eternal consciousness, but consciousness without personality. Which is worse, to be an unreal name/shadow, or a nameless awareness? The metaphysics are hard to solve. Ged's final insistence, however, is that human beings are indeed dual, as people have long thought, but not by being bodies and souls, rather bodies and names. Of the hero Erreth-Akbe he says, that though his image has been summoned by Cob it was still "but a shadow and a name." When he died, his name descended to the shadowland, but the essential part of him remained in the real world.

> There he is the earth and sunlight, the leaves of trees, the eagle's flight. He is alive. And all who ever died, live; they are reborn, and have no end, nor will there ever be an end. All save you. For you would not have death. You lost death, you lost life, in order to save yourself. Yourself!
> (FS ch. 12)

It is ironic that Ged in the end proposes a Kargish doctrine of reincarnation. But one should note its limitations. Ged says only that dead men return to their elements; he does not say they will be reborn *as persons*, or reborn with memory, or reborn in any process of justice. He says no more than any agnostic can accept, but strives to make it a positive affirmation.

We are on our own; living is a process not a state; reality is to be endured not changed: precepts of this nature underlie the *Earthsea* trilogy. Of course it is not the business of literature to hutch such moral nuggets, nor of criticism to dig for them, and especially not when dealing with books as full of the sense of place and individuality and difference as Mrs. Le Guin's. Nevertheless it has to be said that these three books clearly aim at having some of the qualities of parable as well as of narrative, and that the parables are repeatedly summed up by statements within the books themselves. Mages appear to think in contrasts. "To light a candle is to cast a shadow," says one; "to speak, one must be silent," says another; "There must be darkness to see the stars," says Ged, "the dance is always danced . . . above the terrible abyss." In their gnomic and metaphorical quality such remarks are alien to modern speech; and yet they turn out to be distinctively modern when properly understood, the last one for example relying strongly on our rediscovery of the importance of social ritual (the dance), and our new awareness of the extent of time and space (the abyss). A reader may start on *A Wizard of Earthsea* for its spells and dragons and medieval, or rather pre-medieval trappings; he would be imperceptive, however, if he failed to realise before long—however dim the realisation—that he was reading not just a parable, but a parable for our times.

It is tempting to lead on and declare that Mrs. Le Guin is a "mythopoeic" writer (an adjective many critics find easy to apply to fantasy in general). The truth, though, seems to be that she is at least as much of an iconoclast, a myth-breaker not a myth-maker. She rejects resurrection and eternal life; she refutes "cathartic" and "intellectualist" versions of anthropology alike; her relationship with Sir James Frazer in particular is one of correction too grave for parody, and extending to "The Perils of the Soul" and "The Magic Art" and even "The Evolution of Kings," his sub-titles all alike. As was said at the start, she demands of us that we reconsider even our basic vocabulary, with insistent redefinitions of "magic," "soul," "name," "alive," and many other semantic fields and lexical items. One might end by remarking that novelty is blended with familiarity even in the myth which underlies the history of Earthsea itself, the oldest song of *The Creation of Éa* which is sung by Ged's companions in at least two critical moments. "Only in silence the word," it goes, "only in dark the light. . . ." By the end of the trilogy we realise that this is more than just a rephrasing of our own "Genesis" as given by St. John. Mrs. Le Guin takes "In the beginning was the Word" more seriously and more literally than do many modern theologians; but her respect for ancient texts includes no great regard for the mythic structures that have been built on them.

JAMES W. BITTNER

Persuading Us to Rejoice and Teaching Us How to Praise: Le Guin's "Orsinian Tales"

In 1951, the year Ursula Kroeber entered Columbia to begin graduate work in French and Italian Renaissance literature, she invented an imaginary Central European country and wrote her first Orsinian tale. The country's name—Orsinia, or the Ten Provinces—and its creator's name have the same root; *orsino*, Italian for "bearish," and *Ursula* came from the Latin *ursa*. Le Guin explains rather dryly that "it's my country so it bears my name."

After marrying Charles Le Guin in 1953, she abandoned her academic career to concentrate on writing. By 1961, she says in an autobiographical essay, she had completed five novels, four of them set in Orsinia, "as were the best short stories I had done." When these novels and stories, classifiable as neither fantasy nor realism, were submitted to publishers like Knopf or Viking, or to magazines like *Harper's, Cosmopolitan, or Redbook*, they came back with the remark "this material seems remote." It *was* remote, says Le Guin:

> Searching for a technique of distancing, I had come upon this one. Unfortunately it was not a technique used by anybody at the moment, it was not fashionable, it did not fit any of the categories. You must either fit a category, or 'have a name,' to publish a book in America. As the only way I was ever going to achieve Namehood was *by* writing,

From *Science-Fiction Studies* 3, vol. 5 (November 1978). Copyright © 1978 by R. D. Miller and Darko Suvin.

I was reduced to fitting a category. Therefore my first efforts to write science fiction were motivated by a pretty distinct wish to get published.

Orsinia did not go entirely unnoticed. A poem and a story were published in little magazines in 1959 and 1961. But just as a couple of Le Guin's minor Orsinian pieces were appearing in print, she discovered Cordwainer Smith, rediscovered science fiction, which she had read as an adolescent, and, intent on getting published, started writing fantasy and science fiction for *Fantastic* and *Amazing*. By 1963 she had begun her explorations of Earthsea and the Hainish worlds, and was on her way to Namehood. Now, of course, with numerous awards from both inside and outside science fiction, she has achieved it; twenty-five years after her Orsinian tales started collecting rejection slips, her *Orsinian Tales* (1976) received a nomination for the National Book Award for fiction.

I go into all this—the date of the earliest Orsinian tales, and their place vis a vis categories like "realism," "fantasy," and "science fiction"—to dispel the notion that *Orsinian Tales* is Le Guin's attempt to extend the range of her talents beyond the boundaries of fantasy and science fiction. If anything, the opposite is the case. *Orsinian Tales* includes chunks of the bedrock that lies beneath Le Guin's other imaginary countries and worlds. Or, using another metaphor, I would suggest that a trip through Orsinia may lead us to those underground streams that nourish the imagination that created the Earthsea trilogy (1968-72), *The Left Hand of Darkness* (1969), and *The Dispossessed* (1974).

Relationships between *Orsinian Tales* and the rest of Le Guin's fiction will be one of my concerns here. Some of these tales were written before Le Guin discovered-invented Earthsea and the Hainish worlds, some were written at the same time she was writing fantasy and science fiction, and they were all collected, arranged, and published after she had written the works that brought her Namehood. We cannot, therefore, try to understand *Orsinian Tales* as a discrete stage or step in Le Guin's development, for the parts and the whole were composed at different times. Accordingly, my approach will be eclectic. In the first section below, I will treat the book as a whole, discussing Le Guin's synthesis of aesthetic and historical perspectives, and arguing that Le Guin's historical understanding is mediated by the literary form that structures most of her fiction, the circular journey or romance quest. Then, I will look at the country Orsinia as an imaginary construct whose fluid boundaries enclose both fantasy and realism, and also as a *paysage moralisé* which manifests the same qualities we find in Le Guin's other imaginary landscapes. In the final two sections, I will concentrate on "Imaginary Countries" and *"An die Musik,"* two tales Le Guin wrote in 1960, before she turned to fantasy and science fiction, reading the first as the central tale in the collection, and the second as an early formulation of a problem that continues to be prominent throughout Le Guin's career, the conflict between her deep devotion to art and her strong commitment to ethical principles.

I

Orsinian Tales, Le Guin's second collection of short fiction, is radically different from her first. In her "Foreword" to *The Wind's Twelve Quarters,* Le Guin explains that it is "what painters call a retrospective": the stories are assembled in the order they were written to give us an overview of her artistic development. The tales in *Orsinian Tales,* however, are not arranged in order of their composition, so this is not another Le Guin retrospective. But if "retrospective" does not describe the collection, then another word from painting, "perspective," may indicate something about the nature of the tales and may help to reveal the ordering principles embedded in their arrangement.

After we finish reading any story, we step back from it as though we were stepping back from a painting, adjusting our vision to get an impression of its total design and meaning. This is aesthetic perspective, the desired effect of any technique of distancing. The distancing technique Le Guin uses in *Orsinian Tales,* the technique she developed in the fifties before she began writing for *Amazing* and *Fantastic,* is derived from Isak Dinesen's tales and from Austin Tappan Wright's *Islandia.* This technique does something more than create an aesthetic perspective; it creates a twofold perspective—aesthetic and historical.

Le Guin achieves aesthetic distance from her materials by writing *tales,* not stories (notwithstanding the publisher's dust jacket subtitle "A Collection of Stories"). *Orsinian Tales* does not belong in a class with Joyce's *Dubliners* and Anderson's *Winesburg, Ohio;* rather, its title recalls the tradition that includes Scott's *Tales of My Landlord,* Hearn's *Tales Out of the East,* Dunsany's *A Dreamer's Tales,* and Dinesen's *Seven Gothic Tales* and *Winter's Tales.* Le Guin's title is a clear echo of Dunsany's and Dinesen's titles. A tale does not pretend to represent everyday reality as faithfully as a story does; more than a story, a tale calls attention to itself as a work of art, closed off from the world, and in its tendency to state a moral more overtly than a story usually does, it has affinities with fables, parables, and legends. A tale offers a clearer understanding of the shape and action of the moral order we dimly perceive in our sometimes disordered daily experience, and it does this because it detaches itself from the contingencies of a particular time and place. The discovery and delineation of moral laws, in fact, may be the most important goal of the teller of tales, and the pattern of those moral laws cannot be separated from the aesthetic forms which enable the artist to discover them and communicate them to others. As ethical choices in our everyday lives are not free from history, those in a tale are bound by aesthetic forms. A tale offers a perspective that combines aesthetics and ethics in a single vision.

Yet at the same time that Le Guin creates this aesthetic perspective, she negates it by regrounding her tales in history, seemingly, contradicting, yet really complementing the ahistorical qualities of the tale with precise historical connections. Le Guin sets her tales in an imaginary country, to be sure, but that country is in *Mitteleuropa*, not *Faerie*: Orsinia is in the "sick heart" of modern Europe and knows at first hand what Mircea Eliade, a native of Romania, calls the "terror of history." Le Guin therefore evokes as the larger setting of her tales some of the darkest, most chaotic, and most violent history available. Like Hardy's Wessex, Faulkner's Yoknapatawpha County, and Wright's Islandia, Le Guin's Orsinia may be imaginary, but it is profoundly affected by real historical forces.

At the end of each tale we discover a date; these dates, ranging from the early Middle Ages (1150) to the recent past (1965), locate each tale at a precise moment in Orsinia's (and Central Europe's) history, and invite us to step back from our involvement with a character's experiences, to insert those experiences in a definite historical context, and to understand them in a historical perspective. It is significant that the dates are at the *end* of each tale; they appear *at the very moment* we are stepping back from the tale to see aesthetically. At that moment, history and aesthetics, two modes of seeing and knowing, become one.

The process of reading the eleven pieces of *Orsinian Tales*, then, is the process of forming and re-forming this two-fold aesthetic and historical perspective, progressively enlarging our understanding of the relationships among individual tales and deepening our understanding of the relationships between any one moment in the lives of individual Orsinians and the whole web of Orsinian history. As we finish the collection, we realize that the two perspectives are not contradictory, but complementary; the one being the dialectical negation of the other, art and history combine to create a single vision. "Heroes do not make history," says the narrator of "The Lady of Moge"—"that is the historians' job." *Orsinian Tales*, however, offers abundant evidence that the job is not the sole responsibility of historians: it is shared by artists. Le Guin's tales are as historical as Scott's Waverly novels are, and her history is as much an aesthetic invention as are Dinesen's finely crafted tales. As Le Guin's art in *Orsinian Tales* redeems her history from meaningless contingency and hopeless determinism, her history redeems her art from amoral escapism.

Le Guin's arrangement of the tales embodies a complex organic vision of history. If they are not arranged as they were written, neither are they arranged as history courses are, to give the impression that chronology and historical causality are somehow synonymous. Nor are they randomly mixed up just to give us the exercise of reconstituting Orsinia's history. Le Guin's ordering of the tales guides us through the history of Orsinia so that we move forward *only* by circling back to the past; we understand any present moment only as we understand it to be an organic part of its past and future. After beginning in 1960 ("The Fountains"), we return to 1150 ("The Barrow"), move forward to 1920 ("Ile Forest" and "Conversations at Night"), then on to 1956 ("The Road East"), back to 1910 ("Brothers and Sisters"), forward beyond 1956 to 1962 ("A Week in the Country"), back to 1938 ("*An die Musik*"), forward beyond 1962 to 1965 ("The House"), back to 1640 ("The Lady of Moge"), and finally forward to 1935 ("Imaginary Countries"), coming to rest, at the end of the collection, at the chronological *center* of these eleven tales: five are set before 1935, and five after 1935. As I will show later, this is not the only way in which "Imaginary Countries" is the central tale in *Orsinian Tales.*

The pattern of this movement through these tales that *are* Orsinia's history—a synthesis of circularity and linearity, a series of returns which are also advances—is not only the configuration of Le Guin's sense of history; it is also the aesthetic structure that informs most of her fiction. The romance quest which is at once a return to roots and an advance is Ged's path (way, Tao) in Earthsea; it is the route taken by Genly Ai and Estraven from Karhide over the Gobrin Ice to "The Place Inside the Blizzard" and back to Karhide; and it is the form of Shevek's journey from Anarres to Urras and back home again. In *Orsinian Tales*, this pattern is present not only in the shape of the whole collection; it is present also in individual tales: Freyga, Count of Montayana, returns to pagan sacrifice then advances the cause of Benedictine monks; Adam Kereth returns to Orsinia after "defecting" at Versailles; and Mariya returns to her husband Pier Korre in Aisnar after searching for independence and freedom from marriage in Krasnoy.

These circular journeys are in one way or another versions of the Romantic quest for home, freedom, and wholeness. What Le Guin's characters learn on their quests is that freedom and wholeness are not to be found in individualism, but in partnership, and further, that freedom from historical necessity comes not from escaping history, but from returning to roots. This is the moral message that takes shape when we see Le Guin's fiction from the perspective created by her distancing techniques. It is the ethical principle discovered by Sanzo Chekey and Alitsia Benat, by Stefan Fabbre and Bruna Augeskar, and by Mariya and Pier Lorre. In Le Guin's fantasy and science fiction it is discovered by Ged and Vetch, Tenar and Ged, Arren and Ged, Genly Ai and Estraven, George Orr and Heather Lelache, Shevek and Takver. In *The Dispossessed*, we find Le Guin's most concise statement of the principle, chiseled into Odo's tombstone: "to be whole is to be part: / true voyage is return." It is the ethical foundation of Le Guin's fiction, even as it is aesthetic form and historical consciousness.

Ethics, art, and history, along with religion, philosophy, politics, and science, are what Joseph Needham calls "moulds of understanding." Each one, taken by itself, offers a limited and limiting mode of comprehending and experiencing the world. *Orsinian Tales* is one of Le Guin's attempts to formulate a unified mould of understanding that integrates artistic, ethical, and historical modes. Convinced that the worlds we experience, from subatomic to cosmic levels, whether material or imaginative, are all integrated parts of an ordered whole, a continuous process, Le Guin has from the beginning of her career tried to fashion fictional techniques to comprehend that order. The hybrid of realism and fantasy in *Orsinian Tales*, the fantasy of the Earthsea trilogy, and the science fiction of the Hainish novels are all different means to the same end: a realization of the unity of the world we live in. The end, unity, and the formal means, a circular journey, are cognate. In one sense, Le Guin uses different genres; but in another sense, those genres are merely distinct, though not radically different, constellations of moulds of understanding. Just as the artist and historian in Le Guin collaborate in *Orsinian Tales*, artist and scientist work together in her science fiction. Genly Ai opens his report from Gethen with these remarks:

> I'll make my report as if I told a story, for I was taught as a child on my homeworld that Truth is a matter of the imagination. The soundest fact may fail or prevail in the style of the telling: like that singular organic jewel of our sea, which grows brighter as the woman wears it and, worn by another, dulls and goes to dust. Facts are no more solid, coherent, round, and real than pearls are. But both are sensitive.

Ai then proceeds to weave together his own story; extracts from Estraven's journal; an anthropological report; and Gethenian legends, folktales, and myth. Each presents only a partial view of the truth; together they come closer to Truth. For Le Guin, the real and the fantastic, fact and value, art and history, myth and science are neither separate nor even separable realms and modes of discovery; they are complementary and internally related parts of the same realm. "How can you tell the legend from the fact?" asks the narrator of *Rocannon's World*. The answer, of course, is "you can't." Another answer, an ethical one, is "you shouldn't." Le Guin's fiction denies the walls we build with different moulds of understanding; it denies the reification and dehumanization that a fragmented and compartmentalized way of life produces. Like the music Ladislas Gaye hears at the end of "*An die Musik*," "it denies and breaks down all the shelters, the houses men build for themselves, that they may see the sky"

II

The Italian sociologist and economist Vilfredo Pareto was disturbed by the shifting and sometimes contradictory meanings of Marx's words and concepts:

> If you raise some objections against a passage in *Capital*, a passage whose meaning seems to you incontestable, someone can quote another, whose meaning is entirely different. It is the fable of the bat all over again. If you embrace one meaning, someone tells you
>
> > I am a bird; see my wings;
> > Long live the flying things!
>
> And if you adopt the other, someone tells you
>
> > I am a mouse; long live the rats;
> > Jupiter confound the cats!

Much the same can be said—indeed has been said, though in a positive rather than in a negative sense—about the ideas and concepts in Le Guin's fiction. In his essay on the Earthsea trilogy, T.A. Shippey may not argue that Le Guin's words are, like bats, both birds and mice, but he does note that Le Guin's story embodies an "argument" against "conceptual barriers" that result from "the very sharpness and hardness of modern concepts." Not only does Le Guin make "covert comparisons between 'fantastic' and 'familiar,' " says Shippey, she also shifts the meanings of familiar concepts: at times magic in Earthsea seems to be a science, at other times an art, and at still other times, it is ethics. The "oscillation between concepts" that Shippey sees in the Earthsea trilogy is not peculiar to Le Guin's juvenile fantasy; it permeates nearly everything she has written, from her individual sentences to her major themes, images, and even characters. Were Pareto alive, he might consider Le Guin's Gethenians just as bat-like as Marx's concepts: if he tried to see them as men, they would become women, and if he tried to see them as women, they would become men. Le Guin wants to teach readers like Pareto (and characters like Genly Ai) to think both-and (or even, perhaps, neither-nor) rather than either-or. She started doing just that in the fifties and sixties when she was writing her Orsinian tales.

Long before Le Guin wrote a sentence like "The king was pregnant" (LHD), she was writing sentences like this one in *Orsinian Tales*: "On a sunny morning in Cleveland, Ohio, it was raining in Krasnoy and the streets between grey walls were full of men." This sentence first situates us in a familiar time and place, then erases the distinctions we make between a real country like the USA and an imaginary country like Orsinia. Cleveland and Krasnoy do not exist in the same world. Or do they? Le Guin's sentence creates a new world, neither our familiar one, nor an entirely fantastic one, but a world which is both realistic and fantastic. The point of this sentence is not that one thing is real and the other is imaginary; the point is that they are both in the same sentence. The world of Le Guin's fiction is not a realm of well-defined, discrete things and places and times and ideas; rather, it is a realm where categories and perspectives are fluid, a world which is ordered process in which nothing, except change itself, can be taken for granted as certain. Orsinia's location, its political history, even its geology, are all in flux.

Orsinia can be placed on two different maps. Darrell Schweitzer says that "in *Orsinian Tales* Le Guin seems to be trying to do a *Dubliners* set in an unnamed central European country (clearly Hungary, complete with a revolution against foreign conquerors in 1956)." Le Guin's brother Karl Kroeber, on the other hand, tells us "not to seek in Bulgaria for the setting of 'Brothers and Sisters.' The curious growthless plain of limestone quarries is not East of the Sun and West of the Moon, just a little south of Zembla and north of Graustark." Though Kroeber is mostly right in placing Orsinia on the same map with Nabokov's distant northern kingdom in *Pale Fire* and McCutcheon's Balkan kingdom, rather than in a totally fantastic realm ("East of the Sun and West of the Moon"), and though Schweitzer is mostly wrong in identifying Orsinia with Hungary, neither of these two mappers takes full account of Le Guin's "oscillation," as Shippey might call it, between Joycean naturalism and the escapism of McCutcheon's *Graustark* or Hope's *The Prisoner of Zenda*. Literary naturalism and Ruritanian romances were contemporary phenomena at the turn of the century when many writers and readers were making clear distinctions between realism and romance. Le Guin's fictional techniques dissolve those distinctions; the boundaries between the real and the fantastic disappear when we understand them to be complementary and internally related parts of the imaginary.

Le Guin herself says that Orsinia is an "invented though non-fantastic Central European country." Le Guin's invented worlds, whether set in Europe or in the Hainish universe, still contain accurate and naturalistic facts, history in the first instance, science in the second. To make the transition from writing Orsinian tales to writing science fiction was no major step for Le Guin; all she had to do was replace one social science (history) with another (anthropology), and integrate some elements from the hard sciences. In fact, some of the Orsinian tales were written at the same time she was writing the Hainish novels.

There are, certainly, ample naturalistic facts in *Orsinian Tales* to justify looking for Orsinia on a map of Europe. We visit Versailles, hear of Croatian microbiologists, get a glimpse of the conflict between Teutonic paganism and Christianity in the early Middle Ages; we see the social and economic dislocation caused by late nineteenth-century industrialization, watch the suffering of a World War I veteran, and hear about an insurrection in Budapest in October, 1956. But just when we become secure with our identifications between the fictive and the real, the things we see change (like Pareto's bat), and we're in places that appear on no map of Europe. Conversely, when we suspend disbelief and get comfortable in Krasnoy or Sfaroy Kampe or Aisnar, we learn, with a clerk-composer in Foranoy (who has a sister in Prague), that Hitler is meeting Chamberlain in Munich in September, 1938. One city in Orsinia seems to have a foot in both worlds: Brailava could be as real as Bratislava, Czechoslovakia, or it could be as imaginary as Sfaroy Kampe. The point, however, is this: we must not read *Orsinian Tales* the way blind men read an elephant. To avoid seeing either a tree trunk or a wall or a rope, we must see the whole, be sensitive to the *relationships* among parts that characterize an organic whole. Relationships, not discrete things, are the subject of all of Le Guin's fiction. In "A Week in the Country," Stefan Fabbre recalls the story of a Hungarian nobleman. The wars between the Ottoman Empire and Hungary were real; the story is a legend; and Stefan Fabbre is a product of Le Guin's imagination. They are all related. "How can you tell the legend from the fact?" "Truth is a matter of the imagination."

The political entities in Central Europe, like the boundaries between the familiar and the fantastic, have been fluid, and this is probably one reason that Le Guin chose Central Europe as the location of Orsinia. Orsinia's name does more than play on it's creator's name; it echoes names like Bohemia, Silesia, Moravia, Galicia, and Croatia. The singular fact of political experience for these people is that while they have tenaciously preserved their nationality, they have never had lasting political independence. Orsinia shares with these countries a position on the battlegrounds of European and Asian imperialism, from Attila to the present. Orsinia may have come under Hapsburg domination in the sixteenth century (Isabella, "the Lady of Moge," has a Spanish-sounding name) and was probably threatened by the Ottoman Empire in the sixteenth and seventeenth centuries. In the eighteenth century Austria and Prussia could have fought a war in Orsinia; in the nineteenth century, Napoleon probably crossed Orsinian soil; and up to World War I, Orsinia was probably part of the Austro-Hungarian Empire. Then in the twentieth century, after a short-lived political independence, Orsinia was probably overwhelmed from the west by Hitler, and then a few years later, from the east by Stalin. This long historical nightmare of violent political change and oppression by authoritarian states only brings into sharper relief one of the major themes, if not *the* major theme, of these tales: the struggle of the individal to win a sense of freedom and wholeness in a prison-like society, and his heroic (the word is not too strong) efforts to maintain a sense of identity and self-respect. It is but a short step from this to the thematic center of *The Dispossessed.*

Le Guin's imaginary countries are not finished creations in which the landscape, geological or moral, is set for all time. The glaciers and volcanoes on Gethen, the earthquakes on Anarres, as well as Orsinia's limestone bedrock, are notable examples of geological flux. As Genly Ai and Estraven are ascending a glacier (a fluid solid) past the active volcanoes Drumner and Dremegole to reach the Gobrin Ice, Estraven records in his journal,

> We creep infinitesimally northward through the dirty chaos of a world in the process of making itself.
> Praise then Creation unfinished.

(LHD)

Orsinia's topography may not change as dramatically as Gethen's but it is nevertheless also in flux; it too is "in the process of making itself." One of the striking features of the Orsinian landscape is the Karst, the setting of "Brothers and Sisters." Karst topography is characterized by rocky barren ground, caves, sinkholes, underground rivers, and the absence of surface streams and lakes, resulting from the work of underground water on massive soluble limestones. Originally the term "karst" was applied to the Kras, a limestone area along the Adriatic coast of Yugoslavia. (The principal city of Orsinia, Krasnoy, may take its name from the

Kras, and the name of Foranoy may be related to foraminiferan tests, the raw material from which limestone is formed.) There are no hymns like "Rock of Ages" in Orsinia. The rocks dissolve in water.

Like all of Le Guin's imaginary countries, Orsinia is a *paysage moralisé*. The moral and psychological resonance of the settings and landscapes in Le Guin's science fiction has already been recognized. What she does in the Hainish worlds and in Earthsea is anticipated in *Orsinian Tales*. Like the chasm beneath the Shing city in *City of Illusions*, like the forests in "Vaster than Empires and More Slow" and *The Word for World is Forest*, like the islands and seas of Earthsea (another solid-liquid combination), the Karst in "Brothers and Sisters," the forest in "Ile Forest," and the mountains in "The Barrow," as well as the decaying house and garden on the Hill in Rákava in "Conversations at Night," are both images and symbols: they are at once themselves even as they refer beyond themselves to moral and psychological values and meanings. If Orsinia's bedrock can be dissolved and reconstituted, so can moral values. Dr. Adam Kereth steals freedom and is then drawn back to Orsinia by mere fidelity; Count Freyga sacrifices a Christian priest then aids Christian monks; and Dr. Galven Ileskar, who believes that murder ought to be an unpardonable crime, loves a murderer who turns out to be his brother-in-law, and brother, too.

The thematic significance of the fluidity of Le Guin's political, topographical, psychological, and moral landscapes is this: her human actors are free to choose and to be personally responsible for their choices. No less than the rocks in her landscapes, Le Guin's characters are "in the process of making themselves." Neither reality nor ethics is handed to them on adamantine tablets (though some of them may think they are); whole cultures as well as individuals dissolve and reconstitute themselves as they change and grow. This happens repeatedly in her science fiction: Terrans and Tevarans cease to exist as independent cultures in *Planet of Exile*, Gethenian cultures are on the brink of a major change in *The Left Hand of Darkness*, and reality itself is repeatedly reconstituted by George Orr's effective dreams in *The Lathe of Heaven*. It goes without saying, of course, that the society on Anarres is a society in the process of making itself which offers the individual the most freedom to make himself (thereby remaking the society), as long as it does not petrify. Faxe the Weaver speaks for Le Guin when she-he says "the only thing that makes life possible is permanent, intolerable uncertainty: not knowing what comes next" (LHD). Life is making choices; if we knew what comes next, we could not choose.

But what certainties can Le Guin offer in the midst of all this flux? Human relations: fidelity, constancy, and love. In "A Week in the Country," Stefan Fabbre and Kasimir Augeskar, on their way to visit the Augeskars' summer home, exchange these words in a train compartment:

> "So here we are on a train to Aisnar," Kasimir said, "but we don't know that it's going to Aisnar. It might go to Peking."
> "It might derail and we'll be killed. And if we do come to Aisnar? What's Aisnar? Mere hearsay."—"That's morbid," Kasimir said . . . —"No, exhilarating," his friend answered. "Takes a lot of work to hold the world together, when you look at it that way. But it's worthwhile. Building up cities, holding roofs up by an act of fidelity. Not faith. Fidelity."

What at first appears to be merely an academic discussion by two students to pass the time takes on new meanings by the end of the tale. After Stefan falls in love with Bruna Augeskar, after he hears Joachim Bret sing an English lute song,

> You be just and constant still, Love may beget a wonder,
> Not unlike a summer's frost or winter's fatal thunder:
> He that holds his sweetheart dear until his day of dying
> Lives of all that ever lived most worthy the envying,

after he sees Kasimir killed by the secret police, and after he is tortured himself—after all that, when Bruna comes for him, he knows that there is "No good letting go, is there. . . . No good at all." Fidelity—being just and constant still—and love hold the world together in ways Stefan had not imagined. And the more precarious existence becomes, the more necessary fidelity becomes. In "Conversations at Night," Sanzo Chekey and Alitsia Benat are little more than beggars, and their hope, like Stefan's and Bruna's, lies in the personal fidelity that holds their world together:

> "Lisha," he [Sanzo] said, "oh, God, I want to hold on . . . Only it's a very long chance, Lisha."
> "We'll never get a chance that isn't long."
> "You would."
> "You are my long chance," she said, with a kind of bitterness, and a *profound certainty*. . . .
> "Well, hang on," he said. . . . "If you hang on, I will."
>
> (my emphasis)

"Betrayal and fidelity were immediate to them," Le Guin says of the Augeskar family in "A Week in the Country." Like many Le Guin characters, the Augeskars live out on the edge; they live near the Iron

Curtain, in a political climate that makes their existence as perilous as the Gethenians' is in their barely habitable natural climate. It is worth remembering that Le Guin says that *The Left Hand of Darkness* is "a book about betrayal and fidelity." Betrayal and fidelity are as immediate to Ai and Estraven when they trek across the Ice and when they seek aid from Thessicher, as they are to the boxes: Le Guin includes in a collection of tales set in an imaginary country a tale entitled "Imaginary Countries," which includes characters who live from time to time in imaginary countries. . . . "Imaginary Countries" is the central tale in the collection in the same sense that the point at which the snake's tail disappears into its mouth is central; or, it is central in the way that the intersection of two mirrors that produce an infinitely regressing image is central.

So "Imaginary Countries" is central in *Orsinian Tales* in more ways than just being the middle tale chronologically. If we read Le Guin's Orsinian tales as Ursuline tales, then our reading of them becomes at once a journey into Orsinia's history and a journey into the history of Le Guin's invention of Orsinia's history. The work created and the creative work become one. Just as Le Guin's arrangement of the tales directs us back into Orsinia's past even as we move forward into the collection, "Imaginary Countries" returns us to the roots of the imagination that created the book we have just finished reading: the last tale concludes the collection at the same time it looks toward the creation of the collection by showing us a portrait of the artist as a young girl. When Le Guin placed "Imaginary Countries" at the end of *Orsinian Tales*, she was saying, in effect, "In my beginning is my end" and "In my end is my beginning" (the first and last lines of T.S. Eliot's "East Coker"). *Orsinian Tales*, then, has the same organic structure that *The Dispossessed* has. The alternating chapters on Anarres and Urras are put together so that when we come to the end of Shevek's story on Anarres, he is ready to begin the trip to Urras that opens the novel; and when we come to the end of Shevek's story on Urras and his return to Anarres, we see him ready to leave Anarres. Le Guin would probably accept what another Romantic, Coleridge, says about the function of poetry:

> The common end of all *narrative*, nay of *all*, Poems is to convert a *series* into a Whole; to make those events, which in real or imagined History move on in a *strait* Line, assume to our Understandings a *circular* motion— the snake with it's Tail in it's Mouth.

Orsinian Tales does this for the imaginary history of Orsinia at the same time it does it for the real history that is Le Guin's career as a writer.

It could be that Professor Egideskar, who writes narratives of "real" history, as well as his creator, who writes narratives of imagined history, would agree with Coleridge. An observer of history as sensitive as the baron would have seen that the idea of Progress, the ever-ascending "strait Line" of history that was born in the Enlightenment, was not working in the ethics and politics of the twentieth century; by studying early medieval times, he may be trying to understand history not in strictly linear terms (chronology and causality), but in circular terms as well (returns and rebirths). The baron could not be unaware of the goings on to the west of Orsinia in the thirties. Nazi barbarism, in fact, may be the silent subject of his history of Orsinia in the Early Middle Ages. Among the events he is studying and interpreting would be incidents like the one Le Guin describes in "The Barrow," set in 1150. His assistant Josef Brone reads from "the Latin chronicle of a battle lost nine hundred years ago;" one of the incunabula Josef and the baron pack in a trunk probably contains the "bad Latin of [the Benedictine] chronicles of Count Freyga and his son," mentioned at the end of "The Barrow." Count Freyga lived at the time when pagan ethics and Christian ethics clashed; although he is nominally a Christian, he reverts to sacrificing a priest to "Odne the Silent" to relieve his terrifying anxiety about his wife and unborn child. The baron lives at a time when a nominally civilized culture is reverting to barbarism. Understanding medieval Orsinia, going to historical roots, may help Egideskar understand twentieth-century Europe.

Some readers may think that the baron, who calls his wife Freya and his summer home Asgard, is implicated in the revival of Norse myth used by the Nazis to legitimate their ideologies. That would be doing the baron a disservice, for he does know the difference between a unicorn's hoofprint and a pig's, and there is as much difference between a true myth and a false myth as there is between a unicorn and a pig. The baron faces the problem that any serious student of history and culture sooner or later faces: he is part of what he is trying to understand. He needs a technique of distancing. He can get it by spending his summers away from Krasnoy, by participating in his family's imaginary countries, and by studying the history of Orsinia in the Early Middle Ages. In order to get free of the distorting fog of subjectivity and idealogy, he needs an Archimedes point from which he can get "a view in"; he needs to see from a place "a very long way from anywhere else." The baron, that is to say, encounters the same problems as a historian that Le Guin faces as a writer, and this is yet another way in which "Imaginary Countries" is the central tale in *Orsinian Tales*. In a book that is in many ways about history, we have a portrait of a historian: still another instance of the circularity of fantasy.

But "Imaginary Countries" is more than the central tale in the collection. Earlier I said that a trip through Orsinia may take us to the underground streams that nourish the roots of the imagination that created Earthsea and the Hainish worlds. Coming at the end of the trip, "Imaginary Countries" brings us as close as we are likely to come to those streams, Le Guin's childhood experience of Norse myth and folklore.

Written in 1960, after Le Guin had been exploring Orsinia in novels and tales for a decade, and before she turned to stories that fit publishers' categories, "Imaginary Countries" is a tale in which Le Guin returned to the myths that informed her childhood play and nourished her imagination. Like "the Oak" in Stanislas' "kingdom of the trees," the whole body of Le Guin's fiction can be seen as Yggdrasil, the Norse world-tree, with its roots in Orsinia and its branches and leaves in the far-away galaxies of the Hainish universe. When Josef follows Stanislas into "the Great Woods," Stanislas guides him to "the Oak":

> It was the biggest tree [Josef] had ever seen; he had not seen very many.
> "I suppose it's very old," he said; looking up puzzled at the reach of the branches, galaxy after galaxy of green leaves without end.

In this story, which precedes by three years Le Guin's invention-discovery of the Hainish universe, she was already using the language of science fiction with Norse myth. That is exactly how she created the Hainish worlds: in "The Dowry of Angyar" ("Semley's Necklace" in *The Wind's Twelve Quarters*), she wove together the Einsteinian notion of time-dilation with the Norse myth of Freya and the Brisingamen Necklace. That story became the germ of *Rocannon's World*, her first novel, and from that the rest of the Hainish novels followed. The Earthsea trilogy evolved in much the same way.

After Le Guin started writing science fiction, she returned to Yggdrasil again and again. In *Planet of Exile*, Rolery gazes at a mural representing Terra and "the other worlds":

> The strangest thing in all the strangeness of this house was the painting on the wall of the big room downstairs. When Agat had gone and the rooms were deathly still she stood gazing at this picture till it became the world and she the wall. And the picture was a network: a deep network, like the interlacing branches in the woods, like interrunning currents in water, silver, gray, black, shot through with green and rose and a yellow like the sun. As one watched their deep network, one saw in it, among it, woven into it and weaving it, little and great patterns and figures, beasts, trees, grasses, men and women and other creatures, some like farborns and some not; and strange shapes, boxes set on round legs, birds, axes, silver spears with wings and *a tree whose leaves were stars.*

Here is an actual landscape (spacescape?) painting (which, incidentally describes Le Guin's fiction as well as any critical article has), a *paysage moralisé*, representing an imaginary landscape, the Hainish worlds, seen through the eyes of a native of Gamma Draconis III, a person whose ways of seeing have been shaped by the landscape of her native world, itself another of Le Guin's *paysages moralisés*. The tree in this painting, "the Oak" in "Imaginary Countries," and all the other trees in Le Guin's fiction, from the rowan tree in *The Farthest Shore* (Chap. 1) in Le Guin's "Inner Lands" to the forests on Athshe in *The Word for World is Forest* in her "Outer Space"—they all have the same roots.

Like the painting we see through Rolery's eyes, Le Guin's prose landscapes are full of *things*. Could it be that her artistry in representing abstract concepts derives from her childhood moulds of understanding, moulds like those of Zida Egideskar, who builds a unicorn trap from "an egg-crate decorated with many little bits of figured cloth and colored paper . . . a wooden coat hanger . . . an eggshell painted gold . . . a bit of quartz . . . a breadcrust" Rilke, who believed that thinking of the human in terms of *Dinge* is characteristic of the child, would answer yes. Like Zida's unicorn trap, Le Guin's fiction is built by an artisan from a "mess of images and metaphors, domes, stones, rubble" to catch imaginary beasts, imaginary people, imaginary countries, androgynes, mythic archetypes, truth. Zida Egideskar is indeed a portrait of the artist as a young girl.

When Josef Brone asks Stanislas what he does in "the Great Woods," Stanislas answers, " 'Oh, I map trails.' " That answer is profoundly meaningful, for it describes what Le Guin herself does in her fiction. Her discovery-invention and mapping of imaginary countries has been her artisitc solution of the epistemological problem that confronts everyone in the human sciences: like anthropologists, historians, psychologists, sociologists, and students of art, Le Guin is part of the social and cultural and historical situation she wants to write about. In this position, objectivity and truth seem impossible ideals, especially when the culture debases language and fictional forms, the writer's only tools for discovering truth. Because Le Guin is an artist, this philosophical/ideological/ political problem presents itself to her as an artistic problem requiring an artistic solution. And because artists are supposed to tell the truth, it is an ethical problem. Inventing imaginary countries and mapping them has been Le Guin's solution to her artistic/ethical problem. Lies are the way to truth. The real subject of Le Guin's fiction is not life in any of her imaginary countries, in Orsinia or on Gethen or Anarres or Gont or Havnor; these are metaphors, landscapes, *Dinge*, thought experiments, what Kafka (in a letter to Max Brod) calls "strategic considerations":

It sometimes seems to me that the nature of art in general, the existence of art, is explicable solely in terms of such 'strategic considerations,' of making possible the exchange of truthful words from person to person.

Seen in this light, "Imaginary Countries" is not only the central tale in *Orsinian Tales;* it is also central to the whole body of Le Guin's writing, and more than that, to the act of writing itself.

III

Even if Le Guin's strategic considerations do make possible the exchange of truthful words, what if no one wants to publish them? What good are truthful words if they are not exchanged? What's the use of writing? What's the use of art? Questions like these may have been in Le Guin's mind around 1960 when she wrote "An die Musik." Like Ursula Le Guin herself, who had been writing Orsinian novels and tales for ten years without seeing them in print, Ladislas Gaye (whose name faintly echoes his creator's) has been writing songs and a Mass for ten years and has very little hope of ever hearing them performed. If "Imaginary Countries" includes a portrait of the artist as a young girl, "An die Musik," written at the same time, includes an oblique portrait of the artist as a grown woman. Like the Earthsea trilogy, it is "about art, the creative experience, the creative process." "An die Musik," however, is much more than self-portraiture, for it raises questions about the relationship between art and politics—questions fundamental not only to any serious discussion of Le Guin's later works, but fundamental also to any serious discussion of the social role of art in the twentieth century.

The tension between "public and private imperatives" in Earthsea and the Hainish worlds is a reflection or a projection of an ethical conflict in Le Guin herself, and that conflict—between her duty as an artist to serve her art and her commitment to a social ideal—is at the center of "An die Musik," and continues to be prominent in her later fiction, even when an artist is not the central character. A theoretical physicist like Shevek or a mathematician like Simon in "The New Atlantis" is as much an artist as are the musicians that appear throughout Le Guin's fiction. Le Guin does, of course, define the problem in radically different ways in "An die Musik" and in *The Dispossessed* or "The New Atlantis." But even if her formulations of the artist's problem have changed, her conception of the purpose of art has remained constant and steady. With Auden, she believes that the end of art, its final cause, its *raison d'être*, is to persuade us to rejoice and to teach us how to praise. Answering Tolstoy's question "What is Art?" Le Guin defines the job of art with one word: "celebration."

If Le Guin's trilogy of imaginary countries—Orsinia, Earthsea, and the Hainish universe—manifests the same circularity that her fantasy trilogy does (and I think it does), then we can apply her injunction "dreams must explain themselves" to the whole body of her fiction. In order to begin an exploration of the problematic relationships in her later fiction between creativity and politics, between the demands of the imagination and the demands of everyday life, or, more broadly, between the individual and society, we can do no better than return to "An die Musik," her first published story. It is the first of many works in which Le Guin dramatizes the problems she herself faces whenever she sits down to write. This is not the place to make a comprehensive survey of the ways Le Guin has handled these issues in all of her fiction; all I will do here is look carefully at one of her earliest formulations.

As she would do in *The Left Hand of Darkness* when she constructed a thought experiment to explore sexuality, in "An die Musik" Le Guin creates a character—a composer with an "absolutely first rate" talent—and places him in a setting—Foranoy, Orsinia, in 1938, a "dead town for music . . . not a good world for music, either"—in order to ask three related questions: (1) should an artist, as a private individual, ignore the demands of his family to meet the demands of his art, (2) should an artist use his public voice to serve art or a political idea, and (3) what is the function of art.

When Le Guin puts Gaye in a cramped three-room flat and gives him a bedridden mother, an ailing wife, and three children to support on his wages as a clerk in a steel ballbearing factory, and when she makes him a talented composer with a compulsion to rival Berlioz and Mahler by writing a grandiose Mass for "women's chorus, double men's chorus, full orchestra, brass choir, and an organ," she formulates the question in such stark either-or terms that Gaye's conflicting ethical duties are simply irreconcilable. At the same time, she dramatizes each of these claims on Gaye so skillfully that neither can be denied: Gaye cannot abandon his Mass because, as he tells Otto Egorin, "I've learned how to do what I must do, you see, I've begun it, I have to finish it," and he cannot abandon his family because he is "not made so." If neither obligation can be denied and if their conflicting claims are so polarized that they cannot be reconciled, then Gaye's moral dilemma cannot be resolved; it can only be transcended, and then only for a moment. Moreover, by setting the tale in 1938, Le Guin polarizes the artist's public duties as severely as she polarizes his private ones. His only choices are to write apolitical music

(*Lieder* or a Mass) or socialist realism (a symphony "to glorify the latest boiler-factory in the Urals.")

Le Guin's formulation of Gaye's moral/aesthetic dilemma is thoroughly dualistic: it rests on the belief that a devotion to art, like the devotion to a religious creed, is absolutely incompatible with everyday life. In "*An die Musik*" art is religion; if it traffics in social issues, it debases itself. Just as Jesus Christ called on his disciples to abandon all family ties if they wanted to follow Him (Matt. 10:34–39; Mark 3:31–35; Luke 14:25–26), Egorin, who believes that "if you live for music you live for music," suggests to Gaye that he "throw over . . . [his] sick mother and sick wife and three brats" if he wants to write his Mass and hear it performed. And then quoting Christ directly, he tells Gaye:

> You have great talent, Gaye, you have great courage, but you're too gentle, you must not try to write a big work like this Mass. You can't serve two masters [Matt. 6:24; Luke 16:13]. Write songs, short pieces, something you can think of while you work at this Godforsaken steel plant and write down at night when the rest of the family's out of the way for five minutes. . . . Write little songs, not impossible Masses.

But Gaye, like Kasimir Augeskar, another Orsinian musician, is an "enemy of the feasible" (OT). He must write the Mass. He will continue to serve art and his family, Godly art and a Godforsaken steel plant, even if the tension tears him in two. All he wants from Egorin is the recognition of his identity as a musician; that gives him the strength and freedom he needs to endure the conflict he can neither escape nor resolve.

Finally exasperated by "the arrogance, the unreasonableness . . . the stupidity, the absolute stupidity" of artists, yet recognizing Gaye's talent and wanting to encourage him and to produce some of his work, Egorin gives Gaye a volume of Eichendorff's poetry. " 'Set me some of these,' " he tells Gaye, " 'here, look, this one, 'Es wandelt, was sir schauen,' you see—that should suit you.' " It is one of Eichendorff's religious lyrics:

> Es wandelt, was wir schauen,
> Tag sinkt ins Abendrot,
> Die Lust hat eignes Grauen,
> Und alles hat den Tod.
>
> Ins Leben schleicht das Leiden
> Sich heimlich wie ein Dieb,
> Wir alle mussen scheiden
> Vor allem, was uns lieb.

Was gäb' es doch auf Erden,
Wer hielt' den Jammer aus
Wer möcht' geboren werden,
Hielt'st du night droben haus!

Du bist's, der, was wir bauen,
Mild über uns zerbricht,
Dass wir den Himmel schauen—
Darum so klag' ich nicht.

Things change, whatever we look at,
Day sinks into sunset glow,
Desire has its own horror,
And everything dies.

Into life steals sorrow
As secretly as a thief,
We must all be separated
From everything that loves us.

What is there of value on earth,
Who could endure the misery,
Who would want to be reborn,
Dost Thou not promise a home above!

It is Thou, who, whatever we build,
Gently breakest down over us
That we may see Heaven—
And so I do not complain.

Why should this "suit" Gaye? Egorin sees Gaye's personal dilemma as hopeless and wants to offer him the consolation that things change: " 'Es wandelt.' Things do change sometimes, after all, don't they?" He wants to offer Gaye some way of enduring the suffering he cannot escape. The religious belief of Eichendorff, a Roman Catholic, is Egorin's solution to Gaye's personal problems as an artist.

Egorin can offer no consolation whatever to Gaye to help him out of his public dilemma. Because his conception of art forces him to separate it from politics, Egorin's attitude toward the possibility that art can change things in 1938, can make something happen, is completely defeatist:

"Gaye," said Otto Egorin, "you know there's one other thing. This is not a good world for music, either. This world now, in 1938. You're not the only man who wonders, what's the good? who needs music, who wants it? Who indeed, when Europe is crawling with armies like a corpse with maggots, when Russia uses symphonies to glorify the latest boiler-factory in the Urals, when the function of music has been all summed up in Putzi playing the piano to soothe the Leader's nerves. By the time your Mass is finished, you know, all the churches may be blown into little pieces, and your men's chorus will be wearing uniforms and also being blown into little pieces. If not send it to me, I shall be interested. But I'm not hopeful. I am on the losing side, with you. . . . music is no good, no use, Gaye. Not any more. Write your songs, write your Mass, it does no harm. I shall go on arranging concerts, it does no harm. But it won't save us. . . ."

Perhaps because she has a hindsight Egorin does not have, Le Guin does not share his defeatism. And as we discover at the end of the tale, Gaye does not share Egorin's defeatism either. Music does save him, though not in the sense Egorin has in mind.

In the final scenes, Le Guin brings all the questions about the artist and art together, forces Gaye's tensions to the breaking point, and then resolves them not by answering any of the questions she has raised, but by creating an epiphany which transcends the questions. On the afternoon of the day that Chamberlain meets Hitler in Munich to give him the Sudetenland, Gaye is trying to finish his setting of "*Es wandelt*" and his wife is demanding that he do something about their son Vasli who has been caught with some other boys trying to set a camp on fire. Gaye's cry "let me have some peace" is both his and Europe's: private and public merge. A moment later, European politics, the coming war, his family problems, and his Mass all converge as he consoles Vasli, with the sound of his mother's radio coming from the next room:

All cruelty, all misery, all darkness present and to come hung round them. . . . In the thick blaring of the trombones, thick as cough-sirup, Gaye heard for a moment the deep clear thunder of his Sanctus like the thunder between the stars, over the edge of the universe—one moment of it, as if the roof of the building had been taken off and he looked up into the complete, enduring darkness, one moment only.

In the evening, as he sits at the kitchen table with his wife, who is mending and listening to the radio (full of news of Munich, no doubt), Gaye tries to recapture the accompaniment to the last verse of "*Es wandelt*" so he can write it down and send it to Egorin in Krasnoy. At the moment when "the total impossibility of writing was a choking weight in him," at the moment when he thinks "nothing would ever change" he hears Lotte Lehmann on the radio singing Schubert's "*An die Musik.*" The barrier between inner and outer worlds evaporates as he initially mistakes the music on the radio for the unwritten music in his mind:

He thought it was his own song, then, raising his head, understood that he was actually hearing this tune. He did not have to write it. It had been written long ago, no one need suffer for it any more. Lehmann was singing it,

> Du holde Kunst, ich danke dir.

He sat still a long time. Music will not save us, Otto Egorin had said. Not you, or me . . . ; not Lehmann who sang the song; not Schubert who had written it and was a hundred years dead. What good is music? None, Gaye thought, and that is the point. To the world and its states and armies and factories and Leaders, music says, 'You are irrelevant'; and, arrogant and gentle as a god, to the suffering man it says only, 'Listen.' For being saved is not the point. Music saves nothing. Merciful, uncaring, it denies and breaks down all the shelters, the houses men build for themselves, that they may see the sky.

Gaye's epiphany rises not only from the identification of inner and outer music; it also depends on the conjunction of the words in the last stanza of Eichendorff's "*Es wandelt*" and the words in the lyric set by Schubert, Schober's "*An die Musik.*" Here is Schober's poem.

> Du holde Kunst, in wieviel grauen Stunden,
> Wo mich des Lebens wilder Kreis umstrickt,
> Hast du mein Harz zu warmer Leib' entzunden,
> Hast mich in eine bessre Welt entrückt!
>   In eine bessre Welt entrückt.
>
> Oft hat ein Seufzer, deiner Harf' entflossen
> Ein süsser, heiliger Akkord von dir,
> Den Himmel bessrer Zeiten mir erschlossen
> Du holde Kunst, ich danke dir dafur!
>   Du holde Kunst, ich danke dir.
>
> O kindly Art, in how many a grey hour
> when I am caught in life's unruly round
> have you fired my heart with ardent love
> and borne me to a better world!
>   Borne me to a better world.
>
> Often, has a sigh from your harp,
> a chord, sweet and holy, from you
> opened for me a heaven of better times;
> O kindly Art, for that I thank you!
>   O kindly Art, I thank you.

Gaye has been suffering, trying to write the music for the last stanza of Eichendorff's poem, which Le Guin renders as "It is Thou in thy mercy that breakest down over our heads all we build, that we may see the sky: and so I do not complain." In the afternoon, Gaye had heard the thunder of his Sanctus like thunder between the stars "as if the roof of the building had been taken off." Now, in the evening, as he hears his own unwritten tune in Schubert's, Gaye also hears Eichendorff's and Schober's lyrics simultaneously, the first inside his head and the second outside, sung by Lehmann on the radio. He experiences the synchronicity of a poem addressed to God and a poem addressed to Art: Eichendorff's God, who breaks down what men build that they may see heaven, becomes Schober's kindly Art, realized by Schubert and performed by Lehmann, opening for Gaye a heaven of better times. "Arrogant and gentle as a god," music, not God, "breaks down all the shelters, the houses men build for themselves, that they may see the sky." It fires his heart with love and carries him to a better world. Art renews the possibility of utopia. The paradox at the core of Gaye's epiphany is religious: what he suffers for releases him from suffering for it. Music does save him. Le Guin saves Gaye from the conflict of "public and private imperatives" as she merges inner and outer worlds in a palimpsest of art and religion, of immanence and transcendence.

Gaye's epiphany does not, however, unravel the Gordian knot of his ethical dilemmas. It cuts right through them. Otto Egorin, who believes that "music is no good, no use . . . not any more," has a defeatist attitude because he retains vestiges of a belief that music *is* of some good, that it is of some use. Gaye's flash of insight saves him from defeatism by wiping out entirely the question of the success or failure of an artist's attempts to do some good. The world's states, its armies, its factories, and its *Fuehrers* are all simply irrelevant; politics and economics are of no concern to the artist. The function of art is not to save anything or to make something happen or to change the world. Its function is to deny the world, to detach people from politics and history so they can receive visions of a better world, and perhaps redeem politics and history with that vision. Art mediates a negative dialectic; it removes the obstacles that block the way to a better world, but it does not bring that world into being. That is the task of the artist's audience.

So, as he sits in Foranoy, Orsinia, in September, 1938—as Hitler is meeting Chamberlain and as "Europe is crawling with armies like a corpse with maggots"—Gaye concludes that "music saves nothing." A few months later, after Chamberlain had returned to London proclaiming "peace with honour . . . peace for our time," W.B. Yeats died. Auden, who had wrestled throughout the thirties with the problem of the artist's duty, came to a position in his elegy on the death of Yeats that is nearly identical with Gaye's:

> For poetry makes nothing happen: it survives
> In the valley of its making where executives
> Would never want to tamper, flows on south
> From ranches of isolation and the busy griefs,
> Raw towns that we believe and die in; it survives,
> A way of happening, a mouth.

If poetry makes nothing happen, what then is the proper duty of the poet? What should he do in a world where

> In the nightmare of the dark
> All the dogs of Europe bark,
> And the living nations wait,
> Each sequestered in its hate;
>
> Intellectual disgrace
> Stares from every human face,
> And the seas of pity lie
> Locked and frozen in each eye.

Auden's answer is

> Follow, poet, follow right
> To the bottom of the night,
> With your unconstraining voice
> Still persuade us to rejoice;
>
> With the farming of a verse
> Make a vineyard of the curse,
> Sing of human unsuccess
> In a rapture of distress;
>
> In the deserts of the heart
> Let the healing fountain start,
> In the prison of his days
> Teach the free man how to praise.

This is, I would argue, what Le Guin does, not only in "An die Musik," but throughout Orsinian Tales and the rest of her fiction as well. With "all cruelty, all misery, all darkness present and to come" hanging about him, Gaye hears his Sanctus and looks into "the complete, enduring darkness." In each volume of the Earthsea trilogy, Le Guin journeys into the "nightmare of the dark," to the "bottom of the night," and emerges to rejoice and to praise. Genly Ai and Estraven go into "The Place Inside the Blizzard" and Shevek's quest takes him into a cellar with a dying man. Each of the Orsinian tales describes a similar journey into darkness. And there is, moreover, a sense in which every story Le Guin tells is an Orsinian tale; they all bear her name. In that sense, the trip into darkness that most of her characters make is a trip she herself makes as an artist whenever she writes a story. Along with some other modern writers, Le Guin is a lineal descendant of Orpheus. Sometimes the map of her journey is historical, as in Orsinian Tales; sometimes it is psychological and ethical, as in the Earthsea trilogy; sometimes it is political, as in The Word for World is Forest and The Dispossessed. It is always an aesthetic journey. In each case, the message Le Guin returns with is a version of the invocation Estraven murmurs every night as he goes to sleep: "Praise then darkness and Creation unfinished" (LHD).

If we could abstract from Le Guin's practice the ideas that define for her the proper duty of an artist, if we could formulate a statement of the ethics that guides her when she practices her art, it would probably come close to Rilke's definition of the artist's role:

> Art cannot be helpful through our trying to keep and specially concern-
> ing ourselves with the distresses of others, but in so far as we bear our
> own distresses more passionately, give now and then a perhaps clearer
> meaning to endurance, and develop for ourselves the means of expressing
> the suffering within us and its conquest more precisely and clearly than is
> possible to those who have to apply their powers to something else.

Le Guin has consistently occupied herself with her own inner life. She has always written fantasy, searching not in the outside world, but in her own creative unconscious, for the subjects of her fiction. The course of her development from the early sixties into the middle seventies has been a series of attempts to develop for herself the means of expressing her own suffering (which, of course, can be ethical and political as well as psycho-logical), and its conquest more precisely and clearly. She would probably agree with Rilke's repeated assertion that we are "only just where we persist in praising." But she also feels the need to blame. The strength of her convictions and her ethical principles demands that. When her fiction blames, however, as *The Word for World is Forest* does, it is less just.

Ultimately, the real subject of "*An die Musik*" and the rest of Le Guin's fiction that explores ethical problems is not a group of ethical questions. These are means, not ends. Her purpose is to ask them, not to answer them. The real subject of "*An die Musik*" is celebration; the tale is a celebration of Gaye's devotion to his art, and beyond that, a celebration of art itself. That is the meaning of its title. Like Estraven, Shevek, Kasimir Augeskar, and many other Le Guin characters, Gaye is an "en-emy of the feasible." Le Guin places so many obstacles between him and his music not merely to wrestle with questions about the duty of the artist and the function of art, but to dramatize more vividly Gaye's capacity to endure and survive, and to pursue an ideal without compromising either himself or his goal. Like Auden's "In Memory of W.B. Yeats," which, in Samuel Hynes's words, "transforms calamity into celebration by an act of the imagination, and so affirms the survival of art in a bad time," "*An die Musik*" and *Orsinian Tales* are acts of imagination that transform the calamity of history that is Central Europe into a celebration of the individual's ability to survive bad times.

VICTOR URBANOWICZ

Personal and Political in "The Dispossessed"

To say that *The Dispossessed* is about an anarchist society is rather like saying that *Paradise Lost* is about the Christian notion of the Fall: such a statement ignores the strong partisanship of the author of the piece. As Milton made no secret of his Christianity, Ursula K. Le Guin has said that anarchism "is the most idealistic, and to me the most interesting, of all political theories." In the same place she also says that her conscious purpose in writing *The Dispossessed* was "to embody it [anarchism] in a novel, which had not been done before" (here, incidentally, is the epic writer's claim to do the yet unattempted). *The Dispossessed* is an anarchist novel, then. Further, it reveals the author's broad and sympathetic understanding of anarchist theory, with emphasis on the idea that the personal and political growth of the individual must be not only compatible with but also complementary to each other.

The setting of the novel is one indication of Le Guin's familiarity with anarchism. The action seems to be divided between two planets to make plausible the existence of a thriving anarchist society in a civilization like ours, despite the fate of anarchist communities in the twentieth century. Urras is divided much like today's earth. On it the nation of A-Io corresponds to the USA or perhaps some Western European power. As the Ambassador from Terra observes, "The government here is not despotic. The rich are very rich indeed, but the poor are not so very poor. They are neither enslaved nor starving" (Chap. 11). There is some social mobility

From *Science-Fiction Studies* 2, vol. 5 (July 1978). Copyright © 1978 by R. D. Miller and Darko Suvin.

under a state-regulated private capitalist economy; consumer goods are elaborately packaged and displayed; some women use their sex appeal for power games. Thu, A-Io's rival, corresponds to the USSR: its government, though the product of a popularly-based socialist revolution, is highly centralized and totally controls the economy. There is also a Third World of unaligned poor nations. One of these, Benbili, is the novel's Vietnam: when insurrection breaks out there. A-Io and Thu intervene to support opposed sides.

Urras is not a scrupulous copy of our earth. A-Io on the one hand is more Victorian than the contemporary West, with servants abounding and the universities closed to women, and on the other hand more advanced, for the government has succeeded in saving the natural environment from the predations of free enterprise. The greatest sociopolitical difference from our world is on Anarres, the habitable if somewhat arid "moon" of Urras, which has been settled by an autonomous colony of Odonians—communist anarchists of Urrasti origin. This colony, over 150 years old when the story begins, has from its start severely limited contact with Urras. Such an arrangement enhances the plausibility of an anarchist experiment so old and successful. In the twentieth century both authoritarian (Marxist-Leninist) communists and the bourgeois-democratic nations have proven quite willing to tolerate if not actually bring about the obliteration of actual libertarian communist societies. No Western power intervened to protect the Ukrainian peasant communes, which were consciously anarchist and anti-Bolshevik, from domination by Moscow in 1920, though White Russian reactionaries received US aid. In 1936 the USSR supported the pro-republican forces in Spain at the expense of the Spanish anarchists, who had broad popular support and who had speedily collectivized industry and agriculture over wide areas of the country. Anarchist militia and labor unions had to contend against not only the Falangists, but the Republicans and Stalinists among their allies as well. The Anarresti, occupying their own planet and trading mineral ore for a few necessities and toleration from Urras, are in a much better position for survival than were these hapless Terran anarchists.

Anarresti society reflects the ideas of many major anarchist thinkers and theoretical tendencies. One important feature is the communist anarchism of Peter Kropotkin. Unlike the collectivist anarchism of Michael Bakunin, communist anarchism does not demand that the individual work in exchange for necessities. These are available free, and one chooses among available work assignments ("postings") offered by a computerized hiring hall ("Divlab") in response to personal preference, social needs, or, lacking these, the desire for approval from peers and neighbors.

Factories and the like are democratically controlled by the workers. Of special importance to the novel's plot is the possibility of "free enterprise": one may form one's own syndicate to undertake an original project, with the right to requisition needed materials and equipment.

Formal education and day-to-day personal conduct on Anarres follow the ideas of two writers later than the "classical" anarchists, namely Herbert Read (1893–1968) and Paul Goodman (1911–1972). The following passage from *The Dispossessed* is a fine precis of Read's treatise on libertarian schooling, *Education Through Art.*

> Learning centers taught all the skills that prepare for the practice of art: training in singing, metrics, dance, the use of brush, chisel, knife, lathe, and so on. It was all pragmatic: the children learned to see, speak, hear, move, handle. No distinction was drawn between the arts and the crafts; art was not considered as having a place in life but as being a basic technique of life, like speech.

(Chap. 6)

The general administration of education would also please the ghost of Goodman. For young children, schooling is combined with the work of the local community, and advanced studies follow the decentralized organization of the medieval university as Goodman saw it: founded upon a personal relation of teacher and student, unencumbered by grades, credits, and standard required courses. Students obtain courses they desire by requesting a teacher to offer them.

In accordance with norms Goodman established on the basis of his work in Gestalt theory, physical attraction and physical hostility on Anarres are left to the self-regulation of the organism. Sexually, anything goes between consenting adults or adolescents, and coyness is replaced with an open invitation to "copulate." As for less gentle impulses, the Anarresti, though innocent of weapons, accept nonlethal physical hostility so casually that a hand-to-hand fight has to be "interesting" to draw spectators. The loser of a fair fight is neither expected nor inclined to harbor a grudge, any more than one partner in a sexual encounter makes a claim on the other of the "Does this mean we're engaged?" sort: the fight, like the sex, is a "gift."

But it is not a utopia Le Guin portrays. At the age of one hundred and seventy the Odonian colony on Anarres has in some respects lapsed from its earlier ideals. Its prolonged isolation has made it xenophobic towards Urras, quite against anarchist ideals of human cooperation and solidarity across political boundaries; the administrative syndicates have developed informal hierarchies, hardening into bureaucracies and clinging to powers acquired during long-past emergencies; custom has made most persons ashamed to refuse postings even when acceptance means being separated for years from a mate or from one's chosen work. This state of affairs, however, is not to be read as an implied criticism of anarchist theory. That institutions promoting freedom can decline into hierarchical and authoritarian ones is freely acknowledged by anarchists generally, notably by Kropotkin in his discussion of the medieval guilds in *Mutual Aid*. Anarchists regard social (but not state) control of the means of production and decentralized, federal organization of society as highly desirable but not infallible means to a libertarian end; social life is regarded as a continual striving against both tyranny and decadence of freedom alike.

The principal action of *The Dispossessed* does not criticize anarchist theory at all, but clarifies it and portrays its strengths: Shevek, the protagonist, aided by his libertarian upbringing as much as hindered by it, becomes aware of his society's defects and moves effectively to repair them. It is particularly significant that this process grows out of his insistence on pursuing his chosen work (theoretical physics), publishing his findings and communicating with colleagues on Urras as well as Anarres over the objections of his compatriots. Braving a hostile mob and supported only by his own group, the Syndicate of Initiative, he even takes the unprecedented step of boarding an ore freighter to Urras to facilitate communication with the Urrasti. His development as a constructive rebel against conservative forces in his society is organically linked with his development as a physicist and as a human being. The effects of his visit to Urras are revolutionary in more than physics, and the structure of *The Dispossessed* emphasizes that these effects are organically linked with the prior period of Anarres.

In this way Le Guin makes her novel a vehicle for a central moral principle of anarchism, commonly called that of the unity of means and ends: a better society should not and cannot be achieved by using methods today which would be intolerable once it was a reality. Thus Bakunin insisted against Marx that authoritarian means could not achieve a free society and that a revolutionary dictatorship would be indistinguishable from a state. Since the time of Bakunin—and rather against his temperament and character—a non-violent and even pacifist tendency has grown up in the movement. On the personal level this principle excludes drastic renunciations (though not all heroism) for the sake of hastening the revolution. Emma Goldman "did not believe that a Cause which stood for a beautiful ideal, for anarchism, for release and freedom from conventions and prejudice, should demand the denial of life and joy"—and she refused to give up dancing. In a similar vein, Paul Goodman found that "professionals, at least, become radicalized when they try to pursue their professions with integrity and courage—their professions are what they know and care about—and they find that many things must be changed." Goodman, of course, states Shevek's case exactly. In *The Dispossessed* symbolism, structure, and plot stress the unity of personal, professional, and political in Shevek as an individual acting in and upon his society.

During his childhood and later, Shevek recurringly dreams of a wall, the symbol of his major personal barriers and difficulties. His solitary, abstractly meditative character is a wall between himself and others, and he feels himself always alone, even when surrounded by comrades. Another is the impenetrability of the problem in temporal theory that is his chosen field in physics. A third is the self-isolation of Anarres from Urras, somewhat justified in prudence but maintained to a degree that thwarts international solidarity and frustrates Shevek professionally. The different walls are overcome one by one; the conquest of one seems to be related to that of another, and increasingly all walls appear to be one, and the least personal of Shevek's difficulties, his work in physics, is closely identified with the most, his attempts to form and feel a bond with others. This outcome is prefigured early in the novel by a unique version of the dream. At the foot of the wall is a stone, on or inside which

> there was a number; a 5 he thought at first, then took it for 1, then understood what it was—the primal number, that was both unity and plurality. "That is the cornerstone," said a voice of dear familiarity, and Shevek was pierced through with joy. There was no wall in the shadows, and he knew that he had come back, that he was home.
>
> (Chap. 2)

The structure of the novel also stresses the unity of personal and political. The action is divided into two distinct phases. The chronologically earlier phase comprises Shevek's childhood, youth, and early manhood on Anarres, when he discovers and pursues temporal physics and in doing so comes up against problems stemming from his own solitary nature and the increasingly rigid, bureaucratic tendencies in Odonian mores and institutions. Attracted to the Simultaneity school of temporal physics, he finds that physicists of the opposed Sequency school are well entrenched: they style themselves the true Odonian physicists, and tend to block the publication of Shevek's papers. During these difficulties he forms a life partnership with a woman named Takver, who encourages him to form his own syndicate to publish his papers and to talk by radio with Ioti physicists. An earnest Odonian, Shevek has by now become convinced of the social utility of such a course, and even decided to travel to Urras, where he has gained a reputation among Ioti physicists and where he might benefit from resources and colleagues that Anarres cannot match. His physics, his politics, and his personal relationships are all one. A train driver remarks to him that where promiscuity becomes monotonous, monogamy guarantees variety: "It isn't changing around from place to place that keeps you level. It's getting time on your side. Working with it, not against it" (Chap. 9). The temporal physicist agrees. This exchange takes place as Shevek is en route to rejoin Takver and their child after four years' separation. Their lovemaking upon reunion is compared to "planets circling blindly, quietly, . . . about the common center of gravity, swinging, circling endlessly" (Chap. 9). In this Shelleyan image Le Guin links the most private part of Shevek's life with the most public: Urras and Anarres are precisely such planets, for they revolve about each other, each the other's moon, and the human societies on them have long been separated.

On Anarres, then, Shevek grows from weakness and isolation to strength and a bond with others (Takver and his syndics), and renews his society by rebelling against established order. Paradoxically, all these things grow out of the work he must pursue in isolation. The action on Urras is closely parallel, and chapters narrating it alternate with the Anarres chapters. Such organization solves the structural problem of two successive and complete actions, and is appropriate for other reasons. One is that Shevek's brand of physics stresses the simultaneity of events that usually are seen as successive, a fact which in turn points to the theses of this essay. On Urras his development is chiefly public and political, as befits a man of forty. He completes his General Temporal Theory but withholds it from the Ioti, whom at this point he understands well enough to distrust. Illegally and secretly leaving the university where he has been working, he addresses a mass political demonstration which is then brutally suppressed. Virtually wading through blood, he gains asylum in the embassy of Terra, whence he manages to return to Anarres. While the alternation of Anarres with Urras chapters stresses the organic relationship of his actions on the two planets, the Urras phase contains the climax of the action as a whole and demonstrates the unity of all phases of the anarchist's life.

Shevek's political purpose in visiting Urras is to open communications between the two planets, but at first he is thwarted in this, as in the perfection of his theory. As the anarchist from the Moon he is besieged with social invitations, but in accepting these he does not succeed in gaining understanding for his society and its values. One reason he fails is that the Ioti government maintains a wall between Shevek and the lower classes. Unaccustomed to alcohol, he gets drunk at a party attended by upper-class Ioti and his tongue is loosened into scathing eloquence concerning the relative advantages of Anarres and A-Io. The response to his speech epitomizes the way the Ioti have been responding to and using him: the attractive hostess takes him to a bedroom and "rewards" him by leading him on sexually until he spurts semen on her dress, whereupon she dismisses him angrily. Back among the guests he vomits, passes out, and is taken home. After this he confines himself to science and, paradoxically, all walls come down. He completes the essential outlines of the General Temporal Theory by using a tactic which also has sociopolitical significance: instead of continuing to try to prove simultaneity, he instead postulates it to see how things work out—just as, he has learned, the Terran "Ainsetain" postulated the velocity of light as a limiting factor and achieved two relativity theories which are "as beautiful, as valid, and as useful as ever after these centuries . . ." (Chap. 9). The error in his earlier approach is akin to that being made by all of Anarresti society in its choice of total isolation from the rest of the human community: "He had been groping and grabbing after certainty, as if it were something he could possess. He had been demanding a security, a guarantee, which is not granted, and which, if granted, would become a prison" (Chap. 9). Because he hypothesizes, taking a risk as he has taken a risk in leaving Anarres, the prophecy of his childhood dream is fulfilled:

> The wall was down. The vision was both clear and whole. What he saw was simple, simpler than anything else. It was simplicity: and contained in it all complexity, all promise. It was revelation."
>
> (Chap. 9)

Even the wall of interplanetary human community is down, for technological use of his theory will make possible instantaneous communication over interstellar distances. At the moment of discovery he even feels at home on Urras.

> —for at this instant the difference between this planet and that one, between Urras and Anarres, was no more significant to him than the difference between two grains of sand on the shore of the sea. There were no more abysses, no more walls. There was no more exile. He had seen the foundations of the universe, and they were solid.
>
> (Chap. 9)

The events following immediately upon this, the turning point in the novel, are the triumphant consequences (attended by disaster) of Shevek's single-minded and socially responsible insistence on his right to pursue his calling. Somewhat run down from the exhausting mental effort he has just put forth, Shevek becomes panicky and apprehensive that Ioti spies might learn he has completed his theory. He does not want A-Io to use the theory in the service of its imperialistic designs on the Nine Known Worlds. Confiding his fears to Efor, the manservant assigned to him in his university rooms, he immediately gains the other's confidence in return, as he could not in all his months of being lionized as the eminent physicist from the Moon. Efor nurses Shevek through his illness skillfully and instructs him how to slip away from the university and get in touch with the political leaders of the lower classes.

Efor's behavior confirms and exemplifies an insight about brother-hood—today's Terran anarchists would say solidarity—which Shevek re-ceived as a youth, while sitting with an accident victim for whom no relief was available and who was dying of severe burns: "I saw that you can't do anything for anybody. We can't save each other. Or ourselves." For him this means not isolation and despair, but rather that brotherhood "begins in shared pain" (Chap. 2). As I interpret this, the basis of human solidarity is not only the necessity and desirability of mutual aid, but something more existential: the sympathy and solace we can offer each other in the common fate, that each must face death alone. Efor, seeing Shevek's genuine fear and need, feels a bond with him for the first time and confides in him what life is like for the lower classes in A-Io.

The same insight justifies Shevek's isolation by showing how an individual's solitude need not work against solidarity. It seems quite consistent with anarchism, nicely stating the basis for both the individual-ity and the sociality of human nature in a way that harmonizes rather than opposes the two. Le Guin indeed defines freedom in this novel as "that recognition of each person's solitude which alone transcends it" (Chap. 9). Shevek's speech to the demonstrators in the city of Nio grows out of this insight and for this reason is eloquent—despite his foreign accent—and effective: "He spoke their mind, their being, in their language, though he said no more than he had said out of his own isolation, out of the center of his own being, a long time ago" (Chap. 9). A late bloomer socially, he reknits a bond between revolutionary movements separated for over a century and a half. He does not do this by spouting what has become on Anarres the Odonian party line; it is anarchism, but it is no less his unique and stubborn self.

In a libertarian communist society, Le Guin says in *The Dispossessed,* freedom is more fragile than communism, and the spirit of freedom can easily lapse into one of conformity. When this happens, the first to suffer are likely to be those creative individuals whose work must be solitary—precisely those, in other words, who are the best justification of freedom.

Such is the case on Anarres with Shevek and a number of creative artists. But it is to his society's credit that rebels still grow up in it and that rebellion is not very difficult. Shevek and his syndics are advised not to speak by radio with Urrasti, but they cannot be forbidden to do so. On Anarres there is no barrier analogous to passports and State Department clearance to keep Shevek from boarding the freighter to Urras, though he must brave an angry crowd to do so, and though one of the Defense guards dies while protecting him. At the end of the novel an angry crowd is again waiting for him as his ship returns to Anarres Port; but in his busy absence he has renewed the revolutionary ferment that should be the essence of a libertarian society, so that the number of his partisans in the crowd is also large. A Maoist proverb is strangely appropriate to his situation: "There is great disorder under heaven, and all is well."

The idea of human nature in *The Dispossessed*, then, is in large part the anarchist idea of the relation between personal and political, i.e., between individual and social nature implied in Proudhon's aphorism "Freedom is the mother, not the daughter, of order": we are essentially social, so that the free exercise of personal initiative is not only compatible with but positively conducive to the benefit of society. To ensure this compatibility, the order of society must be equitable: useful work and the necessities of life must be available to all; reward and responsibility must be shared out equitably; the concentration of power must be minimal and always shifting, so that, ideally, there is no power but function. Under such conditions human nature blossoms. Shevek repeatedly startles and moves the Ioti with a magnetic charm and a directness and purity of character that he owes to being nurtured in a society without private property, social classes, unemployment, and useless work; where all are brothers and sisters; and where he was taught, more perfectly by precept than by example, that he need recognize no initiative but his own.

It is possible to dig deeper and wider into the anarchist sources of *The Dispossessed*. The affinity of anarchism and Taoism is not, of course, lost on Le Guin. The fact that all political violence in the story is initiated by reactionaries reflects the progression of anarchism from the terrorism of the 1890's to the position of Kropotkin and others that violence as a direct method is counterrevolutionary in effect, though sometimes genuinely revolutionary methods provoke violence. It is beyond the limits of this essay to explore these sources; but Le Guin's exaltation of poverty, a trait of the Christian anarchism of Tolstoy and the Catholic Worker movement, is central to the novel, as indicated by the title (which is also a sideswipe at Dostoevsky). Freedom is legitimately exercised to create and to achieve, but not to accumulate material wealth. It is justified as necessary to the full development of the individual, but the negative freedom from petty privations and the need to work must yield to the general good. In Paul Goodman's words, "we must understand freedom in a very positive sense: it is *the condition of initiating activity*. Apart from this pregnant meaning, mere freedom from interference is both trivial and *in fact cannot be substantially protected*. . . . The justification for freedom is that initiation is essential for *any* high-grade human behavior. Only free action has grace and force." Shevek's Ioti students have only the negative freedoms of leisure and privilege, and their behavior as future physicists is not "high-grade": they are careerists. Shevek, by contrast, has had a hard-scrabble life among a really (if imperfectly) free people: "He had not been free from anything; only free to do anything" (Chap. 5). Thus, "the less he had, the more absolute became his need to be" (Chap. 10). George Woodcock, a literary critic and a long-time anarchist, accordingly sees in *The Dispossessed* a "moral" that is basic to Buddhism and anarchism alike: "those who have shed desire are liberated." When human beings are free *from* being dominated by others and from their own desire to dominate and possess, they become free—and able—to respond to physical necessity in the most efficient way, banding together in pacts of mutual aid and creating on that basis a social structure in which each individual can strive, alone or with others, for full self-realization.

Such a social order is not likely to be perfectly realized, or expected to be. If it were, there would be no need for continuing revolution as an integral part of society. This necessity exists in part because the demands of the individual can never be perfectly reconciled with those of society, but only balanced in a dynamic, conflictful equilibrium. There is always a danger of either excessively subduing the individual on the one hand or of fragmenting society on the other. An artist who is committed to this social vision will portray a libertarian communist society critically as well as lovingly, and has no excuse for failing to develop characters fully or to integrate them into the action and setting. The author of *The Dispossessed* needs no excuses. Proceeding on a utopian's impulse with the conscience of a realist, she has considerably enriched speculative fiction.

ERIC S. RABKIN

Determinism, Free Will, and Point of View in "The Left Hand of Darkness"

The heart of Ursula K. Le Guin's novel, *The Left Hand of Darkness*, at least from a Western point of view, is a paradox. To borrow the title metaphor, on one hand the book seems to teach us how fully determined is the world in which we imagine ourselves, our attitudes and destinies controlled by accidents of sex, of environment, and even of language. On the other hand, the book is clearly didactic, urging us implicitly to will away the imperatives of biology, of physics, and even of our minds. Determinism and free will are classic antagonists in our philosophic tradition, and one cannot, of course, have things both ways. In every respect the left hand and the right reverse each other. The Western, scientific, Aristotelian point of view is that one can trace the sequences of cause and effect and come to understand the roots of how things are by learning how they were determined. To work within the deterministic assumptions of Western culture would seem to destroy the possibility of free will. But in Le Guin's artistic practice, and in the philosophy of the Eastern world, the left hand and the right form a unity by virtue of their difference. Whether one sees reversal as antagonism or fulfillment is, in a profound sense, a matter of point of view. By manipulating the reader's expected acceptance of the importance of determinism, Le Guin channels his mind into a new direction. This direction is not the simple reversal of determinism, the celebration of free will, but a

From *Extrapolation* 1, vol. 20 (1979). Copyright © 1979 by The Kent State University Press.

coordination—to use the Ekumen's term—of determinism and free will within a wider concept, point of view itself. Le Guin's remarkable achievement is that she can manipulate our habitual point of view so that we come to see things from a new point of view, that for which point of view itself is central.

The most famous—and obvious—determinism explored in this novel is sexual. Each Gethenian is sexually inactive during most of each month ("somer"), but when the period of estrus comes ("kemmer"), a person becomes a highly active male or female, the physiological development depending on the state of those around "him."

> The kemmer phenomenon fascinates all of us Investigators, of course. It fascinates us, but it rules the Gethenians, dominates them. The structure of their societies, the management of their industry, agriculture, commerce, the size of their settlements, the subjects of their stories, everything is shaped to fit the somer-kemmer cycle. . . .
>
> Consider: Anyone can turn his hand to anything. This sounds very simple, but its psychological effects are incalculable. The fact that everyone between seventeen and thirty-five or so is liable to be . . . "tied down to childbearing," implies that no one is quite so thoroughly "tied down" here as women, elsewhere, are likely to be—psychologically or physically. Burden and privilege are shared out pretty equally; everybody has the same risk to run or choice to make. Therefore nobody here is quite so free as a free male anywhere else.

In keeping with the determinism inherent in her exposition of this situation, Le Guin indeed shapes the society, industry and even folk tales of Gethen to reflect this biological fact. Such tailoring is not of value merely for itself, however, but to further certain philosophic ends. " 'Fundamentally Terra and Gethen are very much alike' " and so we are to draw conclusions about our own world from our insight into this other world. As Le Guin writes in her introduction, "Science fiction is not predictive; it is descriptive." The world she describes, despite its admitted oddities, is, beneath the appearances, our own.

In order to help us see beneath those appearances, she provides us with one normally sexed human being, Genly Ai, a black man from Terra who is the "Mobile" of the Ekumen sent to invite Gethen to join the confraternity of inhabited worlds. As the Investigators had noted in scouting the planet,

> The First Mobile, if one is sent, must be warned that unless he is very self-assured, or senile, his pride will suffer. A man wants his virility regarded, a woman wants her femininity appreciated, however indirect

and subtle the indications of regard and appreciation. On Winter [English for Gethen] they will not exist. One is respected and judged only as a human being. It is an appalling experience.

And Genly Ai is duly appalled—and confused and mistaken. Yet, at the same time that Le Guin is exposing a deterministic situation, it is clear from her very exposition that she invites the exercise of free will to overcome it. Surely it is more important to be judged "as a human being" than as either a man or as a woman; surely we would not want to misread people as Genly Ai does simply because we are overly fixated on mere matters of sex. Yet, it must be admitted that sex does determine a great deal about a person and " 'It's extremely hard to separate the innate differences from the learned ones.' " How then to see beneath appearances? Typically in this novel, it is by rising above them, seeking a wider context:

> . . . in the end, the dominant factor in Gethenian life is not sex or any other human thing: it is their environment, their cold world. Here man has a crueler enemy even than himself.

In switching our attention from the determinism of sex to the determinism of environment, Le Guin is forcing us to change our point of view.

Genly Ai postulates that the killing cold of Gethen makes survival so chancy that the institution of war is counteradaptive. Thus, the Gethenians' lack of such an institution might be "explained" by environmental determinism. Certainly Genly Ai, whose point of view we ought most to share, explains Gethenian law in that way: "Life on Winter is hard to live, and people there generally leave death to nature or to anger, not to law." He even explains the failures of imagination by reference to the environment: why don't Gethenians have flying machines? "How would it ever occur to a sane man that he could fly? Estraven said sternly. It was a fair response, on a world where no living thing is winged." Even Estraven, the Gethenian, indulges in deterministic explanation. In predicting the weather for the impending cross-glacial trek, Estraven explains that

> The good weather, you know, tends to stay over the great glaciers, where the ice reflects the heat of the sun; the storms are pushed out to the periphery. Therefore the legends about the Place inside the Blizzard.

The key word here is "therefore": determinism seems to explain everything, whether it be a determinism of sex or a determinism of environment.

Le Guin goes much further than these explicit passages in validating determinism. If she is overtly creating a world in which the existence of a certain folk narrative is explained, then she can actualize that world by offering the folk narrative itself as part of the novel. She does this in chapter two. What must be remembered, however, is that nothing *determines* that Le Guin will offer such a tale: she makes it up out of her own mind and we readers who recognize that we are involved with fiction know it to be made up. As readers we admire the skill that not only presents the story in the "folk" form but later justifies it meterologically. We also respond, even if only unconsciously, to the obviously conscious patterning of the novel that comes about in part through the re-use of this image: in the folk narrative of "Estraven the Traitor," the hut in which Arek and Therem meet is a place inside the blizzard, in the Orgota creation myth, the house of corpses is a place inside the blizzard, and in the story of the glacier-crossing, the tent in which Therem and Genly Ai first mindspeak is a place inside the blizzard. In the original folk narrative, the place appears at first as both good and bad since it is both the locale of a desired reunion and the land of death. What shall be our point of view on it? As Terrans—Westerners—we are confused, but upon rereading, after having come to understand that suicide is a paramount crime on Gethen, we realize that such a death is irredeemable in all cases. Hence the boon of reunion tips the balance toward good. On a first reading we would not see this, not yet having learned to adopt a Gethenian point of view, but we learn to adopt such a point of view by reading the novel. In understanding the tale of "Estraven the Traitor," the hut must be seen by Westerners as good because it supports a strong conventional value: the conquest of family feuds by love. If we have been raised on *Romeo and Juliet,* we know what point of view to take on this place in the blizzard. Then in the Orgota creation myth, the hut of corpses, manifestly a place of death, is made the place of creation. Thus, the connectedness of life and death is added to our previous approbation of the image of the place inside the blizzard. To this point of view we may add, among other values, the traditional value of honesty in the mindspeaking episode because mindspeech allows for no lies. Hence, when all this is followed by a meteorological explanation, what is a matter of chosen—manipulated— point of view has come also to seem a determined part of the narrative world. Hence, our recollection of the folk narrative confirms both determinism and free will: the tale as such is fit but its inclusion and narrative uses are matters of choice. By implication, Le Guin shows us that both fitness and choice depend on point of view.

She is similarly subtle in her incidental creation of cultural artifacts:

> On a world where a common table implement is a little device with which you crack the ice that has formed on your drink between drafts, hot beer is a thing you come to appreciate.

Of course, there is no such world; there are no such artifacts. Le Guin makes up the world and then, instead of saying "it was so cold that they had to serve table implements to crack the ice off their drinks," she turns matters around, assumes in a deterministic way what the implements would be in such a world, and then has Genly Ai observe not the fitness of the implement but the fitness of the warm drink. Thus, the fitness of the implement is tacit and serves to increase our sense of a deterministic world without the need of explicit speculations such as those of the Investigators.

Perhaps the subtlest tactics of all are exhibited in the very language of the novel, as indeed they should be since novels, finally, are made of nothing but words. We are told, in the overt way we have already noted, that

> Gethenians often think in thirteens, twenty-sixes, fifty-twos, no doubt because of the 26-day lunar cycle that makes their unvarying month and approximates their sexual cycles.

This explicit observation is implicit later in Estraven's narration: "Forgery of papers is risky in Orgoreyn where they are inspected fifty-two times daily . . ." An American would say, for whatever cultural reasons, "one hundred" or "a thousand" while a Frenchman would say "thirty-six," but the canonical number for exaggeration in Karhidish is obviously fifty-two. That this is fit is determined by the earlier, overt observation about thinking in thirteens; that Le Guin chose to actualize that observation in this way is a matter of personal, and highly skillful, choice.

Other factors of environment also determine the language of this novel. The enormous importance of keen meteorological observation for survival on Gethen is reflected in both Karhidish and Orgota having numerous words for many different types and conditions of snow, sleet, and so on. The parallel fact about Eskimo is often adduced by linguists to indicate that Eskimos actually see more distinctions among snowfalls than, say, speakers of English. The suggestion that language is not only shaped by reality but conversely shapes it is known as the Sapir-Whorf hypothesis:

> The relation between language and experience is often misunderstood. Language is not merely a more or less systematic inventory of the various items of experience which seem relevant to the individual, as is so often naively assumed, but is also a self-contained, creative symbolic organization, which not only refers to experience largely acquired without its help but actually defines experience for us by reason of its formal completeness and because of our unconscious projection of its implicit expectations into the field of experience.

Genly Ai implicitly accepts this hypothesis as true when he wonders "How could I explain the Age of the Enemy, and its aftereffects, to a people who had no word for war?" Le Guin implicitly accepts this hypothesis by creating and using such terms as "kemmer" and "shifgrethor" and "hieb" and "nusuth" and "dothe", by constructing an elaborate "Gethenian Calendar and Clock," and then by using its terminology throughout the novel. Thus is a Gethenian reality created, freely chosen and thereafter determined. In an implicit and thus profound way, reading the language of this novel makes one adopt a point of view that accepts the notion that one can at least in part choose how one's world is determined.

The delineation of point of view is often a problem in understanding language and is a central problem in this novel. Let us consider, for example, the word "traitor." Like the image of the place inside the blizzard, "traitor" is part of the pattern of the novel. Thus, it both determines and is determined while its several artistic uses imply the will behind the work. This word first occurs when Argaven addresses the Stabiles on Hain via ansible, a communications machine, " 'Ask your machine there what makes a man a traitor.' " The answer comes, finally: " 'I do not know what makes a man a traitor. No man considers himself a traitor: this makes it hard to find out.' " Although some readers may believe that some traitors know themselves as such, the text clearly asks us to accept this as a wise answer. If we do, we see that it puts point of view even above the question of language. When Ashe approaches Genly Ai after Estraven's exile in hopes of getting the Mobile to bring money to the deposed Prime Minister, Genly Ai does not know who is meant when Ashe calls himself " 'a friend of one who befriended you' " because he has never understood that Estraven was his friend. Hence we readers, knowing Genly Ai's ignorance and Ashe's devotion, read the irony in Ashe's clarification: " 'Estraven, the traitor.' " From the point of view of the character, which we must momentarily adopt, the word is a stigma wrongly applied by the king. In the folk narrative called "Estraven the Traitor", the title character is a traitor because he ceded land to the neighboring Domain of Stok and thus ended a feud. However, from our point of view he is no traitor, first because his birth was the result of placing humanity over politics when his mother-to-be gave help to his sorely disabled father-to-be and second because the cession of territory is precisely what the Estraven with whom we are concerned, and whom we admire, suggests as a solution to the conflict over the Sinoth Valley. In both cases, moreover, from a wider point of view than that of the Domain or of Karhide, from the point of view of the Ekumen, the acts of cession would restore order and serve a wider human purpose than aggrandizement: peace. Understanding this point of view, we see that Estraven has fully understood the Ekumenical point of view when he can be self-ironic in making plans with Genly Ai to bring down the Star Ship and promise to keep himself out of sight for a while since " 'I am Estraven the Traitor. I have nothing to do with you." Since Genly Ai and Estraven have come to share a point of view, they have a common use of the language and thus can say without misunderstanding that Thessicher, who turns Estraven into Tibe, is a "traitor." And finally, we understand the bitterness of loss which Genly Ai nearly indulges by putting himself before his dead friend after Estraven's self-sacrifice: ". . . the traitor. He had gone on by himself, deserting me, deserting me." Depending on point of view, a word can mean so many things.

Le Guin uses the language of the novel to determine her readers' points of view, manipulating us and leading us from beginning to end. For example, we come to accept the possibility of paradoxical truth through the many aphorisms in the novel. " 'The admirable is inexplicable.' " The aphorisms themselves often implicitly support the determinism we have seen in the vocabulary and usage practices of the novel. " 'The Glaciers didn't freeze overnight.' " " 'We must sully the plain snow with footprints, in order to get anywhere.' " These are the sayings of a frigid world. Le Guin deterministically justifies a narrative world fraught with aphorism:

> Estraven [told] the whole tale of our crossing of the Ice . . . as only a person of an oral-literature tradition can tell a story, so that it becomes a saga, full of traditional locutions.

Yet, here again we see determinism implicitly serving the will of the author, for Le Guin's novel itself is told with traditional locutions, the aphorisms we are reading, and yet comes from a purely fictive realm. This is a paradox which we feel quite as strongly as we might feel the paradoxical truth of any of the aphorisms themselves.

Just as the environment may determine the language, the characters may determine language. And just as Le Guin turns the former process around by first assuming the world with the ice-cracking table implement, so she turns character around by first conceiving the characters and then having them speak as their characteristics ought to determine. Yet, of course, their speeches are chosen by Le Guin—and we know it. Estraven, who is clearly the noblest character in the book and most in touch with his world, speaks in aphorisms of his own invention: "Do you know the saying, *Karhide is not a nation but a family quarrel?* I haven't [sic], and I suspect that Estraven made it up; it has his stamp.' " Estraven is similarly pithy in distilling the experience of his exile: " 'Banished men should never speak their native tongue; it comes bitter from their mouth.' " By contrast, Tibe and Obsle, both of whom oppose Estraven at the book's political level, must self-consciously borrow their aphorisms: ". . . poor relations must be in good time, as the saying is, eh?" and ". . . we can pull a sledge together without being kemmerings, as we say in Eskeve—eh?" Genly Ai, who will come to share a point of view with Estraven, speaks sometimes in aphorisms, even giving their Ekumenical source, but is not self-conscious about the need to gain wisdom from someone else's experience: "One voice speaking truth is a greater force than fleets and armies" and "As they say in Ekumenical School, when action grows unprofitable, gather information; when information grows unprofitable, sleep." Finally, having experienced enough himself, Genly Ai grows and this growth is reflected (determines) his speaking in aphorisms of his own invention: "It is good to have an end to journey towards; but it is the journey that matters, in the end." The use of aphorisms, apparently determined by the characters, in fact reflects the characteristics that Le Guin wills and wishes to communicate.

We work our way back through the logic of determinism to understand this narrative world as one of potential wisdom, and we work our way back through the logic of invention to understand this narrative world as serving an author's freely willed purpose. Both conclusions are subsumed by the concern for point of view. Point of view can determine how the world appears to someone: mad Argaven is " 'a king, and does not see things rationally, but as a king.' " Although Estraven says this, he does not follow up his insight carefully enough. " 'Mr. Ai, we've seen the same events with different eyes; I wrongly thought they'd seem the same to us.' " Le Guin, however, who has created both Estraven and his lapse, makes no such error herself; the entire novel is structured by an awareness of point of view.

The opening lines of the novel show this awareness: "Truth is a matter of the imagination . . . the facts seem to alter with an altered voice . . . yet none of them are false, and it is all one story." True to this word, the novel proceeds by presenting the story first in one voice and then in another, first from one point of view, then from another. The first chapter begins with an italicized document heading, *"From the Archives of Hain."* This heading includes the words, *"Report from Genly Ai."* We do not know who Genly Ai is at this moment, of course, but when we read the first roman-faced word of the novel, "I," we know that it is Genly Ai speaking. Since this is a first person narration, chapter one inevitably forces us into a sympathetic, even if only partial, sharing of Genly Ai's point of view. The second chapter begins with an italicized announcement that we are about to read a " 'hearth-tale' " as told by an unknown narrator. We quickly switch our point of view to take on the perspective necessary to an understanding of this chapter. The third chapter begins without italics but with the word "I." The human mind loves to generalize an instance into a law; having seen a chapter beginning with "I" turn out to be narrated by Genly Ai, we are likely to assume that this chapter is narrated by him as well. But even if we are not so quick to fix things, the text fixes them for us within the first sentence:

> I slept late and spent the tail of the morning reading over my own notes on Palace etiquette and the observations on Gethenian psychology and manners made by my predecessors, the Investigators.

The fourth chapter is again announced in italics as a "story", and so when the fifth chapter begins without notice, we assume we are back to Genly Ai's narration. And we turn out to be correct. Le Guin is training us to accept our logic of inference and to generalize the laws determining the novel's structure. Thus, when the sixth chapter begins without announcement, we should assume that it is *not* Genly Ai. And when it quickly becomes apparent that this is a first person narration, we wonder who is speaking. The text quickly pacifies our curiosity: in the third line of the chapter the cook says "in my ear, 'Wake up, wake up. Lord Estraven . . .' " Our guesses about the laws determining the novel's structure have been correct, and the novel has rewarded us with confirmation. All of this is being done for two very important reasons. First, by making the novel itself an example of the truth altering with altered voices, residing in diverse points of view, the very narrative method forces us to accept the novel's opening aphoristic premises. But an equally important reason is much less general and is well worth discussing.

Although Le Guin presents the novel through two first person voices and intersperses a series of other narratives, of folk literature, Investigators' reports and so on, she arranges to have the novel, nonetheless, move continuously forward. Each chapter picks up some point of plot or thought from its predecessors and proceeds. There is only one exception to this: the mindspeaking episode. From the beginning of the story, Estraven has wanted to learn mindspeaking. The novel has been a record of misperception by Estraven of Genly Ai and by Genly Ai of Estraven. But finally, by chapter sixteen, having escaped Pulefen Farm together and struggled up onto the Gobrin Ice, the two principal characters begin to talk more forthrightly. In their tent, the place inside the blizzard, when Genly Ai explains that his visit to Gethen, because of travel in the trans-light speed NAFAL ship, has prevented him from ever seeing his parents again, Estraven realizes that Genly is as much an exile from his birthplace as is the so-called Traitor. They are mutual exiles. " 'You for my sake—I for yours.' " In this chapter, narrated by Estraven, we have not only the isolation of the two together and their sharing of a common and arduous task but Estraven's narration of his kemmer. Since Genly is always male, Estraven becomes female; they feel very close to each other, but they keep that closeness spiritual. Chapter seventeen is "An Orgota Creation Myth" wherein the world of people is the result of copulation between aboriginal brothers in a hut made of death, corpses, within the blizzard. And then in chapter eighteen, "On the Ice," we return to first person narration. It is in this chapter that Genly Ai covers the same ground Estraven had covered in chapter sixteen, both geographically and narratively. The chapter begins with this line: "Sometimes as I am falling asleep in a dark, quiet room . . . ." An alert reader already knows that Genly Ai must live through this adventure since he has made his presence as "editor" of these materials clear in footnotes. An even more alert reader will note that one of the brothers in the creation myth preceding this chapter runs off immediately after copulation, never to return. If that story bears on ours—and it must or Le Guin would not have willed it there—then it is determined that one character must leave, and since that cannot be Genly Ai it must be Estraven. Hence, this recollection from the future must be Genly's and the chapter is indeed in his voice. It too tells of the growing closeness between Genly Ai and Estraven and of the night of kemmer and finally, closeness of closeness, mindspeech. Estraven mindhears Genly speak his given name, Therem, with the voice of his dead brother and kemmering, Arek. As the only event which is covered twice, as the symptom of love, and as the demonstration of the coincidence of Genly and Therem's points of view, this is perhaps the crucial event of the plot. Chapter nineteen, "Homecoming," begins without italics, and though it begins with the first person pronouns, they are not singular:

> In a dark windy weather we slogged along, trying to find encouragement in the sighting of Esherhoth Crags, the first thing not ice or snow or sky that we had seen for seven weeks.

This could be either character speaking, of course, but since Genly Ai narrated chapter eighteen and since the law determining this novel's structure calls for alternation of narrative voices, this must be Estraven speaking. And so we read this in our minds with Estraven's voice, and it fits, until a page goes by and then the speaker indicates that he knows his recollection is correct "by Estraven's journal, for I kept none." The law is broken! And we have mindheard Genly with Therem's voice! By her consummate manipulation of point of view, Le Guin has given us the experience which her novel had described. Suddenly, we fully understand the mutuality of the characters' points of view and therefore understand the beauty of such loss of self. From the point of view of point of view, both determinism and free will seem insignificant. In the middle of the novel, the antagonism of determinism and free will is critical for Genly Ai; he ends chapter eight with this thought about Estraven:

> . . . it crossed my mind . . . that I had not come to Mishnory to eat roast blackfish with the Commensals of my own free will; nor had they brought me here. He had.

But after mindspeaking, their wills are one and the question of determinism is no longer relevant. In making us see this, Le Guin had used determinism—of sex and of environment, of language and style and image and technique and structure—not to create a sense of free will but to subsume both determinism and free will under the recognition that "truth is a matter of the imagination."

As we saw in the characters' use of aphorisms, Genly Ai and Estraven begin the novel as apparently opposed and, although both learn, primarily Genly grows toward Estraven, the two finally coming to an understanding that does not so much reconcile their differences as make them irrelevant by acknowledging and accepting them as necessary for mutual fulfillment. In this regard, the central utterance of the novel is "Tormer's Lay":

> Light is the left hand of darkness
> and darkness the right hand of light.
> Two are one, life and death, lying
> together like lovers in kemmer
> like hands joined together,
> like the end and the way.

This is a part of the literature of the Handdara, the religion of which Estraven is an adept. Only after the mindspeaking does Genly seem to understand it fully and he offers to gloss it by drawing in Estraven's notebook the yin and yang symbol. " 'Light, dark. Fear, courage. Cold, warmth. Female, male. . . . Both and one. A shadow on snow.' " In coming to understand the Handdara, Genly—and the reader—come to understand something of Chinese philosophy, and in particular of Taoism.

"To oppose something is to maintain it," Estraven notes in his typically aphoristic and paradoxical manner. Compare that with this from the *Tao Teh King* of Lao Tzu, the oldest document of Taoism: "In conflicts between opposites, the more one attacks his seeming opponent . . . the more he defeats himself." Not only does Taoism present its message in aphoristic paradox, it also uses anecdote in the ways of this novel. Chapter four, "The Nineteenth Day," tells of a man who wanted to know the length of his life and foolishly asked the Handdarata Foretellers for the day of his death. He is told he will die on the nineteenth—but not of which month or year. This maddens him and to save his sanity his lover offers his own life to learn how long the man will live. He is told that he will live longer than the lover. When he reports this answer, the man becomes murderous because the lover wasted his question. He kills the lover and this so sobers and shocks him that the next month he hangs himself, on the nineteenth. In this parable the Foretellers indeed tell the truth: the lover pays for the prophecy with his life, the man outlives his lover and he dies on the nineteenth. But even though the Foretellers have the skill of predicting the future (which would imply that it is determined), they predict it for a reason of their own: " 'To exhibit the perfect uselessness of knowing the answer to the wrong questions.' " Both the man and his lover would have been much better off to have acted in accord with the Tao, to have lived as long as they would live, and die when they would die. Then, even had they died on the same days, they would have been spared the madness, and perhaps have known peace. Compare that story with this from Chuang-tzu, the most famous interpreter of Tao:

> Hui Tzu said to Chuang-tzu, 'Your teachings are of no practical use.' Chuang-tzu said, 'Only those who already know the value of the useless can be talked to about the useful. This earth we walk upon is of vast extent, yet in order to walk a man uses no more of it than the soles of his two feet will cover. But suppose one cut away the ground round his feet till one reached the Yellow Springs [the land of the dead], would his patches of ground still be of any use to him for walking?' Hui Tzu said, 'They would be of no use.' Chuang-tzu said, 'So then the usefulness of the useless is evident.'

This story teaches that the useless is itself useful, and the Foretelling of the Handdara, although useless in changing the determined course of men's lives by allowing the consequential application of free will is useful in teaching men to live with ignorance. Whether a given parable, or the ground under a man's feet, is of value is a matter of point of view. Value, after all, depends upon the evaluator. To the Tao, sometimes called the Way and sometimes called Nature, all things are equally valuable and valueless because all things are equally true, equally part of the Tao.

In Taoism the best action is informed non-action, allowing people and things to act out their own natures. In ancient China Lao Tzu interpreted the Tao in this way and drew from it not only conclusions about attitudes but even guides to right action in government. He saw the best governors as those who led the people to fulfill their own natures. This is Estraven's gift as well:

> I never had a gift but one, to know when the great wheel gives to a touch, to know and act . . . It was a delight to feel that certainty again, to know that I could steer my fortunes and the world's chance like a bobsled down the steep, dangerous hour.

One cannot help but note that according to legend, when Lao Tzu saw the dynasty about to decline he left and, before disappearing forever, gave his teachings to a gatekeeper. Therem too leaves Karhide when he sees that dynasty—and all dynasties—about to pass. The gate image of Taoism in this novel is seen as the arch image. The novel opens with the ceremony of Argaven setting the keystone to the arch of the bridge that will open the New Road. The mortar is red. Previously that color had come from human sacrifice; now from animals. Therem sees, at that very ceremony, that it is Genly Ai who will " 'show us the new road.' " And, forming a narrative bridge itself, after Estraven's murder by Tibe's agents at the end of the book, Genly Ai returned

> through the Northern Gates to Erhenrang . . . it came plainly to me that, my friend being dead, I must accomplish the thing he died for. I must set the keystone in the arch.

Therem's blood will support this newer and more important bridge—and simultaneously bridge the novel. Things happen as they are to happen. That is the Way.

Chuang-tzu, who came well after Lao Tzu, tried neither to persuade nor advise. He tried to keep out of the affairs of men, preferring to concentrate on the liberating contemplation of the Tao. In this, he is much like Faxe the Weaver, another Handdara adept who understands the uselessness of knowing the answer to the wrong question and who, once Estraven has passed from the scene, must take his place. Chuang-tzu's main object of satire was Confucius because Confucius paid special attention to political problems. In his time,

> the efforts of . . . powerful families to transform the state into family domains conflicted with the desires of lesser nobles and wealthy citizens for a united state to be ruled by men according to their merits, education and character. The latter formed a relatively democratic movement, although it naturally excluded the working people, especially peasants,

from government, relegating them to the role of beneficiaries of paternal-
istic care.

The ideas of this group were fundamentally formulated by Confucius, and his teachings were thus well suited to form the backbone of the
bureaucratic state which developed in China.

The description of the Confucian nation, and its opposition of the organization by "domains," fits Gethen perfectly.

It had been entertaining and fascinating to find here on Gethen governments so similar to those in the ancient histories of Terra: a monarchy,
and a genuine fullblown bureaucracy.

Although *The Left Hand of Darkness* clearly presents a world parallel to our
own, in the matter of governments the parallel is not to our time but to
the time of the legendary Chuang-tzu.

One ought not to conclude, of course, that Le Guin's novel is a
simple *roman à clef.* There are crucial discrepancies between Chinese
history and this narrative, an obvious example being the contemporaneity
of Estraven and Faxe. The use of Chinese philosophy and literature as a
source should not be taken too far. The Orgota creation myth, for
example, that depends upon ice melt, seems much more closely aligned
with the Norse creation myth than with anything in Chinese literature.
Nonetheless, this novel seems clearly indebted to an ancient philosophy
of dynamic opposition and active unity. "If Nature is inexpressible, he
who desires to know Nature as it is in itself will not try to express it in
words." Yet, this is what Lao Tzu did by writing this paradoxical aphorism
and what Le Guin does by writing her book. In all novels the actions of
characters are determined. After all, whatever will have happened to
them by the time we have read the last page has already been written as
having happened to them when we begin to read the first page. Yet, to
become involved in the rightness or wrongness of their decisions, we must
think of them as if they had free will. So, all characters are determined
and all require us to adopt a point of view that sees them as free. In this
book, that fact about narrative becomes a thematic concern, and the
problem of determinism versus free will is set aside by turning to the
notion of point of view. This is a matter of situating one's mind, a matter
at the heart of Taoism.

In its use of paradox, aphorism, historical parallels, and particulars
of philosophy, this novel seems to attempt to bring its readers around to
sharing, experiencing, the Taoist point of view. According to that point
of view, the Tao is whatever it is; things happen as they must. This is
exemplified in the novel by the accuracy of the Foretellers. When Genly

Ai asks them a sufficiently precise question about his mission, will Gethen join the Ekumen within five years, the answer is not at all paradoxical: "yes." One cannot help but wonder, then, if that implies that such an answer also is useless and that Genly Ai and Estraven might have saved themselves the trouble. But the answer to that is equally clear: they had to do what it appeared to their natures to do, that is the Tao way and the novel's point of view. "Intelligence consists in acting according to Nature." By acting out their natures, they accomplished the Taoist goal of coming to understand their own true natures and each other's. In this way, as the *Tao Teh King* asserts, they can guide the world they live in and finally bring other people's points of view into conformity with their own. The boundaries of nations crumble because these two could come to understand, mindspeak, each other. When in the last chapter Genly Ai goes to see Estraven's homeland and to offer what solace he can to his friend's relatives, Estraven's father wants to know about the journey across the ice, but his son, in whom Genly Ai sees "the flash of my friend's spirit," asks, " 'Will you tell us how he died?—Will you tell us about the other worlds out among the stars—the other kinds of men, the other lives?' " "It is natural for man to be born and to die." Therem and his son both know this, and both are ready for the great adventure, into death and into the stars, an adventure of the body, to be sure, but much more an adventure of the mind. Mankind's perpetual struggle has been to change the world, to understand how it is determined and to impose human will upon it. According to the Tao and according to Le Guin's novel, this struggle ceases, and peace and liberation follow, when a person holds to and accepts the Nature of things. What one needs is to expand one's mind, to gain flexibility in adapting one's own point of view to the nature of the people and things around one, to learn to see people not as men and women but as people, to see the world for what it really is and for what it really does to us, to understand the languages of mankind as the reflections of mankind, to see that all things fit, as in a novel, into a pattern. And to be open to seeing more of the pattern. To come to this understanding is not useless at all, but neither is it the answer to a question spoken by a character. This is not an answer in the novel; it is the novel.

JEANNE MURRAY WALKER

Myth, Exchange and History in "The Left Hand of Darkness"

The theories of Claude Lévi-Strauss provide an access to understanding the workings of the myths in Ursula Le Guin's *The Left Hand of Darkness.* Among other things, the French anthropologist calls attention to the oppositional structure of myth and to its function in social exchange. He points out that myths are a particularly valuable key to the collective thought of a society because they offer an unusually clear code which classifies and interrelates the data of social experience of the peoples to whom those myths belong. They reinforce and verify the economic, cosmological, and kinship norms of a given society in compressed, almost algebraic fashion. The myths reflect, and reflect upon, the problems and contradictions which arise in practical, everyday life. According to Lévi-Strauss, such thought, inevitably, is highly structured. Myth incorporates in story form pairs of images which represent contradictions lying at the center of the society. The story then develops in such a way as to allow those oppositions common ground. It qualifies or mediates their differences. By mediating between opposites, as they cannot be mediated in real life, myth temporarily overcomes contradiction.

The relationship Lévi-Strauss outlines between myth and lived experience (or human history) corresponds to that between the chapters in LHD which are distinctly mythic and others which might be called historical. The myths in LHD, it can be assumed, represent the collective

---

From *Science-Fiction Studies* 2, vol. 6 (July 1979). Copyright © 1979 by R. D. Miller and Darko Suvin.

thought of Karhidian and Orgotan societies, respectively, about their most vital and puzzling social dilemmas. They are, in fact, models which share many of the symbols, themes, and names found elsewhere in the fiction. That these myths have many narrators (e.g., "Estraven the Traitor") or that their narrators remain unknown (e.g., "The Place Inside the Blizzard") indicates that they have been distilled and shaped by an entire society. Bearing the authority of the social collective (commanding, that is, the broad assent of contemporaries and also of ancestors) these myths assume a normative function in the novel. By means of them the most crucial social problems touched upon in LHD can be identified and the ideal solutions to those problems defined. Furthermore, the underlying structure of the myths—the reconciliation of opposites—typifies the structure of LHD as a whole. Thus the myths both anticipate and act as ideal models for the "historical" events in Le Guin's fiction.

If the *process* Lévi-Strauss pinpoints in myth is mediation of opposites, the *theme* he finds at the heart of myth is the social version of that process: exchange. Exchange between human beings in effect constitutes society. Such exchange takes place at the economic level, when people swap goods and services; at the linguistic level, when they give words to one another in conversation; or at the level of kinship, when they marry into one another's families. Each kind of exchange is governed by rules which vary from one society to another. The value of exchange goes far beyond that of the items involved: the exchanges an individual makes, when taken together, form a pattern which defines his social status, his role. Therefore, each individual is the sum and product of the social exchanges in which he participates, and no individual can avoid being defined in this way since no individual can totally escape social exchange.

Of all exchanges, those which define kinship are the most basic. As Lévi-Strauss points out, "the rules of kinship and marriage are not made necessary by the social state. They *are* the social state itself, reshaping biological relationships and natural sentiments, forcing them into structures implying them as well as others, and compelling them to rise above their original characteristics." Societies depend for their very existence on kinship rules—rules of descent, rules about dwelling, prohibition of incest, and so on. Even more importantly, kinship rules, which almost universally prohibit incest, force the biological family to extend itself, to ally itself with other families. Because of the incest prohibition (a negative rule) and the prescription for legitimate partners (a positive rule) marriage results in complex alliances arising among human beings. Such alliances are essential if families are to endure, for food and shelter and physical defense require larger units than single families. Kinship alliances insure that the interests of individuals will lie in supporting the group and ultimately in sustaining the society.

Unlike the openended corpus of actual myths that anthropologists examine, the corpus of myths in LHD is closed and complete. Therefore, it is possible to analyze the entire set of Gethenian myths and establish the ways in which they are connected. Kinship exchange, in the Lévi-Straussian sense, comprises their dominant theme. In them, Le Guin articulates the theme of exchange by employing contrary images—heat and cold, dark and light, home and exile, name and namelessness, life and death, murder and sex—so as finally to reconcile their contrariety. The myths present wholeness, or unity, as an ideal; but that wholeness is never merely the integrity of an individual who stands apart from society. Instead, it consists of the tenuous and temporary integration of individuals into social units.

The Orgota creation myth investigates beginnings, locating the origin of man between pairs of unstable oppositions. "In the beginning there was nothing but ice and the sun" (chap. 18). Under duress of the sun, the ice gave way, melting into three great iceshapes. The iceshapes created the world and ultimately sacrificed themselves ("let the sun melt them") to give men consciousness. With consciousness, however, came fear. Edondurath, the tallest and the eldest of the men, awoke first and fearing the others, killed 38 of his 39 brothers. With their bodies he built a hut in which he waited for the 39th, who had escaped him. That last and youngest brother returned when Edondurath lay in Kemmer and they coupled, engendering the nations of men. Edondurath asked his kemmering why each of the men was followed by a piece of darkness, to which his kemmering replied:

> Because they were born in the house of flesh, therefore death follows at their heels. They are in the middle of time. In the beginning there was the sun and the ice, and there was no shadow. In the end when we are done, the sun will devour itself, and shadow will eat light, and there will be nothing left but the ice and darkness.
>
> (chap. 17)

This myth explicates that essential mystery, creation, in a way which emphasizes the difference between men as social creatures and men as isolated individuals. Edondurath, the oldest, "the first to wake up," behaves in a totally isolating, egocentric way. Because he fears his brothers when he sees them begin to waken, he kills them, thereby eliminating the necessity of confronting them as individualities. Then, to build himself a dwelling, he stacks them up like objects, which they are because he has refused to accord them the status of conscious beings. Into this dwelling comes a being who is his opposite both because he is youngest and because he is sexually different. The biological urgency of Edondurath's kemmer results in his integration with this other human consciousness. The language of the myth suggests that such biological intercourse brings about social intercourse. "Of these two were the *nations of men* born" (chap. 17; emphasis added). When men exist in nations—that is, in society—they exist in time, or more precisely "in the middle of time." So the creation myth equates the temporal median with social mediation. Social exchange is the invariable condition of men in time; the lack of exchange—totally egocentric behavior—is equated with nonbeing at the beginning and end of time.

The logic of man's social exchange is further explicated in "The Place Inside the Blizzard." Two brothers in the androgynous world of Gethen vow kemmering for life, a vow which is illegal. In the Hearth of Shath, where they live, brothers may stay together only until they have produced one child. The brothers produce a child. Then the Lord of Shath commands them to break their vow. One brother despairs and commits suicide. The other, Getheren, assigned the great public shame of the suicide, suffers exile. He departs Shath to seek his death on the ice, but before he goes he thrusts his name and his guilt onto the town. Then, wandering deep on the Pering ice, Getheren meets his brother, all white and cold, who asks him to remain and keep their vow. Getheren declines, replying that when his brother chose death, he broke the vow. The brother tries to clutch Getheren, seizing him by the left hand. Getheren flees and several days later he is discovered in a province which neighbors Shath, speechless. He recovers, but his frozen arm must be amputated. Then he leaves for southern lands, calling himself Ennoch. During his long stay there, no crops will grow in Shath. When Ennoch finally becomes an old man, he tells his story to a kinsman from Shath and reclaims the name Getheren. Immediately, thereafter he dies, whereupon Shath returns to prosperity.

The brothers' crime is loving one another so excessively that they exclude the community. Because they swear permanent vows to one another, their love is defined by law as a crime. Lifelong incest is prohibited, but not for the biologically based reason that incest results in weakened offspring (on Getheren brothers are permitted to produce off-spring). Rather, lifelong vows of sexual loyalty between brothers are prohibited because they prevent vows with others outside the family. In the *Elementary Structures of Kinship* Lévi-Strauss makes this point:

Exchange—and consequently the rule of exogamy which expresses it—has in itself a social value. It provides the means of binding men together, and of super-imposing upon the natural links of kinship the henceforth artificial links—artificial in the sense that they are removed from chance encounters or the promiscuity of family life—of alliance governed by rule.

Exchange of permanent marriage vows is the most significant of all social exchanges, since it knits the participants together in mutual obligation and in concern for their offspring. The vows which bind men of different families create a complex network of loyalties and interrelationships which define the Hearth. Without such a network, based on exchange, the Hearth could not function cohesively; it would disintegrate into solitary, isolated—perhaps warring—families. Therefore, the law which requires sexual exchange is fundamental to the existence of the Hearth.

This law of the community competes with the powerful human desire for personal integrity: the need "to keep to oneself." Keeping to oneself is Lévi-Strauss's pun: it means both remaining isolated, alone, and retaining one's kin by not allowing them to marry outside the family. The brothers' need to keep to each other in the intimacy of the sexual act is so strong that they vow kemmering to one another for life, thereby defying the law which is fundamental to the continued existence of the Hearth. They force a deadlock between the existence of self and the existence of the social group. When the Lord of the Hearth breaks the deadlock in favor of the social group, one of the brothers performs the ultimate act of keeping to himself: he commits suicide, thereby depriving the social group of all further exchange with him. Thus suicide repudiates the law of exchange which makes social groups in LHD possible.

Once the individual places himself at odds with the community, the balance shifts back and forth between the individual and the community until one or the other is destroyed. The community defines the absolute repudiation of exchange—the suicide of the brother—as the worst possible crime and lays the guilt for this crime on Getheren, the remaining brother. On Getheren the Hearth levies exile, the punishment which fits the crime. Exile robs Getheren of the right to exchange anything with his community, as his brother's suicide had robbed the community of the right to exchange anything with him. In response, Getheren bestows his name on the Hearth.

In this myth, as is the case more explicitly in Le Guin's *Earthsea* trilogy, an individual's name signifies his identity, his moral credits and debits. Therefore, when Getheren curses the Hearth with his name, he, on the one hand, transfers responsibility for the suicide of the brother to

the Hearth and on the other denies himself identity as an individual. His
journey to the Ice signals his movement away from the community to
himself. The center of the ice, the place inside the blizzard, signifies
absolute lack of community, a place where "we who kill ourselves dwell"
(chap. 2), as the brother says. Such absolute isolation is rejected by
Getheren. He takes an alternative name and identity, participating in
another society as "Ennoch." Meanwhile, the Hearth, which enforced its
own rule of exchange at great cost to one of its members, undergoes
famine. This lack of physical sustenance is a metaphor for the lack of
social sustenance which occurs when a member of a social group cannot
participate in its activities of exchange. The group experiences depriva-
tion and potentially death. But when Getheren hears of the famine in the
Hearth he reassumes his name and with it, responsibility for the suicide of
his brother. His own death, restoring plenty to the Hearth, follows
immediately.

The mutual dependence between a group and its members is so
imperative, the myth shows, that death follows when that dependence is
denied. Human beings have urgent needs both for privacy and for communal exchanges. As the contradiction between the brother's vows and the
law of Hearth demonstrates, these needs are sometimes mutually exclusive. When they are, the rule of exchange must override the need to keep
to oneself. If the rule of exchange is broken, someone must pay. The
community in the myth tries to make Getheren pay by exiling him, while
Getheren tries to make the community pay by cursing it with his name.
The community cannot survive in health with its law of exchange thus
challenged. Getheren himself can survive only by assuming a role and
joining another community—that is, by reaffirming the social law of
exchange. In the end, Getheren, rather than the Hearth, assumes responsibility for the suicide which denied the law of exchange. When he bears
the guilt he removes its onus from the Hearth. But the myth clearly shows
that if he had not done so the whole community might have perished.
The vow of the brothers initiates a *negative* exchange—the suicide, the
exile, and the curse. The myth shows that such denials of the law of
exchange result in the death of either the individual or the community
because both individuals and communities require exchange, not merely
for psychological health, but for continued existence.

A third myth in LHD explores the logic of exchange in a broader
context, between rather than within communities. Involved here is a
dispute over land between the Domain of Stok and the Domain of Estre
(chap. 9). One day Arek, the heir of Estre, skating over the ice, falls in,
barely pulls himself out, stumbles to a cabin nearby, and is discovered

nearly dead from the cold by Therem, the heir of Stok. Therem brings
Arek back to life by warming him with his own body. When the two lay
their hands together, they match. The two mortal enemies swear kemmering
together. After several days some of Therem's countrymen of Stok come
to the hut and, seeing Arek, murder him. But after a year, someone
arrives at the door of Arek's father, hands him a child, and tells him "This
is Therem, the son's son of Estre." Many years later this young man, who
has been named heir of Estre, is attacked on the ice by his three brothers,
who wish to reign themselves. All but dead from his fight with them he
enters a hut. There Therem of Stok binds the wounds of Therem of Estre.
Their hands match and they vow peace. When Therem of Estre recovers
and, after many years, becomes ruler of Estre, he gives half the disputed
lands to Stok and reconciles the two domains. Because of this action he is
called Estraven the Traitor.

Here the concept of exchange is demonstrated positively rather
than negatively; the ideal of unity is achieved, but at a price. The young
heirs, because they belong to warring domains, are not merely strangers
but mortal enemies. Yet instead of perpetuating destructive exchange
between their domains, they vow kemmering. Because they are the heirs
of their respective domains, their doing so mediates, metonymically, the
quarrel over the lands. Yet each respective domain refuses to follow the
rule of the heirs, preferring instead the rule of the domain, which, in
order to protect its own people and customs, denies the value of any
others. To this rule of exclusivity the heirs' love is sacrificed: Arek is
murdered and that act permanently separates the two heirs. Yet, because
Therem of Stok gives the son of that union to Estre, the breach between
the domains is healed. The warring communities are reconciled by that
gift, the son of the two enemies' love. His very name, Therem of Estre,
mediates between the two domains. His ironic title, "Estraven the Traitor," signifies the sacrifice involved in any system of positive exchange
between communities, between competing social systems. In order for a
man to reconcile competing social systems it is necessary to transcend the
definition of both,—that is, he must sacrifice his own social definition
and status in either.

A fourth myth, "On Time and Darkness," describes Orgota's god,
Meshe, who is said to be the center of time, the universal One. This ideal
of the One, which is apparent in the symbol of Meshe, stands behind all
the myths in LHD, and also behind the historical sections of the novel. In
the historical sections the ideal appears as both the political ideal, the
Ekumen, and the personal ideal, human intimacy. These ideals are social,
not supernatural. Rafail Nudelman has argued that the figure of Meshe,

like other symbols in LHD, implies a "second universe" where "objects and phenomena lay bare their hidden universal significance and supra-historical law of being." But Le Guin's myth relates to human beings. "We are the pupils of his Eye. Our doing is his Seeing: our being is his Knowing" (chap. 12). Meshe is supra-historical only in the sense that he is an imagined, mythical character. He is the image of exchange, which brings about the unification of individuals into communities and of communities into states and of states into the Ekumen. This kind of exchange may represent an ideal whose attainment is difficult, perhaps impossible; but it is not supernatural.

LHD finally rejects all static versions of the ideal, all temptations to escape time, even in its myths. The latter do not follow the tautological pattern either of the eternal return or of the eternal wandering. Instead, they define alienation within and between communities and then, without engaging in perfectly ideal solutions, demonstrate healthy systems of social exchange at work. The exchange is presumably endless, for new selves emerge, new choices are made, new oppositions are defined in the continuing process of history. And so new unities must be constantly achieved. These unities are fragile and momentary. Perfect coalition between men in LHD cannot be formalized in documents or solidified in government structures. Yet, as "On Time and Darkness" shows, such perfect coalition exists as a permanent ideal.

The myths of Getheren serve as a means for exploring the ideal of exchange by first embodying contradictories and then reconciling them. But the same myths also reflect normative patterns of exchange which actually appear in the "historical" sections of LHD. Estraven's unwillingness to pursue Karhide's interest in the Shinoath border dispute repeats the action of his ancestor, "Estraven the Traitor," who gave half the disputed land to Stok. "Estraven the Traitor" also predicts and illustrates the sacrifice involved in initiating such an exchange. Estraven fails as his ancestor, Therem of Stok, failed; before Karhide and Orgota unite, Estraven actually dies in the cause, as his ancestor, Arek of Estre, died. Before dying, he suffers the indignity of exile, recapitulating the pattern of "The Place Inside the Blizzard." Although the actions recounted in that myth replicate those of the novel's historical section, their meaning is there reversed. Estraven is exiled from Karhide not for "keeping to himself," an act which actually challenges the social system, but rather for exactly the opposite, for political exchange with a stranger. His exile leads to his journey on the ice. There, in a place inside the blizzard he meets Genly Ai: not a brother, but a stranger. In this intimate place they discover how to "mindspeak" one another's names. The exile Estraven, who bears responsibility for initiating not only his own but his country's exchange with the stranger, dies like the exile Getheren, who bears responsibility for refusing to exchange. Ironically, the penalty of initiating exchange and for refusing to exchange is the same. This is because too much exchange with "strangers"—those outside the community—produces the same outcome as too little exchange within the community. In either case, the community feels cheated of the full benefit of its member. Thus the pattern of exchange which the myths set up is repeated—sometimes with ironic outcome, sometimes not—in the historical content of the novel.

Other patterns set up in the mythic sections of LHD are also repeated in the historical ones. Although the history is told by specific perceivers, it is told by two distinct voices: an "alien" and a "traitor." Early in the book Genly Ai instructs the reader that the many voices are "all one, and if at moments the facts seem to alter with an altered voice, why then you can choose the fact you like best: yet none of them are false, and it is all one story" (chap. 1). This corresponds to the collective voice which the myths in the novel assume. Furthermore, the symbols in the historical sections are conspicuously the same as those in the myths: in both, Le Guin employs the same (aforementioned) contraries.

Most importantly the patterns set up in the myths serve as rules which guide and define the behavior of characters in the historical section. For example, when Estraven learns of his exile from Karhide, he considers returning home to Estre, but he does not. Instead, he quickly concludes "I was born to live in exile and my one way home [is] by way of dying." This easy conclusion seems not to tally with his courageous, stubborn political behavior in Karhide. But shortly after this episode we discover that his self-exile may have more to do with real guilt over incestuous vows than with the trumped-up political charge that he is a traitor. Estraven remarks to his kemmering that their vows were false because "the only true vow of faithfulness I ever swore was not spoken, nor could it be spoken" (chap. 6). Much later, at the conclusion of the novel, we discover that Estraven's earlier "true vow of faithfulness" was made to his brother. The vow, even though it is never verbalized, represents Estraven's reluctance to participate in the most important aspect of social exchange, the importance of which the reader will know from having read "The Place Inside the Blizzard." Accepting the logic of that myth, Estraven judges himself guilty and himself enforces the penalty which the myth prescribes, exile and eventual death. Of course, Estraven's guilt involves an intention, not an act. But the important thing is that the myths provide both the characters in the historical sections and the reader with rules for judging human behavior and with the logic behind such rules.

The most important rule is that of exchange, and its paradigmatic figure in the historical sections of the novel is Faxe the Weaver. He shows that it is possible to connect categorically unique human beings in religious ritual. Early in the novel Genly Ai describes this ritual, which thrives on "an old darkness, passive, anarchic, silent . . ." (chap. 5). Genly Ai himself becomes drawn into the web, which is masterfully woven and controlled by Faxe. This weaving ritual of brilliant intuitive intensity is paralleled very late in the book by Faxe's cool appearance as a politician in Karhide, expediting the official exchanges between citizens. Faxe the Weaver is the Karhidian equivalent of the Orgoreyn god, Meshe. At the level of politics and at the level of religion he promotes exchange—in some sense he symbolizes exchange. But it is always in history, in real human events not in some distant unchanging place or time.

The novel's imagery of the weaver and weaving shows that any ideal which attempts to fix the movement of time or to make human relationships rigid must be suspect. Productive human exchanges which weave people together into healthy communities are contrasted in the novel with quick, superficial unity: Estraven is replaced in Karhide by Tibe, whose dramatic appeals for unity depend upon his cooked-up threat of war. His superficial resemblance to both Meshe and Faxe the Weaver shows in his face, which is "masked with a net of fine wrinkles" (chap. 8). However, Tibe's face, along with his communications network, the radio, parodies the book's true relationships. A second parody of the novel's ideal becomes evident in the houses of Mishnory, which are "all built to a pattern" (chap. 8). The mesh is distorted into an optical illusion, focusing not on the connecting strands, but on the boxes they form. It emphasizes the emptiness, the vacuity, the unproductiveness of rigid order. Such rigidity is manifest in the Orgotan way of categorizing people and keeping track of them with papers. But perhaps the most powerful representation of unproductive human relationships is the cold trip Genly Ai takes with twenty-six silent Orgotians in the back of a truck which he describes as a "steel box" (chap. 13). In it he is taken to Pulefen Farm, where he and the other prisoners are kept in dull conformity by anti-kemmer drugs. Such imagery represents social ideals which do not take account of real exchange. Without such exchange the social structure calcifies and becomes rigid. According to Estraven, who brings about personal and political unity, that unity must be brought out of change: "The unexpected is what makes life possible," he tells Genly Ai (chap. 8). And he confesses in his notebook that his one gift is the ability to take advantage of flux and change: "I never had a gift but one, to know when the great wheel gives to a touch, to know and act" (chap. 14). Illegitimate unity suffocates, the novel shows; legitimate unity arises out of spontaneous human exchange.

Most crucially, then, the myths in LHD assert the impossibility of retreating from history and from human society. They insist that the goal of "keeping to oneself" in a fixed, temporal place is an impossible fantasy, a fantasy that must be sacrificed to the demands of communal exchange in history. This is implied by the pattern of exchange, the mediating of opposites, which underlies all myths. Truth arises out of conflict; the only legitimate unity is fragile and momentary. So Le Guin rejects static, cyclical structures. In her myths, as in the myths which Lévi-Strauss interprets, the oppositions define human problems, particularly problems with exchange; their mediation creates or maintains community. That these myths are fundamental to the meaning of the book is evident in the fact that the patterns they define account for most of the plot in the historical sections of the novel. The novel thus locates significance not in some static, timeless place, but in history; and its myths reflect social ideals which continually—and with difficulty—emerge from that history.

SUSAN WOOD

Discovering Worlds: The Fiction of Ursula K. Le Guin

Ursula K. Le Guin makes maps. The worlds she presents to her readers are various: Rocannon's World, where golden-haired warriors ride winged cats; Gethen, where ambisexual humans have built a civilization perfectly adapted to perpetual cold; Earthsea, where innumerable islands are home to wizards and dragons, goatherds and kings; Anarres, where anarchists strive to maintain life in the desert, and freedom in that life. Yet all the exotic, complex and varied societies Le Guin presents are really aspects of one world: ours, now. In the nine novels and numerous short works which she has written between 1962 and 1976, the exploration of imaginary worlds has provided a framework for an exploration of the varieties of physical life, social organizations, and personal development open to human beings. At the same time, this richness and variety suggest the ethical concept underlying her work: a celebration of life itself, through a joyful acceptance of its patterns. This concept is expressed not only in the works themselves, but in her vision of the artistic process which brought them forth.

It is easy to think of the science fiction and fantasy writer as a god: one who can create a world, fill it with life for the readers' amusement, and rest on the seventh day. Le Guin's working mode, however, is organic and intuitive, rather than planned; she acts like one of her League ethnographers, observing and reporting on the life form of new planets. She explains, for example, that she had no outlines, no plans of the island-world Earthsea and its languages, when she began to write her fantasy trilogy. She discovers people and places as they exist—in the writer's subconscious, in the truth and reality of their own being:

> This attitude towards action, creation, is evidently a basic one, the same root from which the interest in the *I Ching* and Taoist philosophy evident in most of my books arises. The Taoist world is orderly, not chaotic, but its order is not one imposed by man or by a personal or humane deity. The true laws—ethical and aesthetic, as surely as scientific— are not imposed from above by any authority, but exist in things and are to be found—discovered.

In turn, the discovery of this intrinsic order, on a personal level, forms the action of Le Guin's major works. In general, her characters are engaged in a quest, both a physical journey to an unknown goal which proves to be their home, and an inward search for knowledge of the one true act they must perform. The development of the plot, then, takes on a deeper significance than is usual in science fiction, with its emphasis on action for the sake of entertainment. The Le Guin character often initiates actions which have personal and social conseqences. The student-wizard Ged, in his pride, looses a spirit of unlike; the Ekumen envoy Genly Ai refuses to trust the one person who trusts him: and the fates of whole worlds are altered, as surely as they are by George Orr, who, in an effective dream, can wipe out six billion people. More important than the pattern of plot, however, is each character's movement to an understanding of this pattern: to an acceptance both of the integrity of each individual life, and of the place of each individual within the overall pattern of life.

This metaphor of discovery, of course, has limitations. A romantic definition, perhaps overly so, it appears to de-emphasize the importance of skill and craft in writing fiction. Discoveries, after all, may involve a slow and patient search for the right word: perhaps, as in the Earthsea trilogy, for the true name which will control the essence of the thing. Le Guin's work resonates with such definitive words: in *City of Illusions*, the presentation of the Shing stronghold, Es Toch, as a city "built across a chasm in the ground, a hollow place," both a literal chasm and a moral "abyss of self-destruction," a self-deluding lie; in *The Lathe of Heaven*, the description of George Orr in terms that recall *Tao* 37, as "a block of wood not carved," perfect in its integrity. A central and recurrent image is that of life as a pattern or web, with individual points of life joined by lines of communication. This image, with its strong ethical overtones—each life is, like a Gethenian, "singularly complete," but none exists in isolation—is echoed in a variety of symbols: the patterning frame, a foretelling device in *City of Illusions;* the web of tensions and communications woven by the Foretellers in *The Left Hand of Darkness;* the spells woven of words, movements, and human understanding in the Earthsea Trilogy; and the description of the Ekumen, the framework of human communication which Le Guin's future worlds evolve, as a "network" for trade in goods and ideas. Overall, the books are unified by the patterns formed from seeing black and white, darkness and light, self and other, death and life, not as opposites but as necessary complements in the harmony of existence. These recurrent image patterns, significant in themselves, serve also to describe and reinforce the underlying concepts of integrity and interdependence. All Le Guin's fiction works through imagery as well as content to question what a character in *The Left Hand of Darkness* sees as "the whole tendency to dualism that pervades human thinking."

In fact, Le Guin's fictions themselves are webs, woven of words, recurrent images and thematic patterns, moving always closer to an expression of a human truth, a vision of life. Her central figures—scientist, wizard, designer, or traveller—embody aspects of the artist seeking truth and expressing its patterns. Any full appreciation of her work, then, must embody an appreciation of its conscious craft: the patterning of *The Left Hand of Darkness* around the myth of its own world; the balancing of *The Dispossessed* between two planets and one movement of discovery; the careful cadencing of sentences. Le Guin's apparent delight in language becomes another means of celebrating human life. Thus style and structure are important elements of her work; her skill at handling them is a major contribution to the maturity of the field.

Le Guin's weakness is a paradoxical tendency to impose moral and ethical patterns on her work, so that form and content work against her philosophy. This didacticism is most evident in "The Word for World is Forest" (1972), "The Ones Who Walk Away from Omelas" (1972), and passages of *The Dispossessed.* The author's statement of values precludes their discovery, in contrast to the process, most notable in the Earthsea books, whereby the reader shares naturally in the characters' growing awareness of the right direction of their lives. Such a tendency is inevitable, however, given Le Guin's serious concern with human experience and conduct. It is this concern, usually embodied convincingly in individuals' actions and perceptions, which has made her one of the most notable writers to choose science fiction as a framework for discovery.

Ursula Le Guin's work, then, is mature art: rich and varied in content, skillful in presentation, joyous in its celebration of life, and, above all, thoughtful in approach, rooted in and developing a significant personal philosophy. The maturity is literal as well as literary.

Ursula Kroeber Le Guin was born in 1929, the daughter of anthropologist and author, A. L. Kroeber, and writer, Theodora Kroeber. The self-portrait she gives in an autobiographical essay in the British sf journal *Foundation* is that of a child happily surrounded by people who appreciated both other cultures and the spoken and written word as an augmentation of life. She collected her first rejection slip when twelve, from John W. Campbell, then editor of *Astounding*. The following twenty years included a Master's degree in French and Italian literature from Columbia, marriage to historian Charles Le Guin, the birth of three children, and the production of several published poems and unpublished novels. By the early 1960's when Cele Goldsmith Lalli began to buy such fantasies as "April in Paris" (1962), "The Word of Unbinding" (1964), and "The Rule of Names" (1964) for *Fantastic* and *Amazing*, Le Guin was an accomplished writer, expressing valuable insights with grace and humour.

Her rapid development as a writer from that point is best seen in *The Wind's Twelve Quarters* (1975), a collection of seventeen short stories first published between 1962 and 1974, highlighted by "Winter's King" (1969), "Nine Lives" (1969), and "Vaster Than Empires and More Slow" (1971). All are notable stories in which scientific extrapolations—sublightspeed travel and alien biology in the first and third stories, cloning in the second—provide a framework for powerful psychological studies.

In Le Guin's first three novels, *Rocannon's World* (1966), *Planet of Exile* (1966), and *City of Illusions* (1967), innovative and entertaining fictions develop on the solid conceptual basis of human values affirmed. *The Left Hand of Darkness* (1969) confirms its author's status as one of the major forces in contemporary science fiction. A work of great emotional power, impressive technical skill, and genuine social and psychological extrapolation, it won both the 1970 Nebula award of the Science Fiction Writers of America and the Hugo award of the 28th World Science Fiction Convention as the best novel of the year. It presents a new world in the distant future to challenge our view of the present, in particular our assumptions about male and female roles, about sexuality and love.

The next novel, *The Lathe of Heaven* (1971) brings readers back to to an all-too-possible near-future Earth: polluted, disease-ridden, self-destructive. Yet it avoids easy "relevance" to offer, again, a genuine alternative for human life: not a social blueprint, but a personal philosophy of right living. "The Word for World is Forest," which appeared in 1972 in Harlan Ellison's *Again, Dangerous Visions*, is unfortunately less successful in avoiding the limitations of moral outrage at contemporary problems. In Le Guin's most recent sf novel, *The Dispossessed* (1974), two worlds, the anarchist society of Anarres and a capitalistic nation on its sister-planet Urras, are tested through a scientist's search for truth, a couple's discovery of joy.

By 1975, Ursula Le Guin was acknowledged as a leader of the science fiction field: winner of three Nebula awards and three Hugo awards, she was the Guest of Honour at the 33rd World Science Fiction Convention in Melbourne, Australia—which presented her with a fourth Hugo for *The Dispossessed*. It seems fitting, however, that the major work of this mature writer, who is bringing a new adult concern with the living of life to science fiction, should be a work nominally for children: the Earthsea trilogy, composed of *A Wizard of Earthsea* (1968); *The Tombs of Atuan* (1971), a Newbery Honor Book; and *The Farthest Shore* (1972), winner of the National Book Award for Children's Literature. This work, which has won praise and professional honours, reconfirms the importance of fantasy as a timeless vehicle for examining basic human concerns: growth, maturity, and death.

The central concerns of Le Guin's work are evident in her first novel, *Rocannon's World*. The genesis of this colourful heroic fantasy is a short story, "The Dowry of Angyar," published in *Amazing* in 1964 and reprinted as the novel's Prologue. This story, Le Guin writes, became "the germ of a novel" when a minor character asserted his importance: " 'I'm Rocannon. I want to explore my world.' " It also introduced thematic concerns and characteristics of style developed in the later novels.

Most notable, perhaps, is the richness and variety of the world presented. Fomalhaut II is seen in a dual perspective, through the superficial "objective" summary of the League's *Abridged Handy Pocket Guide to Intelligent Life-forms* and the romantic presentation of Semley's heroic culture, scanned and dismissed by the League investigators. That culture is a tapestry of proud warriors on winged cat-like steeds; beautiful golden-haired women; laughing elfin creatures of sunlight, the Fiia; and lumpish troll-like creatures of night, the Gdemiar or Clayfolk—or, to the League scientists who so casually interfere with the destiny of planets, "the trogs."

The story unfolds with tragic inevitability. Semley, a highborn Angyar lady, seeks her dowry, a legendary necklace of sapphire and gold. Courageous, yet blindly arrogant, she trusts herself to the Clayfolk, whose technology she refuses to comprehend; thus she remains unaware that they have sent her on a sub-lightspeed flight of sixteen years to the nearest League world, Ollul. Here, Rocannon gives her back her necklace. Returning home after one subjective night, Semley discovers the cost of her quest: her husband long dead, her daughter grown, her dowry the burden

188 • SUSAN WOOD

of loss and madness. The mythically appropriate pattern of her fate is achieved (as is Argaven's in "Winter's King") by the scientific realities of sub-lightspeed travel; time, like other human truths, is subjective, mutable.

Semley's action, then, has consequences for herself and her kinfolk; and Le Guin, in her awareness of these consequences, finds the beginning of her novel. Semley's situation, in turn, had been partly created by League interference in her world. Rocannon, whose reading of the cursory League summary of the planet's cultures is ironically counterpointed by his growing interest in Semley, interferes in his turn with the planet's destiny—and so is claimed by the "tragic myth" Semley suggests to him. He forbids League contact while he mounts an ethnographic survey; and thus, in the years which elapse while he makes his sub-lightspeed journey, the unprotected planet is over-run by rebels who wipe out his expedition.

Rocannon, acknowledging his responsibility for events, undertakes a destructive quest for revenge. Like the Le Guin heroes who follow him—Falk, Estraven and Ged, especially—he becomes part of a mythic pattern, his destiny linking past and future to present. Seeking across unmapped continents for his enemies, he learns the secret of "mindhearing," a form of telepathic communication which enables him to complete his mission. Yet, like Semley, he must pay with the loss of that "which you hold dearest and would least willingly give," his friend Mogien's life. Mogien, however, is a warrior who senses, and joyfully accepts, the heroic death which fate holds for him. Moreover, Rocannon, in losing everything—friends, possessions, even his identity—is reborn from Zgama's fire as Olthor, the Wanderer, a hero of Angyar legend. His mission completed, he gains a new home on the world ultimately given his name. Where, then, does the freedom of individual action end, and the pattern of consequences merge into the pattern of fate or of myth? "How can you tell the fact from legend, truth from truth?" asks the storyteller beginning Semley's tale. The question foreshadows the specific opening of *The Left Hand of Darkness*, with its strikingly similar plot of journey through annihilation of self and sacrifice of life to new awareness and integration. It also announces one general thematic concern of Le Guin's novels: the nature of truth.

The most important element of *Rocannon's World*, as of *Planet of Exile* and *City of Illusions*, is not, however, philosophical speculation, but the richness and variety of the life presented. A whole novel could be written, for instance, about the telepathic Fiia, a humanoid race who "chose the green valleys, the sunlight, and the bowl of wood" when their kin, the Clayfolk, chose "night and caves and swords of metal"—and who know they have, by this choice, made themselves incomplete, "the Half-People." (In fact, the choices suggested here do gain fuller development in the fallen-Eden tale of "The Word for World is Forest.") Even within the limits of a short formula narrative, Le Guin exhibits a remarkable ability to communicate the essence of a culture—as, for example, when she sums up the proud Angyar as "lacking any first-person forms for the verb 'to be unable.' "

The language, too, complements the world it depicts. The ritual beauty of the Fiia's greetings of Semley—"Hail, Halla's bride, Kirienlady, Windborne, Semley the Fair"—contrasts effectively with Ketho the League curator's mumbled "She wants something we've got here in the museum, is that what the trogs say?" As the prosaic account of Rocannon evolves into the heroic tale of Olthor the Wanderer, the language becomes more rich and cadenced. Thus he is first seen looking at a "very tall, dark-skinned, yellow-haired woman" accompanied by "four uneasy and unattractive dwarves." He is last presented in language no more ornate, but subtly different, as he is different—the stuff of legend:

> When ships of the League returned to the planet, and Yahan guided one of the surveys south to Breygna to find him, he was dead. The people of Breygna mourned their Lord, and his widow, tall and fair-haired, wearing a great blue jewel set in gold at her throat, greeted those who came seeking him. So he never knew that the League had given that world his name.

Though Le Guin's style has evolved towards simplicity, it is still characterized by this flowing quality, a skillful use of cadence and sound patterns, and a flexible use of compound and complex sentences to state, elaborate, and qualify the variations of life and truth.

The exile's quest, a journey which leads physically home and spiritually to harmony, becomes Le Guin's basic narrative pattern. In *Planet of Exile,* the movements to integration are biological, as Terran genes slowly adapt to the alien world Werel; social, as Terrans and native Teverans ally at last against their common enemies, the marauding Gaal and the 5,000-night-long winter; and, most important, personal, as Jakob Agat and Rolery defy cultural taboos to marry. Both races, both individuals, thus gain a new "chance of life" in the midst of death. This life is affirmed in the sequel, *City of Illusions.* Here the exile Falk crosses a far-future North America, in the process stripped, like Rocannon, of every shred of his last life, including his name. His goal is the city of the Shing, his enemies who give him back his true name—Ramarren, Agat's heir, a leader of the high civilization his hybrid race has evolved on Werel. As the dualminded Falk/Ramarren, he resists Shing mind control, and thus exposes the lie by which they rule on Earth. Ramarren's return to Werel will bring, in turn, freedom back to the home world Terra, and to the League.

Another aspect of Le Guin's concern with harmony is her emphasis on communications devices and techniques, both for themselves and for their symbolic importance. Sub-lightspeed travel can bridge the abyss of space. The ansible, a device which "will permit communication without any time interval between two points in space," allows ideas to "leap the great gaps of spacetime." Mindspeech, or paraverbal communication, bridges the isolation of individuals "like a touch across the abyss." All these suggest, finally, the state of being "in touch": that primary communication within the self, the integration of conscious and unconscious minds and the self-knowledge which, repeatedly, enables the central character to cross the abyss of despair, to "get through nothingness and out the other side."

The multiplicity and inter-relationship of these concepts, and the flexibility of the image expressing them, provides a useful insight into Le Guin's process of exploring ideas. The Dispossessed, for example, opens with Shevek crossing the void of space like a flung stone, an image suggesting his social and physical exile by recalling both the rocks flung at him as he leaves and his last sight of Anarres as "a ball of white stone falling down into blackness." His awareness of this isolation plunges him into a depression, presented in images corresponding with his physical situation aboard the interplanetary freighter: "For hours or days he existed in a vacancy, a dry and wretched void without past or future. The walls stood tight about him. Outside them was the silence." The abyss is thus associated with the book's local image of the ambiguous wall, the created and chosen prison cutting off all human communication. In fact, Shevek's primary isolation here is from his own sense of integrity, the awareness of freedom and accompanying responsibility basic to Odonian society. He feels that "he had given up his birthright of decision. It was gone, fallen away from him along with his world, the world of the Promise, the barren stone." Despair is deepened by a fever in which he hangs "in a limbo between reason and unreason, no man's land."

The flung stone, however, also suggests Shevek's independent discovery of Zeno's Paradox, and thus his role as physicist. By asserting his right to work and to share the results of that work, he transcends the abyss of despair—and gains freedom to create. In turn, by transcending the "prison" of provable theory, he achieves the vision in which he sees the fundamental unity, not only of two apparently opposed views of reality, but of the universe itself; "at this instant the difference between this planet and that, between Urras and Anarres, was no more significant to him than the difference between two grains of sand on the shore of the sea. There were no more abysses, no more walls. There was no more exile. He had seen the foundations of the universe, and they were solid." In personal and scientific terms this vision of "simplicity which contained in it all complexity" is "the way clear, the way home, the light." Its practical application is the ansible which makes possible the League of All Worlds and the Ekumen, webs of communication stretched across the abyss of space and cultural difference.

Le Guin's science fiction also presents a future history consistent with its philosophy in stressing both the interdependence of life and the variety of its possible forms. Intelligent human life, in this cosmography, arose millenia ago on the planet Hain, which established innumerable colonies. Each colony-planet became "the world" to "the men" after Hainish civilization collapsed. By 2300 A.D., which Ian Watson postulates as the date of *The Dispossessed*, a revived Hainish culture possessing sub-lightspeed travel has contacted eight worlds. The ansible facilitates creation of the League of All Worlds, a trade union and super-government. In "The Word for World is Forest," scientists of the eighteen-year old League end Terran exploitation of Athshe. "Vaster Than Empires and More Slow," set in "the earliest decades of the League," shows the Terrans, who resent the fact that Hainish "not only founded but salvaged" their civilization, mounting expeditions to seek "truly alien worlds." In an effective image, the misfits of the Extreme Survey crew are pictured entering their vessel by wriggling through the coupling tube one by one "like apprehensive spermatozoa trying to fertilize the universe." What they discover is a perfectly integrated alien intelligence, the tree-world 4470; what they learn from it is the need, not to dominate the universe, but to accept and love another being unreservedly. "Nine Lives," also set in the early years of Terran expansion, presents the same discovery as two mining engineers isolated on a hostile world, learn to respond to an alien/human being, the ten-clone John Chow, and in turn teach love of the other to one unit of that clone. In its extrapolation of the psychological implications of a biological advance, as well as in its characterization and skillful narration, this is probably Le Guin's finest short story.

Rocannon's World, set some 300 years after the League's foundation, chronicles two major developments. The League appears to have developed as an authoritarian government, levying taxes on new worlds to equip forces against the mysterious alien Enemy; inevitably its unthinking use of power breeds rebels. On the positive side, however, Rocannon does learn the teachable skill of mindhearing, with its potential for creating true understanding. In *Planet of Exile*, set in "year 1405 of the League of All Worlds," the Terran colony on Werel has been isolated for 600 Earth-years by the Shing advance; in *City of Illusions*, 1200 years later, the end of this isolation begins when Werel sends an expedition back to the homeworld. As Zove tells Falk, the latter's mission is to restore hope to a world which fears its own past greatness as much as it fears the Shing: "We keep a little knowledge, and do nothing with it. But once we used that knowledge to weave the pattern of life like a tapestry across night and chaos. We enlarged the chances of life. We did man's work." In *The Left Hand of Darkness*, the Hainish worlds have been undertaking this work for 1491 Ekumenical years.

The Ekumen, like the viable anarchistic society of Anarres, reveals Le Guin's power to envision genuine alternatives to present human organizations. Genly Ai, the Ekumen envoy, describes the government he serves as "not a kingdom but a co-ordinator, a clearing-house for trade and knowledge" uniting 3,000 nations on eighty-three worlds, seeking an alliance with the Gethenian nations for many reasons: " 'Material profit. Increase of knowledge. The augmentation of the complexity and intensity of the field of intelligent life. The enrichment of harmony and the greater glory of God. Curiosity. Adventure. Delight.' " Ai's own experience of exile and acceptance enables him to understand the Ekumen and its reasons for sending him to Gethen alone:

> Alone, I cannot change your world. But I can be changed by it. . . . Alone, the relationship I finally make, if I make one, is not impersonal and not only political: it is individual, it is personal, it is both more and less than political. Not We and They; not I and It; but I and Thou. Not political, not pragmatic, but mystical. In a certain sense the Ekumen is not a body politic, but a body mystic. It considers beginnings to be extremely important. Beginnings, and means. Its doctrine is just the reverse of the doctrine that the end justifies the means. It proceeds, therefore, by subtle ways, and slow ones, and queer, risky ones; rather as evolution does, which is in certain senses its model.

The promise of this "mystical" and individual relationship with the human community of the Ekumen motivates Estraven to sacrifice his life to further Ai's mission. This promise finds its expression in the love which bridges the abyss between Ai and Estraven; its fulfillment in "the delight, the courage" with which individual Karhiders welcome "the coming of men from the stars"; and its symbol in the bridge whose keystone is mortared with blood.

The future Earths of other works—notably *The Lathe of Heaven* and

"The New Atlantis" (1975)—exist in different cosmogenies. They are, however, broadly consistent with the post-collapse Terra of the League's formative years, a "discord" in which life continues only through "the absolute regimentation of each life towards the goal of racial survival." More important, the action and underlying values of the non-Hainish works, especially of the Earthsea trilogy, always point to the same philosophy of harmony and balance.

Le Guin's Hainish future history resembles, in broad outline, the pattern of spaceflight-Galactic Empire-Interregnum-Rise of a Permanent Galactic Civilization which Donald Wollheim identifies as basic to science fiction. Yet the very fact that Hain, not ruined Terra, is the prime world challenges readers' assumptions. Even the League involves not domination of the universe by our descendants, but acceptance of a larger pattern of life. The Ekumen, in turn, offers a genuine alternative to the standard idea of the military/economic empire evolving to "challenge" creation.

Criticism of xenophobia, the racial expression of fear of the other, is implicit in Le Guin's future history. The opening pages of *Planet of Exile*, for example, call into question the nature of "humanity." The centre of consciousness is Rolery, a native woman exploring, with fear and fascination, the city "imagined by alien minds." These others, the "grinning black false-men" with their eyes of an "unearthly darkness," are soon revealed to be "human" in the reader's terms. They are Terran colonists who, even after 600 years, hold aloof from the natives whom they regard contemptuously as non-human, "just hilfs." The separation of these races, and their potential for union, is powerfully suggested when Rolery and Jakob Agat touch light palm to dark palm in "the salute of equals." Specifically the gesture recalls Agat's rescue of Rolery from the abyss and foreshadows their communication in love and mindspeech "like a touch across the abyss." Generally it foreshadows the interbreeding of races to produce the new civilization which restores the League. This basic human gesture of touching hands recurs throughout Le Guin's work. In *The Lathe of Heaven*, for example, Heather Lelache confirms her liking for George Orr with a handshake which reminds her of her mother's SNCC button, black and white hands joined.

The Left Hand of Darkness, in particular, questions the nature of "humanity" by challenging assumptions about sexuality and sex roles. King Argaven rejects alliance with "all those nations of monsters living out in the Void" as "a disgusting idea . . . I don't see why human beings here on earth should want or tolerate any dealings with creatures so monstrously different" from the Gethenian ambisexual norm. Here, too, the action presents Genly Ai—specifically as "earth-coloured," darker-skinned than the Gethenians—learning to accept and "touch" one member of an alien race. The wholeness in dualism which Gethen offers is, in turn, expressed through images of touch in Tormer's Lay:

> Light is the left hand of darkness and darkness the right hand of light.
> Two are one, life and death, lying together like lovers in kemmer, like
> hands joined together, like the end and the way.

The touch confirming the acceptance of the other, then, is part of the larger image pattern of light and darkness, opposition and integration, which resonates throughout Le Guin's work. In specific terms, it signals a social and personal harmony. Thus the movement of *Planet of Exile* is a joyous one, culminating in Agat's realization that "these were his people. He was no exile here." The counterbalancing movement is tragic, tracing the consequences of disharmony in dislocation and breakdown. In "The Word for World is Forest," notably, the world-dominating Terran culture is represented by the soldier Don Davidson. Disastrously insecure in his identity, he believes that "the only time a man is really and entirely a man is when he's just had a woman or just killed another man." Davidson is so completely unbalanced that he can only continue to exist by imposing his will on the external world, clearing the forest which he fears and killing the Hainish-stock humanoid natives whom he dismisses as sub-human "creechies." In contrast, the Athshean world is harmonious. The forest presents a delicate ecological balance of trees and water, shadow and sunlight; its people maintain sanity "not on the razor's edge of reason but on the double support, the fine balance, of reason and dream."

Inevitably, Davidson's insanity grows; the paranoid conviction that every living thing is his enemy leaves him in a mental isolation confirmed by physical exile to the Terran-made desert of Dump Island. The real tragedy, however, is not his fate but the perpetuation of his madness in Athshean culture. Led by Davidson's counterpart, the dreamer Selver, the Athsheans learn to preserve themselves by exterminating their killers—whom they identify, ironically, as non-human "yumens." Their real fall into the world of experience comes, the story suggests, not with the actual acts of murder but with the prior process of objectification. This produces a split between the I and the not-I, and thus makes the idea of murder possible. If, as Northrop Frye suggests, the basic reaction of the (Western) human mind is to "see the world as objective, as something set over against you and not yourself or related to you in any way," then Le Guin's novels in all their elements—cosmography, imagery, character development, resolution—offer an alternative to that process.

It is evident, then, that Ursula K. Le Guin's work possesses a thematic and conceptual interdependence consistent with her philosophy. Discussion of any one element, or any one novel, quickly leads to a branching network of cross-references and examples. Nevertheless, within the overall pattern, each work explores a unique aspect of the human problem of right living, on and in response to a unique world.

Gethen, named Winter by the Ekumen's investigators, is the most richly detailed of Le Guin's worlds, and the strangest. Here, human beings have evolved complex civilizations which have been profoundly influenced by two factors: a physical condition of almost perpetual winter, and a human condition of periodic ambisexuality. These realities, in turn, provide metaphors which echo the central movement in from imbalance to harmony, as the alien/human Genly Ai, Ekumen envoy to Gethen, learns to accept the winter-world, to love one of its alien/human people, and to know harmony and joy within his divided self.

The first investigators named the new planet Winter, and noted that "the dominant factor in Gethenian life is not sex or any other human thing: it is their environment, their cold world. Here man has a crueler enemy even than himself." Life exists in a precarious balance with death. Individuals move as tiny dark shadows across a blinding backdrop of white, and move through their society in the complex prestige-relationships of *shifgrethor*, a term which "comes from an old word for *shadow*." They seek refuge from the "bright winter, bitter, terrible and bright" in the warm dark circle of the communal Hearth, whose unity forms their primary social organization. The Hearth's fires exist, however, "to warm the spirit and not the flesh," since the Gethenians rely on adaption, "physiological weatherproofing," rather than central heating. In thirty centuries of technological progress, they have developed electricity and other efficient devices like the Chabe stove, which emits heat and light; yet change proceeds slowly, carefully, and Winter remains "a world where a common table implement is a little device with which you crack the ice that has formed on your drink between drafts." Gethenians are, however, losing this precarious balance. Having evolved to some degree of control over their world, they are becoming each other's enemies: family Hearths are uniting into the large rival nations of Orgoreyn and Karhide, abandoning their local feuds to mobilize for war. Love of one's own country is becoming "hate of one's uncountry." Estraven, Prime Minister of Karhide, the only Gethenian who trusts Ai, welcomes him for bringing a "new option": unity for Gethen within the diversity of the Ekumen. Yet, ironically, the Envoy sent alone to form a personal bond with Gethen is an individual unable to make that rapport. "I've been cold ever since I came to this world," he tells Estraven, walking away from their crucial meeting "cold, unconfident, obsessed by perfidy, and solitude, and fear." Self-alienated, he can only see Estraven as an alien, and mistrust him on, ultimately, the basis of his own sexual confusion.

Estraven, as a Gethenian, is potentially ambisexual, a man (a wielder of power) who is also a woman. Ai, even after two years on Gethen, can only see a Gethenian "self-consciously . . . first as a man, then as a woman, forcing him into those categories so irrelevant to his nature and so essential to my own." Yet human women are truly aliens to him. Thus he mistrusts Estraven, regarding those signals and actions which arise from the complications of shifgrethor as a "womanly" performance, "all charm and tact and lack of substance, specious and adroit. Was it in fact this soft supple femininity that I disliked and distrusted in him?"

Gethenians, in fact, are neither men nor women, but potentially either. Sexually neutral and androgynous most of the month, each regularly enters an estrus period, *kemmer,* becoming male or female as hormone changes dictate. Thus sex roles and their corresponding social behavior cannot exist; and responsibilities, notably parenthood, are shared. Dualism becomes not the sexual alienation Ai feels, but the basic relationship of "I" and "thou."

Yet the dualism persists for the reader. Prime ministers and secret agents, pulling sledges, wearing breeches in the cold, represented always in Ai's narrative by the masculine/generic pronoun "he": the Gethenians too easily seem men who, jarringly, are sometimes women. "The king was pregnant." The reader's own preconceptions, plus Le Guin's admitted failure to show "the 'female' component of the Gethenian characters in *action,*" make it too easy to envision a Gethenian as Ai does, forcing each into the "irrelevant" categories of man and woman.

It is not possible, as David Ketterer suggests, to paraphrase the action of *The Left Hand of Darkness* adequately without mentioning Gethenian ambisexuality. That action, echoing the novel's central concepts, is unified, a circle; yet it is also dual, internal, and external. Genly Ai completes his journey from Karhide, through Orgoreyn, over the Ice, back to Erhenrang where—with dramatic rightness, but perhaps unconvincing haste given his earlier hesitations—he completes his mission by welcoming the Ekumen ambassadors to the planet. This action fuses the archetype of the winter-journey through death to rebirth with specific Gethenian myths of "The Place Inside the Blizzard" and "Estraven The Traitor": tales of betrayal and higher loyalty which, in turn, find literal expression in Estraven's own fate. In this fusion, the action unites the inner and outer worlds. Ai's journey is not just a simple hero-tale of Man against Ice, though the physical hardships are effectively presented, as the thermometer drops each morning to "somewhere between zero and − 60°" and the sledge sticks yet again. Rather, the shared exile and danger of that journey enable him to move, at last, to an understanding of Gethen, made possible only by an acceptance of the individual's, Estraven's, sexuality.

Genly Ai, like most narrators, unconsciously reveals his own character in his observations about others. The reader assumes the Ekumen envoy will be wise, experienced. It is a shock to realize that Ai is only thirty, and naive, especially in his dealings in Orgoreyn. His chief limitation is the ignorance and fear of female sexuality which lead him to mistrust, not just Estraven but most Gethenians, seeing them as males with certain negative traits he identifies as female. Thus he describes his building superintendent, father of four, as "my landlady, a voluble man," an individual "feminine in looks and manners" with "a soft fat face and a prying, spying, ignoble, kindly nature." His profound mistrust of Estraven continues even after the latter has rescued him from certain death in Pulefen Voluntary Farm. Both sit, exiles, aliens, in a tent on the Ice, in warmth and light surrounded by death: alone. Ai muses:

> What is a friend, in a world where any friend may be a lover at a new phase of the moon? Not I, locked in my virility; no friend to Therem Harth, or any other of his race. Neither man nor woman, neither and both, cyclic, lunar, metamorphosing under the hand's touch, changelings in the human cradle, they were no flesh of mine, no friends: no love between us.

Yet just as the reality of Gethen shaped its societies and the myths by which its people express human truths, so the actual experience of the winter-journey enables Ai to accept Estraven, to forge the personal bond uniting worlds. His awareness of the Gethenians as "isolated, and undivided" on a hostile world lacking even highly-evolved animals, leads to an understanding of their holistic worldview and Terran dualism: matters which do "go even wider than sex . . ." He also begins to recognize his own sexual alienation. Significantly, the episode is presented from Estraven's point of view, emphasizing the isolation of each individual, their growing understanding. When the physical realities of tent life force the two to deal with the sexual tension between them, Ai is finally able to accept Estraven as the latter has always accepted him: as a whole human being. Their trust and love are confirmed not by sexual contact which "would be for us to meet once more as aliens," but by the subtler touch of mindspeech:

"a bond, indeed, but an obscure and austere one, not so much admitting further light (as I had expected it to) as showing the extent of the darkness."

Finally, when Ai tries to walk in the white void of shadowless snow, the place "inside the blizzard" where even the senses are traitors, he fully comprehends the dualism which complements Gethenian wholeness. " 'We need the shadows in order to walk,' " even though each shadow, in the Orgota creation myth, is the death which follows each mortal over the eternal ice of the world. Ai sees the Gethenians as uniting all opposites, like the Terran yin-yang symbol: "Light, dark. Fear, courage. Cold, warmth. Female, male . . . Both and one. A shadow on snow'."

Unfortunately Ai's insight, like his rapport with Estraven, remains incomplete. By the novel's end he can accept Faxe the Weaver as a "person," but, like Gulliver, he rejects his fellow human beings as "great apes with intelligent eyes, all of them in rut, in kemmer." Ironically, it is as a self-made alien again that he brings the unique humans of Gethen into the fully human community of the Ekumen—an action confirming that dualism and harmony which only Estraven fully understands. In turn, these concepts, central to Le Guin's work, arise naturally from the interplay of action, setting, metaphor and myth.

The narration which Ai presents embodies another of Le Guin's concerns. "I'll make my report as if I told a story, for I was taught as a child on my homeworld that Truth is a matter of the imagination," he begins. Indeed, his viewpoint influences the reader's view of the Gethenians. Moreover, as he adds, "The story is not all mine, nor told by me alone." Balancing perspectives are provided, for example, by the scientific, yet inevitably personal, comments of the Investigator Ong Tot Oppong in Chapter 7. The introduction of Estraven's journal, beginning with the chapter "One Way Into Orgoreyn," alternating with Ai's account of the same events, starting with the chapter "Another Way Into Orgoreyn," creates irony and suspense. It also develops the theme of communication, as misunderstanding, mistrust, and misplaced trust build to their crisis. Most important, Estraven's diary develops an understanding of his character as he methodically records their progress and reviews his life—all the while making his own winter journey to the death which will end his exile from Estre, which will reunite him with Arek his brother and lover whose "shadow" follows him through life.

The introduction of the Gethenian myths lifts the individual actions on which they comment into the wider context of human truth. In what sense, for example, was Estraven a "traitor"? In what sense was his fate freely chosen (and possibly, in Gethenian terms, a contemptible suicide)? In what sense was it the inevitable end of a pattern of conflicting loyalties and loves, since, as he writes, "I was born to live in exile . . . and my one way home was by way of dying"? In what sense is the whole account another journey made by Genly Ai, trying to rediscover the joy he knew on that painful journey which was "the real center of my own life"?

All of Le Guin's major novels, in fact, present protagonists who are trying to find the "real center" of their lives. George Orr of *The Lathe of Heaven* loses his intrinsic balance when, involuntarily, he begins to create worlds. The novel's opening view of an overcrowded, polluted, rainwashed Portland of April 2002 is depressingly plausible. Yet it is also Orr's creation. Since puberty, he has had "effective" dreams—dreams which become reality. He alone possesses the knowledge of other truths. One is of a world which ended in nuclear holocaust in April 1998: the reality of the void, in which there is "nothing left. Nothing but dreams." Heather Lelache, who loves him and has stood with him at the center of reality as worlds shifted, denies this truth in a fury of fear:

> Maybe that's all it's ever been! Whatever it is, it's all right. You don't suppose you'd be allowed to do anything you weren't supposed to do, do you? Who the hell do you think you are! There is nothing that doesn't fit, nothing happens that isn't supposed to happen. Ever! What does it matter whether you call it real or dreams? It's all one—isn't it?

The novel's crisis develops as Orr's worlds cease to be "one," losing their continuity as the psychiatrist William Haber plays God with his dreams.

George Orr, the dreamer, is "the man in the middle of the graph," whose perfect balance may be seen as either "self-cancellation" or "a peculiar state of poise, of self-harmony." His proper occupation is as a designer, one whose talent is "the realization of proper and fitting forms for thing." His effective dreams may follow this function; but if they are manipulated, they create chaos. Characteristically, Orr recognizes his power, and his "obligation" to "use it only when I must." Heather Lelache, needing strength, is drawn to Orr, recognizing in him the "wholeness of being" of "a block of wood not carved . . . He was the strongest person she had ever known, because he could not be moved away from the center." Yet even she, who believes like Orr that "there is a whole of which one is a part, and that in being a part one is whole," is moved by compassion to undertake the "unimaginable responsibility" of using his power. Her interference precipitates the Alien invasion, which brings immediate disaster and ultimate aid.

To an individual with "no center to him," who (like Don Davidson) defines himself "solely by the extent of his influence over other people," Orr's power is irresistibly tempting. William Haber represents the rational, progressive Western mind, trying to "make a better world." His arguments sound so familiar, so acceptable that even Orr doubts himself, and so yields up responsibility to his irresponsible "bear-god-shaman." "What's wrong with changing things?" Haber asks. Orr can only reply that:

> We're in this world, not against it. It doesn't work to try to stand outside things and run them, that way. . . . There is a way, but you have to follow it. The world *is*, no matter how we think it ought to be. You have to be with it. You have to let it be.

His words, like Heather's perception of him, unconsciously paraphrase the Tao, though as a true sage he has no formal knowledge of the Eastern philosophies Haber so contemptuously dismisses. The Taoist philosophy of unaction infuses the novel; quotations from Lao Tsu and Chuang Tse introduce specific chapters; yet *The Lathe of Heaven* is not a philosophic tract but a novel whose characters and events illustrate the wisdom which Orr and the Aliens know: "What comes is acceptable."

Haber, in his "conscious, careful planning for the good of all," dismisses individuals: Orr, whom he despises as a tool; Heather, whose death he, chillingly, welcomes. Thus the worlds he creates are all flawed, lacking freedom, joy and, finally, validity. They reflect the "void" at the center of his being, which, in his "effective nightmare," spreads to engulf reality. In this crisis Orr, by "the power of will, which is indeed great when exercised in the right way at the right time," acts as he must. Supported by the love he shared with Heather, and "a little help from [his] friends" the Aliens, he moves through the void to end the breakdown caused by Haber's dream. Following his necessary way through certain loss, he finds that, as E'enemenen Asfah observes, "There are returns"—to Heather, and to joy.

When Gaveral Rocannon, in despair, asserted that "In times like this . . . one man's fate is not important," his companion Mogien retorted: "If it is not . . . what is?" Each of Le Guin's novels shows the importance of individual life. In *The Lathe of Heaven*, as in *The Left Hand of Darkness*, form works with content, as the constantly changing point of view allows Haber and Heather Lelache (who is intensely alive in some worlds, non-existent in others) to add their interpretations of reality to Orr's. The style, too, emphasizes the ordinary, the human. When Heather, rediscovering Orr, asks if "this mess" is the best world he can dream, he replies: "It'll have to do." The exchange is typical, phrased in the everyday language of real people—in contrast with the heightened language with which Le Guin describes Orr's heroic, necessary act. The characters move through events of increasing drama and unreality, but it is their lives, and not those events, which matter after all. Thus Orr and Heather, in the wilderness, debate the nature of reality. However, it is by scrupulously sharing the five eggs which his depopulated dream-world has provided for them that they assert reality—the validity of individual perception and experience.

Local images drawn from the novel's world, and from nature, also serve as ties to a basic reality. (Significantly, though the political and social situations Haber creates by his manipulations grow worse and worse, human nature and the shape of the continents remain unchanged.) The erupting volcano, Mt. Hood, literally and metaphorically suggests the destructive force of Haber's irresponsible will to power. The constant Portland rain and mist suggest the uncertainty, the fluidity of life itself. Another recurring image is that of the sea, of time and the unconscious, in which the turtle-like Aliens, who can control effective dreaming, swim in their element. Orr, to Haber an irresponsible "moral jellyfish," is also at home in this sea, like a fragile creature which "has for its defence the violence and power of the whole ocean, to which it has entrusted its being, its going and its will." *The Lathe of Heaven,* like Le Guin's other novels, shows that this chosen surrender is the right "way" for human life to follow.

"To go is to return," observes E'enemenen Asfah; and Odo, whose search for freedom begins a revolution, also knows that "True journey is return." The Odonian Shevek of Le Guin's most recent novel, *The Dispossessed,* crosses other oceans of space and time, following his way home. His story, in structure and in theme, can in fact be represented by the green Circle of Life, symbol of the Odonian movement.

The controlling image of *The Dispossessed,* however, is the divisive wall of uncut rocks surrounding the spaceport on Anarres. For the Odonians, the anarchists whose ancestors colonized the planet seven generations before, the physical boundary represents the ideological wall separating them from the anarchist societies of their homeworld, Urras. "Like all walls it was ambiguous, two-faced. What was inside it and what was outside it depended upon which side of it you were on." Thus the wall functions as a political, social, and personal symbol, not of the absence of freedom, but of the rejection of freedom. Choice, and the acceptance of human commitments, are basic to Odo's vision of freedom. Thus "a promise is a direction taken," fidelity a chosen limitation "essential in the complexity of freedom." Yet the world of the Promise has become a world of imposed denial: of truth, of the past, of the future. The Odonians are taught, from 150-year-old films, to reject Urras utterly as "disgusting, immoral, excremental." They will not return from their self-exile to offer Urras the hope of their new society; nor will they let Urrasti individuals or ideas cross their walls. Thus Odo's ongoing revolution goes nowhere: "To deny is not to achieve." In general, the Odonians increasingly are rejecting freedom, in particular freedom of thought, for the rule of custom and of bureaucracy. Equally, the Urrasti have rejected the future represented by the Odonians, hiding them on the Moon just as they hid poverty and misery under the gracious trappings of their world.

Individual Odonians, too, reject freedom by denying responsibility for their actions. Sabul, who steals Shevek's ideas and blocks his development, is a self-aggrandizing hypocrite. Shevek, too, gives up his book to Sabul and his freedom to the Urrasti, accepting an authority he does not recognize as valid; as a result he becomes psychologically incapable of creating until he reasserts his own will. Thus the walls are not built by any failure of Odonian theory, but by flaws in human nature, especially "the will to dominance [which] is as central in human beings as the impulse to mutual aid is."

Shevek and the other members of the Syndicate of Initiative are unique in their commitment to the autonomy of conscience, and in their acceptance of the social ostracism with which Odonians punish the unofficial crime of "egoizing" or being different from the group. Shevek's social function as a dissident proceeds, as it must, from his personal experience of imprisoning a fellow-student and learning how "disgusting" such power over another could be. Even earlier, the wall became a nightmare symbol for him, triggered by a teacher's rejection of his creativity but associated also with his mother Rulag's denial of her promise to him and her partner. In the nightmare, the wall vanishes when a "voice of dear familiarity" shows him "the cornerstone . . . the primal number" and he knows with a "rush of joy" that he is "home." The episode foreshadows the vision which enables him to see the unity of time and, in a visionary and literal way, go "home."

Thus Shevek's actions as a scientist and Odonian are rooted clearly in individual experience. Like George Orr, he derives the strength to act from the personal bond of human love. He and Takver share a partnership which brings them deep suffering when the social emergencies of the Famine separate them; but which also brings them, in their reunion, "joy . . . the completion of being." This joy brings Shevek a wider social vision of human beings stepping outside the selfish search for pleasure—"a closed cycle, a locked room, a cell"—into "the landscape of time, in which the spirit may, with luck and courage, construct the fragile, make-shift, improbable roads and cities of fidelity: a landscape inhabitable by human beings." On the intellectual level, this suggests Shevek's scientific theory, which, like loyalty, binds "time into a whole." On the political and philosophical level, Takver and Shevek's partnership is mirrored in and by the Odonian experiment itself, in which individuals, working in solidarity, have transformed the desert into a human world. In fact, Shevek, like Odo, embodies the anarchist ideal. Takver suggests that the Syndicate of Initiative should walk away from the wall of convention and "go make an Anarres beyond Anarres, a new beginning." Shevek offers the Urrasti revolutionaries, and all the Hainish worlds, his freedom to "be the Revolution." His success is signalled when the Hainish officer Ketho accepts the risks of walking through the wall on Anarres, to experience freedom for himself.

The multileveled symbol of the wall, then, like the single figure of the man Shevek, ties together the complex strands of the stories Le Guin presents: of the man growing up to find his true way, of the partner affirming his fidelity, of the anarchist embodying an ideal of freedom, of a scientist developing a theory which, in practical terms, will unify human civilizations. This interwoven structure suggests and reflects the unity of Odonian society, composed of complex and multileveled bonds between the self and others.

Dualism, the self-exiling division between self and surrounding world, is also an important idea which provides Le Guin with a structural concept. Most of the important background information is presented in debate: for example in Shevek's discussion with Oii's family in Chapter 5. The initial discussion between Shevek and Kimoe establishes the sexism and social inequality of Urras, the equality of Anarres. Bedap's angry debate with Shevek in Chapter 6 clarifies the flaws in Odonian society. The book begins with the physical clash at the spaceport wall as the Odonians attack the traitor/revolutionary Shevek. It culminates in the violent confrontation between the Urrasti marches and the armed govern-ment forces; and in the personal confrontation between Keng and Shevek, who forces her to abandon the inertia of despair for the commitment of hope.

Above all, *The Dispossessed* employs an overall structure of opposi-tion and reconciliation. The first chapter presents Shevek leaving his home; the last, his return, "the promise kept," to Anarres. Like Rocannon, Falk/Ramarren, and especially Genly Ai—who brings the end of the old world "with him in his empty hands—Shevek appears as the messianic "Forerunner . . . a stranger, an outcast, an exile, bearing in empty hands the time to come." Between, the even-numbered chapters chronicle his growing disillusionment with Urras; the odd-numbered chapters, in a long flashback, tell the parallel story of his disillusion with Anarres, so that the moment of his decision to go to Urras is presented immediately before his return. As the Australian critic George Turner observes, this structure not only allows a point-by-point comparison of the two cultures, but points to a general political/philosophical concern: how can a strong individual like Shevek fit into *any* system, or successfully reconcile the public and private morality?

Though *The Dispossessed* seems to imply that the individual and social worlds, like Anarres and Urras, cannot be united, its tone is not despairing. Perhaps its finest achievement is its tough-mindedness, the willingness to pose difficult questions, accept the impossibility or failure of solutions, and still, with hope, seek answers. Anarres is neither a utopia, an impossible no-place, nor a dystopia; rather it is a functioning, and convincing, society. Shevek and Takver are recognizable Le Guin characters—the truth-seeking scientist, the artist and complete person who intuitively senses the unity of life. Yet they are individuals, shaped by Odonian society, which comes alive through them.

The Dispossessed is an ambitious novel, attempting to present an individual, two societies, and an ideal of human life. Inevitably, Le Guin cannot maintain equal control and depth throughout; and so the idea dominates. Urras, the ur-world, is much less convincing than Anarres. Too arbitrarily the antithesis of Odonian ideals, too closely a critique of contemporary North America's flaws, it cannot present an effective challenge to test Anarres. Moreover, it is presented entirely through Shevek's extremely limited perceptions; the uprising in Nio Esseia surprises him, and fails to convince the readers.

Shevek's speculations on government and on human relations, too, often become uncomfortably didactic—or move into generalized discussions and analyses. The novel moves in a confusing manner between center-of-consciousness narration with an individual voice presenting ideas rooted in specific human actions and perceptions, to omniscient narration from an undefined point of view and background, presenting generalized observations. For example, a three-page discussion of partnership within Odonian society contains such general statements as:

> To maintain genuine spontaneous fidelity in a society that had no legal or moral sanctions against infidelity, and to maintain it during voluntarily accepted separations that could come at any time and might last years, was something of a challenge. But the human being likes to be challenged, seeks freedom in adversity.

This is less convincing than, and made redundant by, the succeeding presentation of Shevek and Takver's four-year separation, their acceptance of it and their reactions. *The Dispossessed* relies too heavily on the idea expressed and analysed rather than embodied and shown. Despite powerful emotional scenes, particularly those between Shevek and Takver, it evokes a distanced intellectual appreciation of its theme and structure rather than the intuitive understanding of shared human feeling characteristic of Le Guin's other novels.

Conversely, Le Guin's best work, the Earthsea trilogy, derives its great strength from the direct translation of ideas into shared experience. Fantasy is, as Le Guin recognizes, "a journey into the subconscious." The truth found there can be communicated directly, without the intervening barriers of social and philosophical constructs; but first the writer must find an appropriate style, one exhibiting the "permanent virtues" of clarity and simplicity. The Earthsea novels clearly exemplify this ideal.

The patterning of the Earthsea trilogy is that of a human life: growth, the acceptance of power, mature action, the abdication of power, death. Within this circle of experience, each book presents another pattern: a quest through death's realm to adult knowledge and power. Like the magic of Earthsea itself, the books draw their strength from the specific knowledge of individual things. The life they present, while universal in its implications, is always particular: that of the mage Sparrowhawk, whose true name is Ged.

Though *A Wizard of Earthsea* opens in the context of legend, it moves quickly from the evocation of the shadowy figure "who in his day became both dragonlord and Archmage," to the daily life of the goatherd boy of Gont as he discovers his power to call down hawks and to shape the fog. The complementary patterns of *The Tombs of Atuan* and *The Farthest Shore*, too, are firmly rooted in the individual stories of Tenar, Priestess of the Nameless Ones who becomes White Lady of Gont, and Arren, prince of Enlad who becomes King of All the Isles. Ged, in these books, is presented from the outside as a mature and somewhat enigmatic figure of power, performing actions whose significance the young protagonists can only half comprehend. Yet he remains a sharply-realized individual: the Sparrowhawk indeed, with his "reddish-dark" face, "hawk-nosed, seamed on one cheek with old scars," and his "bright and fierce" eyes. He and his companions eat dry bread, and suffer hunger; they sail the world's seas and are parched by its sun; they act rashly and, when they must call on magic to restore the balance they have upset, they suffer exhaustion and pain. Their actions have the inevitable rightness of myth, always supported by the credibility of human feeling.

Earthsea, too, like Gethen and Anarres, is a fully-realized world. From the actuality of its wave-washed islands comes its strength as metaphor. An archipelago, Earthsea stretches some 2,000 miles from the cold North Reach south to the warm waters of the raft-people, the Children of the Sea; and another 2,000 miles from Selidor where the skull of the Erreth-Akbe lies amid the bones of the dragon Orm, east to the semi-barbaric Kargad Lands. These islands hold many kingdoms and several races; the trilogy presents each particular of life—fisherman and sorceress, goat and dragon, appletree and sparkweed—in all its richness. Yet Earthsea is a finite world. The Children of the Sea still dance the midsummer Long Dance, "one dance, one music binding together the sea-divided lands." Yet they move on fragile rafts above, and upon, a waste of limitless ocean, in celebration of the human spirit whose dance of life always moves "above the hollow place, above the terrible abyss." Ged sails Earthsea from edge to inhabited edge, seeking beyond the world for the shores of death's realm. Thus the physical islands of Earthsea exist in a delicate balance with the sea; the known human world lies surrounded by the unknown; and all life exists defined by death. This balance is central to the magic, and the meaning, of Earthsea.

Though secular rulers, kings, and lords govern the people of Earthsea, true power rests with the mages: men whose inborn power is augmented by long study to know the essence of each created thing, the "true name" by which it can be controlled. Though they can summon and use "the immense fathomless energies of the universe," the most important aspect of their art is the recognition of its natural limits, of "the Balance and the Pattern which the true wizard knows and serves."

Magic is an art which must be learned, patiently. A *Wizard of Earthsea* and *The Farthest Shore* show gifted apprentices at school on Roke Island, learning to weave spells with gestures, unseen powers, and the words of the Old Speech now spoken only by wizards and dragons. Le Guin's wit, and a gift of humor rare in fantasy, find full scope in the School of the Island of the Wise, as Gamble teases Prince Arren with tales of enchanted dinners, and Ged shoots arrows made of breadcrumbs and spells after Vetch's chickenbone owls.

Magic must not be used lightly, however; for evil, in Earthsea, is a "web we men weave" by the misuse of power. In A *Wizard of Earthsea*, Ged, who believes that a mage is "one who can do anything," must, like Le Guin's other protagonists, learn painfully that "as a man's real power grows and his knowledge widens, ever the way he can follow grows narrower; until at last he chooses nothing, but does only and wholly what he *must do* . . . ." In pride and anger, he summons a spirit of the dead; and so he lets a dark spirit of unlife enter the world. To name, to control that Shadow, he must journey over the oceans of Earthsea, into his own spirit, to confront and accept his "black self." His companion Vetch, watching, understands that Ged:

> by naming the shadow of his death with his own name, had made himself whole: a man: who, knowing his whole true self, cannot be used or possessed by any power other than himself, and whose life therefore is lived for life's sake and never in the service of ruin, or pain, or hatred, or the dark.

In the later books of the trilogy, Ged's power is founded in abnegation; he has learned to "desire nothing beyond my art," and to do only "what is needful"—even to relinquish that art.

In contrast to the heroic sweep of A *Wizard of Earthsea*, with its sparkle of sun on waves and roar of dragons, *The Tombs of Atuan* offers the narrow, intense focus of psychomyth: Le Guin's own term for her explorations in the timeless regions of the human mind. With its single action, setting, and central character, the novel powerfully suggests the claustrophobia of its controlling metaphor: the dark labyrinth beneath the Tombs, the dark passages of the human spirit inhabited by the " 'powers of the dark, of ruin, of madness.' "

The narrative opens with a symbolic death as the child Tenar becomes Arha, "the Eaten One," priestess of the Nameless Ones. The impersonal ritual of her sacrifice effectively suggests the denial of human life in the world of the Tombs. Tenar exists behind stone walls in a barren desert, her life and sexuality expressed only in ritual dances before the Empty Throne: celebrating death as the Long Dance celebrates life. Her only freedom is to wander her labyrinth, "the very home of darkness, the inmost center of the night," a place of corrupted power suggesting the fear, hatred, and utter loneliness which imprison her spirit. Her only right is to kill the men imprisoned there—and then live with her terrible nightmares of guilt.

Ged comes to the labyrinth seeking the Ring of Erreth-Akbe with its lost Rune of Peace, bringing the gift of "life in the place of death." Just as the light of his wizard's staff reveals beauty in the dark caverns, so his wizard's knowledge reveals Tenar's true name. When he, in turn, shares his true name with her, the gift of human trust is complete: a treasure more potent than the restored Ring. By its power, Tenar can choose freedom for them both. The novel ends with rebirth, as she walks from the crumbling Tomb into "the huge silent glory of light," accompanying Ged into the human world "like a child coming home."

The Farthest Shore completes the trilogy with Ged's third and final journey through the realm of death, accompanied by Prince Arren who thus fulfils the prophesy of Maharion: "*He shall inherit my throne who has crossed the dark and living and come to the far shores of the day.*" Its action is a sombre, ironic balance to that of *A Wizard of Earthsea*. Just as the Archmage Nemmerle gave his life to close the door which Ged, by his rash act, opened between life and death, so Ged gives his power to close the door which the wizard Cob opens in his attempt to escape death. Death is not, in itself, evil; rather, it is necessary, "the price we pay for our life, and for all life." Cob's denial of death, however, has evil consequences, for he denies life and thus destroys the essential balance of creation.

Le Guin suggests the evil effects of Cob's action in vivid, specific terms: Hort Town's foul disorder, the former wizard Hare's drugged ramblings; and especially the creeping mistrust, the numbing despair, which slowly dim Arren's shining devotion to Ged. Enduring these symptoms of imbalance, Ged and Arren come to their cause: the open door through which the light and joy of the living world flow into the lands of death. Again, the controlling images are resonant archetypes, evoking the sterility of denial and despair: the Dry River where only night flows, the Dry Land filled with "dust and cold and silence." Yet though even "the springs of wizardry have run dry," the human love and faith which are "the springs of being" do not fail. Arren, by his courage and devotion, leads Ged over the Mountains of Pain; and both regain life once more. The trilogy ends, not with triumph as Arren is crowned, but in a more appropriate mood of serenity. Ged, dragon-borne, vanishes from the world of action; and his story returns, full circle, to the timeless cadences of legend.

Peter Nicholls, in common with many critics, has praised Le Guin for her "telling precision of imagery," her ability to achieve "the strongest emotional reasonances . . . by capturing the individuality of a particular situation or character," as in the account of Arren's descent among the dead:

> All those whom they saw—not many for the dead are many, but that land is large—stood still, or moved slowly and with no purpose . . . They were whole and healed. They were healed of pain, and of life. They were not loathesome as Arren had feared they would be, not frightening in the way he had thought they would be. Quiet were their faces, freed from anger and desire, and there was in their shadowed eyes no hope.
>
> Instead of fear, then, great pity rose up in Arren, and if fear underlay it, it was not for himself, but for all people. For he saw the

mother and child who had died together, and they were in the dark land together, but the child did not run, nor did it cry, and the mother did not hold it or ever look at it. And those who had died for love passed each other in the streets.

Yet it is not just the details—the mother not looking at her child—which make this section moving. The simplicity of the language, its directness, and the sonorous cadencing of phrase and sentence into a timeless lament all combine with the specific images to make the passage unforgettable.

In Le Guin's work, even lamentation becomes a celebration of life, of the human spirit's power and desire to express its uniqueness.

"I must go where I am bound to go, and turn my back on the bright shores. I was in too much haste, and now have no time left. I traded all the sunlight and the cities and the distant lands for a handful of power, for a shadow, for the dark." So, as the mageborn will, Ged made his fear and regret into a song, a brief lament, half-sung, that was not for himself alone . . .

Like the mageborn, Ursula K. Le Guin also finds words of power, and weaves them into complex evocative patterns of human truth. In the limitless imaginative world of science fiction and fantasy, she finds:

precise and profound metaphors of the human condition . . . the fantasist, whether he used the ancient archetypes of myth and legend or the younger ones of science and technology, may be talking as seriously as any sociologist—and a good deal more directly—about human life as it is lived, and as it might be lived, and as it ought to be lived.

This seriousness of purpose, combined with rare skill and a determination to continue "pushing out toward the limits—my own and those of the medium" have established Le Guin as a major artist, exploring a unique vision of human life.

DENA C. BAIN

The "Tao Te Ching" as Background to the Novels of Ursula K. Le Guin

The intuitive approach that comes before thought is the only fruitful one with regard to the Chinese sages, and an explicative paper on the basic precepts of the *Tao Te Ching* will reveal nothing about Tao and a great deal about the writer. The Chinese sages taught through poetic paradox, not through the rational dualism of analysis and synthesis, and the importance of Ursula Le Guin's contribution to science fiction lies in her ability to use a distinctly Western art form to communicate the essence that is Tao. In many of her novels, Tao is the universal base upon which societies and individual characters act. The fact that Tao exists not in rational systems but in life and the imaginative construct of life that we call art makes the critic's task of revealing the methods and materials of Le Guin's imaginative integration a very difficult one. Nonetheless, I hope to avoid the traps inherent in the process of analysis as much as possible in giving some definition to the Taoist mythos that permeates the three novels—*City of Illusions*, *The Left Hand of Darkness*, and *The Dispossessed*—which I think best communicate it.

Unlike Western religious thought, which sees the universe as real and God as a person, Eastern tradition sees the universe as illusory and God as an impersonal force. In both Eastern and Western mysticism, however, the mystical experience is nothing less than direct intuition of Ultimate Reality—a supreme being in the West, a supreme state in the East. In Taoism—and in using this term, I am always referring to the

From *Extrapolation* 3, vol. 21 (1980). Copyright © 1980 by The Kent State University Press.

philosophy, not the later organized church—the supreme state is Tao, and its most common representation is as the line joining/dividing the yin and yang principles in the circle of life. Tao is the essence, the ultimate unity of the universe. It is the perfect balance point that encompasses all and nothing. In the *Tao Te Ching*, Tao is real, although no more real than the universe it governs; yet it is very definitely the governing force of the universe: the Mother, the One, Being, the Way. Tao "gave birth to the One; the One gave birth successively to two things, three things, up to Ten Thousand." Not-being, or the Something Else, the Self-So, the Nameless, stands outside time, ready, as Holmes Welch suggests, to produce new universes ruled by Tao, and maintaining the Tao that rules this one. Nonetheless, it and Tao are aspects of one another. It is in this sense that Tao encompasses all and nothing, or as Lao Tzu says: "For truly Being and Not-being grow out of one another." I would like to quote at greater length from Chapter II of the *Tao Te Ching* as translated by Arthur Waley, as it not only contains several important concepts, but also leads into a discussion of the underlying conflict of *City of Illusions:*

> It is because every one under Heaven recognizes beauty
> as beauty, that the idea of ugliness exists.
> And equally if every one recognizes virtue as virtue, this
> would merely create fresh conceptions of wickedness,
> For truly Being and Not-being grow out of one another;
> Difficult and easy complete one another.
> Long and short test one another;
> High and low determine one another.
> Pitch and mode give harmony to one another.
> Front and back give sequence to one another.
> Therefore the Sage relies on actionless activity,
> Carries on wordless teaching. . . .

If we had no preconceptions of beauty, nothing would appear ugly; one thing is made high only at the expense of making something else low, and so on. Similarly, in human affairs every challenge provokes a response, and when anyone tries to act upon humans the ultimate result is the opposite of what he is aiming at. Thus, the Sage, faced with a statement of action that is one side of a duality, must not support that side either directly or indirectly by taking the other side and thereby reinforcing the duality. Lao Tzu believes that challenges are to be ignored and that to cope with them by responding is the greatest of mistakes. According to his teaching, no one can achieve his aims by actions that create the rhythmic oscillation between opposites so common in human affairs. How, therefore, is the Sage to achieve his aims? The answer is *wu wei*—actionless activity. The Sage's lack of response to aggression is his wordless teaching. His passivity negates argument and teaches the aggressor to break the circle of cause and effect, and shows him that "To yield is to be preserved whole," like Shevek, the physicist protagonist of *The Dispossessed,* whose "gentleness was uncompromising; because he would not compete for dominance, he was indomitable." This actionless activity can succeed because it is the exemplar of the Taoist ideal of *tz'u*—love in the sense of compassion—coupled with humility. This attitude sets up a state of attraction rather than compulsion. Actionless activity is an attitude rather than an act, a state of being rather than doing, and this is the basis of its attraction. The Sage "becomes the model for the world"; his complete relativism absorbs aggression. He "approves of the good man and also of the bad man: thus the bad becomes good." First, then, the Sage never tries to do good, since a concept of good implies a concept of evil, and supporting the concept of evil only makes it stronger and more difficult to combat. Secondly, the cycle of cause and effect is so strong, so pervasive in human affairs that good done to one person may well be evil done to another; and third, by the Sage's wordless teaching, his compassion and humility, and his complete relativity in which good and evil are subjective, he can consider any man's criteria as valid as his own, "believing the truthful man and also believing the liar . . . thus all become truthful."

The question of truth is the central issue of *City of Illusions,* and the question is focused around Mindspeech, which is called the Last Art. The word "art" is used in the sense of a Zen or Ch'an art. Zen, or Ch'an, is descended psychologically if not doctrinally from early Taoism, and like it became the "conductor," as Waley says, for the same force engendered by actionless activity and developed in what Lao Tzu calls the Uncarved Block, or true nature. In man's true nature, in the compassion and humility of the Uncarved Block, there is neither good nor evil, beauty nor ugliness, truth nor lie: only Tao. Mindspeech draws upon this true nature—it is impossible to dissimulate in Mindspeech because there is no gap between "thought" and bespeaking, as there is between thought and speech. Zove, who is one of the several characters in Le Guin's work closely resembling Lao Tau's Sage, teaches, like Lao Tzu, by paradox. It is he who points out to the protagonist Falk the paradox of Mindspeech, which is that "In truth manhood lies." Whatever the bespeaker believes to be true will impact with all the conviction of belief, though it may be completely erroneous.

It seems, however, that the Shing introduce a new element, the mindlie. In Le Guin's cosmogony, the Shing are the Enemy, the alien race that broke the power of the old League, twelve hundred years before the action of *City of Illusions,* in a pyrrhic victory that left them isolated on Earth, rulers of a place that is forever alien to them. If true nature is an extension of the order of the universe, and if to be in harmony with the one is to be in harmony with the other, imagine the shock felt at the time of the War by the League members, practitioners of the Last Art, when this people arrived whose inner nature seemed to contain the capacity to distinguish between the truth or falsehood of their beliefs and to choose falsehood. The operative word is "choice." If the Shing believed what they bespoke, they would not be evil, merely consistent. Their introduction of dualism into the Uncarved Block gave them an advantage over the League that could not be fought.

This is what the Forest People believe, and it is the story that they teach to Falk, the protagonist, whose mind at the beginning of the book, like the reader's, is a blank slate to be written upon; it is not necessarily the truth.

Falk is actually Ramarren, leader of the first spaceship to travel from the planet Werel to Earth since the destruction of the League. All but one of his shipmates, a child, were destroyed by the Shing, and he himself was mind-razed and turned out to die. Rescued by Zove's Forest People, Falk must eventually leave those whom he now loves to find and complete the destiny that was interrupted. In his search for the truth, Falk is actually hunting for clarity, for an end to the ambiguity of the lives and words of the Shing. This ambiguity is indeed overwhelming: Falk is thrown into intimacy with Estrel, the first Shing he meets. Yet she is always "a gray shape in grayness" to him; she "kept nothing from him and yet her secrecy remained untouched." The attitude of the Shing to life and death, shown by their Law against killing which Falk calls a lie, is a reflection of the vagueness that shades everything about them. They are not capable of definitive action; even their murder is not complete. They will wipe an enemy's mind completely clean, obliterating personality, knowledge, and experience, but they consider themselves innocent of killing because they leave the body untouched. Yet there is beauty in the illusory nature of their reality, though Falk will not accept it, preferring his own illusion about reality. When Falk awakes in the Shing palace for the first time, he is in a room where:

> There was no furniture. Walls, floor and ceiling were all of the same translucent stuff, which appeared soft and undulant like many thicknesses of pale green veiling, but was tough and slick to the touch. Queer carvings and crimpings and ridges forming ornate patterns all over the floor were, to the exploring hand, nonexistent; they were eye-deceiving

paintings, or lay beneath a smooth transparent surface. The angles where walls met were thrown out of true by optical-illusion devices of crosshatching and pseudo-parallels used as decoration; to pull the corners into right angles took an effort of will, which was perhaps an effort of self-deception, since they might, after all, not be right angles. But none of this teasing subtlety of decoration so disoriented Falk as the fact that the entire room was translucent. . . . A blot of shadow somewhere in the green depths suddenly rose and grew less, greener, dimmer, fading into the maze of vagueness. Visibility without discrimination, solitude without privacy. It was extraordinarily beautiful, this masked shimmer of lights and shapes through inchoate planes of green, and extraordinarily disturbing.

Of course, it is disturbing to Falk, for whom the city of the Shing is not, as it is for Estrel, a place among places, and though a voice from the mirror in the room in which he wakes tells him to "Wait a moment more, Falk. Illusions are not always lies. You seek truth," he cannot endure or admit the truth offered him in the hallucinogenic dream-play. Lord Kradgy presents Falk with the same paradox about truth that the Sage Zove had:

> I am a Shing. All Shing are liars. Am I, then, a Shing lying to you, in which case of course I am not a Shing, but a non-Shing, lying? Or is it a lie that all Shing lie? But I am a Shing, truly; and truly I lie. Terrans and other animals have been known to tell lies also; lizards change color, bugs mimic sticks and flounders lie by lying still, looking pebbly or sandy depending on the bottom which underlies them.

Falk ought to have gone alone, as Zove, the Bee-Keeper, the Prince of Kansas, the Listener in the forest all had told him. By trusting that Estrel had his good at heart, he opened the possibility for her to do him ill. Yet had she done him ill by bringing him to the Shing? He is so clouded by emotion and attached to his preconceptions that he believes this to be the truth, merely because it seems that the Shing are trying to do him ill, and merely because the Shing are alien and enormously remote, bringing with them the "hues, the mood, the complexity of a lost world, a planet of perfumes and illusions, of swamps and transformations. . . ."

The Shing succeed in giving Ramarren back his identity, in hopes that they can find out from him the location of Werel in order to destroy it. They do not know, however, that Ramarren has succeeded in retaining his Falk identity as well and, because he has the two sets of information, is aware of their plans. Like all seekers, however, Falk-Ramarren must go through a transformation before being able to complete his mission. He has to learn that Estrel speaks truth when she says: "There is no Enemy, and I work for him." There is no Enemy, only another way to the truth. The transformation takes place just before the climactic scene in which Falk-Ramarren overcomes the Shing Ken Kenyek, and regains his ship. It is made possible because Falk leaves all conscious, rational thought to Ramarren and sinks into a state similar to the trance state he had earlier put himself into to save his identity as Falk. He attains the Tao, the Way, the state of actionless activity, by emptying himself of all conjecture and all thought. Thus, while Ramarren tries with all his trained intelligence to find a way to escape the Shing, the thought, based on his Kelshak upbringing, crosses his mind that:

> there is in the long run no disharmony, only misunderstanding, no chance or mischance but only the ignorant eye. So Ramarren thought, and the second soul within him, Falk, took no issue with this view, but spent no time trying to think it all out, either. For Falk had seen the dull and bright stones slip across the wires of the patterning frame, and had lived with men in their fallen estate, kings in exile on their own domain the Earth, and to him it seemed that no man could make his fate or control the game, but only wait for the bright jewel luck to slip by on the wire of time. Harmony exists, but there is no understanding it; the Way cannot be gone. So while Ramarren racked his mind, Falk lay low and waited. And when the chance came he caught it.

Falk-Ramarren comes to the realization that illusion, the world of the Shing, has its own truth, its own reality, and should, therefore, also be heard by the Werelians. The hatred Falk had always felt for the Shing is replaced by compassion and pity for the profound, irremediable lack of understanding that is the essence of their lying. They could not get in touch with men, and had used that as a weapon, the "mindlie." Yet after twelve centuries of trying to rule these men "whose minds made no sense to them and whose flesh was to them forever sterile," they are left "Alone, isolated, deafmutes ruling deafmutes in a world of delusions. *Oh desolation. . . .*" Thus, in the compassion that leads to true understanding, Falk-Ramarren says that: "There's always more than one way towards the truth," and takes Ken Kenyek with them to tell his story as well.

As the ship left Earth, the dawn coming over the Eastern ocean "shone in a golden crescent for a moment against the dust of stars, like a jewel on a great patterning frame. Then frame and pattern shattered, the barrier was passed, and the little ship broke free of time and took them out across the darkness." These images of light and darkness, which begin and end the book, figure very strongly not only in Lao Tzu but in all Chinese thought as the two halves of the yin-yang symbol. The terms literally mean the "sunny side" and "dark side" of a hill. Yin is the light, male, active, Being principle, and yang is darkness, the female, quiescent, Not-being. Being and Not-being are aspects of the same thing; together they are Tao and cannot be separated.

Though the images of darkness and light pervade all of Le Guin's work, they are most important in the novel that uses the concept as its title: *The Left Hand of Darkness*. The title is taken from a Lay of the planet Gethen:

> Light is the left hand of darkness
> and darkness the right hand of light,
> Two are one, life and death, lying
> together like lovers in kemmer,
> like hands joined together,
> like the end and the way.

According to a prehistoric Orgota creation myth, there was in the beginning nothing but the ice and the sun. When the nations of men were born to the giant Edondurath, however, each child had a piece of darkness that followed him. When Edondurath asked his kemmering why this was so, he was answered: "Because they were born in the house of flesh, therefore death follows at their heels. They are in the middle of time. In the beginning there was the sun and the ice, and there was no shadow. In the end when we are done, the sun will devour itself and shadow will eat light, and there will be nothing left but the ice and the darkness." Man lives in light, therefore, but must carry a piece of darkness with him in order to be man. At one point in their journey across the ice, Genly Ai and Estraven must travel for days through complete whiteness, through an "even, white, soundless sphere," where there are no shadows, no darkness. Genly Ai draws the yin-yang symbol and shows it to his companion, who has never seen it before. "It is yin and yang," Ai explains, "*Light is the left hand of darkness* . . . how did it go? Light, dark. Fear, courage. Cold, warmth. Female, male. It is yourself, Therem. Both and one. A shadow on snow."

The Handdara, the spiritual discipline that has shaped the country of Karhide, is its shadow. Behind the politics and parades and passions of this nation of mad kings and feuds "runs an old darkness, passive, anarchic, silent, the fecund darkness of the Handdara." As Lao Tzu says, "He who knows the male, yet cleaves to what is female / Becomes like a ravine, receiving all things under heaven / . . . He who knows the white, yet cleaves to the black / Becomes the standard by which all things are tested. . . ." The Handdarata cleave to the black. Though they will, if necessary, leave their Fastnesses to take up public life, living in the brightness of the society of men, and, as they say, taking back their shadows, they devote themselves to unlearning, to the ignorance which is the beginning of wisdom. "Learning consists in adding to one's stock day by day," but the practice of Tao, Lao Tzu says, "consists in subtracting day by day, / Subtracting and yet again subtracting / Till one has reached inactivity. / But by this very inactivity / Everything can be activated." The Handdarata practice the same sort of return to a state of Void or Quietness that Lao Tzu teaches. The approach to trance is never by external stimulation or action of any sort, but always by quiet and inaction. When Genly Ai first meets Faxe the Weaver, he and another are standing like statues in the full sunlight of a wide green meadow. Ai says that "They were practicing the Handdara discipline of Presence, which is a kind of trance—the Handdarata, given to negatives, call it an untrance—involving self-loss (self-augmentation?) though extreme sensual receptiveness and awareness."

It is this discipline of Presence that enables Faxe the Weaver to be one of the Foretellers. As the Weaver of the group, he stands at the center, at the balance point and point of transference, and eventually becomes the focus of the energies developed by the conflict between the Pervert and kemmerer, and augmented by the time distortion of the Zanies, who are in opposition to the Presence of the Celibates, with their total apprehension of immediate reality. He controls the empathic and paraverbal forces at work among the others, and at the moment of the Answer, there is "in the center of all darkness Faxe: the Weaver: a woman, a woman dressed in light." Though it would seem that the Handdarata, who do not want answers and who avoid them, are paradoxically the Answerers, yet their reason for answering questions is in keeping with their philosophy of unlearning. They have perfected Foretelling, Faxe says, "To exhibit the perfect uselessness of knowing the answer to the wrong question." In other words, there is no such thing as a right question. Like the king who might ask who would serve him best as prime minister, without understanding what "serving him best" may mean; like the Lord Berosty who asked "on what day shall I die?" and thereby caused his own death to occur on the day named by the Foretellers, any Asker who phrases his question in hopes of receiving a particular answer defeats the purpose of asking by his expectations. Indeed, the very process of asking questions, of adding to one's store of knowledge rather than subtracting from it, is never fruitful, as Ai, whose mission is no less difficult for the affirmative answer his question receives, learns. Faxe explains why:

"The unknown," said Faxe's soft voice in the forest, "the unforetold, the unproven, that is what life is based on. Ignorance is the ground of action. If it were proven that there is no God there would be no religion. No Handdara, no Yomesh, no hearthgods, nothing. But also if it were proven that there is a God, there would be no religion. . . . Tell me, Genry, what is known? What is sure, predictable, inevitable—the one certain thing you know concerning your future, and mine?"

"That we shall die."

"Yes. There's really only one question that can be answered, Genry, and we already know the answer. . . . The only thing that makes life possible is permanent, intolerable uncertainty: not knowing what comes next."

The Yomeshta, who seek light where the Handdarata praise darkness and Creation unfinished, are a variation of the basic philosophy that lies behind the Handdara and therefore all of Gethen. Their belief, however, is that the Weaver Meshe, at the moment of answering the Question of the Lord of Shorth, became trapped, like a filament in a vacuum, in the burning light of timelessness created by the Zanies. In that instant, Meshe stood in the Center of Time, seeing past, present and future as one whole:

Meshe is the Center of Time. That moment of his life when he saw all things clearly came when he had lived on earth thirty years, and after it he lived on earth again thirty years, so that the Seeing befell in the center of his life. And all the ages up until the seeing were as long as the ages will be after the Seeing, which befell in the Center of Time. And in the Center there is no time past and no time to come. In all time past it is. In all time to come it is. It has not been nor yet will be. It is. It is all.

At the Center of Time there is no darkness, only light:

Meshe saw all the sky as if it were all one sun. Above the earth and under the earth all the sphere of sky was bright as the sun's surface, and there was no darkness. . . . Darkness is only in the mortal eye, that thinks it sees, but sees not. In the Sight of Meshe there is no darkness.

Therefore those that call upon the darkness* (*The Handdarata) are made fools of and spat out from the mouth of Meshe, for they name what is not, calling it Source and End. . . . There is neither darkness nor death, for all things are, in the light of the Moment, and their end and their beginning are one.

Though the Handdarata seek the Not-being aspect of Tao, while the Yomeshta deny the connection between the Being and Not-being aspects, the Handdarata answer their charges, typically, by saying *nusuth*, it does not matter. It does not matter because their philosophy contains the same concept of an eternal present, though they have no dogma like the Yomeshta. In practicing their discipline of Presence, in seeking to leave untrodden the snows of ignorance, they become like Faxe, who looks at Genly Ai "out of a tradition thirteen thousand years old: a way of thought and way of life so old, so well established, so integral and coherent as to give a human being the unself-consciousness, the authority, the completeness of a wild animal, a great strange creature who looks straight at you out of his eternal present."

Gethenian society as a whole exists at the center of time—it is always the Year One, and dates future and past change accordingly each year. The people are much more concerned with presence than with progress, as Genly Ai remarks in a comparison of Gethenians with Terrans. Perhaps the ability to foretell is, as Genly Ai suspects, really the power of "seeing (if only for a flash) *everything at once:* seeing whole." This same pattern of viewing time as an eternal present is also a theme of *City of Illusions.* The patterning frame used by Zove and his sister Buckeye, and by the Prince of Kansas, is "a fortune-teller, a computer, an implement of mystical discipline, a toy." Patterning frames serve the same function as the foretelling trance, except that they incorporate representations of the physical world (the Ten Thousand Creatures created by Tao). The energies that build up between the frame and the empathic Listener are finally released into a shifting of the patterns as, in the instant of attaining Tao—the Center of Time—past, future and present are coexistent and all three can be read in the patterns of the "jewels of life and death." Thus, the Prince of Kansas plays on his frame, and sees the pattern of Opalstone's (Falk's) life in its entirety. He sees that Opalstone should have died a century ago among the stars from which he came, and he sees him shooting off from time's frame back to the stars, as indeed he does in the concluding passage of the novel.

The nature of time is central to *The Dispossessed,* and again the concept of presence is important, both in Shevek's temporal theories and in his own life. For Shevek, past and future together equal the present, so that we always live at the center of time. For example, Shevek comes to this realization during the time of his great happiness with Takver:

> It was now clear to Shevek, and he would have thought it folly to think otherwise, that his wretched years in this city had all been part of his present great happiness, because they had led up to it, prepared him for it. Everything that had happened to him was part of what was happening to him now. Takver saw no such obscure concatenation of effect/cause/effect, but then she was not a temporal physicist. She saw time naively as

a road laid out. You walked ahead, and you got somewhere. If you were lucky, you got somewhere worth getting to.

But when Shevek took her metaphor and recast it in his terms, explaining that, unless the past and future were made part of the present by memory and intention, there was, in human terms, no road, nowhere to go. . . .

Time, according to Shevek's Simultaneity Theory, is a function of the conscious mind. He explains to the businessman Dearri that babies have no time; they cannot distance themselves from the past and understand how it relates to the present, or plan the future on the basis of its relation to the present. The unconscious mind of the adult, that is, the Uncarved Block, is like that still. He says: "In a dream there is no time, and succession is all changed about, and cause and effect are all mixed together. In myth and legend there is no time. What past is it the tale means when it says 'Once upon a time'? And so, when the mystic makes the reconnection of his reason and his unconscious, he sees all becoming as one being, and understands the eternal return." This brings us again to the *Tao Te Ching:* "In Tao the only motion is returning; / The only useful quality, weakness. / For though Heaven and Earth and the Ten Thousand Creatures were produced by Being, / Being was produced by Not-being." Having made the connection between time and the conscious and not-time and the unconscious, backed by the shy man's quotation from Tebores ("The unconscious mind is coextensive with the universe"), Shevek goes on to discuss Sequency in terms of the conscious mind's linear time, and Simultaneity in terms of cycles:

> One cycle, one orbit around the sun, is a year, isn't it? And two orbits, two years, and so on. One can count the orbits endlessly—an observer can. Indeed such a system is how we count time. It constitutes the time-teller, the *clock.* But within the systems, the cycle, where is time? Where is beginning or end? Infinite repetition is an atemporal process. . . . The little timelessnesses added together make up time. . . . So then time has two aspects. There is the arrow, the running river, without which there is no change, no progress, or direction, or creation. And there is the circle or the cycle, without which there is chaos, meaningless succession of instants, a world without clocks or seasons or promises.

Shevek's temporal theory, then, is to be a general field theory that will unite the two concepts and use the simultaneous aspect of time in the same conscious way that we use linear time. The result will be the ansible, a field in which a communication can exist in two places within the circle of time.

One of the underlying assumptions behind the philosophy of

Anarresti society is that the whole is comprised of two inseparable opposites. As it says on Odo's Tombstone: "To be whole is to be part; / true
voyage is return." Shevek also, "would always be one for whom the return
was as important as the voyage out. To go was not enough, only half
enough." Yet the source of the problem between Urras and Anarres, who
are surprised to find that the Hainish and Terrans call them jointly the
Cetians, is that the voyage out was made two hundred years earlier by the
Odonians, but the return has never been effected. Instead, a wall was
built, a wall which, depending on one's point of view, encloses Anarres,
or encloses the rest of the universe. Shevek's job is to unbuild walls with
his empty hands, to unite the centrality of Anarresti functional anarchism
with the spendor of the Urrasti; the past of Urras with the future that is
Anarres. Where Falk has many teachers to help him along his way, and
Genly Ai has two Sages of the Handdara, Estraven and Faxe the Weaver,
Shevek has only himself. We see his development against the backgrounds
of both sides of the conflict into a "perfected man" who teaches the
imperfect with a wordless teaching: by example, by love, humility, compassion, and by a mysterious but natural power of his personality. Like
Falk and Genly Ai, the solution to Shevek's problem becomes clear to
him only when his situation is so reduced that action on his part is no
longer possible. Caught up in the politics of Urras; seemingly more distant
than he has ever been from joining the two elements; seemingly involved
in an action that can only strengthen the wall, Shevek is caught at a
point of such total reduction that luck takes over and he is whisked to the
best place for him to be in order to complete his mission, the neutral
Terran embassy. Not surprisingly, his general field theory of time becomes
clear to him at the same time of low ebb in the fortunes of his mission.
Sitting in his luxurious cell at the University, Shevek realizes first of all
that he had to come to Urras to write his theory of time, to his enemies,
who could give him something he could not get from his friends and
brothers: knowledge of the foreign, of the alien, of the other side of the
circle. He begins to see also that the flaw in his approach to his physics
has been the same—he has been too narrow:

> He had been groping and grasping after certainty, as if it were something
> he could possess. He had been demanding a security, a guarantee, which
> is not granted, and which, if granted, would become a prison. By simply
> assuming the validity of real coexistence he was left free to use the lovely
> geometries of relativity; and then it would be possible to go ahead. The
> next step was perfectly clear. . . . How could he have stared at reality for
> ten years and not seen it? There would be no trouble at all in going on.
> Indeed he had already gone on. He was there. He saw all that was to

come in this first, seemingly casual glimpse of the method, given him by his understanding of a failure in the distant past. The wall was down. The vision was both clear and whole. What he saw was simple, simpler than anything else. It was simplicity: and contained in it all complexity, all promise. It was revelation. It was the way clear, the way home, the light.

Once he sees his way clear before him, it is his obligation and desire to share that clarity with everyone, like the Sage who must always return to live in the world and teach. When he stands in Capitol Square surrounded by a vast crowd, the crowd becomes a single great creature that listens to the speakers, "not hearing and understanding in the sense in which the individual rational mind perceives and understands, but rather . . . as a thought perceives and understands the self." When Shevek speaks, he is speaking the mind, the being, the language of the self gathered in the Square, out of the center of his own being. He tells the crowd that in order to become full, they must be empty, like the Anarresti who have nothing but their freedom and therefore have everything that the Urrasti lack. The Anarresti are the future because they do not cling to the past:

It is our suffering that brings us together. It is not love. Love does not obey the mind, and turns to hate when forced. The bond that binds us is beyond choice. We are brothers. We are brothers in what we share. In pain, which each of us must suffer alone, in hunger, in poverty, in hope, we know our brotherhood. We know it, because we have had to learn it. We know that there is no help for us but from one another, that no hand will save us if we do not reach out our hand. And the hand that you reach out is empty, as mine is. You have nothing. You possess nothing. You own nothing. You are free. All you have is what you are, and what you give.

I am here because you see in me the promise, the promise that we made two hundred years ago in this city—the promise kept. We have kept it, on Anarres. We have nothing but our freedom. We have nothing to give you but your own freedom.

Shevek holds in his empty hands the tool that will destroy not only the wall between Anarres and Urras, but the wall of space that divides all the known worlds, and he gives it to all freely. His theory means nothing to him. "Weigh it in the balance with the freedom of one single human spirit," he says to Ambassador Keng, "and which will weigh heavier? Can you tell? I cannot." And so, having given all he had to give, he returns to Anarres, his hands empty, as they had always been.

There is, then, a basic mythos underlying each of the novels based on the Quietist philosophy of Lao Tzu's Taoism: the concepts of wholeness, of presence, of reconciling forces which appear totally opposed, but which, in the moment of complete reduction and return to the Uncarved Block, are invariably revealed to be necessary complements. Thus, Falk-Ramarren attains to the compassion which enables him to understand the illusory reality of the Shing, instead of despising its falseness in his false search for an impossible truth, and open the doors that have remained closed for twelve hundred years; thus Genly Ai, reduced to possessing nothing but his shadow on snow, is able to effect the unification of the darkness and light principles on Gethen and open the door to contact with the Ekumen; and finally, Shevek unbuilds the wall that stands between Anarres and Urras, and changes the lives of all the billions of people in the nine Known Worlds with the "simple matter" he holds in his empty hands.

Le Guin is a deliberate, conscientious writer who not only creates fully developed cultures in each of her novels, but who has woven them together into an entire cosmogony, giving, in the course of all her novels and stories, a history of the spread of civilization from Hain-Davenant to the Ekumen of eighty worlds, of which Terra is a part. She weaves social and political commentary into her cultural presentation, as in the conflicts between Karhide and Orgoreyn in *The Left Hand of Darkness*, or Anarres and Urras in *The Dispossessed*, always set within the larger scale of humanity as an integral part of the balance of the cosmos. Finally, her style mirrors the balance of her themes. Her writing moves gently but inexorably. To use another analogy from Lao Tzu, it is like a deep pool of water, seemingly inactive, but actually teeming with life. She, too, like the Sage, influences by actionless activity. The value of her work lies in the combination of all these elements, and others, into a complete overview of what it means to be human, no matter on what world, in what cultural subdivision, humans find themselves.

BARBARA BROWN

"The Left Hand of Darkness": Androgyny, Future, Present, and Past

Much of the impact of Ursula K. Le Guin's *The Left Hand of Darkness* (1969) results from the fact that the novel is an exploration of the concept of the dichotomous/androgynous one on three time levels: future, present, and past. First and most obviously, it is future directed, presenting a possible androgynous world on the planet Winter. Second, it is rooted in the present. As Le Guin affirms in her introduction to the Ace edition, the purpose of her science fiction is descriptive, not predictive: "I'm merely observing, in the peculiar, devious, and thought-experimental manner proper to science fiction, that if you look at us at certain odd times of the day . . . we already are [androgynous]." Third, *The Left Hand of Darkness* is directed to the past. In her exploration of androgyny, Le Guin examines a subject whose origins are buried deep in our mythic past.

The term androgyny, itself, reflects the past, present, and future orientation of the novel. Increasingly, we hear the word used in the present by writers like Carolyn Heilbrun in *Toward a Recognition of Androgyny* and June Singer in *Androgyny*. They, and other sociologists, use the term to describe a present theory of human sexuality that will provide a viable future pattern for psychological and cultural evolution if we can synthesize the ancient, past knowledge of our androgynous beginnings with our contemporary experiences.

From *Extrapolation* 3, vol. 21 (1980). Copyright © 1980 by The Kent State University Press.

The very origins of the word, lying in our past, in ancient Greece suggest a beginning definition. Androgyny is a combintion of *andro* meaning male and *gyn* meaning female. It suggests by its form a blending in which human characteristics of males and females are not rigidly assigned. One might simply assert then that the androgyne is the dichotomous one, incorporating male and female psychological duality in one physical entity. There are, though, more complex ideas currently associated with the word. Androgyny is an affirmation that humanity should reject all forms of sexual polarization, emerge from the prison of gender into a world in which individual behavior can and is freely chosen.

We need a word of caution here. Androgyny is not a prescription for blandness, for homogeneity, for the submerging of differences. Human experience will always be paradoxical, containing opposite energies and qualities. According to Jungians, the life system works as a result of the dynamics of the interaction of the opposites. We must have this tension. In androgyny, however, the source of the dynamics is not the opposition of male and female but rather the alternating thrust and withdrawal of the masculine and feminine principles within each individual psyche.

In practical terms, then, the theory of androgyny affirms that we should develop a mature sexuality in which an open system of all possible behavior is accepted, the temperament of the individual and the surrounding circumstances being the determining factors, rather than gender. In some aspects androgyny involves the reacquisition of what Freud defines as the polymorphously perverse body of the child. In this situation the individual considers every area, not just the genital, as potentially erogenous. He or she develops beyond gender limitation.

The preceding interpretation of androgyny in the present is certainly part of what concerns Le Guin. However, her presentation of the androgynous beings in *The Left Hand of Darkness* also encompasses the original archetypes. These archetypes express the underlying human conviction that man had once experienced a unity that is now denied by the basic division into male and female. Any review of the creation myths reveals an astounding number of androgynous situations. June Singer in her excellent study of the subject includes a detailed analysis of these creation stories. Some of the more obvious examples are briefly referred to here. Consider that the Bible includes two versions of creation. In Genesis I, it is an androgynous God who creates both man and woman in his image. In the second version in Genesis, it is the hermaphroditic Adam who produces Eve from his side. The patriarchal Jewish society emphasized this latter version.

Both the early Gnostic writings and Kabalistic literature present pictures of the androgynous origins of man. Traditional pictures of Adam Kadmon, the first man, according to Kabalists, show the genitals combining male and female organs. Eventually, as this complicated myth develops, primal man is torn apart and the male and female become opposites.

There is also an androgynous version of creation in Plato's *Symposium*: "[The] original human nature was not like the present, but different. The sexes were not two, as they are now, but originally three in number; there was man, woman and a union of the two, having a name corresponding to this double nature, which once had a real existence, but is now lost, and the word 'Androgynous' is only preserved as a term of reproach." As this creation story unfolds the gods are attacked by this unified creature. The punishment for its defiance is division into the two parts of man, male and female. Each part then continues to desire the other half, trying to gain completion.

Similarly, this concept of the paradoxical, split yet unified, male and female principle is found in Chinese mythology. This traditional belief is embodied in the *I Ching* or *Book of Changes* dated sometime between 2000 to 1300 B.C. Here the supreme ultimate generates the primary forms, the Yin and the Yang. All nature then consists of a perpetual interplay between this primordial pair. They are Yang and Yin, heat and cold, fire and water, active and passive, masculine and feminine.

While Le Guin works out of this mythic/religious background, she also continues "the hidden river of androgyny" in literature so well discussed in Carolyn Heilbrun's book *Toward a Recognition of Androgyny*. One might interpret the triumph of Orestes and Athena in the *Oresteia* as the union of the male and female dualities. Later, the deification of the Virgin Mary in the medieval period balances the principle of the deified masculine in God. There are androgynous women throughout Shakespeare. They choose to defy social conditioning and assert masculine temperaments: the ambitious Lady MacBeth, the sexually determined Desdemona, the lustful Goneril and Regan. Moll Flanders in Defoe's eighteenth-century novel is an androgynous figure in her defiance of the traditionally passive role assigned to women of the time as is Hester Prynne in *The Scarlet Letter* and Nora in *A Doll's House*. Consider *Orlando* by Virginia Woolf. Here Woolf makes explicit the androgyny she so favors in the concluding chapters of *A Room of One's Own*. For a real life account of androgyny read Jan Morris' *Conundrum*. This androgynous passage in Herman Hesse's *Siddhartha* confirms how a conviction of the androgynous potential for man appears in unexpected places. When Siddhartha dreams of meeting his friend Govinda:

He dreamt that Govinda stood before him, in the yellow robe of the ascetic. Govinda looked sad and asked him, "Why did you leave me?" Thereupon he embraced Govinda, put his arm round him, and as he drew him to his breast and kissed him, he was Govinda no longer, but a woman and out of the woman's gown emerged a full breast and Siddhartha lay there and drank . . . it tasted of woman and man, of sun and forest, of animal and flower. . . .

According to the perceptions of many writers, we are, indeed, male and female. This recognition of androgyny as our ideal is buried in our mythology, in our literature, in our subconscious, and in our cells. Ursula Le Guin draws upon this past tradition of the mythic and literary androgyne and her recognition of the androgynous behavior in our present society when she writes her future-based novel, *The Left Hand of Darkness.*

Le Guin is aware how difficult her readers will find acceptance of the androgynous principle. To make explicit the need for such a non-Western interpretation of experience, she first establishes the movement from duality to unity on all levels of Genly Ai's experience, then depicts his increasing sensitivity to the peripheral ambiguities of truth that contradict the central facts.

We begin with duality into unity in terms of imagery, setting, characters, action, and philosophy. Traditionally, the right side has been associated with light representing knowledge, rationality, and the male principle; the left with darkness, ignorance, and the female principle. In *The Left Hand of Darkness* the initial description of the setting immediately establishes this light/dark, left/right polarity. The novel opens with "Rain clouds over dark towers . . . a dark storm-beaten city." Yet there is one vein of slowly winding gold. This is the parade. Genly, the protagonist, sees these as contrasts, separate facets of the scene. They are, though, part of one unified vision of the world of Winter.

The wider universe is depicted in terms of light and dark. The mad Argaven, King of Karhide, mentions that the stars are bright and blinding, providing a traditional account of the universe. Continuing the description, he expands it, insisting on the surrounding void, the terror and the darkness that counterpoint the rational light of the interplanetary alliance of the Ekumen that Genly symbolizes. The glacier, the heart of Winter, is so bright on the Gobrin Ice it almost blinds Genly and his travelling companion, Estraven, the proscribed first minister of Karhide. Yet it is dark and terrible when they are caught between Drumner and Dremegale, the volcanos, spewing out black smoke and ash.

The action in the novel is often described in terms of dualities. At Arikostor Fastness, Genly specifically mentions the thin strips of light that creep across the circle. They are the counterpoints of the slats of dimness. The weaver, Faxe, a man, is seen as a woman dressed in light in the center of darkness. The foretellers are a part of a bright spider web, light against dark.

Toward the conclusion of his journey, both Genly and the reader perceive the merging pattern of dualities on these levels of setting and action. Light and dark, left and right, and, by implication, male and female become whole. Estraven quotes Tormer's Lay to Genly:

> Light is the left hand of darkness
> and darkness the right hand of light.
> Two are one, life and death, lying
> together like lovers in kemmer,
> like hands joined together,
> like the end and the way.

Genly and Estraven yearn for the dark of the shadow when they are in the antarctic void of the white darkness. Without shadow, without dark, there is a surfeit of light. They cannot see ahead to avoid the threatening changes in the terrain. In total understanding, Genly draws for Estraven the Yang and the Yin, the light and the dark. "Both and one," he says; "A shadow on snow." Both are necessary. Ultimately, Genly recognizes their crossing of the ice is both success and failure: union with the Ekumen, death for Estraven. Both are necessary.

But light and dark, left and right are not the only polarities that are unified as preparatory patterns for the central sexual unification. There is political duality in the opposed states of Orgoreyn and Karhide. Karhide has a slow steady pace of change. In many ways it is disunited. While it speaks to the people's sense of humanity, fostering a sense of strong individualism and family loyalty based on the conception of the hearths, like many democracies it harbors within it the possibility of the rise of fascism and a susceptibility to demagogues.

Orgoreyn is more socialist. Burdened down by the rivalries of its Commensalities, the extensiveness of its bureaucracies, the pettiness of its inspectors, it nonetheless is ordered and unified. It conveys a sense of progress. Still, it terrifies Genly with its failure to respect the rights of the individual. These political polarities exist not only between the two states but also within each, since the individual systems are at the same time both rational and irrational.

Genly, disgusted with this ambiguity, embraces Karhide, then rejects it; accepts Orgota, then flees from it. He seeks a consistent rational pattern. There is none. This is precisely Le Guin's thesis. Ambiguous duality must exist if unification is to occur.

This state of political polarity is unified by the agency of the Ekumen. Not a kingdom but a co-ordinator, it serves as a clearinghouse for trade and knowledge for the eighty-three nations within its scope. Mystical in nature, the Ekumen works slowly, seeking consensus. Estraven immediately recognizes that the Ekumen is a greater weaver than the Handdara. It has woven all aliens into one fabric that reflects both the unity and diversity of the civilized world.

This pattern of unifying dualities is clearly related to the central concern of androgyny. Without an awareness of the possibility of unifying opposites on the imaginative, physical, and political levels, we would not be as willing to alter the present sexual dichotomy we experience. According to Ursula Le Guin, at times we already perceive the androgynous possibilities within us. She suggests we are, nonetheless, unable to explore fully this unified duality. One reason for this limitation is the restrictive way the western mind interprets human experience. (A similar view is promulgated by Taoism and Zen.) This linear approach, characterizing western thought, focuses on scientifically provable facts. As a result it is narrow and exclusive. It fails to incorporate our peripheral senses which through intuition and mystical awareness, also contribute to knowledge. Through the action in *The Left Hand of Darkness,* Le Guin suggests that by utilizing this peripheral vision we, like Genly, can learn to accept life with all its ambiguities, its paradoxes, its flow, its unknowable qualities, with all its androgyny.

At the beginning of *The Left Hand of Darkness,* Genly is limited by the western mode of thought. As a scientist observing a subject, there is a tacit assumption of superiority on his part. He admits early in the first chapter that he judges the Gethenians as aliens. His detached manner leads him mistakenly to assert that the rivalry between Tibe, the traitorous cousin of the King, and Estraven is irrelevant to his cause. He dislikes Estraven because he is obscure, not an easy subject for scientific research. Notably, Genly's poor judgment of Winter's cultures results from his desire to gather the facts and proceed to logical conclusions. He is skeptical of anything that cannot be labeled and categorized.

Only by abandoning his devisive scientific approach can Genly achieve the unification of the warring philosophical and sexual elements within him. First, however, there are many ambiguities he must accept. One of these is Shifgrethor, an ambiguous conveying of information and intent. Not lying, it is a viable mode of behavior, conveying one aspect of truth. The wheel of experience, as Estraven insists, is not factually knowable. It turns independent of human control. On the Gobrin Ice, Genly must accept this ambiguity. No one can predict his success or failure on the glacier. As well, Genly eventually perceives that opposites are not exclusive, not contradictory. Estraven is both patriot and traitor. Genly is both patriot and traitor. Loyal to his mission, he brings Winter into the Ekumen; yet he betrays Estraven by permitting the landing of the starship before forcing Argaven to recall Therem's condemnation. Life is not linear as Genly first believes. Since it is process, the Gethenian system of measuring time is not alien but rather a logical emphasis of the individual's perception as the center of meaningful experience.

Finally, Genly accepts the ambiguous flow of events that makes it an impossibility to contain truth in language. In discussing Therem's behavior with Argaven, he says, "As I spoke I did not know if what I said was true. True in part; an aspect of truth." Often it is the west that affirms that there is one truth that can be logically explicated. It is the east that perceives that truth is flowing and ebbing, inexplicably diffuse, androgynous.

Ironically, this recognition of the many facets of truth is revealed in the beginning of *The Left Hand of Darkness*. Here the enlightened Genly, now looking back with wisdom on his experiences on Winter, declares that truth is a matter of the imagination (eastern) but one can write a report on events (western) containing facts (western). However, those facts, since they are neither solid nor coherent, will glow or dull according to the speaker (eastern).

The unification of all these dualities, the acceptance of these ambiguities, prepares both Genly and the reader to accept the central thematic unity of the sexual hermaphroditism of the Gethenians. In his response to the aliens, Genly reveals what Le Guin assumes the reader's feelings might be to these dichotomous characters. Estraven is first described as "the person on my left." Appropriately he is involved in feminine intrigue; however, he is wearing green, gold, and silver. These are colors not usually associated with both the right (the masculine) and with the left (the feminine). [Later] Estraven is on Genly's right, all male now, but defying the traditional symbolism of right and left, he is a dark, shadowy figure. Associated with both light and dark, with left and right in a deliberately reversed symbolic order, Estraven is also an ambiguous figure. Neither Genly Ai nor the reader can interpret such a character according to traditional concepts. This world of Winter denies the established polarities of the light and dark, left and right, male and female.

Initially, the mobile responds to this confusion on the basis of his cultural conditioning. While he is repelled by the sexual duality of the Karhiders, he can neither overtly reveal his feelings to his hosts nor covertly admit his distaste to himself. His language, his responses, though, record his uneasiness. Genly first describes Estraven in these revealing terms declaring he was "Annoyed by [his] sense of effeminate intrigue." Later he calls Estraven a strange alien. He is oblivious to the fact that Estraven is the Karhider who has most attempted to befriend him. In a patronizing manner, Genly mentions that his landlady seems male on first meeting but also has "fat buttocks that wagged as he walked and a soft fat face, and a prying, spying ignoble, kindly nature. . . . He was so feminine." In commenting on the lack of war on Gethen, Genly observes, "They lacked, it seemed, the capacity to mobilize. They behaved like animals, in that respect; or like women. They did not behave like men or ants." Finally, in describing Therem in their later relationship, he affirms, "There was in his attitude something feminine, a refusal of the abstract, the ideal, a submissiveness to the given which displeased me."

At the beginning of *The Left Hand of Darkness*, Genly divides these unified creatures into polarities. He perceives the Gethenians in single bodies responding as both male and female. This merging of the stereotyped roles and responses first shocks and then revolts him.

The completion of his mission, however, brings him to full understanding of the nature of all dualities. They are extremes on a continuum, separated but nonetheless joined, unified. Duality can be unity. Genly must accept this fact and find ease in it. For him the crossing on the ice is a journey to self and universal knowledge. Genly begins by sharing supplies with Estraven; moves to encompassing him with mindspeak; concludes by totally accepting Estraven's nature and, by extension, the androgyny of his own. Toward the conclusion of their journey, Genly admits,

> What I was left with was, at last, acceptance of him as he was. Until then I had rejected him, refused him his own reality. He had been quite right to say that he, the only person on Gethen who trusted me, was the only Gethenian I distrusted. For he was the only one who had entirely accepted me as a human being; who had liked me personally and given me entire personal loyalty, and who therefore had demanded of me an equal degree of recognition, of acceptance. I had not been willing to give it. I had been afraid to give it. I had not wanted to give my trust, my friendship to a man who was a woman, a woman who was a man.

By later drawing the symbol of the Yang and the Yin, light and dark, masculine and feminine, Genly makes visible his emotional and intellectual acceptance of Estraven: the two in the one.

Le Guin, however, does not conclude with Genly's recognition of the androgynous possibility. Her ending suggests that this state of unified duality is a preferable, superior state of existence. In the final chapter, Genly no longer relates to his own species nor they to him. He is alien to the Terran arrivals. Uneasy in his new perceptions, Genly calls the representatives of the Ekumen "a troupe of great, strange animals of two different species, great apes with intelligent eyes, all of them in rut, in kemmer . . ." He is happy to return to the company of the young Gethenian physician who is described in these terms: ". . . and his face, a young serious face, not a man's face and not a woman's, a human face, these were a relief to me, familiar, right."

In *The Left Hand of Darkness* Ursula Le Guin suggests we too should accept as right, as familiar, the archetypal androgyny within us. Transcending male, transcending female, we can become fully human.

BRIAN ATTEBERY

"The Beginning Place": Le Guin's Metafantasy

Most writers of fantasy reach a point where they start to defend what they have written against charges of irrelevance or meaninglessness. There are essays by George MacDonald, J. R. R. Tolkien, C. S. Lewis, and many other fantasists that say, "This is real. It matters. My stories are born from and reflect back upon the outside world of perception and action." The impulse is understandable: many readers and, unfortunately, a few writers mistake fantasy's alteration of reality for an evasion of reality. Such readers fail to note how carefully the best fantasists order their creations—how they limit the magical possibilities and bind them to a stringent moral order. Ursula K. Le Guin, in one of these defenses of fantasy, says that "fantasy is true, of course. It isn't factual, but it is true. Children know that. Adults know it too, and that is precisely why many of them are afraid of fantasy. They know that its truth challenges, even threatens, all that is false, all that is phony, unnecessary, and trivial in the life they have let themselves be forced into living."

Le Guin's best known fantasy is the Earthsea trilogy: three tales of wizardry and self-discovery set in a world of islands inhabited by men, dragons, and lesser beings. The high quality of these stories has been recognized in a number of critical essays, in major awards—a *Boston Globe—Horn Book* Award for *A Wizard of Earthsea*, a Newbery Honor Medal for *The Tombs of Atuan*, and a National Book Award for *The*

From *Children's Literature*, vol. 10 (1982). Copyright © 1982 by *Children's Literature*, An International Journal, Inc.

Farthest Shore—and in the response of the children and adults who read them. What kind of response? The same kind that Le Guin, in another essay, tells of having arisen in her upon reading, at age ten, a fairy tale by Hans Christian Andersen: ". . . It was to that, to the unknown depths in me, that the story spoke; and it was the depths which responded to it and, nonverbally, irrationally, understood it, and learned from it."

But having located the truth of fantasy in the unconscious, how can we act consciously in accordance with it: what is the use of a dream upon awakening? That is a question that Le Guin and her predecessors have skirted in their essays. However, Le Guin's most recent fantasy novel, *The Beginning Place*, is largely about the relationship between fantasy and ordinary, daylight reality. It tells, in a sense, what happens when we close the book and drift back from Middle Earth or Narnia or Earthsea. Le Guin explores this relationship by establishing not one but two fictional realms, one fantastic and one modeled on the world we live in. Her protagonists, Irene Pannis and Hugh Rogers, cross from one world to the other, like fictional representatives of the reader as he picks up a work of fantasy and puts it down, adjusting his eyes and his expectations each time to a new order of being. In their actions and reactions Le Guin embodies her notion of the ways fantasy can be used either to evade or to achieve psychological growth.

The Beginning Place opens in a setting that is sharply detailed and yet impossible to locate, for it is set in standardized American suburbia. Its supermarkets, freeways, and apartments, its Kensington Heights, Pine View Place, and Raleigh Drive might encircle virtually any medium-to-large city in America. All is bland, uniform, ersatz. It is a horrible place, but no one in the story seems consciously to recognize the horror, not even the hero, Hugh, a young supermarket checker. Hugh's unconscious, though, is at work. Unruly and fertile, as our unconscious minds tend to be, it protests one evening as Hugh sits at home heating a frozen TV dinner and waiting for his brittle, demanding mother to come home. Choosing as its defense not neurosis but escape, Hugh's unconscious stirs him to panic, drives him out the door, and sets him running:

> Right down Oak Valley Road, left onto Pine View Place, right again, he did not know, he could not read the signs. He did not run often or easily. His feet hit the ground hard, in heavy shocks. Cars, carports, houses blurred to a bright pounding blindness which, as he ran on, reddened and darkened. Words behind his eyes said *You are running out of daylight.* Air came acid into his throat and lungs, burning, his breath made the noise of tearing paper. The darkness thickened like blood. The jolt of his gait grew harder yet, he was running down, downhill. He tried

to hold back, to slow down, feeling the world slide and crumble under his feet, a multiple lithe touch brush across his face. He saw or smelled leaves, dark leaves, branches, dirt, earth, leafmold, and through the hammer of his heart and breath heard a loud continual music. He took a few shaky, shuffling steps, went forward onto hands and knees, and then down, belly down full length on earth and rock at the edge of running water.

The stream whose music Hugh hears is not in the world of TV dinners and carports. It is across the threshold into the world of dreams, magic, ritual, and renewal. With a careful orchestration of prose rhythms and precise images, Le Guin has deftly drawn us into an altered reality. Just before Hugh begins running he finds himself saying, without willing it, "I can't, I can't." His need takes him to a place where he can—can breathe, can think, can luxuriate in smells and touches of nature, and ultimately, can bring himself to a new order and understanding.

Part of his understanding involves another person, a fugitive like himself. Irene has been coming to this twilight land for several years. It is her sanctuary from an awkward living situation and a threatening family life. Unlike Hugh, she has ventured beyond the stream which is the beginning place of the title, the threshold, and has gone on to explore some of the country beyond. She has met its inhabitants and begun to learn their language. The pastoral town of Tembreabrezi, perched high on a dim mountainside, is her adopted home. The innkeepers Sofir and Palizot keep a set of clothes for her and call her "dear child." Time on this side of the threshold differs from time on the mundane side, so she has been able to spend a day with her friends and yet have been gone only an hour, or spend a week in a single night. She has gone trading in the next town with Sofir and has learned to sew with Palizot. She has met Lord Horn in the manor at the edge of town and has come to know and secretly love the Mayor or Master, Dou Sark.

Because this world has for so long been her own place—she has named it, in her mind, "the ain country," from a Scottish ballad—she resents the intrusion of a stranger. She greets Hugh with a "No Trespassing" sign, hides his camping gear, threatens him with a rock. Hugh retreats, though thereafter he begins exploring the land on his own.

Irene becomes aware that there is a problem in the ain country, a lurking fear that has gradually closed off travel and communication so that only the outsiders Hugh and Irene are free to come and go outside the town boundaries. And Irene discovers, to her frustration, that the townspeople look not to her but to Hugh as their appointed deliverer (or possibly, according to certain hints, scapegoat). She is necessary only to guide him to the confrontation with whatever obscure evil he is supposed to face. Neither Hugh nor Irene can get a clear idea of its nature. Nevertheless, Hugh is willing to go, partly because he has fallen in love with Lord Horn's daughter Allia and partly because it is the first chance in his life to do something of worth. Irene has discovered that her beloved Master Sark is weaker than she had thought, and untrustworthy. She is willing to go with Hugh primarily because she no longer has reason to stay. She has also begun, in spite of herself, to respect Hugh's courage and integrity.

So the two strangers take leave of the village of Tembreabrezi and set out to fight what might as well be called a dragon. Seeing them off are a wise old man, a blonde princess, and a dark traitor. The land of their retreat, the refuge found for them by their unconscious minds, has thrown them into an archetypal conflict, a fairy tale. No refuge is without cost, and the realm of the unconscious is entered only at great peril, because it is the home of dragons, ogres, and the other monsters that lurk in the dim corners of our minds. This particular monster turns out to be a sort of undifferentiated essence of monster. Its weapon is raw fear and its form, as Lord Horn forewarns, is dependent on the beholder.

Seen through Irene's eyes it is gross, grotesque, humanoid, and female—Grendel's dam. To Hugh, though, it is apparently male:

> "You call it 'her,' " he said.
>
> "It was." She did not want to speak of the breasts and the thin arms.
>
> He shook his head, with a sick look, pallor increasing. "No, it was—The reason I had to kill it—" he said, and then put out his hand groping for support, and staggered as he stood.

The reason hinted at here seems to be that it was obscenely male and threatening to Irene. Each sees in the monster a mirror of his worst, hidden self, the monster self that Le Guin calls, in *A Wizard of Earthsea,* the shadow. ("Shadow" is an important term in Jung's model of the psyche. Le Guin had not read Jung when she wrote *A Wizard,* but she has since found many of his ideas useful in discussing the nature and value of fantasy.)

After Irene challenges the monster and Hugh kills it, Irene tends Hugh's wounds and together they make their way back to the threshold. There is no return to the village; Allia and Sark are forgotten. Hugh and Irene are bound together by their experience, their former hostility replaced by a liking growing rapidly into love. Halfway down the mountain, stopping for food, they make love, rather to their own surprise. Home again in the daylight world (only it is night this time, and raining), they remain together and plan to leave the suburb for the city, their lives no longer in stasis, with no more need for this particular escape.

What has Le Guin said about fantasy in this story? First, she reemphasizes her belief that it is valuable, even necessary to human well-being. Hugh, before he finds the threshold, is becoming dangerously dissociated into a robotlike persona and an unacknowledged, unhappy, explosive inner self. Irene is torn between love and resentment for her dead father, her aloof brother, and her abused mother, and her conflicting feelings leave her perpetually angry, afraid, and unable to make necessary changes in her own life. By escaping to the other world, both are granted respite from the demands of others and an opportunity to examine their lives from a distance. The inner strength that both possess is allowed to surface. Within the twilight world Irene and Hugh can be seen to stretch and straighten like newly emerged seedlings.

Le Guin indicates, secondly, that the magic world is potent. It is not there merely for the convenience of visitors, or for their amusement. It is full of hidden dangers and rules. Le Guin represents the danger primarily through her monster, drawing upon such horror conventions as eerie sounds (a "high gobbling scream far off in the woods,") and silences ("The wind had died. Nothing moved. It was like deafness,") and the ambiguous but unquestionably awful physical appearance of the creature. The rules, and the visitors' problems in learning them, she shows in several interesting ways. First of all, it is not a simple matter to get in and out across the threshold. Hugh can always enter, but Irene cannot, though she could when she was younger. Irene can always get out, but Hugh twice finds himself simply walking on into more twilight forest where he should have made the transition into sunlight and the sounds of cars and airplanes. Only together are they sure of finding both ways open, just as it takes both of them to defeat the monster.

Language serves as an analog to knowledge of the workings of the ain country. Irene has learned much of the language of Tembreabrezi, but there are areas where her knowledge fails her. She knows the words for familiar objects, common activities, and personal relationships, but she is not sure of the significance of more formidable words. She is not sure whether the word she has translated "king" means that or something quite different. She is unfamiliar with the word that may refer to the monster and might have been a clue to its nature. She is unable to ask about the differences between the twilight world and her own: why there is no sun or moon; why the language includes words for morning and night.

Hugh and Irene are most in ignorance about the rules governing good and evil, which in this—as in most fantasies—are wound around with magic. There is the monster: it is evil or at least brings evil about. There is the never-seen City with its maybe King: it is almost certainly good. Lord Horn tells Irene that it is because he has been to the City that he is called Lord. There was some sort of compact made with the monster or what it represents a generation ago. A child was sacrificed and the fear driven back temporarily, only to return stronger than before. Irene and Hugh know nothing of how any of this came about or how it relates to the closing of the roads. Irene thinks to herself, "He, and she, and all of them here, were subject to the law of the place, laws as absolute as the law of gravity, as impossible to disobey and as difficult to explain." And yet they do, they must, reach some kind of understanding in order to act for good and not evil. They begin to understand in the same way Le Guin says a child can understand the deeper significance of a fairy tale: nonverbally, irrationally, below or beyond the level of consciousness. Though the arcane mysteries of the twilight world remain mysteries, it is enough for the moment to know where they must go and what they must do. Irene realizes that it is wrong for her to return to the village; Hugh knows that he must make his stand against the monster. Having learned something about themselves, they understand at least their own rules in the fairy tale they are enacting, even though the history and nature of the fairy tale world elude explanation.

That is not to say that there is no connection between experience in our own world and experience in the other. Le Guin is especially subtle in drawing two kinds of connection—parallels and contrasts—between the two worlds. Physically there are many contrasts: daylight and twilight; pavement and forest; clutter and clarity; and, if time can be considered physical, hurried-up time and deliberate time. All of these make the ain country a kind of commentary on our own lives. We can also see areas in which the two lands are parallel, and that too helps us to see our world from a new perspective. We see in the lives of Hugh's mother, Irene's brother, and other people in the daylight world the same kind of bargaining with fear that has circumscribed the lives of the people of Mountain Town. Le Guin avoids too-obvious analogs—Hugh's sword equals X, the trail they follow is really Y—because allegorical elements that might just get by in an ordinary fantasy would be obtrusive in this sort of half-and-half tale. Nonetheless, there is enough continuity from world to world to make each a usable mirror of the other. What Hugh and Irene learn, about fear, about love, about themselves, they still know when they return.

One thing they learn, and another of Le Guin's points about fantasy, is that it is, despite parallels, not the same as waking life and should not be experienced in the same way. To do so is to trivialize it. What is rich and mysterious in twilight may seem flimsy in daylight. Both Hugh and Irene are guilty at first of this misunderstanding or misusing of the fantasy experience.

In an essay on style in fantasy, Le Guin proposed that we "consider Elfland as a great national park, a vast and beautiful place where a person goes by himself, on foot, to get in touch with reality in a special, private, profound fashion. But what happens when it is considered merely as a place to 'get away to'?" That is just what happens in *The Beginning Place*; indeed, that question could well have been the seed of the novel. What happens is that the cool, mysterious solidity of the beginning place gives way to the oddly insubstantial, conventionalized, fairy tale world of Tembreabrezi. The name of the place may be a clue. Though it has a respectable etymology, a compound of words for "mountain" and "town," the name sounds like nonsense, especially the kind of nonsense that shows up in cheap, pseudo-Dunsanian fantasy. It is not Le Guin's usual sort of name: "One place I do exert deliberate control in name-inventing is in the area of pronounceability. I try to spell them so they don't look too formidable (unless, like Kurremkarmerruk, they're meant to look formidable) . . ." Names in Earthsea are on the order of *Ged, Pendor, otak, rushwash tea*. The name *Kurremkarmerruk* is different because it belongs to the wizard who is Master Namer—and as such has the only name which means nothing.

In Tembreabrezi, both Hugh and Irene fall in love with people who are merely reflections of themselves: Irene with dark, intense Dou Sark, Hugh with pale, quiet Allia. In Jungian terms these are animus and anima: projections of the masculine component of the female psyche and the feminine component of the male. This is not real love, in Le Guin's universe. Her stories show, over and over, the reaching out to the dissimilar Other which is the beginning of mature love. When Hugh and Irene discover one another, it is a different matter. But Allia and Sark are not even portrayed as real, full characters. We see nothing of their lives unconnected with Hugh and Irene, overhear none of their thoughts. They are daydreams, My Ideal Man/Woman. To underscore the point, Hugh's and Irene's feelings toward them are described in a deflatingly parodic style: "He felt in himself the longing, the yearning to give so greatly to the beloved that nothing was left, to give all, all. To protect and guard her, to serve her, to die for her—the thought was unendurably sweet; again he caught his breath as if a knife had gone into him, when that thought came to him." This is not emotion but the mask of an emotion tried on for size. Love, says Le Guin, can enter into a fantasy world, but it cannot be found there, only representations of it.

J. R. R. Tolkien took his fantasy creation very seriously indeed, devoting much of his life to its development and defending it in the essay "On Fairy-Stories" and the story "Leaf by Niggle." But he never lost sight of its nature, and he began to be disturbed by those who tried to make of it something other than a story. He wrote to a friend, "I am not now at all sure that the tendency to treat the whole thing as a kind of vast game is really good." Those who do so are the people who are reluctant to emerge from the fantasy. Not content with what Tolkien calls Secondary Belief as they read, they attempt to mix the waking world and the dream. They print bumper stickers about hobbits and write stories that are strikingly like Hugh's mawkish musing on Allia. Le Guin, too, disapproves of the alteration of fantasy into a game. A fantasy world, she says in *The Beginning Place*, is not where you live your life, but where you go to begin to comprehend it.

The Beginning Place works better as metafantasy, or commentary on fantasy, than as a fantasy tale. In showing how to emerge from the world of the unconscious, how to, as it were, wake up again, Le Guin is obliged rather to slight the dream. It is a frustrating book to read because Irene and Hugh's story only touches briefly on the story, or history, of the fantasy world. If they truly belonged to the twilight world and were actually, as they seem briefly to be, its culture heroes, its saviors, then we would learn the fate of that world in learning of their adventures. That is the way it is with Frodo and Middle Earth or Ged and Earthsea. In this case, however, the individual drama, the coming of age of Hugh and Irene, is worked out without any corresponding solution of the problems of Tembreabrezi and its countryside. We are left asking questions: What happens to Horn, Sark, Allia? Where is the City and what is it like? Is the twilight a perpetual state or does it mark a long-delayed transition to dawn or utter night? Why are there no birds, no flowers, no songs? Hugh and Irene do not need to know, having reached their goal, but the reader would like to. We are too accustomed to grand finales and happily-ever-afters; like children greedy for more bedtime story we want to know "what happened after that?" We accept Irene and Hugh's return to reality and the implied message about times to dream and times to wake up, but we do so grudgingly, with many a backward glance.

Perhaps Le Guin will return to the beginning place, as she did to Earthsea, and take up the loose threads of its tapestry. Until then, *The Beginning Place* is most satisfyingly read, first, as a tale of two striking characters and their inward growth, and, second, as a fantasy about fantasy, just as *The Lathe of Heaven* is her science fiction novel about science fiction. *The Beginning Place* can tell us much about the richer world of Earthsea and how, like all fully developed fantasy worlds, it may properly be used not as an escape from, but as a means of reimagining, of reseeing the world we live in.

CAROL McGUIRK

Optimism and the Limits of Subversion in "The Dispossessed" and "The Left Hand of Darkness"

He hunted through an overflowing drawer and finally achieved a book,
a queer-looking book, bound in blue. . . . The title was stamped in gold
and seemed to say Poilea Afio-ite, *which didn't make any sense, and*
the shapes of some of the letters were unfamiliar. Shevek stared at
it, took it from Sabul, but did not open it. He was holding it, the thing
he had wanted to see, the alien artifact, the message from another world.

— The Dispossessed

Le Guin coolly subverts "pulp" exoticism: it is a prosaic (though queer-looking) textbook and not the star-washed ship viewscreen of space opera that offers young Shevek his first glimpse of a wider cosmos. Yet the passage also suggests the limits that Le Guin places on her portrayal of the alien—the "other"—in her two finest science fiction novels. Shevek's "alien artifact" is, in fact, from no alien world: it is a text in his own field, physics, by a scientist of Urras, the planet from which Shevek's own ancestors migrated some 170 years before the events described in *The Dispossessed*.

The people of Urras are of the same stock as the people of Anarres: the two worlds are not so much alien as estranged. Representing not the unknown but the previously known and rejected, Urras is to Shevek's people a rejected mother-world: the formidable solidarity of the Anarresti originated in their shared hatred of Urrasti oppression. (Similarly, on the level of characterization, Shevek himself is shown as having matured through his conscious rejection of Rulag, his own non-nurturing mother.)

Repeatedly in the "Hainish" novels, the apparent alien becomes, on better acquaintance, really a repressed, rejected, or earlier phase of the self. When the Earth envoy Genly Ai reaches his Gethenian friend Therem Harth telepathically, it is the voice of his dead brother that the terrified Lord of Estre "hears." An analogous paradox structures Freud's analysis of the uncanny: the world "*heimlich*," he notes, grades easily into its opposite: *unheimlich*, not homelike, terrifying. Le Guin's vision of the alien works in a more optimistic direction, seeing beyond apparent "otherness" to a connectedness—she sometimes calls it "human solidarity"—that goes beneath and beyond apparent difference. This model is, as Le Guin has noted, Jungian and romantic (the collective unconscious is the source of individual identity) rather than Freudian and ironic. (To Freud, such "oceanic" certainties are simply memories of one's deluded sense of omnipotence in infancy.)

The first level of optimism in Le Guin, then—and the primary reason for her suppression of the alien—is psychological. In *The Left Hand of Darkness*, the Gethenians are, like the people of Anarres and Urras and indeed like the Earth envoy Genly Ai, all of common ancestry. Earth, like Gethen—and like the Cetian solar system described in *The Dispossessed*—was seeded with sentient life by the proto-human colonizers called the Hainish. In Le Guin's cosmos, as in Cordwainer Smith's, there is no true "other"—all intelligent life has a common origin and a common humanity. All advanced species have the capacity for "mindspeech," or telepathy—science fiction's most powerful image of communion. Since the human psyche is notably flawed, planetary cultures may well evolve in troubling ways: social injustice is a central concern in Le Guin's fiction. Yet the final message always seems to involve the ultimate bridgability of difference—at least by characters of heroic capacity. Le Guin's heroes are strong enough to resist the pressures of xenophobia (the hatred of apparent difference), and wish enough to take as their goal the greater good of humanity; this often requires the "betrayal" of some smaller group. One such character is Shevek, the exile/traitor/hero of *The Dispossessed*: "I want solidarity, human solidarity. I want free exchange between Urras and Anarres." Another is Therem Harth of Estraven, the exile/traitor/hero of

The Left Hand of Darkness: "Do you think I would play *shifgrethor* when so much is at stake for all of us, all my fellow men? What does it matter which country wakens first, so long as we waken?"

Such heroes are not pasteboard saints: they are self-willed individuals whose magnanimous loyalties lead them past temptation and well into transgression. In his youth, Therem Harth breaks the incest taboos of his planet by vowing *kemmering* (marriage) with his brother; later, he breaks other social codes when he steals and, perhaps, when he chooses to die. Shevek, too, despite his fierce love for Anarres, is often, because of his genius, incapable of satisfying its egalitarian principles. At two, he is reprimanded for claiming that the sun belongs to him; at eight, he is punished for "egoizing" in his study group. At forty, he will donate his scientific breakthrough, the theory of simultaneity, to the Hainish, in order to prevent it from being put to partisan uses. Such heroes are intuitive, and their intuitions are vindicated. Their allegiance to an idealized human community protects them from misanthropy, yet their clear-sighted openness to the "message from another world" comes from their habitual sense of distance from their native groups—another of Le Guin's paradoxes. Genly Ai says of Therem Harth: "He was always ready. It was, no doubt, the secret of the extraordinary political career he threw away for my sake; it was also the explanation of his belief in me and devotion to my mission. When I came, he was ready. Nobody else on Winter was."

Le Guin's conception of heroism, then, is—like the ubiquity of human values in her cosmos—admirably enlightened yet somehow also fundamentally optimistic, denying the ineluctable difference of the truly alien by making the central feature in heroic behavior a refusal to *be* alien-ated. Le Guin's heroes insist on the negotiable status of difference; the plots both of *The Dispossessed* and *The Left Hand of Darkness* involve successful negotiation. Le Guin's Hainish cosmos is thus tailored to demonstrate the power of individual heroes, the altruism of their heroic impulse, the advancement of society through violation of its laws, and the persistence of humane values despite often unfavorable cultural conditions. (Genly Ai, imprisoned in totalitarian Orgoreyn and moved by the special treatment given him by fellow-prisoners, muses: "It is a terrible thing, this kindness that human beings do not lose.")

Above all, Le Guin's cosmos is ethical, designed to provide a setting for the drama of human choice. Fredric Jameson has called her procedure "world reduction," but it also involves an inflation of individual human agents. Shevek's renegade physical research—the transgression of one man—leads to the theory of simultaneity. The Ekumen establishes contact with newly discovered worlds by sending a single Envoy: "The first news from the Ekumen on any world is spoken by one voice, one man present in the flesh, present and alone." Isolation is power: as Therem Harth warns Obsle of Orgoreyn, the unarmed defenseless Envoy "brings the end of Kingdoms and Commensalities with him in his empty hands." This Hainish cosmos is a vigorously enabling one—and it consistently rewards those heroes and cultures that tolerate diversity. It is Cetian physics that penetrates the mysteries of space and time, because Cetian science—unlike that of hapless "Ainsetain of Terra," a genius trapped in a less enabling world—has always encouraged eclecticism:

> The Terrans had been intellectual imperialists, jealous wall-builders. Even Ainsetain, the originator of the [relativity] theory, had felt compelled to give warning that his physics embraced no mode but the physical and should not be taken as implying the metaphysical, the philosophical, or the ethical.
>
> *(The Dispossessed)*

By contrast, in Le Guin's refreshingly anti-imperialist cosmos, "the strongest, in the existence of any social species, are those who are most social. In human terms, most ethical." This is fundamentally a Renaissance or humanist cosmology—the Universe, like the text, is constructed to incarnate Man ("one man present in the flesh"). Humanity is the subject and the object of all texts and all messages: the ansible, like the radios of Karhide and like "mindspeech," transmits a single human voice.

Scholars who approach Le Guin through the field of utopia/eutopia/dystopia—a flourishing academic specialty in recent years—find her idealized, humanized cosmos less problematic than some other factions in science fiction studies (one might term the dissidents "hard science" fundamentalists or cosmological gnostics). Such critics are prone to fears that utopia is not now the avant-garde literary form that it was in 1516, and that—however enlightened humanism's original secularization of value—the Renaissance emphasis on the reasonableness of human nature and the intelligibility of the cosmos detracts from some of the more powerfully subversive symbolic possibilities of the science fiction genre.

The eloquent if splenetic Stanislaw Lem has summed up this viewpoint succinctly in a general indictment of American SF's tendency to "domesticate" the cosmos. In his view, which is taken from the standpoint of contemporary cosmology, "it makes no sense at all to look at the universe from the viewpoint of ethics":

> The universe is a continued explosion extended over a time of twenty billion years [that] could appear as a majestic solidification only to the

eyes of a transient being like man. . . . Thanks to time travel and FTL [faster than light spaceships], the cosmos [of American SF] has acquired such qualities as domesticate it in an exemplary way for storytelling purposes; but at the same time it has lost its strange, icy sovereignity. . . . The fact that a domestication of the cosmos has taken place, a diminution that [has] whisked away those eternally silent abysses of which Pascal spoke with horror, is masked in SF by the blood that is so liberally spilt in its pages. But there we already have a humanized cruelty, for it is a cruelty that can be understood by man, and a cruelty that could finally even be judged from the viewpoint of ethics. . . . We [thus] come to understand what SF has done to the cosmos: for it makes no sense at all to look at the universe from the viewpoint of ethics. Therefore the universe of SF is not only miniscule, simplified and lukewarm, but it has also been turned towards its inhabitants, and in this way it can be subjugated by them, losing thereby [its] indifference. . . . In the universe of SF there is not the slightest chance that genuine myths and theologies might arise, for the thing itself is a bastard of myths gone to the dogs. The SF of today is a "graveyard of gravity," in which that subgenre that promised the cosmos to mankind, dreams away its defeats in onanistic delusions and chimeras—onanistic because they are anthropocentric.

(*SF Studies* 4 [1977])

Although Lem's charge of excessive violence is hardly applicable to the consistently responsible and pacifistic fiction of Le Guin, his attack on the "domestication" of the cosmos does suggest a troubling limitation in her vision—an optimism that too easily tames the universe by denying its perilous otherness. Thoroughly secular, admirably ethical, Le Guin's universe nonetheless achieves its balance and coherence through a diminished emphasis on the unknowable, the alien; the "silent abysses of which Pascal spoke with horror" are made, perhaps too readily, to speak to us here and now. This may be what David Ketterer means in *New Worlds for Old* when he criticizes *The Left Hand of Darkness* for the overt didacticism that he calls "insufficiently displaced myth." Lem's critique is broader: in general, American SF's pastoral parables of a hero-enabling, navigable cosmos indulge in downright misrepresentation of the physical universe—and thus fail to delineate our real existential dilemma:

The space surrounding a neutron star cannot be passed closely in a spaceship even at parabolic velocity because the gravity gradients in a human body increase . . . and human beings explode until only a red puddle is left, just like a heavenly body that is torn apart from tidal forces when passing through the Roche limit.

Le Guin has said that she does "not like to see the word 'liberal' used as a smear word," and given the often reactionary leanings of popular

SF (of which, more later) there is courage and risk in her liberal stance. Still, if Darko Suvin's definition of SF as "the literature of cognitive estrangement" is correct (as I think it is), there is also some evasiveness— some stopping short of radical re-visioning—in Le Guin's humane liberalism. Science fiction, with its potentially powerful imagery of voyages into the unknown and encounters with the alien, is probably better designed to subvert than to validate human-centered norms and values. (Indeed, Le Guin's androgynes in *The Left Hand of Darkness* are used, early in the novel, in such a subversive way. The Gethenians, with their lack of institutionalized sexism and gender anxiety, force readers to ponder their own preconceptions about gender and identity. Yet while strongly making that point—and, along the way, joyously puncturing a number of SF's most cherished sexist cliches—Le Guin finally imposes, over her subversive surface, a humanist/Taoist fable of oneness and reconciliation. There is a humanity beyond gender difference, evident in mindspeech, in the Gethenians' "human" pronoun, and in Genly Ai's final ability to understand and love Therem Harth. Subversion of traditional gender roles in this novel, then, ultimately serves the purpose of affirming a familiar progressive value: tolerance for diversity.)

Le Guin's liberalism, in short, while admirable in questioning stereotypes and rejecting the easy violence and repellant social Darwinianism of so much popular SF, is nonetheless content to dwell on the knowable (indeed, heroic) capacities of human nature, never striking into the heart of true darkness: the morally problematic existence of intransigent evil, and the cosmologically problematic fact that our universe poses literally unimaginable dangers. Lacking these dark intonations—or rather given her Jungian/Taoist value for darkness as a benign and necessary balance to light—Le Guin's human-centered, progressive vision can degenerate, as Samuel Delany has noted, into sentimentality. This is an occasional flaw in the portrayal of life on Anarres (e. g. "However pragmatic the morality a young Anarresti absorbed, yet life overflowed in him, demanding altruism, self-sacrifice, scope for the absolute gesture"—the implied definition of "life" here forces its idealism on readers). Sentimentality sometimes strikes a false note even from the scrupulously honest, plain-spoken, unforgettable narrators of *The Left Hand of Darkness*: "They were as sexless as steers. They were without shame and without desire, like the angels. But it is not human to be without shame and desire." The words are spoken by Genly Ai, but in their tacit assumption that humanity is the endpoint of creation they are worthy of *Star Trek*'s constantly thwarted but incurably anthropocentric Dr. McCoy.

The real limit to subversion in Le Guin, then, is her tendency to an unexamined humanism: human capacities are given, rather too readily, a cosmic heroic stature. This is common among practitioners of "soft" SF, intent on replacing the technological emphasis of "hard" SF with a reemphasis on characterization. (It is also common among SF's libertarians, confident that institutions and laws are unnecessary restrictions on liberty, given the fundamental decency of individual human consciences.) Yet there are alternatives to an optimistic, utopian cosmology available in the popular science fiction tradition. A brief discussion of Cordwainer Smith and Arthur C. Clarke—two writers who in different ways exploit SF's more radical possibilities—may help to place Le Guin's mediating liberalism. It will also introduce the final topic of this essay: Le Guin's ambivalent relationship to popular SF and her most consistently subversive activity—her energetic reversal of science fiction's common stock of tropes.

Cordwainer Smith was the pseudonym of Paul Linebarger (1913–1966), a Johns Hopkins professor, foreign affairs consultant, and military intelligence expert (he coined the term "psychological warfare"). Le Guin dates her adult interest in SF from 1960, when she encountered "Alpha Ralpha Boulevard," her first Cordwainer Smith story: "I don't really remember what I thought when I read it, but what I think now I ought to have thought when I read it is, "My God! It can be done!" (*Foundation* 4 [1974]). Although ultimately the differences are more striking, there are many similarities between Le Guin and Smith. In Smith, as in Le Guin, all sentient life has a common source, although it is Terra, not Hain: the descendants of Earth colonists have settled the galaxy, and all intelligent life is Earth-derived. (There are intelligent animal species, genetically enhanced to serve as slaves to man, but the species are native to Earth. There are also true aliens, possibly from another galaxy—the elegant architects called the Daimoni—but they do not figure prominently in the stories.)

In Smith, as in Le Guin, the shared humanity of intelligent species is metaphorically underscored by universal latent telepathic abilities, called "hiering" and "spieking" in Smith. Le Guin, like Smith, sets her "Hainish" novels in different eras of a consistent future cosmos. (In a special Le Guin issue of *SF Studies* [1978], Rafail Nudelman praises the "originality" of her "future history drawn with a dotted line," but here Le Guin follows the practice not only of Cordwainer Smith but also of numerous other SF writers, from Asimov and Heinlein—who began the trend under the guidance of their editor during the 1940's, John W. Campbell—to H. Beam Piper and Frank Herbert.) Finally, like Le Guin, Smith is far more concerned with enduring human problems than with new technological solutions. In *Norstrilia*, the hero's trusty family retainer—a computer—answers Rod McBan's simple question "Who am I?" with a burst of eloquence:

> You are Rod McBan the hundred and fifty-first. Specifically, you are a spinal column with a small bone box at one end, the head, and with reproductive equipment at the other end. Inside the bone box you have a small portion of material which resembles stiff, bloody lard. With that you think—you think better than I do, even though I have more than five hundred million synaptic connections. You are a wonderful object, Rod McBan.

Cordwainer Smith's universe is thus, like Le Guin's, designed to explore and analyze the human psyche.

The difference is that Smith's analysis of the human dilemma is gloomier—his vision is religious rather than secular, fatalistic rather than optimistic and progressive. In Smith, unlike Le Guin, space is not easily navigable; monstrous adaptations are necessary to convey humans from planet to planet. In "The Game of Rat and Dragon," huge invisible "Rats" prey upon unprotected spacecraft; in *Norstrilia*, Rod McBan voyages to earth pickled and disassembled, packed in a crate the size of a hatbox. In "Scanners Live in Vain," set early in Smith's future history, something called the "Pain of Space" infects all early voyagers with a suicidal "need to die"—a problem that Smith solves fancifully by lining the walls of his ships with oysters, living tissue that absorbs the hostile cosmic vibrations and dies so that humans can retain their sanity. (Animals who martyr themselves in the cause of man form a recurring theme in Smith; this may well be *his* area of sentimentality.)

Smith's pessimism is as consistently represented by his cosmos as Le Guin's progressive optimism by hers. In Smith, the rulers of Earth achieve eutopia only to find that humanity is on the decline: immortality, prosperity and peace have destroyed the suffering that Smith regards as essential to human identity. The rulers of the Instrumentality are forced to initiate the Rediscovery of Man, an emergency measure that re-introduces to earth the necessary human realities of war, disease, hatred and death. For all its emphasis on humanity, then, Smith's is a far less enabling cosmos than Le Guin's; in his postlapserian universe, human nature is to be redeemed through divine providence, not through social planning. In *Norstrilia*, the promise of redemption is represented by enslaved animals called the Underpeople, whose leader, the E'telekeli ("Entelechy," in Montaigne's paraphrase of Aristotle, is "the soul, or perfection moving of itself") is a fugitive, a failed genetic experiment—part eagle and part

Daimoni. E'telekeli, father of E'kasus, is that quality, outcast from humanity and "other" than humanity (Daimoni are aliens), that nonetheless can redeem humanity. The politics are reactionary here (in that they suggest that the human condition is not improvable through political means), but the vision is radical in that evil is alive and awake in this universe. The reality of uncanny peril imbues the struggles of Smith's heroes with an authentic, if eccentric, intensity. What is subverted in Smith is precisely that eutopian dream of a perfectible—or at least reasonably nurturant—human community that is so strongly conveyed by Le Guin in such central images as the beneficent Ekumen. Ironically, Smith's religious conservatism leaves more room for mystery—for SF's exploration of "cognitive estrangement"—than Le Guin's more enlightened but less alienated humanist idealism.

Smith's is a High Church universe, hierarchical and paradoxical: the last shall be first. *Childhood's End*, Arthur C. Clarke's finest novel, offers a similar paradox couched in mystical rather than religious terms. Since Le Guin has been called a mystic because of her extensive use of paradox (a charge also frequently leveled at Jung), comparison of her work with *Childhood's End* may help to demonstrate the decidedly unmystical centrality of reason in her cosmos. In *Science Fiction: History, Form, & Vision*, Scholes and Rabkin have called *Childhood's End* a utopian novel, but it is actually a parable about the limitations of enlightenment, indicated by the solely transitional value of the Golden Age achieved in its middle section. The real message combines a mystical quietism like that of Stapledon's *Star Maker* (an influence Clarke acknowledges) with the child-as-monster theme beloved in pulp SF and best represented by Lewis Padgett's "Mimsy Were the Borogoves" and many of Ray Bradbury's early stories.

Clarke's consistent mysticism and Le Guin's preference for the rational are most clearly seen in their differing treatments of heroism and telepathy. In Clarke's novel, the exertions of the dare-all hero, Jan Rodricks, are poignant rather than effective. The cosmic rite of passage which humanity is about to undergo—the evolution and absorption of Earth's children into the pure energy entity called Overmind—makes Rodricks' venturesome individuality irrelevant. Nobody over the age of ten is recruited by Overmind: mature individuals are not of interest in this cosmos—they do not get very far. Seven-year-old Jeff Greggson travels further in his early dreams of the Overmind than the superior alien race, the Overlords, have travelled in their spaceships. Indeed, the ethical complexity and brilliant rationality of the Overlords' minds are exactly what makes them unsuitable for further evolution: they know that they will never progress into Overmind. In his conclusion, which Clarke says "repudiates optimism and pessimism alike," earth is destroyed by its departing children, yet the loss is a sign that humanity has evolved beyond the need for bodies, or an earth to contain them.

Clarke's Overmind—the most advanced cosmic entity—paradoxically seeks out immature beings to contact through telepathy. Children are not yet fully socialized; they have fewer barriers, less reliance on earth-bound reasoning, than adults. In Le Guin, by contrast, telepathy is possible only in maturity. As Genly Ai tells Therem Harth: "Except in the case of the born Sensitive, the capacity [for mindspeech] . . . is a product of culture, a side-effect of the use of the mind. Young children, and defectives, and members of unevolved or regressed societies, can't mindspeak. The mind must exist on a certain plane of complexity first. . . . Abstract thought, varied social interaction, intricate cultural adjustments, esthetic and ethical perception, all of it has to reach a certain level before the connections can be made" (*LHD*). Far from embracing mysticism, then—if mysticism be defined as a yearning for self-loss and oneness—Le Guin, by contrast to Clarke, reveals a firm value for mature, rational individualism: in the Hainish novels, the libertarian in her is stronger than the Taoist. Yet, as with Smith's Christianity, Clarke's Buddhist mysticism may well leave more room for those powerful intonations of the unknown and the unknowable that SF is particularly well-suited to generating.

Perhaps the main point here is that utopia/eutopia/dystopia—the enlightened explorations, as in Le Guin, of exemplary societies—is, while clearly related to science fiction, just as clearly an older form, with closer ties to the optimistic assumptions of Renaissance humanism about human capacity. This optimism marks many passages in More's *Utopia*:

> [The citizens of Utopia] hold that happiness rests not in every kind of pleasure but only in good and decent pleasure. To such, as to the supreme good, our nature is drawn by virtue itself. . . . The Utopians define virtue as living according to nature. . . . [Reason] admonishes and urges us to lead a life as free from care and as full of joy as possible and, because of our natural fellowship, to help all other men, too, to attain that end.

In his emphasis on the innate rationality and altruism of human character, More sounds very much like Odo, founder of Anarres—a less ambiguous utopia than the subtitle of *The Dispossessed* would suggest.

Utopia, an inherently anthropocentric form, is not necessarily a genre that encourages its practitioners to use all the symbolic capacities of science fiction. While it may well explore social, sexual, and psychological "estrangement" (as Le Guin certainly does), it will seldom proceed to the cosmological estrangement explored by Clarke or the moral (as opposed to purely ethical) dilemmas posed by Smith. The utopian vision places the cosmos in the background in order to ensure that man remains in high relief; it deals with ethical rather than moral matters—with heroism rather than sin—because of a secular and classical focus inherited from Renaissance humanism. Perhaps another way to put this is to say that a utopia such as Anarres is political and thus dwells on the possible. Ideally, however, science fiction is equipped to range further, into the limits of the conceivable. Both Clarke and Smith, for instance, depict utopias solely to demonstrate their futility and to offer transcendent—if frightening—alternatives.

To emphasize the symbolic potential of science fiction in this way is not, incidentally, to suggest that scores of writers surpass Le Guin in their exploitation of the genre. Although Clarke and Smith do offer a more powerful representation of the cosmos, neither is the literary craftsman that Le Guin is, or comes close to her skill in characterization. Le Guin's limitations are simply those imposed by the optimism of the humanist ideology and its literary offspring, utopia. Yet a large but misguided group within science fiction studies is now trying to legitimize SF by hitching its raffish wagon to a star—the older and, academically speaking, infinitely more respectable genre of utopia—and has encouraged the critical community to praise (in Le Guin and in contemporary utopian fiction generally) the very anthropocentric tendencies that are really limitations on what SF can accomplish.

Carl Yoke, for example, writing in *Extrapolation*, betrays this anxiety about respectability in remarks that sever Le Guin completely from the popular American tradition: "Without question, Le Guin is a writer of the first rank. . . . And she is a writer who is read by people who do not consider themselves to be science fiction fans, who, in fact, scoff at the term 'science fiction.' . . . In this respect, Le Guin has done much to legitimize the genre, and as a result she has achieved 'mainstream' stature, just as H. G. Wells, Aldous Huxley and George Orwell have" (Fall 1980, p. 198). Similar statements are often made and seldom challenged, but they raise at least two problems. The first has already been discussed: a marginal literary form serves highly useful and potentially subversive purposes, especially in its symbolic capaciousness, its greater freedom and fluidity of imagery. Why then should SF aspire to the mainstream? Secondly—and this is a new issue—such statements actually belittle Le Guin's achievement, for the British dystopians were never out of the mainstream in quite the sense that Ursula Le Guin was in 1966, when her first Hainish novel, *Rocannon's World,* appeared with Avram Davidson's *The Kar-Chee Reign* as an Ace Doubles paperback. (The Ace Doubles series was the apotheosis of pulp—two novels published back to back, under one cover, to cut costs. Donald A. Wollheim was the editor, and some fine fiction appeared in this throwaway format: the second Hainish novel, *Planet of Exile,* appeared later in 1966 paired with Thomas Disch's mordant *Mankind Under the Leash.*)

Wells, Huxley, and Orwell may have had their struggles, but they never had to publish their novels in tandem, or to deal with the often conflicting constituencies of American commercial SF: editors demanding quick sales, critics demanding high quality, fans demanding pure enter-tainment and frequent personal appearances at conventions. Le Guin's career has been almost unique in its graceful accommodation of such pressures. *The Left Hand of Darkness* and *The Dispossessed* won both the fans' Hugo and the SF writers' Nebula awards for the years in which they appeared (1969 and 1974); Le Guin is the only author who has twice won both awards simultaneously, demonstrating that these novels satis-fied the highest expectations both of avid amateurs and SF professionals. Le Guin, who now publishes in *Critical Inquiry* and *The New Yorker,* is perceived by critics as a belletristic writer, yet the appeal of her science fiction to her original fannish constituency has never faltered. Indeed, the continuing high popularity of *The Left Hand of Darkness* and *The Dispossessed* among fans may well be founded in a more intelligent response to Le Guin than her current critical modishness, which depends heavily on the unexamined assumption that utopia is, after all, an irreproachable intel-lectual enterprise. The fans, on the other hand, love Le Guin because of her provocative rendition of SF's themes and tropes—her witty reversals and re-visions of the pulp conventions in which fans are learned. The Handdara religion of Karhide says that "to oppose something is to main-tain it," and Le Guin's revisions of the pulp tradition echo this paradox, both challenging and revivifying science fiction's characteristic narrative strategies.

A perspective by incongruity is afforded by Stanislaw Lem, who much resembles Le Guin in the use of reversal, paradox, and strategic understatement, but who is hostile rather than ambivalent toward the SF tradition. Lem's method, like Le Guin's, consists in an ascetic refusal of exoticism. Readers are re-educated and, upon any sudden irruption into the story, will see a cliche *as* a cliche. As a replacement for the standard space-opera sentence "The vast, unexplored planet loomed suddenly on the viewscreen," for instance, Lem offers us this:

On day 1,006, having left the local system of the Nereid Nebula, I noticed a spot on the screen and tried rubbing it off with a chamois cloth. There was nothing else to do, so I spent four hours rubbing before I realized that the spot was a planet and rapidly growing larger.

(*Memoirs of a Space Traveler*)

Retaliating against the mad-computer theme in popular SF (perhaps best exemplified by HAL in Kubrick and Clarke's *2001: A Space Odyssey*), Lem offers fables of sadomasochistic washing machines; and, in *Star Diaries*, of a planet supposedly colonized by a renegade computer but actually inhabited by humans in robot suits, accessories in an insurance scam. Musing on "the fundamental decency of the electronic brain," Lem's voyager Ijon Tichy concludes: "Only Man can be a bastard."

Le Guin's satire is aimed more at exhausted literary conventions than at human nature, but she uses the same tool: subversion of the SF reader's conditioned expectations. Using the SF scenario of the hero seeking refuge among benevolent aliens, for instance, Le Guin offers in *The Dispossessed* Shevek's encounter with *his* first alien—an employee of the Terran embassy on Urras:

"Shevek. My name is Shevek. From Anarres." The alien eyes flashed, brilliant, intelligent, in the jet-black face. "*Mai-god!*" the Terran said under his breath, and then, in Iotic, "Are you seeking asylum?"

On Urras, Iotic is standard and English the "alien" tongue. *The Left Hand of Darkness* similarly reverses space-opera's view of the alien either as a threat to be subdued or a resource to be exploited. It is the Earthborn Genly Ai who is the alien intruder on Gethen, but he comes bearing no arms—just a message from the Ekumen, a clearing house of information about other worlds. Ai's outnumbered status is used to effective ironic purposes: his (in human terms) perfectly ordinary male gender is viewed by Gethenian consensus as a distasteful perversion. Yet, in a further reversal and denial of the exotic, Genly Ai looks so much like a Gethenian (albeit a sexually anomalous one) that he cannot persuade the bureaucrats of Orgoreyn that he *is* from outer space. Therem Harth admits that there are few external tokens of Genly Ai's difference: "[The Orgota] see him no doubt much as I first saw him: an unusually tall, husky and dark youth just entering *kemmer*. I studied the physicians' reports on him last year. His differences from us are profound. They are not superficial. [Yet] one must know him to know him alien". Bug-eyed monsters have not been fashionable in SF for decades, but a tendency to exteriorize "otherness" persists—and Le Guin's characterizations of the alien constitute a penetrating criticism of that tendency.

Le Guin's not-so-alien aliens may have their cosmological limita-tions, as mentioned earlier, but they very effectively challenge the often facile exoticism of popular SF. In conventional usage, the trope of the alien suggests that evil can be embodied somewhere beyond the human norm, and this evil bears an instantly recognizable and hateful shape. A memorable example occurs in Fredric Brown's "Arena," published in 1944 (the pulps became decidedly xenophobic during World War II):

> And he was alone, but not alone. For as Carson looked up, he saw that red thing, the red sphere of horror which he now knew was the Outsider, was rolling towards him.
>   Rolling.
>   It seemed to have no legs or arms that he could see, no features. It rolled across the blue sand with the fluid quickness of a drop of mercury. And before it, in some manner he could not understand, came a paralyzing wave of nauseating, retching, horrid hatred.
>   (*SF Hall of Fame*, Vol. I, p. 287)

In tacit response to this SF theme of alien-as-menace, Le Guin describes the country folk of Karhide in *The Left Hand of Darkness*, who welcome Genly Ai calmly and without curiosity: "An enemy is not a stranger, an invader. [In Karhide] the stranger who comes unknown is a guest. Your enemy is your neighbor." Thus, in Le Guin, evil is political, not racial: it is embodied in the secret police of Orgoreyn and Urras; in all-too-familiar, not in strange-looking shapes.

Social Darwinianism—the notion that in society as in nature, only the fit survive—is often rendered in popular SF as a rationale to support competitiveness, aggression, and imperialism. This theme, like that of the exteriorized alien, is analyzed and disposed of in Le Guin's science fiction. The Hainish universe is a sadder but wiser place in which the adaptive purposes of aggression have been demonstrated to be nil. The Earth ambassador to Urras tells Shevek:

> My world, my Earth, is a ruin. A planet spoiled by the human species. We multiplied and gobbled and fought until there was nothing left. We controlled neither appetite nor violence; we did not adapt. We destroyed ourselves. But we destroyed the world first. . . . You Odonians chose a desert; we Terrans made a desert. . . . We survive there, as you do. People are tough! There are nearly half a billion of us now. Once there were nine billion. You can see the old cities still everywhere. The bones and bricks go to dust, but the little pieces of plastic never do—they never adapt either. We failed as a species, a social species. We are here only because of the charity of the Hainish.

When Fredric Jameson calls *The Left Hand of Darkness* an "anti-*Dune*," he suggests Le Guin's revisionary relationship to popular SF. Indeed, although both Herbert and Le Guin are libertarians, Le Guin precisely reverses the notion prevalent in the *Dune* series (and widespread in SF) that personal identity is achieved primarily in the struggle to subjugate or be subjugated—that all life is a holy war or Jihad. By contrast, the persecuted Odonian community on Urras is said to be striking, not for better wages, but "against power." And in "American SF and The Other," Le Guin strongly expresses in critical terms the stance of her Hainish Fiction, which consistently rejects popular SF's aggrandizement of power as a route to personal identity:

> If you deny any affinity with another person or kind of person, if you declare it to be wholly different from yourself—as men have done to women and class has done to class, and nation has done to nation—you may hate it, or deify it; but in either case . . . you have made it into a thing, to which the only possible relationship is a power relationship. And thus you have fatally impoverished your own reality. You have, in fact, alienated yourself.
> This tendency has been remarkably strong in American SF. The only social change presented by most SF has been toward authoritarianism, the domination of ignorant masses by a powerful elite—sometimes presented as a warning but often quite complacently. . . . Military virtues are taken as ethical ones. Wealth is assumed to be a righteous goal and a personal virtue. Competitive free-enterprise capitalism is the economic destiny of the entire Galaxy. In general, American SF has assumed a permanent hierarchy of superiors and inferiors, with rich, ambitious, aggressive males at the top, then a great gap, and then at the bottom the poor, the uneducated, the faceless masses, and all the women. The whole picture is, if I may say so, curiously "un-American." It is a perfect baboon patriarchy, with the Alpha Male on top, being respectfully groomed, from time to time, by his inferiors.
> Is this speculation? Is this imagination? Is this extrapolation? I call it brainless regressivism.
>
> (*The Language of the Night*)

It is appropriate that discussion of the inventor of Anarres and Odo should finally come full circle. Le Guin's most consistently subversive activity lies in her polemical reversals, in her ironic rendition of the popular SF tradition. Yet the source of her popularity and of her narrative power, as well as of her ideological limitations, lies in her calm but persistent placement of the human individual—never at war but always at risk—in the live center of her cosmos. The physics of Le Guin's Hainish cosmos are thus really metaphysics, although such scientists as Fritzjof Capra would certainly endorse them:

> Most of today's physicists do not seem to realize the philosophical, cultural and spiritual implications of their theories. Many of them actively support a society which is still based on the mechanistic, fragmented world view, without seeing that science points beyond such a view, towards a oneness of the universe which includes not only our natural environment but also our fellow human beings.
>
> (*The Tao of Physics*)

Le Guin's metaphysics stress harmony rather than Capra's "unity"—a resonance of disparate but cooperative parts rather than an immolation of identity. (This is strongly imaged in *The Left Hand of Darkness* in her description of Foretelling—a communal activity that utilizes abnormal energies, making an orchestration of aberrations necessary to producing valid prophecy.) In *Devotions*, John Donne wrote that: "Man consists of more pieces, more parts, than the world. . . . And if those parts were extended, and stretched out in man as they are in the world, man would be the giant and the world the dwarf; the world but the map and man the world." Le Guin's rendition of human presence in the cosmos employs an analogous paradox, reversing the usual SF positionings of micro and macrocosm.

Le Guin once jokingly wondered why no researcher had yet prospected among the archives at Radcliffe and Columbia for nuggets from her early academic work. While researching this essay at Columbia's Butler Library, I did look up her master's thesis, "Aspects of Death in Ronsard's Poetry"; in fact, it suggested the focus of this discussion. Perhaps Le Guin's defense of Ronsard's optimism stands as the best rejoinder to any emphasis here on limitations:

> To say Ronsard saw life as good . . . is not to make of him a kind of Pollyanna of the Renaissance. Scholars are sometimes condescending, perhaps, in their opinion of Renaissance optimism. Ronsard was as aware as any Platonist of his time that there seems to be a fundamental flaw somewhere, that perfection does not exist and happiness does not last, in this world.

Ronsard's optimism, like that of the Hainish series Le Guin would conceive ten years after writing her thesis, is firmly founded in a value for reason. Ronsard "moved on classical ground . . . and if he saw the grave as dark, it was with the unmysterious darkness of earthly night." Both in their humanism, which is also a demystification of superstition and regressivism, and in their harmonious, "unmysterious" rendering of darkness, the Hainish novels do suggest Le Guin's continuing and in some ways problematic value for an enlightened Renaissance optimism.

Chronology

1929	Born October 21 in Berkeley, California, to Theodora Kroeber, the author of *Ishi in Two Worlds*, and Alfred L. Kroeber, a noted anthropologist.
1947–51	Radcliffe College.
1951–53	Graduate work in French at Columbia University.
1953	Marries Charles Le Guin in Paris, on December 22.
1957	Birth of daughter, Elizabeth, in Moscow, Idaho.
1959	Birth of daughter, Caroline, in Portland, Oregon, subsequently the residence of the family.
1960	Death of Alfred L. Kroeber.
1964	Birth of son, Theodore, in Portland.
1966	*Rocannon's World. Planet of Exile.*
1967	*City of Illusions.*
1968	*A Wizard of Earthsea.*
1969	*The Left Hand of Darkness.*
1971	*The Lathe of Heaven. The Tombs of Atuan.*
1972	*The Farthest Shore. The Word for World is Forest.*
1974	*The Dispossessed.*
1975	*Wild Angels. The Wind's Twelve Quarters.*
1976	*Very Far Away From Anywhere Else. Orsinian Tales.*
1978	*The Eye of the Heron.*
1979	*Malafrena. The Language of the Night.*
1980	*The Beginning Place.*
1981	*Hard Words.*

Contributors

HAROLD BLOOM, Sterling Professor of the Humanities at Yale University, is the author of *The Anxiety of Influence*, *Poetry and Repression* and many other volumes of literary criticism. His forthcoming study, *Freud: Transference and Authority*, attempts a full-scale reading of all of Freud's major writings. He is the general editor of *The Chelsea House Library of Literary Criticism*.

DAVID KETTERER teaches at Concordia University, Montreal. He is the author of *The Rationale of Deception in Poe* and *New Worlds for Old: The Apocalyptic Imagination, Science Fiction and American Literature*.

DOUGLAS BARBOUR is a member of the English Department at the University of Alberta.

ROBERT SCHOLES is the chairman of the English Department at Brown University. He is the author of *Structural Fabulation: An Essay on the Fiction of the Future*, and other books on science fiction and American literature.

IAN WATSON is the author of *The Gardens of Delight* and *Sunstroke and Other Stories*.

FREDRIC JAMESON is Professor of French and Humanities at Duke University. He is the author of *Marxism and Form*, *The Prison House of Language* and *The Political Unconscious*.

GEORGE E. SLUSSER is the curator of the J. Lloyd Eaton Library of Fantasy and Science Fiction at the University of California at Riverside.

GÉRARD KLEIN is the author of *The Day Before Tomorrow*.

T. A. SHIPPEY, of St. John's College, Oxford University, is the author of *Beowolf* and *The Road to Middle Earth*; he has translated *Poems of Wisdom and Learning in Old English*.

JAMES W. BITTNER teaches at the University of Northern Iowa and is the author of *Approaches to the Fiction of Ursula K. Le Guin*.

ERIC S. RABKIN is Professor of English at the University of Michigan. He is the author of *The Fantastic in Literature* and has edited anthologies of science fiction.

JEANNE MURRAY WALKER teaches at the University of Delaware at Newark and writes science fiction.

SUSAN WOOD is a member of the Department of English at the University of British Columbia. A winner of the Hugo award, she has written widely on science fiction.

DENA C. BAIN has written on R. A. Lafferty and William Blake.

BARBARA BROWN of Toronto is a teacher, writer and editor.

BRIAN ATTEBERY teaches English and music at the College of Idaho and is the author of *The Fantasy Tradition in American Literature*.

CAROL McGUIRK is Associate Professor of English at Florida Atlantic University. She is the author of *Robert Burns and the Sentimental Era*.

Bibliography

Annas, Pamela J. "New Worlds, New Words: Androgyny of Feminist Science Fiction." *Science Fiction Studies* 2, vol. 5 (1978): 143–55.

Arbur, Rosemarie. "Le Guin's 'Song' of Inmost Feminism." *Extrapolation* 3, vol. 21 (1980): 223–26.

Attebery, Brian. "On a Far Shore: The Myth of Earthsea." *Extrapolation* 3, vol. 21 (1980): 269–77.

Bailey, Edgar C., Jr. "Shadows in Earthsea: Le Guin's Use of a Jungian Archetype." *Extrapolation* 3, vol. 21 (1980): 254–61.

Bickman, Martin. "Le Guin's *Left Hand of Darkness*: Form and Content." *Science Fiction Studies* 1, vol. 4 (1977): 42–47.

Bittner, James W. *Approaches to the Fiction of Ursula K. Le Guin, Studies in Speculative Fiction*, no. 4. Ann Arbor: UMI Research Press, 1984.

Bucknall, Barbara J. *Ursula K. Le Guin*. New York: Frederick Ungar, 1981.

Cameron, Eleanor. "High Fantasy: *A Wizard of Earthsea*." *Horn Book* 47 (April 1971): 129–38.

Cogell, Elizabeth Cummins. *Ursula K. Le Guin: A Primary and Secondary Bibliography*. Boston: G. K. Hall, 1983.

Delaney, Samuel R. "To Read *The Dispossessed*." in *The Jewel-Hinged Jaw*. Elizabethtown, N.Y.: Dragon Press, 1977.

Fekete, John. "*The Dispossessed* and *Triton*: Act and System in Utopian Science Fiction." *Science Fiction Studies* 2, vol. 6 (1979): 129–43.

Galbreath, Robert. "Taoist Magic in the *Earthsea Trilogy*." *Extrapolation* 3, vol. 21 (1980): 262–67.

Huntington, John. "Public and Private Imperatives in Le Guin's Novels." *Science Fiction Studies* 3, vol. 2 (1975): 237–48.

Lake, David J. "Le Guin's Twofold Vision: Contrary Image-Sets in *The Left Hand of Darkness*." *Science Fiction Studies* 2, vol. 8 (1981): 156–64.

Moylan, Tom. "Beyond Negation: The Critical Utopias of Ursula K. Le Guin and Samuel R. Delaney." *Extrapolation* 3, vol. 21 (1980): 236–53.

Nudelamn, Rafail. "An Approach to the Structure of Le Guin's SF." *Science Fiction Studies* 3, vol. 2 (1975): 210–21.

Olander, Joseph D. and Greenberg, Martin Harry, eds. *Ursula K. Le Guin*. New York: Taplinger, 1979.

Porter, David L. "The Politics of Le Guin's Opus." *Science Fiction Studies* 3, vol. 2 (1975): 243–48.

Remington, Thomas, J. "A Time to Live and a Time to Die: Cyclical Renewal in the *Earthsea Trilogy*." *Extrapolation* 3, vol. 21 (1980): 278–86.

Rosinsky, Natalie M. *Feminist Futures: Contemporary Women's Speculative Fiction,*
Studies in Speculative Fiction 1. Ann Arbor: UMI Research Press, 1984.

Scholes, Robert. *Structural Fabulation.* Notre Dame, Ind.: University of Notre
Dame Press, 1975.

Slusser, George Edgar. *The Farthest Shores of Ursula K. Le Guin.* San Bernardino,
Ca.: The Borgo Press, 1976.

Spivack, Charlotte. *Ursula K. Le Guin.* Boston: Twayne Publishers, 1984.

Suvin, Darko. "Parables of De-Alienation: Le Guin's Widdershins Dance." *Science
Fiction Studies* 3, vol. 2 (1975): 265–74.

Theall, Donald F. "The Art of Social-Science Fiction: The Ambiguous Utopian
Dialectics of Ursula K. Le Guin." *Science Fiction Studies* 3, vol. 2 (1975):
256–65.

Turner, George. "Paradigm and Pattern: Form and Meaning in *The Dispossessed.*"
SF Commentary 41/42 (February 1975): 65–74.

Acknowledgments

"Ursula K. Le Guin's Archetypal 'Winter-Journey' " by David Ketterer from *New Worlds For Old* by David Ketterer, copyright © 1974 by David Ketterer. Reprinted by permission.

"Wholeness and Balance in the Hainish Novels" by Douglas Barbour from *Science-Fiction Studies* 3, vol. 2 (Spring 1974), copyright © 1974 by R. D. Miller and Darko Suvin. Reprinted by permission.

"The Good Witch of the West" by Robert Scholes from *Structural Fabulation: An Essay on Fiction of the Future* by Robert Scholes, copyright © 1975 by University of Notre Dame Press. Reprinted by permission.

"The Forest as Metaphor for Mind: *The Word for World is Forest* and 'Vaster Than Empires and More Slow' " by Ian Watson from *Science-Fiction Studies* 3, vol. 2 (November 1975), copyright © by R. D. Miller and Darko Suvin. Reprinted by permission.

"World-Reduction in Le Guin: The Emergence of Utopian Narrative" by Fredric Jameson from *Science-Fiction Studies* 3, vol. 2 (November 1975), copyright © 1975 by R. D. Miller and Darko Suvin. Reprinted by permission.

"*The Earthsea Trilogy*" by George E. Slusser from *The Farthest Shores of Ursula K. Le Guin* by George E. Slusser, copyright © 1976 by George E. Slusser. Reprinted by permission.

"Le Guin's 'Aberrant' Opus: Escaping the Trap of Discontent" by Gérard Klein, translated by Richard Astle, from *Science-Fiction Studies* 3, vol. 4 (November 1977), copyright © 1977 by R. D. Miller and Darko Suvin. Reprinted by permission.

"The Magic Art and the Evolution of Words: *The Earthsea Trilogy*" by T. A. Shippey from *Mosaic* 2, vol. 10 (Winter 1977), copyright © 1977 by University of Manitoba Press. Reprinted by permission.

"Persuading Us to Rejoice and Teaching Us How to Praise: Le Guin's *Orsinian Tales*" by James W. Bittner from *Science-Fiction Studies* 3, vol. 5 (November 1978), copyright © 1978 by R. D. Miller and Darko Suvin. Reprinted by permission.

"Personal and Political in *The Dispossessed*" by Victor Urbanowicz from *Science-Fiction Studies* 2, vol. 5 (July 1978), copyright © 1978 by R. D. Miller and Darko Suvin. Reprinted by permission.

"Determinism, Free Will, and Point of View in *The Left Hand of Darkness*" by Eric S. Rabkin from *Extrapolation* 1, vol. 20 (1979), copyright © 1979 by The Kent State University Press. Reprinted by permission.

"Myth, Exchange and History in *The Left Hand of Darkness*" by Jeanne Murray Walker from *Science-Fiction Studies* 2, vol. 6 (July 1979), copyright © 1979 by R. D. Miller and Darko Suvin. Reprinted by permission.

"Discovering Worlds: The Fiction of Ursula K. Le Guin" by Susan Wood from *Voices for the Future: Essays on Major Science Fiction Writers* edited by Thomas D. Clareson, copyright © 1979 by Bowling Green University Popular Press. Reprinted by permission.

"The *Tao Te Ching* as Background to the Novels of Ursula K. Le Guin" by Dena C. Bain from *Extrapolation* 3, vol. 21 (1980), copyright © 1980 by The Kent State University Press. Reprinted by permission.

"*The Left Hand of Darkness*: Androgyny, Future, Present, and Past" by Barbara Brown from *Extrapolation* 3, vol. 21 (1980), copyright © 1980 by The Kent State University Press. Reprinted by permission.

"*The Beginning Place*: Le Guin's Metafantasy" by Brian Attebery from *Children's Literature*, vol. 10 (1982), copyright © 1982 by *Children's Literature*, An International Journal. Reprinted by permission.

"Optimism and the Limits of Subversion in *The Dispossessed* and *The Left Hand of Darkness*" by Carol McGuirk, copyright © 1985 by Carol McGuirk. Printed by permission.

Index